The Dark Days of Magic

SECRETS

By

Nelly Harper

The Dark Days of Magic– Book 1
Secrets
Published by Goblin House
www.goblinhouse.co.uk
Paperback
ISBN: 978-1-9996229-1-6

<u>Whilst this book is set in a fictional place,
it was written by a real person, in England, using
British English.</u>

Author's note:
Where certain words have dual meanings, their alternate use has been capitalised. Whilst this is not grammatically correct, it has been done to ease understanding of sentences that could otherwise prove too ambiguous.

1

THERE WAS NO DOUBT THAT THE STRANGE PRICKLING feelings, which had started so faintly in Amelia's fingertips, were growing in intensity. She shot a guilty look over her shoulder. Mrs Lee was stirring one of the huge copper pans on the range and eyeing her with a frown.

"What are you doing over there? You're up to no good, I can tell."

Amelia kept her eyes down as she bent to retrieve the wooden scoop she had failed to keep hold of, grateful that it hadn't been the bowl of rough salt she had dropped. Before she could rise, there was a step behind her. She bit her lip in alarm, tasting blood.

"Hurry up and get back downstairs; I don't want to see you in my kitchen until all that ironwork is spotless."

Amelia ducked a cuff from the back of Mrs Lee's weighty hand and fled. The cook emphasised her annoyance by slamming the door behind her and sliding home the bolt. Amelia sighed with relief to be on her own once more.

The wide, wooden steps were worn from use. The third and tenth creaked as she stood on them; the thirteenth gave a slight wobble. There was character in these stairs; familiar quirks that told her exactly where she was on the dimly lit staircase. The lower door opened up onto a large open-plan basement. In one corner, a couple of looms had been set up alongside a dark mahogany spinning wheel. This was one of Amelia's favourite places, where the majority of her apprentice work with Mrs Forth was carried out. Sunlight flooded down from the high, clerestory windows, making the floating particles of dust dance in the shafts of light. Amelia imagined they were the spirits of all those who would have loved her if only they were still alive.

A number of small bedrooms lined the far wall, including her own. She ignored these and headed over to the cleaning room with its overriding smell of vinegar and polish. On the old, stained table lay a number of filthy iron skillets. Amelia set down the salt but stopped short of picking up the scrubbing brush.

Even knowing she was alone, she cast a quick, wary glance over her shoulder. The walls of this room were only panelled halfway up, the remainder being glazed to allow maximum light in. Satisfied that the basement was indeed empty, she ignored the stool and sank to the floor, tucking herself up hard against the panels, small and hidden. She looked again at her hands. She could see nothing different about them, but the feelings were still there, tingling, itching, and stabbing at her nerves like pins and needles.

For the first time since coming to Marlborough House, Amelia was glad that this was not a classroom day. She usually enjoyed her lessons, taken with the boys in the quiet room at the back of the large mansion. Mr Forth was a fair teacher who, unlike the live-in staff here, never stigmatised them for who they were or what they might become. His only opinion of them was based on the efforts they put into their education, though even he would have struggled to keep his patience when she couldn't keep hold of her pen.

Instead, she had been down here, carding fleece, when she had first noticed the pains. She'd put them down to her own carelessness with the carders to begin with, the sensations not unlike fine metal teeth scraping across her fingertips. When those prickles began burying themselves deeper into her skin, she had been unable to delude herself any longer.

Luckily, Mrs Forth had not been in either, so at least there had been no one to witness her panic. Unluckily, she had somehow managed to get through the whole two sack loads of fleece early. It was more than her life was worth to get caught slacking, so as Mrs Forth would need to check her rolags before she could begin spinning them, she had gone in search of Dorothy, the housekeeper, to find something else to do. Unfortunately, she had been waylaid by Mrs Lee, who had foisted the dirtiest chore she could think of on her.

Leaning her head back against the panel, Amelia closed her eyes. She needed Morgan more than ever, but the older girl had died and left her to cope in this cold, hostile house without her. A tear slid down Amelia's cheek, hot and slow. Morgan would have known what to do. She had been fiery and strong. Even the fact that they were here being watched for signs of 'strangeness' had never dimmed her mood for long.

A memory of her voice echoed in Amelia's mind, "They can watch us all they like, cos there's nothing wrong with either of us. And if something does start to happen, then we'll just have to make sure that no one ever finds out."

For once, the memory did not comfort her.

"How am I supposed to do that?" Amelia whispered into the friendless space around her. "You never told me how." She still had four years left until she reached twenty-one. Four interminably long years before she would be free and out of this watch house for good.

The sound of footsteps echoing down through the open windows brought her back to her senses. She heard humming; Jasper must be busy working out in the yard. Taking a deep breath, Amelia picked herself off the floor, brushed herself down, and set to work. Maybe, if she scrubbed at the skillets hard enough, these dreadful feelings would slough off along with the dirt.

Like toothache, bone-deep and unrelenting, the sensations remained. Amelia began to feel sick, though whether from the paraesthesia or from worry, she had no idea. The head of Marlborough House called each of those he held guardianship for into his office every so often for 'welfare meetings,' where he would question them extensively on how they were feeling. Amelia always found these sessions unnerving, even when she had nothing to hide. Blain Cordright was not particularly tall, but he had hard eyes, the colour of afternoon shadows on tarmac; they glared at her as if they could open up her very mind for him to read.

Though the meetings were infrequent, they were watched all the time and could be sent to Blain at a moment's notice. The implication that they were somehow deviant and untrustworthy was always there, hanging in the air over their heads. Even Dorothy and Johns, the friendliest of the live-in staff, were not above threatening to report them. Mrs Lee would have no hesitation in sending her to Blain if she had even the slightest suspicion that anything was amiss.

As soon as the ironwork was clean, Amelia went up the dark stairway and knocked on the door. Bracing herself for more of Mrs Lee's brisk temper, she was relieved to see Jasper's grinning face. He caught her looking over his shoulder into the empty kitchen beyond and grinned.

"It's okay; there's no one else here just now." He held up his hand to show the remains of a digestive biscuit.

Amelia relaxed. There was no way Jasper would be stealing biscuits if there was any chance of getting caught. At fourteen, he was three years younger than her and had the annoying knack of avoiding trouble. His was a smile that could convince anyone he was above suspicion, and he used it often.

"I better get back before I'm missed," he said through a mouthful of crumbs. "See ya later."

****

"Are you listening?"

Amelia blinked her attention back to the table, where everyone was gathered for the evening meal. "Sorry, Mark. What were you saying?"

"We were clearing shrubbery with Johns and found this old cottage hidden in the wood. It looked like it had collapsed years ago." He paused for a mouthful of food, and Aarav took the opportunity to jump in.

"Part of it was still standing. We went in with Johns for a look. There was a room that still had half its ceiling. I found this cupboard set into the wall. It blended so well with the stonework no one else had seen it." His chest puffed out along with his ego. "The door was locked, but the wood was rotten, and I managed to break it open easily enough."

Jasper's dirty blond hair looked more like he had been the one crawling through bushes and investigating ruins. "I wish I'd been there. Finding secret cupboards is far more interesting than raking gravel."

"Yeah, but kids have to do the kids' jobs." Aarav gave him a smug grin.

Jasper stuck two fingers up at him under the table. He still had a few months to wait before he was fifteen and his own apprenticeship started.

The unrelenting tingling in Amelia's hands seemed to pulse at the word 'secret,' becoming painful and reaching right up and through her wrists. She gripped her fork a little tighter. "What was in the cupboard?"

Aarav had just opened his mouth to answer when the sound of slamming cutlery from the top end of the table made them all jump.

"What?" Mrs Lee was on her feet and glaring at the head gardener seated on her right.

The atmosphere in the room thickened noticeably. Whilst Gipton did not wilt under her iron stare, his voice was not quite as strong as usual when he replied. "There is no harm now, Elsie."

"No harm indeed; well, that remains to be…" She broke off, glaring like Medusa at the gawping faces around her.

"It was a box with a big, iron lock. We couldn't get it open." Aarav finally managed to whisper when Mrs Lee had left the room, and the rest of the staff felt it safe enough to resume talking.

Jasper squirmed in his seat. "What happened to it?" His head bobbed from Aarav to Mark, like an eager dog watching for a treat.

"That's the really interesting part," Aarav said around a mouthful of food. "When Gipton arrived to check on our work and saw the cottage, he went berserk. Started shouting and hollering at Johns, telling him he was a fool who didn't know how to listen to instructions. I've never seen him so annoyed."

"When Johns showed him the box, he went all quiet." Mark flicked a glance up the table. Seeing that everyone else was busy with their own hushed conversation, he leaned a little further forwards. "Then he told us not to say a word of this to anyone. He took the box as if it would explode at any minute and hurried away. He didn't come back for a long time. When he did, he never mentioned the box at all."

From the other end of the table, one hastily uttered word rang out like a door chime, though whether the boys even heard it, Amelia could not be sure.

Magician.

All talk cut off as Mrs Lee returned, her lips crushed into a thin line of anger. She thumped a steaming pot of apple crumble onto the table and began serving out portions with such a firm hand that anyone else would have been accused of trying to break the china.

Opting for safety, the boys moved on to talk about their other find: a dead cat in the underbrush, not far from the cottage. Amelia barely heard them.

Magician.

The word echoed in her mind. She bent her head, willing her grip to remain firm around her spoon.

Magician.

She jumped when Aarav nudged her. "You look as if you're going to cry," he said, with a hint of mockery. "Don't worry, it must have been there for years."

Amelia gave him a weak smile. The bones in her hand were feeling as brittle as her nerves, and she was not in the mood for his teasing.

Magician.

Her mind screamed the word at her, refusing to be ignored. She had been steadfastly trying not to think about magic all day, but there had never really been any doubt as to what was happening to her. It had happened to someone else before, though Amelia had only found out about it by chance. It had been a few years earlier, not long before she had started her apprenticeship. The morning was still as clear in her mind as the day it had happened.

"Amelia, I'm sorry, but I need you to go and clean out the hearths upstairs." Dorothy's cheeks had been flushed with annoyance. "Sheena has failed to turn up for work, and we are running so far behind. It wouldn't matter so much, but Mr Blain has just informed me he has a visitor arriving shortly."

Amelia had donned the cleaner's unused apron, ignoring Morgan's grin of amusement. Just as she had been leaving the last room, she'd heard male voices coming up the main staircase. Dorothy had warned her to stay out of sight, so she'd ducked back behind the door. Eavesdropping had been the last thing on her mind, but the two men had not been quiet with their conversation.

"So she was a Carrier? All this time and right under your very noses. By God, Blain, that is brazen. How did you catch them?"

"My cook was passing their house and by chance saw the child in the garden using powers. Naturally, she came straight back and reported it to me."

Blain's companion's words were staccato-sharp. "It had got that far? Had the child no pains to show what she was?"

Amelia held her breath as they passed the door, afraid she might be caught, even more afraid of what else the men might say.

"Apparently, yes," Blain's voice was tight with annoyance, "but because the grandmother was the one who watched the child when the mother came to work, they were able to hide them until they passed."

"So the grandmother had powers too; are you sure the mother was only a Carrier?"

"It appears so. We were... very thorough."

An involuntary shiver ran down Amelia's spine at the memory. Everyone knew that magicians were taken away and never heard of again. The very thought of having something that made people react in such a way made her eyes prick with tears. She did not want to be bad, to be someone people feared so much. She couldn't be that— could she?

Luckily, Aarav had already turned away, laughing at something Mark had said. Jasper gave her a strange look but tucked into his pudding and said nothing. Amelia blinked and swallowed hard. She needed to get a grip. She was going to give herself away if she carried on like this.

The daughter of the cleaner had not been feared by everyone, a quiet voice at the back of Amelia's mind told her later that evening when she was tucked up in bed. The girl's mother and grandmother had still loved her. They had done their best to hide her, so maybe magicians were not all bad?

Would her own parents have protected her? Amelia had no idea; they had died when she was just a baby. Her aunt was all the mother Amelia had ever known. Aunt T had raised her with nothing but love and compassion until her own death nine years later. The next couple of years had been spent in an orphanage before Blain had brought her to Marlborough House. She knew she was lucky; not every orphan was given such a great education, let alone the opportunity to gain an apprenticeship.

As scary and strict as Blain was, he had at least given her a better life. She owed it to herself not to throw it all away now. She was going to be a weaver, an artisan trade that was in high demand these days. Her life would be a good one, so long as she could keep her head. It sounded like these pains were a passing thing. All she needed to do was keep them hidden and carry on as normal. Besides, the tiny voice at the back of her mind said, having powers might actually be kind of fun.

2

THE SHACKLES AROUND THANIEL'S WRISTS AND ANKLES dug in deeply. He was beginning to regret shouting and struggling so much. All it had done was rub his skin raw and reduce his voice to little more than a hoarse rasp. He slumped against the wall, his resistance as deflated as his energy. His brain still felt as if it were exploding, though thankfully the nausea had settled somewhat.

Cold radiated up through the floor, and he wished he hadn't hurled his blanket and pillow across the room. It had been just as rash as kicking over the water he'd been left. Thaniel's anger flared again at the injustice of it all, but it was short-lived. He was drowning in pain, too defeated to fend off the intolerable pulsing any longer. Sleep grabbed him finally, pulling him into a black, dreamless void that smelled of panic and fear.

When he awoke, aching and sore, his head had eased only slightly, and it hurt to swallow. Judging from the tiny beams of light that crept through the few chips and scratches in the thick paint covering the single small window, it must be daytime. There was a shuffling on the other side of the door. Thaniel felt his adrenaline spike. He jumped to his feet as the door opened and his mother crept silently in. She held a lamp in one hand, a finger of the other pressed to her lips. Her eyes were red and swollen, and she had a bruise on her temple. Protective anger swelled inside Thaniel, along with a strong sense of relief.

She had not been home when his stepfather had caught him curled up in blinding pain on his bedroom floor. Thaniel had expected help, so the hate in Paul Grayson's voice had been a shock. Though they could not be described as close, their relationship had never been confrontational; yet the instant Paul saw the state Thaniel was in, he became incandescent with rage.

Thaniel was too old to be treated like an errant schoolboy, but his stepfather dragged him to his feet anyway. Vomiting with pain, Thaniel had been unable to resist as he was hauled down the stairs and out into the garden. Like a man possessed, Paul had manhandled him across the lawn, through his garden workshop, and into the small storeroom at the rear. On the far wall, he removed an old blue towel, uncovering a double set of chained manacles. They hung like a limp animatronic sea creature discarded long ago. The sight of them sent a sudden dread cascading into Thaniel, almost bringing him to his knees. Paul wasted no time fixing the restraints. As the last manacle was being clamped around his ankle, Thaniel's world went thankfully blank.

The sound of the kitchen door slamming brought him back to his senses. The freakish pain in his head had eased slightly, but his anger at Paul's treatment of him had grown. Who the hell did he think he was, treating him this way? He'd never have managed it had Thaniel not been half out of his wits with pain. Paul Grayson was not that big a man. At eighteen, Thaniel was just as tall and, he thought, probably just as strong.

His stepfather's tirade had thrown words like 'monster,' 'filth,' and 'inhuman' at him. Where on earth had that come from? And how was having a blinding migraine so wrong? On top of both these shocks was the fact that Paul had a set of shackles bolted into his storeroom wall. Why would a self-employed modeller have such things? He made props for stop-motion animation, for God's sake.

Thaniel had braced himself when he heard his stepfather returning. Paul carried a large laundry bag out of which he'd pulled a worn blanket and an old, shabby pillow. He had thrown them down next to Thaniel. Still standing far enough back to remain out of reach, he had taken out a bottle of water and a plastic cup, tossing each onto the blanket. Last of all, Paul took out an old, chipped pot.

"Can't have you pissing on my floor," he said as he pushed it nearer with his foot.

It was all so incomprehensible to Thaniel. "Why are you doing this?"

In response, Paul leaned towards him, eyes blazing, his voice hissing out through gritted jaws. "You should have died with the rest of them. If I'd have known what you were, I would have never taken you in."

He sounded insane.

"What do you mean?"

Paul had braved a step forward, fists raised. "You're lucky I don't kill you myself."

Thaniel raised his own hands in defence. The action made Paul flinch and hastily jump back. Then he was gone, slamming the door and locking it behind him.

"Hey!" Thaniel shouted after him. "Come back and tell me why I'm here. What is going on?" He tugged at the shackles, ignoring the pain it caused. His struggles had become more frantic, but no matter how much he shouted and cursed, Paul Grayson did not return.

The pain had calmed eventually, both in his head and self-inflicted from the restraints. He was angry, confused, and more than a little scared. Now, Ann Grayson stepped towards her son, her voice low and strained. "We haven't got long. You must go, Thaniel. Paul has sent for the oligarchy; they will be here in the morning."

"Mum, what is happening? My head was going to burst, and he just went berserk, dragged me down here, and chained me up. I couldn't even stop him; the pain was so bad." Nervous bile rose in Thaniel's throat, but it was the worry etched across his mother's face that was frightening him more than anything.

"I am so sorry, Thaniel. I had no idea that you would have magic. I thought you would be safe. Your sister never had it; I thought you would be the same."

It had been a long time since Thaniel had seen such a look on her face. So long that he had almost forgotten. "Magic? Mum, what are you talking about? There is no magic now; that was all finished with years ago."

His voice was starting to rise. Ann Grayson shot a hurried look over her shoulder. Her messy bun was coming loose, and the movement made dark strands of hair fall to brush her shoulders. "Shh. Thaniel, listen. There is not enough time to tell you everything. You know that your father was killed because he had magic. Jess didn't have any, but she was with your dad when they got him, so…" Her eyes clouded, and she had to take a deep breath before she could speak again. "Magic killed Paul's family. He would never have married me if he'd thought you would have it too. I am sorry; I never realised just how deep his hatred runs."

All the while she was talking, she was fiddling with the manacles. There was a small click, and one of Thaniel's wrists sprang free, falling to his side like a dead weight. The other soon followed. He winced and rubbed the raw skin as his mother crouched and started on the ones on his ankles.

"This is crazy. Why do you think I have magic? You've never said anything before." Thaniel's panic was rising even faster than his anger had. There were another couple of clicks, and the tight metal bands sprang open. Thaniel kicked them away.

"The pain in your head, it's no ordinary headache. It's your magic starting to awaken. All magicians go through something similar." Ann reached for her son's face. Holding it in both hands, she kissed him firmly but gently on the forehead. Then she pulled back and looked him straight in the eyes. "You must hide yourself. There is a place known only to magicians, Etherea Forest. You will be safe there. Tell them who your father was; they will look after you." She pulled him into a bear hug. Thaniel could feel her trembling as he held her tight.

Ann released her hold. It was breaking her heart seeing her boy come to this. Pressing all the money she had in her purse into his hand, she told him, "You're old enough to take care of yourself now; you will manage just fine. Until you get to the forest, trust no one, and never, ever let anyone see your magic."

Thaniel tried to give it back to her, but she tucked it into his pocket. He rubbed a hand over his forehead, as if he could wipe the pain and the madness away. "I don't know any magic, Mum. I'm not..."

There was a sound in the distance. Ann shook her son, trying to force her words into him. "You are a magician, Than, just like your father. You will work it out, but you must go. Now." It was taking everything she had not to grab his arm and run with him. "I wish I could come with you, but I need to stay here and try to stop anyone from coming after you. You have to trust me. These pains will stop soon, I promise." She wanted to take him in her arms again and hold him so tightly that nothing could ever hurt him. He was her baby, the only one of her precious family that she had left. There was no time.

"I love you; don't ever forget that." She pushed him out of the small room into the adjoining studio.

Thaniel was surprised to see that it was still night, with a bright, full moon making everything through the large, panelled windows glow in ethereal blue light. "I love you too, Mum, but..." He had so many questions all fighting for recognition in his pain-fogged mind. His head was beginning to pulse badly again, and he staggered under the pressure.

"You're not going anywhere, boy."

Too late. Paul Grayson appeared at the workshop doorway, a metal bar in hand. He looked ferocious and scared, his shoulders forward, tensed, ready for trouble.

Thaniel looked around the studio for... what? He knew there was no other way out.

"Paul, please!" Ann stepped in front of her son. "You can't do this." Her hand reached back for Thaniel's, gripping it so hard her knuckles whitened.

Her husband's face curled in disgust. "I always knew the little rat would turn out to be scum like his father. I've been waiting for the day it showed itself." He flicked his head to the side. "Get out of the way, Ann."

She stood firm. "Paul, he's my son. You can't do this. You always said family was everything."

"My family meant everything." Paul's voice was harsh. "Mine. He should have died with the rest of them."

"Paul!" Ann's voice broke on the word.

"Get out of the way. You can't protect him."

Ann was a small woman, but she stood her ground against the man she had loved until now. "No," she told him, chin raised in defiance.

Paul grabbed her by the shoulders and hurled her to the side. She fell hard against one of the workbenches, toppling the part-made model of an intricate cuckoo clock and sending it crashing to the floor beneath her prone body. Thaniel cried out and made to go to her. Paul raised the metal bar.

"Just give me the excuse to do it, rat."

Thaniel stopped dead, unsure if his stepfather was threatening to hit him or his mother. Not willing to take any chances, he stepped unsteadily backwards, bumping into another of Paul's creations and toppling it. Ordinarily, Thaniel would have been sorry. Now he ground his heel into the broken parts, determined to keep the man's attention away from his stricken mum.

Paul didn't even look at it. "Your kind are finished," he spat. "The oligarchy will not tolerate you to live. They will be here in the morning, and you will be chained up, waiting. Your mother will go in shackles too if you try to resist any longer."

"No." Thaniel's shoulders drooped. "Don't hurt her anymore."

With a smug tilt of his chin, Paul bent to take hold of the scarf around Ann's neck. For a second, Thaniel thought he was going to bunch it into a pillow for her head. The almost savage way Paul swiped it from her neck soon disabused him of that thought.

Back in the storeroom, Thaniel allowed himself to be restrained once again.

"Nice of your mother to provide a gag, wasn't it?" Paul forced the material across his stepson's mouth, tying the scarf tightly behind his head.

Strands of Thaniel's hair caught in the knot, pulling on his scalp, though he barely noticed. His head was becoming intolerable again; if this kept up, Paul was going to get his wish. No one could withstand this much and survive for long.

Thaniel had no idea how long he was consumed with pain. When he finally came back to his senses, he was alone and the workshop was silent. His first thoughts were for his mother. He couldn't remember seeing her move after she had fallen. Was she still lying out there on the studio floor? He'd never known his stepfather to be violent. Sure, he could be moody and sullen at times, but in the four years Paul and Ann had been married, Thaniel had never known him to raise a hand to her.

They had always seemed so contented together, and Thaniel had liked seeing his mother happy. She had been sad for far too long. Thaniel had only been nine when his father, Carter Brook, had died. It had been very early on in the civil unrest that had come to be known as the Purge. His sister, Jess, had been fifteen. She had died along with her father, and suddenly their happy little family of four had become two. It had been a hard loss and a time that Thaniel had pushed far to the back of his mind.

They had lived in Harforth then. He could still remember stones being thrown at the house and the insulting graffiti that had been daubed across the walls. For months, he had not been allowed to go outside and play— not that anyone had come to call on him—and his mother had cried a lot. They had moved after that, breaking all connections to the town and the people they had once thought of as friends.

When they had first come to Winterbourne, they had lived in a small, basic flat over the hairdressers where his mother had taken a job. They kept their heads down and their past to themselves. Gradually, they'd settled into their new community, and slowly they both began to heal. Then Ann had met Paul, and two years later they'd been married. Thaniel would rather have kept his mother all to himself, but he would never deny her the happiness she'd found.

Moonlight was still banding into the room through the cracks in the painted window, all too similar to the bolts of pain lancing through his skull. It would be a while until morning. Thaniel felt a knot tighten in his stomach. The oligarchy was coming for him then. Hopefully, they would at least make sure his mother was alright before they took him away.

He had only ever met one member of the ruling organisation before, Oligarch Carswell. Paul had been working on a special animatronic model for one of the man's infamous parties. He had been nice, or so Thaniel had thought at the time. Then again, until last night, he had thought the same of his stepfather.

3

By mid-morning the next day, Amelia had revised her opinion on how much fun having powers might be. The pain in her hand now extended throughout her whole body, and she felt like a firework about to explode. Sooner or later, someone was going to notice. There was a hiss from the stove beside her as Mrs Lee's soup began to boil over. Amelia reached for the pan without thinking.

"Ow, shit." She swore as she dropped it back onto the hob. Her hand was throbbing, the skin red and already starting to blister. For the first time since it had begun, she barely felt whatever was happening inside her body. Before she had time to bring herself to her senses, she gritted her teeth, grabbed the pan, and tipped the scalding liquid right down her front.

"That cloud is looking a bit ominous." Mrs Lee nodded her head towards the town. "Glad I didn't wait to get these herbs cut." She held up a hand, full of fragrant greenery.

"Hmmm." Dorothy put down her heavy shopping bag and flexed her hand. "It sure hurried me along the road. Thought I was going to be in for a soaking."

"You did well to get back in time. Come away in and I'll get the kettle on." Mrs Lee had barely finished her sentence when Amelia's high-pitched scream sounded from the kitchen. Not a sprightly woman, she nonetheless took off

22

running for the door. She barrelled to a horrified halt when she saw her soup splattered all over the floor. "What on earth is going on here?"

As urgent as the cook was rigid, Dorothy dropped her shopping, squeezed past Mrs Lee, and rushed to the sink. She filled a bowl with cold water and poured it straight over Amelia, heedless of Mrs Lee's protest.

"I will clean the kitchen, Elsie," Dorothy admonished in her best no-nonsense tone. Her usual musical lilt returned as she soothed Amelia. "A cool bath is what you need now, girl. Got to take the heat out of your skin, or it will just keep getting worse."

Amelia let herself be led out of the kitchen and up the back stairs to the staff bathroom. Mrs Lee, not content to stay in her ruined kitchen, followed a few paces behind. Once there, Dorothy shoved the plug into the bath and turned on the taps. Then, sparing Amelia no dignity, the housekeeper began to gently peel away her wet clothes. After two days of worry, it was a relief to be able to cry freely at last, and Amelia was not holding back. Her body felt as if it was on fire from the inside out and the outside in.

"I'm sorry." She was crying so much she could hardly form the words. "The soup was boiling over; I was trying to save it."

"Hush now," Dorothy said, giving up on the last piece of clothing. "I think we're going to have to soak this one off."

Mrs Lee looked down at Amelia's reddened, blistering skin, and her face softened. Quietly, she left the room, reappearing a short while later with a pair of dressmaking scissors. She did not speak, leaving the room as quickly as she had come. Dorothy made short work of cutting away the material that had stuck to Amelia's skin until only a few patches remained, obstinately clinging to her stomach like melted candle wax.

"You got to get right under," Dorothy told Amelia, urging her into the bath. "We have to stop it burning, or your scars will be terrible." She held out her own arm, where a long, keloid scar stood out dark and ugly against her brown skin. It was an old burn, a silly accident with a hot iron, but it was ugly, and Dorothy had always felt self-conscious about it.

Amelia gasped as the water lapped at her legs. "I can't."

"You can and you will." Dorothy's hand was like a vice on Amelia's arm, pulling her body down. "It's not too cold; I'm not trying to give you hypothermia on top of your burns, but it has to be cool enough to take the heat out."

Sobbing fit to burst, Amelia lowered herself into the water and lay back, hurting so much that she no longer knew where one pain ended and the other began. If the water were to come right up over her head, she thought, it would only bring blessed relief.

Dorothy stroked her hair away from her face with one hand as she swirled the water around with the other. "The worst is over now, pet. Once the heat is out of your skin, you will feel much better."

Was it, though? Would this mask of burns be enough to hide the magic fighting to emerge inside her body?

Amelia laid back against the cold porcelain of the bath and let her hot tears run down to mingle with the cold water. She felt as exposed and vulnerable as a newly hatched chick.

Slowly, the pain began to ease, and Dorothy was able to slough off the last of the fabric from Amelia's skin without causing too much more damage. "I think you've been lucky. It looks all nasty just now, but I don't think it's too bad, really. There's no need to be sending for an ambulance."

Though Amelia's tears still flowed, relief flickered, washing away the last recriminations of what she had just put herself through. She had done it. She had given herself a reason to be uncomfortable in front of everyone for the next few days. Surely her pains couldn't last much longer than that? A weird kind of euphoria was beginning to grow, deep down in her core. The door opened, and she jumped guiltily.

Mrs Lee dropped a clean nightdress on the chair and set a steaming cup on the side of the bath. "Drink this; it's chamomile. It will calm you down and stop you from catching a chill. Then it's straight to bed with you, my girl. I've spoken to the surgery; the doctor will be out to see you in a little while."

****

The boys came down to see her before dinner. Her earlier excitement had soon dissolved, and she lay feeling sore and sorry for herself. Jasper, always the most caring, held her undamaged hand, looking worried. "Are you going to be alright?"

"Of course she will," Aarav said, winking at Amelia. "She's just wanting a little bit of attention, that's all."

Mark shot him a puzzled look. They had been the best of friends for years, yet even he had to admit that Aarav was being a real jerk lately. "What's with being so sarcastic?"

Aarav gave him an answering smirk and bit at a broken fingernail.

Mark turned to the others. "Mrs Lee was in such a state; she was even crying."

"What?" Jasper and Amelia looked at him in surprise.

Aarav gave a huff of indignation. "Why would she be upset? It's not as if she even pretends to like Amelia, or any of us, come to that." He flicked a thin half-moon of nail at Jasper. "Apart from you, that is."

Jasper ducked out of the way but was too focused on Mark to rise to the bait.

"I heard her say something about it reminding her of her daughters." Mark's voice had taken on a distinctly aghast air. "I couldn't hear it all, but it sounded like something happened to them in the Purge and they died."

"Shit." Jasper's jaw dropped. "Were they scalded too?"

"Yeah, souped to death." Aarav snorted. They all ignored him.

Mark shrugged, "I don't know. I went to grab a flask from the kitchen and overheard her talking to someone in the scullery. She mentioned the word magic, though."

"Magic? What has that got to do with getting scalded?" Jasper frowned at Mark, who had said the word as if it were a dirty stain. "Did magic kill her daughters? I bet that's why she hates magicians so much. I heard her telling Blain once that magic was the work of the devil and should never be allowed to return."

At the talk of magic, the pains in Amelia's body intensified, almost as if they were trying to call out and declare themselves. She swallowed hard and changed the subject. "The doctor said it's going to hurt for a few days, and I'll probably end up with some scarring, but hopefully it won't be too bad."

Aarav rubbed at his throat. "Can I have some of your water?" He reached for Amelia's glass, downing it before she could answer. He looked a little flushed himself. Ducking his head, he rushed out of the door. "I'll go get you some more."

Mark watched him go with a frown. "He's been in a funny mood for the last few days. I don't know what's up with him."

"Maybe he's just sorry for Amelia," Jasper joked, knowing it wasn't true. "Maybe he fancies her?"

Amelia pulled a face. "Shut up, Jasper."

"Ooh, look at you blush. 'Melia and Aarav sitting in a tree, K, I..."

"SHUT UP!" Both Amelia and Mark shouted at him.

Jasper looked at Mark as if he was thinking of trying the same joke on him but thought better of it and just grinned at them instead.

When Aarav came back with the water, he flung himself down on the foot of the bed, trying to act as if he hadn't just behaved like an idiot. Amelia winced as the covers tugged on her raw skin.

"So," he said, not noticing, "how long are you going to milk this for? I bet you'll get to miss a fair few lessons."

Amelia held up her hand, showing him the clean white bandages covering her palm and three fingers. "Well, I'm not going to be holding a pen for a while."

***

Amelia leaned back on her pillows, feeling dreadful. It had been bad enough when she'd had the boys to distract her, but now, alone, she found herself floundering. She closed her eyes, but her mind was filled with a thin, squealing noise—the sound of every cell in her body screaming as they were forced to accept her awakening powers. She still couldn't quite believe that she had really been brave enough—or stupid enough—to pour a pan of scalding soup over herself. Shock, mingled with guilt and the occasional bout of euphoria, still had its enveloping arms around her. Through the turmoil of emotions, the word that had been shouting at her since her pains first started began to settle in and grow roots.

She was a magician. The very thought thrilled her just as much as it terrified her. She wished she knew more about what it meant, but all mention of magic was forbidden in the house, and she had learnt long ago not to ask questions. Footsteps sounded on the stairs. Amelia hastily flicked out her light and closed her eyes. It would be the domestic returning from her day off. She was the only other person who slept down here just now. The bedroom door creaked open a few moments later, and Letty poked her head into the room. She gave a low tut of annoyance at finding Amelia seemingly asleep and quietly closed the door. Not daring to turn the lamp on again and risk the woman's gossipy attention, Amelia stared up at the dark ceiling and tried to focus on anything but how she was feeling.

She drifted into another uneasy night's sleep, filled with vivid dreams. She was trapped, bound tightly, and barely able to breathe. Tiny lights floated all around her. They were not friendly. The ground ahead was a quagmire of mud that bubbled and sucked down everything it touched. The mire edged towards her, and the lights appeared to shine a little brighter with expectation.

It was almost at her toes when she noticed a movement out of the corner of her eye. Someone was peering at her from out of the gloom. Her heart skipped a beat as she looked at him. He seemed just as surprised to see her, yet he paused only a second before rushing forward to help. The mud reached her first. Amelia was alarmed to find that it had the consistency of water yet acted like the implausible quicksand of old movies.

Fear gripped her throat. She was still bound, but now she could move inside the ties, and the more she struggled, the deeper she sank. As the dirty water reached her neck, the lights pricked out. The last thing she saw before darkness engulfed her was a tear running down the boy's face. There was a brush of lips on hers, and the softness of it wrenched at her heart. So this was what love felt like, she thought, as the water closed over her head.

She woke with a gasp of mud-free air and for a few seconds relished the feeling of unencumbered breath flowing into her lungs. Full awareness followed slowly, bringing with it a riot of prickling, stabbing sensations tightly wrapped in skin that felt as if it had shrunk two sizes overnight. Gingerly, she pulled up her nightdress and peeled back the dressing on her stomach.

The skin was beacon-red beneath a liberal scattering of thick, yellowing blisters. Amelia's stomach churned. It looked like a bed of fluid-filled fungi blooming on her skin. She bit back a cry of dismay. *You did this for a reason,* she told herself, closing her eyes against the sight of it. That only served to highlight just how unbearable the inside of her body was feeling. She rested her hands lightly over her stomach as if she could hold herself together. The burns were the perfect mask; without them, she would never be able to hide what was really going on with her, but right now she just wanted to be healed—to be rid of the magic and the burns.

Her hands warmed a little. The internal chaos inside her pulsed, then dissolved into tiny particles, flowing along her arms and evaporating out through her palms like a pressure cooker whose valve had been lifted and the steam released. At the same time, the soreness under her hands eased. Astonished, she pulled them away, and the heat abruptly stopped. She let out a muffled laugh as she checked her stomach. Beneath the loosened dressing was a patch of almost healed skin, right where her hands had been.

There were sounds coming from Letty's room now. Amelia quickly pressed the dressing back in place and covered herself; closed doors meant nothing to the adults of Marlborough House. She lay back on her pillow and waited for the inevitable intrusion. Her mind was buzzing. She had just done magic, and it had felt amazing. The burns on the rest of her body still hurt, but it didn't matter anymore. Without the strange pains in her body, she felt lighter than she had in days. How could anything about healing be bad?

"Well, you're looking a bit perkier," Dorothy said, poking her head round the door.

Amelia jumped. She had been so focused on listening for Letty that she had failed to catch the telltale sound of creaking on the stairs.

"I thought you might have had a bad night." Dorothy came over to the bed and put the back of her hand to Amelia's forehead.

"I had really weird dreams." Amelia pushed her euphoria away and tried to look like she had felt waking up. "I dreamt I was tied up and drowning in mud." She flushed, remembering the boy. She was not going to tell that part to anyone.

"You had a nasty shock yesterday, and being plunged into a cold bath can't have been nice. It was bound to affect you." Dorothy took hold of her injured hand and began to unwind the bandage. She went only as far as to see some of the skin on her fingers. "I thought this was going to be worse."

Shit.

"Your bath must have really helped," Amelia said, a little too quickly.

Dorothy didn't seem to notice as she carefully retied the gauze. "The doctor is coming back tomorrow to check there is no sign of infection, then it will be left to the district nurse to change your dressings every couple of days." As she spoke, she busied herself pulling back Amelia's covers. Amelia bit her lip. This time, however, Dorothy made no attempt to invade her dignity, looking only at her legs and feet. They had escaped much of the damage, though they still looked a livid mess. "I'll put some more cream on for you."

"How are you feeling?" Letty wandered into the room, curling her face up as she saw Amelia's inflamed skin and bandaged hand. "Ooh, that looks nasty. I bet it hurts?"

Dorothy tutted, "Of course it hurts." The golden smell of calendula wafted up, slightly marred by the sour underlying scent of aloe vera. "Make yourself useful and bring down some breakfast."

Rolling her eyes at the back of Dorothy's head, Letty ducked back out of the room. Her footsteps could be heard clonking up the stairs, then the door banged, and the basement was quiet again. Dorothy finished applying the cream and handed Amelia the tub.

"You can do the rest now, I think," she said. "Just on the exposed skin, though, don't go peeking under any of your dressings." She patted Amelia on her good hand. "No schoolwork for you today, so don't you worry about getting up. Mrs Lee says you've to stay in bed for at least a couple of days. I'll keep popping down to see how you are." She rose as lighter footsteps approached. How like Letty to shirk her responsibilities onto someone else.

"I've brought you a book to read as well," Jasper said, putting the tray down carefully. It was swimming in spilt tea. Dorothy swiped him lightly over the back of the head. He aimed one of his dazzling smiles at her. "I might have spilt a little, but it isn't much, honest."

They left her alone to eat. Amelia couldn't remember the last time she'd had breakfast in bed. It would have been quite the novelty if she hadn't felt so despondent. After Dorothy's reaction to her hand, Amelia knew that she was in trouble. As soon as the doctor took a look under the dressings, he would know. She could feel the powers winding up inside her again, yearning for release. Here she was, sitting on the most exciting and unbelievable thing that had ever happened to her, and now she couldn't do anything about it for days.

Food eaten, she set her tray on the floor and leaned back against her headboard, book in hand. She had little time to read usually, so it was going to be a luxury to sit here and lose herself in a story. She stifled a yawn and was reminded again of her broken night's sleep. The boy. Her breath caught in her chest as she thought about him. Other parts of the dream had faded away, but he was so lucid in her mind, he might have just walked out of the room.

He'd had dark, messy hair that looked as if he'd just run his fingers through it, and eyes that had seemed to caress her soul. They were an icy blue that should have appeared cold and hard, but instead they had been full of depth and feeling, like a pale, watery sky in the early morning. Amelia's heart missed a beat. That moment, when he had smiled and her insides had melted. She sighed. What would it be like, running her own fingers through that mop of unruly hair? She knew she would have done it if the mud hadn't taken her.

4

THANIEL JERKED AWAKE AS THE STOREROOM DOOR swung open. Two of the oligarchy's elite security team marched in. They were clad all in navy, one carrying a strange metal rope with large, clear crystal clusters on each end. Thaniel scrambled to his feet, alarm bleeding into the pain in his head, sending sparks of light to fleck his vision.

The crystals began to glow as, without a word, the Guard with the rope wrapped one end around Thaniel, pinning his arms to his sides. He kept a firm grip on the other, holding it as if Thaniel were nothing more than a troublesome dog on a leash. The pain in Thaniel's head ceased immediately, and his vision cleared. His relief was etched with jagged spikes of anxiety as, none too gently, the other man removed the gag from his mouth. He left it hanging around Thaniel's neck like a noose. It smelled faintly of the perfume his mother wore.

The men moved aside to allow enough room for a third to enter. He carried the poise of someone in authority. Although also dressed in dark clothing, he was not in Guard uniform. Nor was he one of the oligarchy.

"Nathaniel Grayson. You have been rep..."

"Brook." Thaniel interrupted him, the casual assumption about his name annoying him far more than it ever had before. "My name is Nathaniel Brook."

"I never gave him my name." Paul Grayson's voice came in quickly from the studio. It carried a smug edge to it, presumably expecting congratulations on his foresight. The man ignored him.

"Nathaniel Brook, you have been reported for possessing magic. You will be coming with us."

Thaniel pressed back against the wall. "I thought one of the oligarchy was coming for me?"

As casually as if he were merely reading his watch, the man backhanded him across the face. "The oligarchs do not trouble themselves with the likes of you."

He held out a hand, and Paul scuttled forward to drop a key into it.

"Where is my mother?" Thaniel shouted at him, ignoring the taste of blood on his lip. "What have you done with her?"

Paul's answer was a mocking sneer. He stepped back into the studio and out of sight as one of the Guard unlocked the cuffs. Once free of his stepfather's restraints, Thaniel lunged forward, but whatever the metal rope was, it held him firmly bound.

"You will only do that once," the man said, taking the end of the rope from the Guard.

"I want to see my mother."

"You will be silent." The man's manner was so cold and unruffled that Thaniel's fears rose even higher. There was no way she would stand by and let this happen.

"I want to know where my mother is. Is she hurt? Did you hurt her?" He shouted the last at the empty doorway, certain that Paul was still hovering close by. Incapacitating pain lanced through Thaniel's body, and he cried out, crumpling to the floor. It was over almost immediately.

"You will be silent," the man said again. Behind him, Paul Grayson reappeared, smirking like a schoolboy getting to play with the bullies.

Thaniel struggled to his feet. Without the use of his hands, it was an undignified scramble. No one helped him. The Guards' faces were blank. If, like his stepfather, they were enjoying this, their feelings were well masked. The man in charge waited until he was upright, then turned and led the way out of the room. The studio beyond was a mess, the destroyed models and components still strewn across the floor. Thaniel's eyes went straight to the place where his mother had fallen. He was relieved yet terrified to see that she was no longer there.

He glared at his stepfather but dared not speak again. Paul raised his eyebrows, shrugged his shoulders, and laughed. One of the Guard pushed Thaniel along, and he turned away before he tripped.

Outside in the garden, the grass was heavy with dew. Footprints trailed across the lawn, the stepping stones ignored by all but Paul.

An urgent tapping from the house made Thaniel look up. His mother was at one of the upstairs windows, tears painting lines of misery down her cheeks. One of her hands pressed against the glass.

"I love you, Nathaniel." Her shouted words muted by the double glazing were only just audible.

He forgot the rope.

"Mum," he yelled, starting towards the house. He only managed a step before the pain hit. It was like being wrapped in a living, pulsing thing. Then his body hit the ground, and the air was knocked out of him. As instantaneous as before, the pain was gone, and Thaniel was left writhing like a worm and gasping for breath.

The man in charge stopped and looked impassively down at him. He waited until Thaniel got back to his feet, then swung on his heel and walked away. Thaniel looked back up at the window. His mother had both hands up at the glass now, screaming his name.

"Nathaniel, Than.."

'*I love you,*' Thaniel mouthed to her as he was pushed on. He never got the chance to see her yell the words back, though her frantic hammering at the window stayed with him all the way across the lawn.

A midnight-blue van was parked by the kerb. It had no markings to identify it as belonging to the Guard, yet there was no doubting whose it was. A small group of onlookers had gathered. Keeping well back, they ogled at the sight of Thaniel, trussed up and being manhandled into the back. Paul Grayson stood by the gate with his arms folded. His vainglorious face was the last thing Thaniel saw as the doors closed.

Thaniel didn't think he had ever felt so helpless or so angry. The darkness of the van's interior did nothing to reassure him. He might have been the only occupant, but the space was full of the lingering apprehension and fear of the countless other occupants who had gone before him.

He lost all track of time and, exhausted after his night of agony, he would have dozed, had the driver not seemed to be doing his level best to hit every pothole that had ever graced the road's surface. Countless times, Thaniel's head smacked against the side panel, and more than once he was sent sprawling to the floor as the van swung around sharp bends with no thought for the safety of the unbelted passenger, bound in the back.

They must have reached a motorway because the going got smoother, and Thaniel soon drifted into an uneasy sleep. It could have been five minutes or five hours; he had no way of telling when he was suddenly jolted awake. The engine revved, and Thaniel struggled to keep his seat as they once again traversed smaller, twistier roads.

Even disoriented, it was clear when the van began to reverse its way down a bumpy track. Thaniel's pulse quickened. The vehicle stopped, and the engine was cut. One of the front doors opened, and the van's suspension shifted as someone got out. A minute later, one of the rear doors was flung wide, and light flooded into the compartment. Thaniel recoiled as his pupils suddenly retracted. He was pulled from the van, staggering a little as his feet touched the floor. The air was fresh on his face after the staleness of the van's interior, but still, Thaniel shuddered as he looked around him.

There were no buildings of any sort in sight, only fields, trees, and a high, formidable fence topped with razor wire. The unmetalled road beyond the substantial gate was more of an overgrown dirt track than anything else. The man in charge walked Thaniel over to a small pedestrian gate, beside which was an aluminium intercom with a backlit keypad. There must have been some kind of facial recognition function because the smaller gate clicked open after only a glance.

Thaniel found himself being pushed through, with the man following close behind. He shuddered as the cord emitted a strange pulse, reacting with whatever current was running through the fence. The van's engine started up again the moment the gate clicked shut behind them. A new spasm of fear clutched at Thaniel's throat as he watched the Guard drive away. Was he about to be killed here in the middle of nowhere, where there were no witnesses?

"You will keep silent and within six feet of me at all times. If you fail to do this, the crystal cord will activate." The man's voice was as hard as his features. Not waiting for an answer, he turned and began to walk.

Thaniel felt the cord around him starting to vibrate and quickly started after him. What was the point in trying to get away? Even if he could free himself from this strange silver binding, there would be no way to get past the enclosing fence.

Ruts had been gouged into the track, leaving deep puddles of muddy water next to which large thistles grew in abundance. They spiked at Thaniel's ankles as he passed. Once he fell, unable to keep his balance with his arms pinned. Pain shot through him as he hurried back to his feet; not quite as bad as before, still it was enough to make him scream.

Trees crowded in around them, dappling the ground with shadows from the dancing leaves above. It was a beautiful place and, apart from the occasional scolding blackbird, a haven of serenity. This sense of peace was so at odds with the predicament Thaniel found himself in that it conversely added to his feeling of foreboding.

The man kept walking, neither speaking nor looking anywhere but directly ahead. Thaniel was so scared, the tightness in his chest intense enough that he didn't know how he was going to take his next breath each time he exhaled. He could feel his heart thumping, the pulses at his throat and wrists thrumming to the same beat. He wondered what it would be like to die. Would he feel those pulses slow and stop, feel his heart give its one last thud? He imagined his vision going black and his hearing gradually fading away to nothing.

He slipped again, landing heavily. It took him a moment too long to recover his senses. The crystals on the ends of the cord glowed brighter, and the metal activated. Thaniel felt the screams tearing out of him. A tree root was digging into his side, and there was a sharp stabbing in one of his knees. Vaguely, he thought his ribs might be broken, but the pain from the cord was so intense he could barely register the injury. He knew he needed to get up; it was the only way to stop the agony, but he was drowning in it. This was the way he was going to die.

Abruptly, the all-consuming pain ended. Thaniel gasped for as much breath as his injured ribs would allow. Two muddy black boots appeared in front of him.

"Open up," the man said, reaching down.

Thaniel warily eyed the small capsule he was holding and clamped his lips closed.

"Either you take this and get back on your feet before I start walking again, or you don't." The man shrugged. "It's your choice. The crystal cord will not kill you, whatever you may think. You will stay in agony, or you will stay within six feet of me."

Thaniel opened his mouth. Dying of poison might be preferable to dying of agony. The taste was something akin to peanut butter, yet fizzing on his tongue as the capsule quickly melted. His pain stepped behind a curtain of stamina. Thaniel was too relieved to worry about how implausible that was. The man gave a brief nod, turned, and strode away. Fingers of hope started to encroach on Thaniel's fear. If this man wasn't trying to kill him, maybe he was taking him to safety? Was there any chance that this could actually be Etherea Forest?

Birds sang all around them: the light, chirruping cries of flocking blue tits and great tits, long-tailed tits, and even a few goldcrests. Then there was the repeating *chiff chaff chiff chaff chaff chiff* from high up in the treetops. The little brown warbler might prefer an open perch to sing his name, but Thaniel couldn't spot him. He did get a glimpse of a turret, though, and then a few steps later, the peak of a gable. Whilst the trees conspired to keep it obscured, Thaniel couldn't help feeling that the building was showing just as much interest in him as he was in it.

When they finally came through the last of the forest and stepped onto a wide, gravel path, the whole of the dark granite mansion came into view. Thaniel gasped in awe. It was like something out of a fantasy book—a cross between a medieval castle and an enormous stately home. Numerous gargoyles and grotesques looked down from their perches, each one seeming to stare at him with interest. A shiver rippled across his body, tingling all the way to his fingertips.

Across the front of the building, midway up the wall, were newer statues of men and women in long, flowing robes, their apathetic gazes oddly blank compared to the rest of the carvings. The man noticed where he was looking and gave a sarcastic noise in the back of his throat.

"There's your oligarchy," he said, nodding towards the row of figures. "You happy now?"

Thaniel's hopes snuffed out like a pinched candle.

The oligarchy had made their stance when it came to magicians. Once he went inside that building, he would never be coming out. His gut clenched around the thought that he would never see his mother again or know what happened to her. She would be left in the clutches of that bastard, Paul, unless she had the ingenuity to escape and start again. She had done it once before, when she'd had him to protect. Now, she had only herself, and Thaniel couldn't be sure she would think herself worthy enough to save.

He drew his eyes away from the statues and back up to the gargoyles. He could almost believe they were sentient. Despite the magic-quelling cord around him, his skin prickled again, then suffocated under the miasma of dread that settled on his heart. This magnificent building was so at odds with everything Thaniel had ever understood about the oligarchy. Yet there it was, proof in stone that this was indeed an oligarchy stronghold.

Despite pointing out the statues, Thaniel's captor was not the type of person to waste time admiring the architecture. He barely even broke step as he led the way along the path towards an inconspicuous door set into the closest wing of the building. Thaniel could feel every hair on his body alive with static as he followed. Their feet crunched on the gravel, grinding Thaniel's spirit further down with each step. Even the birds seemed to have stopped their chatter.

The door had once been a bright red, but the peeling paint had faded over time. A small brass plate read 'Sheldon Wing,' an innocuous name that did not match the looming facade. Every window, including the small one set into the door, was covered in ironwork. It was as if the building was one giant, ominous cage. Thaniel's eyes hooked on the brass-faced knocker set into the door, with its large, round, screaming mouth. His blood ran cold.

The man took hold of the knocker and rapped it three times. The loud, hollow sound was quickly followed by slow, steady footsteps. Thaniel's hands were clammy. Sweat trickled down the back of his neck. The door swung slowly open, and he swallowed hard.

5

AMELIA COULDN'T STAND IT ANY LONGER. IT HAD BEEN two days, and her burns were starting to itch unbearably. The feeling of pent-up magic inside her was almost as bad as when she had dropped the pan in the first place. She needed to release it again. Surely if she only used a little at a time, on the worst parts of her body, who would ever know?

Luck had been watching over her last time. The doctor had been called away on an emergency; his home visits taken over by a locum, who had arrived when both Dorothy and Mrs Lee had been busy. Letty had offered to sit with her whilst the bandages were being changed, but only so that she could flirt with the GP; she had paid no attention whatsoever to the state of Amelia's wounds. No one would notice if she was careful.

Holding her hands over the top of her left leg, Amelia held her breath and waited. Nothing happened. Exhaling, she tried again. Her thigh stayed obstinately damaged. Amelia swore under her breath, a slight feeling of panic beginning to unfurl deep in her stomach. Why couldn't she do it? It had been so easy last time. Frustrated, she reached for her cold tea. Maybe taking a drink would help her swallow the urge to break something? The cup shattered in her hand. The release felt amazing.

"Wow," she breathed, almost soundlessly.

In her hands, the broken pieces of pottery could have been countless accusations about what she had just done or one determined thought to be whole again. She chose the latter, and almost instantly the pieces reformed.

"Yes!" Her exclamation was louder this time.

She ran her thumb over the cup. Apart from a couple of small chips, it was as good as new. Not good enough to escape the wrath of Mrs Lee, though. The buzz of freshly released magic still hummed in her veins, changing Amelia's usual half-empty-glass approach to one of half-full. It took a good few minutes of dedicated searching before she found the two tiny missing pieces of pottery. Another concentrated thought, and the cup was as perfect as it had been when Letty brought it down to her. Amelia's hands were tingling from the expelled power. She turned them over and was surprised to see that the skin on her burnt palm had not changed at all.

The earlier bud of panic in her stomach had unwrapped itself into a kaleidoscope of butterflies, each one carrying a different thought of what could be possible now. She felt as light as air, as if with one dedicated step she could take flight herself. She almost tried, but the skin pulled on her leg as she lifted it, and her common sense returned. A heartbeat later, she was back on the bed, her hand above her thigh. Now that she knew how to focus properly, the healing came as easily as the intention. Restraining herself came somewhat harder. It was almost a relief to hear the heavy tread of Mrs Lee on the stairs.

"Are you feeling alright?" she asked, pressing the back of her hand against Amelia's forehead. "You feel fine, but you look a little flushed." Noticing the spilt tea, she frowned, and her voice sharpened to the tone Amelia was more accustomed to. "What happened here?"

"Sorry." Amelia did her best to look contrite. "I forgot how sore my hand was. I will clean it up."

Mrs Lee's face softened again, and she waved a hand. "Never mind. I will send Letty to clean it. You have a bit more rest this morning, then I think we can start you on something light this afternoon."

The cook might be showing a new side to her nature, but the maid had no such graces. "Not my place to clean up after someone else's carelessness," she grumbled as she wiped away the mess.

Amelia lifted her book out of the way before Letty caught it with her wet cloth. "I did say I would do it."

"Don't see how you've done anything to deserve all this special treatment." Letty sniffed, "It was your own stupid fault if you ask me. Mrs Lee won't stay soft on you for long."

****

"No, no. Elon Kelby cannot possibly sit next to Pazia Olvalroyd." Thomas Grange, Blain's house manager and personal assistant, flicked the offending card away. "She will only draw him out over that unfortunate incident with the Hunters. Come to think of it, better not put the Hunters anywhere near either of them."

"What incident, Mr Grange?" Amelia asked as she slid the name cards to one side.

"That is none of your business," Thomas huffed, studying the layout in front of him. The pressure was on with this dinner party. Overnight, it had gone from a simple affair to a major undertaking, all thanks to that pile of rubble they had uncovered in the woods. Elon had switched engagements with Nirim at the last minute, a move that Thomas was certain would have infuriated Nirim, who was a regular visitor. Elon had also requested invitations for both Peyton Lanford and Pazia Olvalroyd. With Lorena Hunter already confirmed as a guest, there would be four of the seven oligarchs in attendance.

Thomas raised an eyebrow and picked up the next card. "Ahh, Mr Greckham." He made a show of looking at the other names, "He can go next to Isabel Branwell and..." He swiped up Pazia Olvalroyd's card, slapping it down with a flourish.

Mrs Lee cast an eye over the cards. She tapped one. "Lillian Langford has an intolerance to strong smells; better move her. Marcus smokes those awful-smelling cigars, and Lidia Foxwell always wears far too much scent. Stick her between Mr Greckham and Alistair Calvington, Sylvie Cartright will have to move."

"She won't like that," Thomas huffed again, though he did not dispute Mrs Lee's reasoning. It was alright, Blain hosting these sorts of dinner parties, but it was his neck on the line should he get the seating plan wrong and cause a ruckus.

A gust of cold wind lifted the cards from the table as the back door opened, and the boys herded in, looking miserable. They were closely followed by Gipton, who ushered them quickly into the boot room to remove their wet outers. They still resembled half-drowned rats when they tramped into the kitchen.

"Get into the back room where the fire's lit," Mrs Lee ordered them. "I don't want you in here dripping on my clean floor. I'll send Letty along with some tea for you."

"You're a good egg," the gardener said as the boys traipsed out. "Bloody wet out there. It's to be hoped the weather bucks up soon or we wain't be finished in time."

Thomas Grange looked up sharply. "You need to be. Mr Blain intends taking them out to see."

Gipton made a noise in his throat. "I can't work miracles, Thomas."

Mrs Lee shoved the lid onto the teapot and planted her hands firmly on her hips. "What is going on?"

"Now Elsie, t'ain't anything you need to be worrying yourself about." Despite his words, Gipton looked uncomfortable.

"Don't you think I should be the judge of that?" she countered. Snapping her head around, she fixed a gimlet eye on Thomas. "You tell me what is going on, or I will go straight to Mr Blain and ask him myself."

Senior he may be, but no one messed with Elsie Lee when she had her temper up. Thomas straightened his back, bolstering himself against the coming onslaught. "You remember the box the boys found out in that old cottage?"

The rising colour in Mrs Lee's face drained away. Forgetting all about Amelia's injuries, she thrust a tray into her hands, adding cups, biscuit tin, and the heavy pot of tea. "Take this into the back room," she ordered, shooing the girl out of the door. "Go on, and don't come back until you're called for."

"I told you I didn't do it." Jasper's cheeks were flushed.

"Am I supposed to believe they just broke all by themselves, then?" Aarav yelled back at him.

Amelia put the tray down and looked quizzically at Mark. He was making no attempt to join in the row. He rolled his eyes at her. Clearly, this argument had been going on for a while.

Jasper was not backing down. "I never even used your stupid secateurs. I was using the edging spade all afternoon. You know I was."

"Boys." Amelia interrupted, dumping the tray on the table. "Come and have a drink and a biscuit."

"Amelia, you're out of bed," Jasper grinned, turning away from Aarav. "How are you feeling?"

"Still sore, but better. I've been helping Mr Grange do the seating plan for next week."

"I don't know why everyone is getting so het up about it," Mark said, helping himself to a jammy dodger. "It's only a dinner party. He puts one of those on every few months. The way Git-ton is talking, you'd think the house was going to come crashing down around our ears if we don't get everything done."

"They were just saying something about that now. Mrs Lee didn't seem very happy." Amelia wished she had been able to stay in the kitchen a bit longer and hear what was being said.

Aarav, realising that he'd lost everyone's attention, gave up his aggravated stance and joined them at the small table. He shoved two dodgers in his mouth at once, spraying crumbs as he spoke. "Git-ton told us not to talk about the wood in front of her. He wouldn't say why, just that she'd a lot on her plate right now."

"Pig." Mark stirred sugar into his tea, relieved that a plateful of biscuits had finally released the tension. Aarav had been spoiling for a fight all afternoon. It was getting to be a habit.

****

Amelia's nightmare had not been a solitary occurrence. Frequently, she found herself bolting awake, gasping for the breath that would draw her back to the land of the living. Each dream followed a similar pattern. She would find herself alone somewhere beautiful. These havens of calm would swiftly change to scenes of terror as whatever water there was nearby engulfed her. Just before she died, the same boy would appear and try his best to save her. No matter how hard he tried, he always failed. Sometimes, their fingers would touch, and a jolt of excitement would shoot up Amelia's arm like an electric shock.

He intrigued her. Once, years ago, she had read that it was impossible for your mind to make up a face. Anyone appearing in your dreams had to be someone, however inconsequential, that you had already seen. Amelia knew for a fact that she had never seen this person. He was not someone she would ever forget. Maybe a little older than her, with pale, ice-blue eyes and dark, unruly hair. He made her heart race and her stomach fill with wriggling, fluttering nerves that were impossible to control. Every time she awoke from seeing him, he would linger in her mind. It made her heart ache that they could never hold one another.

She found herself thinking of him at odd times throughout the day, earning herself numerous scoldings for daydreaming. The household was all working hard to prepare for Blain's upcoming dinner party. Usually that would have raised Mrs Lee's spirits, but whatever Mr Grange and Git-ton had told her the other night had put her in the foulest of moods. It made her short with everyone, and her newfound sympathy with Amelia had evaporated like mist in the morning sunshine.

Tension in Marlborough House increased as the day for the event drew nearer. Lessons with Mr & Mrs Forth were cancelled for the week so that everyone could focus on the preparations. Every inch of the house had to be swept, dusted, polished, and vacuumed; even those parts that the guests were never likely to see.

"It doesn't do to be slack in these matters," Grange told them. "You never know when an emergency might arise."

Gipton kept all the boys working hard outside. They weren't complaining. It was always fun to get out of the grounds and into the woods. There had been no more finds in the cottage, but Aarav did find an old wooden door nearby, with rusted hinges set deep into a bulge in the ground. When they finally managed to wrench it open, they found a stale-smelling underground cellar room, independent from the house itself.

Inside, they discovered the remains of a makeshift bed with a few disintegrating old clothes heaped on top. Jasper nosed into some wooden crates piled against one wall, finding them all disappointingly empty. In the far corner stood an old metal barrel. Gipton poked a stick inside, then recoiled, coughing. He clicked his fingers at Aarav and Mark. "Drag this outside. It's far too dark in here to see what's in it."

"There's something nasty in there; it smells like dead dog." Aarav gagged, kicking the barrel. "Can't Mark do it on his own?"

Mark bit his tongue. Aarav's moods were really getting on his nerves. They had turned his easy-going pal into an irritable pain in the...

The sound of Johns yelling stopped Mark's thoughts dead in their tracks. Both his friend's irascibility and the barrel were soon forgotten as he raced with the others to see what had happened. They found Johns at the bottom of what would once have been the cottage's garden, one of his legs sunk deep into a hole in the ground.

"Looks like an old well," Mark said, kicking aside the broken cover.

"Hmm. They could have covered it with something better than a mossy bit of wood," Johns grumbled, rubbing at his leg. It had taken two of them to pull him free of the shaft, and his pride was hurting far more than his body.

"I wonder how deep it is?" Jasper dropped a stone down the hole. They counted to four before hearing a splash.

"Good job you didn't go right down," Gipton said, getting down on his hands and knees and peering inside.

Mark was still kicking around at the debris. "Looks like they might have had a bit of a wall around it. You can see where roots have grown through the brickwork, and it's crumbled away. There's some wire here too, and bits of rotten posts."

"Give yourself a few minutes, Johns, and then you and Mark set to and get some kind of covering over that hole. I don't care how pretty it is, so long as it stops anyone falling down it until I can arrange for something more permanent." Gipton pointed to Aarav and Jasper. "You two get back to the root cellar and shift that barrel."

Hitching their T-shirts up over their mouths, they dragged the reeking tub to the doorway, heaving it carefully up the steps and out into the daylight. It was half full of black-looking water, with something pale lurking beneath the surface. The boys looked at each other.

"I'm not doing it," Aarav said. "That bloody thing stinks."

Jasper shrugged and kicked the barrel. It tipped easily, and he jumped back. Aarav wasn't so quick. Stagnant water splashed over his shoes.

"You little shit. You did that on purpose. I ought to..." His words faded away as he noticed the look of horror on Jasper's face.

"It wasn't a dog," Jasper said quietly.

Sitting on the ground in front of them was the unmistakable remains of a human head. It must have been in the barrel a very long time. The hair was all gone, as was the skin. Only the skull remained, covered in a sickly, whitish-grey substance that left a trail of waxy gunk where it had rolled. The smell of stagnant water was overpowered by a rancid, ammonia-like stench, which quickly faded in the fresh air.

Aarav turned away, managing only a couple of steps before doubling over and retching loudly. Hearing him, Gipton marched over. He saw the head and stopped short.

"Johns!" he yelled over his shoulder. "Get Blain. NOW!"

Johns took one look at the lump on the ground and fled.

"I need to get these shoes off," Aarav said as soon as he'd finished being sick. "They're covered in that stuff."

Gipton's eyes remained fixed on the head in front of him, as if he were frightened it might start talking the second he looked away.

"Do you think the rest of the body is here somewhere?" Jasper asked, glancing around, as if to catch sight of a withered limb or two. He felt a little nauseous himself.

"Get yourself back to the house," Gipton said, snapping out of his shock. "Take Mark with you. You're all done for the day."

6

"STANTON MEADS." MRS LEE SET HER TEACUP DOWN with such force that the fine bone china handle snapped clean off. She didn't even notice. "I thought we were done hearing that name. Is it not bad enough that I hear it in my nightmares?" An uncharacteristic wobble slid into her voice.

Gipton lifted a hand as if to touch her arm, then thought better of it. Beside him, Blain tapped a thoughtful finger on the tabletop before speaking. "Elon Kelby is hoping to be able to give us more information when he comes on Thursday. Hopefully, by then, they will know who the head belonged to."

Dorothy shivered, "I am just glad they have taken the wretched thing away. Imagine it being out there all this time, rotting." Her eyes went wide. "Do you think there will be any more... bodies, I mean?"

Mrs Lee closed her eyes, her knuckles white where they gripped the arms of her chair.

Gipton shook his head. "We've scoured the area of the cottage; there was nothing else to find. One of the Guard teams the oligarchy sent even set up a rope and went down the well. It was all clear."

Mrs Lee let out a relieved breath. Blain gave her a reassuring smile. "We have no idea what magical residue may remain, so we will be burning the whole plot as soon as the search is fully complete." A shadow passed behind his eyes as he spoke. Magic was once again being performed at Marlborough House. His sensors had been picking up the signs for days. Young magicians could not contain their emerging magic for long, and soon enough it would be evident who the culprit was. Blain just hoped it would not happen during Thursday's dinner party, but if it did, he would be ready.

He was unsure whether there was any link between finding the magician's cottage and the awakening of one of the teenager's powers; it could just be a coincidence. Where magic was concerned, though, it paid to be vigilant, something that both Mrs Lee and the Fenton area knew to their cost.

About ten years earlier, rumours concerning magic and its practitioners had begun to circulate all across the country. At first, many tried to ignore the malicious talk. After all, people had lived alongside magicians for time immemorial. They were part of the fabric of society: friends, colleagues, family. Somehow, though, no matter how loud the voices of sense and reason, the detractors drowned them out. More people had begun to doubt. Gossip led to fear, which in turn led to intolerance. Magicians began to be targeted, victimised, and hounded. The Guard was set up to quell the rising problems. They trod a fine line in those early days; needing to appear neutral and reassuring to everyone, they nevertheless set about removing every magician provoked into retaliating.

Stanton Meads' semi-reclusive ways and notorious temper had always marked him out as an oddity. Whilst he had by no means been the only magician in the area, he had soon become the natural target for the people of Fenton. As the small town's residents became bolder with their taunts, so Stanton's ill-tempered responses had grown. It had only enhanced people's fears.

After months of animosity and hatred, Stanton had been cornered in the library by a large group of brash young people. Refusing to turn himself over for citizen's arrest, asserting that he had done nothing wrong, the situation had turned nasty. Emboldened by reports of other such attacks on magicals, the youths had advanced, brandishing iron bars, knives, and anything else they could get their hands on.

Stanton had responded with fire, the dry wooden timbers of the old building going up like kindling, causing enough heat to burn three-inch-thick tomes to ashes. Stanton, protected by his powers, had simply walked out through the flames, leaving everyone else trapped inside. None had survived. Blain shuddered at the thought. How on earth did anyone overcome such tragedy?

Stanton had not lingered in the town, hurrying away to his little cottage in the woods where the Guard had found him, barely an hour later. In those days, Fenton Woods had been a light and airy place, where the townsfolk often walked. Stanton quickly put paid to that. His final act had been to curse the area surrounding his dwelling so that it quickly grew into a dense barricade full of impenetrable rhododendron, hawthorn, and holly. Whether he had intended to seal himself inside or to stop anyone from getting to his property once he had been caught, no one knew for sure.

The mass murder of thirty-five young people and two members of staff had been the single biggest atrocity of the Purge and the catalyst the oligarchy had been waiting for. With the majority of the public now lobbying for them to take a much firmer stance, they reluctantly, or so it had appeared to the public, agreed that they would no longer tolerate the use of magic. The role of the Guard was ramped up, and the organised vigilantes who had been stirring up animosity for so long began to terrorise the magical community in earnest.

A year later, tolerance of the troubles was waning fast. The oligarchy found itself coming under further pressure to end the problems once and for all. They made a show of punishing the vigilantes and discouraging anyone else from taking matters into their own hands. Slowly, everything settled down. The Guard continued its work in the background, and no one really noticed that the oligarchy had stopped short of actually outlawing the use of magic.

Marlborough House and its extensive grounds had been abandoned when Stanton's curse had begun encroaching on its borders. Once again, the oligarchy had stepped in, buying up both property and woodland and thereby giving the distraught people of Fenton a welcome buffer between the town and the cursed land. Nominated and supported by the Home Affairs Oligarch, Nirim Elex, Blain had been given residency and the highly trusted new role of Guardian. It was a position he took very seriously.

Around the country, a number of these guardian houses had been put in place. Their public role was to take in those under twenty-one who had been displaced or orphaned by the Purge and give them a first-class education and apprenticeship. Yet despite outward appearances, guardian houses did not take in every waif created by the unrest. Only those possessing a magical bloodline, or whose parentage could not be ascertained, were given into the system.

Powers could begin to show themselves at any time during a magician's growing years but usually began to emerge in the mid to late teens. It was unheard of for magical abilities to develop after the age of twenty. Just to make sure that no one slipped through the net, guardian houses kept their residents until the age of twenty-one. After that, they were deemed adults and free to enjoy life without any further censure.

"And you are sure it is safe to burn it all?" Mrs Lee wrung her hands together, a sure sign of her distress.

Blain opened his mouth to answer, but Gipton got there first.

"It will be," the gardener assured her. "Nothing will be done until the weather conditions are perfect and the fire breaks are in place."

Blain nodded his agreement. He needed people like Gipton and Mrs Lee, those who detested magic and would continue to do so for as long as they lived. He had made a mistake once with a cleaner from the town. Luckily, it had been rectified before any damage had been done, but it must never happen again. There could be no doubts here;

no chance of anyone else sympathetic to magic slipping into his employ. His workers acted as his eyes and ears in both the house and the town. Nothing went on that he did not get to hear about sooner or later.

The muscle by his left eye twitched, and he rubbed it. Mrs Lee's concerns reminded him that he would need to send someone into Fenton to see what, if anything, was being said about them there. The locals always took an interest in the comings and goings at Marlborough House. Blain wouldn't put it past someone to have seen the experts arriving and decided to tattle. He allowed himself a small smile. It would be a simple matter to hint that all the activity was down to security measures. When his guests began turning up for the dinner party later in the week, all speculation would be washed away. Blain did not mind the gossip, so long as he could manipulate what was being said.

He often entertained oligarchs at Marlborough House, along with the usual crowd of socialites. It was rare that anyone new was ever admitted into the ranks of the ruling class, but that did not seem to deter the many bootlickers and hangers-on who had emerged at the first hints of a war with the magicians. Not special enough to have been noticed much before, they now thrived in the spaces created by the demise of those with better talents. Blain was always included in this group, and though he played his part well, he was already exactly where he wanted to be. As one of a select few people who undertook secret work for the ruling body, not even all the oligarchs knew everything that Nirim asked of him.

Blain looked across the table at Gipton; he too played his role well. Marlborough House's gardens were immaculate now, though it had taken two years to bring them back to order. All that while, Gipton had been extending the work out into the surrounding woodland. It was done as part of the boys' apprenticeships, but in reality Gipton's job had always been to uncover the location of the notorious magician's former property.

Mrs Lee was looking tired; what with Amelia's accident and the preparations for the upcoming dinner party, things were clearly taking their toll. They had always prioritised boys at Marlborough House, yet Morgan had been gone over a year now, and it was high time they got another girl to take her place. The number of youngsters coming into the system had dwindled significantly, though it would take many more years before they had contained all the magic that existed. Blain wondered again which one of their current residents was causing the trouble this time.

Gipton cleared his throat. "Will the men be back tomorrow, or are they finished here now?"

Blain shook away his wandering thoughts and brought his attention fully back to the conversation. "They are going to give the area one final check-over in the morning, and then you can burn it. Make sure all the boys are there; the girl can go out too. I want them to see what is done to anything magic. Reinforce the dangers."

Gipton nodded. "Good idea. I get the feeling that Jasper especially is very excited about all these new findings."

"It's only natural." Blain carefully picked a stray hair from his sleeve. "But they need to be made aware that it is only exciting because we are getting *rid* of every trace of magic and the unnatural magician who wielded it."

****

The fire burned hot and fierce, helped along by the liberal amounts of kerosene Johns had poured over everything. Not even the fallen masonry had been spared.

"We will have to make a new cover for the well," Mark said as the hastily arranged wooden boards were licked in flame.

"The well will be getting filled in," Gipton called over. "Can't risk anyone being harmed by drinking from it."

Amelia thought at first that he must be joking, but one look at his face told her he was deadly serious. Johns, too. Surely no one could be harmed by drinking the same water that a magician had once used? If that were the case, then everyone at Marlborough House was in danger from her. The thought made her feel unclean. Was this how lepers had felt when they'd been forced to cover their faces and ring a bell to warn others of their presence?

"You look upset." Aarav flung his arm around her shoulders. "You're not going to be contaminated just by standing here, you know."

"I'm not upset." She shrugged his arm away. Aarav frowned but for once said nothing. "I was just thinking, can you really get hurt from drinking water?"

"You can if it's been tainted by magic," Mark said, orange light dancing in his eyes from the reflected flames. It gave him an oddly ominous air.

Gipton finished prodding part of the fire and came over to them. "We think this place belonged to a magician named Stanton Meads. He killed a lot of young people before they finally got him, including Mrs Lee's two daughters. Burnt 'em all in a raging fire, he did. There's no telling what else the evil bastard might have done before they took him away."

"Cook had two daughters?" Jasper gasped. "I didn't even know she was married."

Gipton shook his head, looking pained. "Her husband died the very next day. Couldn't take the grief, they said. His heart just gave up. You go easy on Mrs Lee these next few days, the lot of you. She ain't taking this easily."

"I could have told my own story, thank you very much."

No one had heard Mrs Lee walking up behind them. She stood watching the flames, her eyes dry and clear, her mouth set in a firm line. She said no more, just watching as the fire caressed her memories.

Mercifully, she had been out of town on the day of the tragedy, visiting a friend a clear five miles away. Though even at that distance she had seen the mass of smoke rising sleepily into the air, not realising at the time that she had been witnessing her daughters' final goodbye.

She looked at the smoke now, pulling upwards from the tips of the flames. She hoped her girls would see it, wherever they were; see it and know that the last remnants of Stanton Meads' life here were burning. She turned away briskly and walked back to the house. She would not cry today. This was the closest she was ever going to get to justice; it was not a day to mourn. It was a day to be thankful for those like Blain, who stopped at nothing to clear the world of such evil.

****

Two days later, the long drive was full of sleek and shiny cars, indicative of the class of occupants they had just delivered. The formal dining room looked immaculate; each precise place setting at the long mahogany table had no doubt been laid using a ruler. Dominating the centre was a long, low arrangement of flowers and greenery, interspersed with candles.

The dinnerware was of the finest china, pure white with an elegant piping of silver scrolling around the edges, matching perfectly with the silver cutlery. The glasses, three to each setting, were all of the best quality crystal. As were the water and wine decanters sitting on the long, mahogany bureau that nestled against one wall.

Blain had brought in professionals to do all the work, sparing no expense for the occasion. Amelia and Jasper had helped carry in the tall floral stands that were now dispersed throughout the hall and reception rooms, but that was about all. The richly scented arrangements of Aurelian lilies, lisianthus, and gypsophila easily covered the lingering smells of floor wax and furniture polish. Mrs Lee had actually smiled as she stood back and let the caterers get on with unloading. The kitchen had soon been full of hams, smoked salmon, and canapés. Succulent joints of sirloin beef and rack of lamb were dressed and ready to go into the heated ovens, and heaps of vegetables were being peeled and prepared.

"Anything could happen tonight," Blain had warned the three boys and Amelia when he appeared downstairs shortly after three pm. "The circumstances of the cottage are unprecedented and not for common gossip." He gave them each a sharp, pointed look. "Obviously the members of the oligarchy are likely to be very interested. This is the first time most of them will be hearing the news. I want nothing to show me up. They will no doubt want to question some of you. You will speak only when spoken to, and then only to answer the questions you are asked. Nothing more."

They each nodded as he looked at them in turn.

"The members of the oligarchy will be arriving half an hour before the other guests. You are to stay silent and out of sight unless called for. Mr Grange will be keeping a *very* close eye on you all."

Amelia looked at her feet, relieved. They were not likely to want to speak with her. She had nothing to do with what the boys had found in the woods. Aarav's elbow dug into her side.

"Are you listening to me, girl?" Blain demanded.

Amelia looked up like a startled lamb.

"You are to present the ladies with a small spray of flowers as they are leaving. You will stand on the front step next to me. Boys, you will stand in line down the steps. It will be very late, so get some rest beforehand. Dorothy, make sure they are all presentable."

"They will be, sir. You have my word."

Blain gave a sharp nod of his head. "Good." He ran his eyes over them all again. Appearing dubiously satisfied, he made a dismissive noise.

Amelia felt herself sag a little with relief.

"A word, Mr Grange, if you would." Blain turned and strode from the room, Thomas hurrying after him.

"I suggest you all go and have a lie down for now." Dorothy looked as if she would enjoy a few minutes' peace and quiet herself. "The guests will be arriving in a couple of hours; there will be no chance after that. We won't be eating until just after eight, so get yourselves something to put you on." She pointed to a tray of neatly cut sandwiches on the sideboard. "Then off you go."

****

Amelia dreamed. She hadn't thought she would even be able to sleep, given all the excitement and the noise, but the moment her eyes closed, he was there waiting for her. Every nerve ending in her body came alive at the sight of him. She longed to touch him, to feel the texture of his skin beneath her palms. Before she could reach him, he was shouting, but his words were torn away by the sudden wind whipping through the tree branches. She spun around, looking for the water. There was always water, waiting to wash her life away.

This time, it was a pretty stream, with sparkling clear water rushing over a pebble bed. The sound of it was suddenly all she could hear. She turned back to where the boy had been standing, but he was gone, leaving her feeling desolate and alone.

Her feet were getting wet. She looked down. The stream was now a river, sweeping wide to draw her in. The current pushed at her, wanting to take her with it. The pressure buckled her knees, and she fell sideways. The water closed over her head. When she couldn't hold her breath any longer, she opened her mouth. Bubbles poured out, and the river rushed in, filling her chest with pain.

Suddenly, a hand reached towards her. The fingers closed around her own and pulled. The next thing she knew, she was on the bank, coughing up mouthfuls of water. Exhausted, she collapsed onto her back, grateful for the sweet air in her lungs. The boy's face appeared above hers, his eyes clouded with worry. Butterflies in her stomach flipped and danced as his hand caressed her face. Closing her eyes, she knew the kiss was coming. She smiled as his breath warmed her skin. Then his scream tore through the air as something dragged him from her, carrying him higher and higher. She was left, shivering on the riverbank, knowing that she would always be alone.

7

THE CANDLE IN FRONT OF ISABEL BRANWELL WAS flickering wildly, sending chaotic shadows dancing over the nearby faces. She blinked, trying to ignore it. Next to her, Peyton Lanford was trying to skewer a reluctant quail's egg with his fork. She watched it skittering around his plate and tightened her grip on her own cutlery. God, she was getting way too intolerant lately. Her premenstrual tension was so out of control that even she could feel how irrational she was. Maybe she should consider seeing the doctor?

"Isabel... Izzy..."

Her attention flicked back to Blain. "Sorry, I didn't catch that." She put her knife and fork together on her plate and pushed it slightly away from her.

"I was asking if you'd heard anything from Armitage?"

As was so often the case, her husband was busy working away. His job took him all across the country, often for weeks on end. It wasn't that he left her struggling; the money his unsociable job earned him was more than enough to ensure that she wanted for nothing. They had a large, ranch-style house sitting in substantial grounds. Two fine thoroughbreds graced her stables, along with a beautiful, flaxen chestnut Arab. Her beloved horses took up a good part of her time, but even so, the loneliness of her life was a constant drain. She painted her usual smile on her face, grateful for the distraction.

"He telephoned me shortly before I left this evening, as a matter of fact." For a moment her eyes brightened, "He is hoping to be home early next week if all goes well. Problems at the company he went to oversee have not been as drastic as he had first thought."

One of Blain's eyebrows raised. "Really? I thought it was quite a big job he was on?"

"Yes, I was quite surprised."

Isabel took a sip of her wine as Blain's attention was briefly taken by one of the waiters. She glanced around the table. She was used to attending functions without Armitage, so rarely was he around to attend them himself. She supposed she should be grateful to be included without him. She looked at Clive Greckham and Alistair Calvington and wondered which one had been invited to make up the numbers this time. It certainly wouldn't have been Elon Kelby sitting down at the other end of the table.

In the background, strains of Tchaikovsky's *Waltz of the Flowers* could just be heard over the chink of cutlery. She hummed along to it, watching as one of the waiters took the flickering candle away to trim the wick.

Blain finished speaking to the waiter and turned his attention back to Isabel. "How is that latest thoroughbred you acquired? A 16.3 bay, I believe?"

Isabel was always happy to discuss her horses; they were the one thing in her life that had consistency. Her face lit up as she launched into a description of her latest acquisition. Blain listened with half an ear, trying to keep abreast of his other guests at the same time. His eye fell on Sylvie sitting down at the other end of the table. She looked as contented as everyone else, but she had been his plus-one far too long for him to be fooled. Usually excellent company, she would no doubt make a point of not looking in his direction all night.

Blain had known the seating arrangements would not be to her liking. He'd hoped that having one of the seats of honour next to Elon Kelby would placate her. Clearly, he had been wrong. He smothered a sigh. Was it any wonder that he had no intention of ever marrying? An attractive woman with excellent social standing, he considered Sylvie a friend, a suitable partner for socialising and functions, but nothing more.

Of all the women he knew, Blain had the softest spot for Isabel. He felt sorry for her predicament, though he didn't want to sleep with her either. Sylvie could be as jealous as she liked; he simply wasn't interested in that sort of thing—with anyone.

"... tender frog, but it seems to be on the mend nicely now."

Blain dragged himself back to the conversation. "Once he stops being lame, let me know. We'll go out for a ride together. I could do with taking Duke out for a long hack. He hasn't been out much lately."

Isabel leaned back and let the waiter take her plate. "That would be lovely, though I probably shouldn't take him too far for a while. I could always bring Lady Rain instead."

Further down the table, the conversation was far more animated.

"It is not natural," Lidia Foxwell was saying. "Half the food available is so heavily processed and tampered with that you don't know what it is you're eating. I swear some of the stuff my Sophie buys is only one step away from being plastic."

Marcus Blatt shook his head. "Soy, jackfruit, tofu... Really, Lidia, you should get your facts right. I admit a lot of vegan foods are highly processed, but it's far from plastic."

"Okay, so tell me, what is the point of vegan eggs? Surely if you don't want to eat eggs, you wouldn't want to pretend to eat them?"

"It's not pretending to eat something; it's just adding variety into their diet. There's nothing wrong with that."

The waiters moved about like ghosts, only half noticed as they cleared the first course and began serving the next. Lidia looked at the thick, succulent slices of pink beef on the plate that had just been placed in front of her. "We have always eaten meat; it's what our digestive systems are set up for. If you want to be more natural, then maybe just cut out dairy. That, I can fully understand. Sophie was already very thin; now her bones are showing even more. How you can tell me that is healthy, Marcus, I have no idea."

"Now Lidia, don't be twisting my words. I never said being so thin was healthy. It doesn't matter what your diet is; if you don't eat the right amounts and balance it out properly, you're going to have problems. I'm just saying that a vegan diet makes a lot of sense. I envy your daughter's dedication." Marcus nodded as a waiter materialised beside him, offering more wine.

"There is no sense in having a diet that you have to supplement with tablets because it cannot give you all the essential vitamins your body needs." Lidia rolled her eyes, looking at Marcus's wife, Lucy, across the table.

Lucy pulled a face back at her. "You might as well talk to a stone," she called over to them. "For what it is worth, I agree with you in part. Some people can live quite healthily on a vegan diet, but unfortunately, not everyone can."

Next to her, Sylvie smiled blandly. How typical of Lidia to drone on about her precious children. Anyone would think they were the only kids in the world. Sure, they had lost their father in a work accident during the Purge, but who hadn't lost someone?

On Sylvie's right, Elon Kelby was deep in conversation with Marlon Hunter, who, for some reason, had swapped seats with one of the other guests and thrown all Thomas Grange's careful seating plan into disarray. Marlon did not seem very happy about something, and it didn't take a genius to work out what. *Cuckold,* Sylvie thought unkindly. She didn't think it could be easy, always playing second fiddle to his powerful wife; now with all the rumours in the press that she was also screwing the Master Oligarch, it must be hammering at his masculinity.

Sylvie wished she could make out what they were saying, but the table was too wide for easy conversation with anyone other than her immediate neighbours. A fact Lucy seemed not to have realised. She should behave with a little more decorum; this was a very illustrious dinner party, after all. No less than four of the seven members of the oligarchy were present: Elon Kelby, Pazia Olvalroyd, Peyton Lanford, and Lorena Hunter. Lucy should be on her best behaviour. There were plenty of other occasions where she could holler across a dinner table and not be frowned upon. Then again, she did have Alistair Calvington on her other side. That man could send anyone's blood running cold. Sylvie could never understand why he was included on anyone's invitation list. It wasn't as if he was on any committees or did anything important. He ran a research centre. Something to do with science, possibly; she had never cared enough to really listen.

Isabel let out a shrieking laugh from the other end of the table. Sylvie took a mouthful of beef and ground her teeth together. That woman grated on her nerves. It was clear to anyone with even half a sense that she was an overly hormonal female desperate for attention. Her husband was rarely ever at home, leaving his wife to swan around the countryside in her skin-tight jodhpurs and woefully inadequate breast support.

Sylvie knew that Blain sometimes accompanied her. She herself could not bear horses; they were smelly and big, with too much gas and no toilet training. She just could not see the attraction so many women had for the beasts. As for men riding, well... that just made her cringe. Surely it was far too painful for men to sit astride a horse like that; their anatomy must surely get in the way? She shook away the thought, only to have it replaced by one of Isabel fawning over Blain. Her teeth clenched even tighter. She would not look; she would not appear to care. She focused instead on her plate; the beef really was delicious. This caterer was first-class; she should get their name before she left.

****

With four options for the guests to choose from at every course, there was plenty of food left over for those downstairs to enjoy. They were having a served banquet of their own, so for once everyone was able to relax and enjoy being waited on.

"I wonder how the news is being taken?" Johns said between mouthfuls.

Mrs Lee gave him a disgusted look. The least he could do was pretend to have some manners whilst they were eating such fine food. She took a sip of her wine. It was not the same quality as that being served upstairs, but still far better than anything the staff would ordinarily be given.

"I doubt they will talk about it at the dinner table," Thomas said in his most supercilious voice. "It is hardly a topic to discuss over one's meal." He put a loaded fork in his mouth, closing his eyes as the flavours melted over his tongue.

Johns rolled his eyes. Mark and Aarav grinned at him.

"Can I have some wine, please?" Aarav asked, holding his glass out hopefully.

"You can have sparkling juice," Mrs Lee said. "You are not twenty-one yet."

Aarav shrugged his shoulders. "Worth a try."

Amelia nibbled at her food, trying to imagine the boy from her dreams sitting here with them. It seemed so ridiculous to call him a boy, as if he were nothing more than a child. What else could she use, though? Teenager? Young man? They were both so... cumbersome. Her stomach fluttered at the thought of those clear blue eyes on her. She just knew that they would warm her, even though they shone like chips of sparkling ice. Gooseflesh rose on her skin, and she tried not to smile.

"Are you alright?" Dorothy was looking curiously at her. "You're hardly eating anything. I just saw you shiver, and you're looking a little flushed. You aren't coming down with anything, are you?"

"I'm okay," Amelia said quickly, flushing even more. "I've never had quail's eggs before; they're so small." She made an effort to push her thoughts away and concentrate on what she was doing. Tonight was not the time to raise anyone's concerns.

8

"THANK YOU." BLAIN SMILED AT THE WAITER. "CAN YOU inform one of my staff downstairs that I want to see Ted Gipton in ten minutes in my study?"

The guests had retired to the large drawing room, where a string quartet was playing quietly in the corner. Lillian Lanford stood near an open window, savouring the fresh air. She had asked for the nearest bouquets, with their heavily scented lilies, to be moved, and the eager young gentleman from the catering company had obliged.

"I am sorry about the flowers, Lillian," Blain apologised, turning back to her. "They certainly are overpowering." He cocked his head to one side, a cheeky grin forming on his face. "Though, I would have thought that given your name..."

Lillian laughed, "I'm afraid the only flowers of my namesake that I can bear are the unscented variety. Is that not right, love?"

Peyton slipped in beside them with two glasses of champagne and an apologetic look for Blain, who raised his own half-drunk glass in response.

"Ah," Peyton said with a nod. He rested his free hand on the small of his wife's back and smiled indulgently at her before turning back to his host. "I have some new varieties of Asiatic lilies in the garden this year. Fragrance-free, they promise a delicate pink colour, and, given our cooler climate, we can expect to have a number of semi-double blooms."

The Lanfords' garden was renowned. Peyton had a huge variety of flowers from all over the world, many of which he had bred himself. Some now even graced the flowerbeds here at Marlborough House. Blain knew next to nothing about the subject; he left all that sort of thing to his gardener. He murmured a vaguely approving response. The thought of Gipton reminded him what he was supposed to be doing. "Forgive us, Lillian; I must whisk Peyton away for a little business."

With a sigh, Lillian watched them leave. Though, after the news Blain had imparted to the oligarchs and their partners when they'd first arrived, she fully understood its necessity. She shuddered, not wanting to think about dismembered heads, then winced inwardly, glancing towards the musicians. She really was not keen on their arrangement of *Greensleeves*. The lead violinist kept adding little flourishes, which jarred with her own expected flow of the music. It was like picking up a well-known book only to find someone had added an extra page of conflicting story to the end of each chapter.

Her mind wandered again; what would Blain do if he realised that he had not been given the whole truth? Would he still be as eager to help them? Probably. People like Blain, nice as he was, were always eager to do whatever it took to feel that bit more accepted than everyone else. Lillian looked sideways at the others left in the room. Not one of them knew as much as they thought they did about the inner workings of the oligarchy. Even her own knowledge was restricted. She was more than happy with that, though, or was it that it just didn't seem important? When her one desire, to be a mother, was one that would never, could never, ever, hold true, how could anything else in the world matter?

That dream had been taken cruelly away many years ago in a tiny fishing village in the southern part of the country when a magician selling charmed wish bracelets had cursed her. Absently, Lillian's hand found its way to her stomach as she remembered. Her fingers fluttered over the silk of her dress, like the faint, tiny beating of a foetal heart, before she clenched her fist tight, crushing the memories into yet more mental confetti. It filled every waking moment and tinged every sleeping thought. She would never be rid of the longing, the memories, or the guilt.

If she had not picked up that bracelet, Peyton and the magician would not have got into an argument, she would not have told them she had changed her mind, and the magician would not have twisted her words. Those colourful flakes of memory would never let her forget the feeling of her womb shrivelling as the magician wrapped the bracelet around her wrist. They would never cease dangling the hope that maybe one day her husband would find a way to reverse what he had done. How could she ever complain about the time Peyton spent chasing down magicians? How could she not support whatever it took to reach their goals?

The musicians had moved on to a rendition of Handel's *Arrival of the Queen of Sheba*, which was much more to

Lillian's taste. She concentrated on trying to pick out the lower tones of the viola. It did not do to dwell too much on lost hope. When she was certain that she was as composed as she could be, she turned to the other guests and began to mingle once more.

****

In the study, extra chairs had been brought in to accommodate Pazia, Peyton, and Lorena. Blain had given his smart captain's chair up to Elon and taken the Gainsborough usually reserved for his visitors. A knock on the door hushed their conversation.

This being his office, Blain was the one to call out, "Enter."

Gipton shuffled in, a little nervous to be in the midst of such company. He knitted his fingers together in front of himself as he faced the large desk. He had scrubbed his hands with a stiff hog hair nail brush, managing to remove almost all of the usual grime that welded to his gardener's hands. Feeling the cracked skin and callouses, he quickly shifted his hands behind his back and tried to relax.

"Now then, Ted," Elon Kelby said, diluting his imposing manner with a welcoming smile. "Can you tell us all about these findings in Fenton Woods, both the fortunate and the unfortunate ones?"

Gipton shot a hesitant look to Blain, who clarified, "The cottage we have been looking for, and the head we were not."

"Ah, yes." Gipton swallowed, his mouth dry. Blain pushed a glass towards him, and he took a welcome drink, the amber whisky burning a path down his throat.

"So who was it that actually found the cottage?" Pazia Olvalroyd focused on the gardener, as if she could draw the information from him with her gaze alone. Her black hair was styled tonight in ombre box braids, tipped in bright scarlet, matching lips and nails providing the only coloured highlights in her otherwise black ensemble.

Gipton thought for a second, "I believe it was Mark." He scratched at his clean-shaven chin. "No, no, it was Aarav. I had left the boys under Johns' care whilst I went into town. They were supposed to be clearing a specific area. I have the wood marked out on a grid, you see, so I can keep an eye on the areas we work, but apparently Aarav wandered off and started clearing the wrong part." He scratched at his chin again. "Come to think of it, I never did get to the bottom of why Johns wasn't watching the boys properly."

"So," Pazia sat a little straighter. "Why do you presume the boy felt the need to start working in that particular spot? Does he usually ignore instructions? Is he a wilful child?"

Elon glanced at Blain, who gave the slightest shake of his head. The movement was not lost on Lorena, who, as always, had half an eye on Elon. It was obvious that both men had already discussed this matter at length. Unlike Pazia and Peyton, Elon had not been at all surprised by the news of the latest find. She hid a smile. Elon might not have told her what was going on here at Marlborough

House, but he had encouraged her to come tonight and warned her to be prepared for a revelation.

It was the only reason she had belatedly accepted Blain's invitation. After the press had snapped photographs of her leaving Elon's hotel room at four in the morning, she had intended to keep her head down for a while. Certain people, Pazia Olvalroyd in particular, would never let such juicy gossip die quietly. Still, the woman had behaved herself tonight, no doubt spending the time since Blain's announcement working out this current line of questioning.

Gipton was shaking his head. "Aarav is a good lad. Never had a problem with him. He can be a bit cocky at times, but you show me a teenage lad who isn't."

Pazia still did not smile. "And who found the head?"

"Aarav and Jasper were the ones who cleaned out the cellar, but it was..."

Pazia's head tilted a little to the side, like an owl listening for a mouse. "Aarav again?"

"Err, well, it was Jasper who really found it, I suppose. Well, he and Aarav brought the barrel full of water out of the cellar like I told them to, but Aarav refused to tip it over to see what was inside."

"And why was that?"

"It was the smell, you see. Stunk something awful that water did, especially once the skin on the surface split. So Jasper had to do it."

Pazia leaned back in her chair. "Hmmmm."

Peyton took up the questioning. "Was there anything else in the cellar?"

Gipton relaxed a little. He shook his head. "Water had been leaking in for a good few years, by the look of it. Everything was ruined, covered in mould, and disintegrated the moment it was touched."

"You are sure?"

Gipton looked surprised. "I'm positive."

"Could the boys have hidden something and not let you know about it?"

Again, Gipton shook his head. "I can't see how. No one was ever alone in the cellar."

Peyton picked up a pen from the desk and rolled it between his fingers. "What about the rest of the house?"

Blain stepped in, answering with smooth efficiency. "There was a box found in a cupboard in the main part of the house. Elon already has that. It was locked; we couldn't open it."

Peyton's eyes widened; he swung around to look at Elon.

"The box was empty," the Master said simply. "You would have been the first to hear otherwise."

"Hmmmph." Peyton let his pen fall to the table, disappointment clear on his face.

Pazia was watching him intently. She had never realised before just how much his neatly trimmed beard, sandy with flecks of white, reminded her of a terrier she had once owned. She had loved Jackson; he had been loyal, obedient, and as aggressive as a fighting dog should any other animal dare to come near her. Unfortunately, it was that misplaced sense of bravado that had got him killed. She wondered idly if the same would happen to Peyton.

The way he defended that little wife of his was not so dissimilar.

"Did this Aarav find that as well?" She asked, turning back to the gardener.

Slowly, Gipton nodded his head. Why had he never connected all this before? He took another sip of whisky and swallowed, not tasting a thing.

"What about the rest of the body?" Lorena spoke into the considered silence that followed.

"No sign of it." Gipton shrugged, gripping his glass tighter.

Lorena shuddered. Why did no one else seem remotely bothered by this?

Elon had loosened his tie and opened the collar of his shirt. "What I want to know," he said, rubbing his neck, "is why the cottage was in ruins in the first place. As far as we were all aware, it had only been hidden by Mead's spell. It was certainly still standing when the man was dragged away."

Pazia's braids swung as her head whipped around. "You don't want to know about the head?"

Elon waved his hand. "My dear, I know as much as is possible to know about the head at this time. I have scientists working on it as we speak. I had hoped to be able to bring you some information tonight, but so far all that can be confirmed is that it did not belong to a magician."

Pazia had to work hard not to roll her eyes. It was just typical of Elon to have kept this news to himself. He expected her to run to him, and him alone, the moment she uncovered anything worth knowing. Clearly that only worked one way.

"So exactly how long have you been sitting on this information?" she asked him. There was a slight inflection in her tone, though what it might be suggesting was unclear to anyone else.

Elon didn't even look in her direction. "It is only natural that Blain should contact me the moment this discovery was found." He had his elbows on the desk now, his fingers steepled against each other. He tapped his middle fingertips together, looking at Gipton. "I think we are done with you now. Can you ask this, err—" He looked down at his notes—"Johns, to come up."

Blain nodded again to Gipton, and the gardener left the room, taking his whisky with him. Safely through the private door leading to the staff stairwell, he leaned against the wall and gulped the rest of its contents. He could cope with one oligarch at a time; maybe even two, he thought, but not a meeting like that.

"I didn't get offered any single malt," Johns complained, throwing himself into a chair in the staff office a short while later.

Gipton grimaced. "Think yourself lucky you weren't in there long enough to need one."

"Pfft!" snorted Johns. "They don't need time to be intimidating, that lot." He ran his hand over his brow. It came away damp with nervous sweat. He rubbed it on the leg of his trousers before remembering they were his best ones. "They wanted to know how well I worked with you."

Gipton looked surprised.

"Wanted to know if I'd defied your instructions on purpose and got the boys clearing the wrong area." He shrugged. "I don't know what that has to do with anything."

"And did you?" Mrs Lee asked him, putting a steaming cup down in front of him.

Johns nodded his thanks. It wasn't whisky, but the hot, sweet tea was welcome nonetheless. "Of course not. Aarav found it when I was busy helping Mark with a massive tree stump. Don't you start. It's bad enough with them upstairs trying to make out problems where they don't exist, without you trying it too."

Mrs Lee squeezed his shoulder. "I meant no harm, lad. This find has got everyone unsettled."

A shudder ran down Gipton's back. For all he had known this find was coming one day; he had never anticipated anything as gruesome as that head. He had seen bodies before; he'd been one of those who'd searched the burnt-out library in town. What had remained of those young bodies, however, had been dry and blackened. The severed head had been a different matter. Its gelatinous substance was almost like the bottom of a bar of soap that had been left in water for too long. He shuddered again. Thank goodness Elsie always bought green soap; he didn't think he would ever be able to use a bar of white again.

9

"Concentrate."

The air fizzled with animosity. There was a sharp crack as the cane whipped down across Thaniel's back. He gasped, tasting blood. He had been able to withstand the blows to start with, so long as they weren't too close to his damaged rib. Now his back was riddled with marks, and each new stroke found an old wound.

The bucket of water, six feet away, was by far the heaviest and most unwieldy thing he had been made to use his magic on so far. His fingernails dug into his palms as he focused. Hot needles of pain stabbed into his temples as the galvanised metal began to lift. The bucket wobbled, sending water slopping over the edge. Pressure was building behind his eyes. He couldn't hold it any longer. He let out a cry, and the bucket thudded down, tipping sideways and spilling its contents over the floor. Thaniel felt a tear trickle from his eye. Wiping it away, he was horrified to see that it was blood.

"Enough."

The instructor had moved to his usual place at the back of the room, by the small table he used as a desk. On the floor in front of him stood a large spotlight pointed in Thaniel's direction. It cast the room behind into deep shadow, out of which the instructor rarely ventured.

Thaniel had seen both his silhouette and his shadow, but never his face.

One of the two female chaperones came scurrying into the room. She handed Thaniel a sachet of sherbet. He took it gladly, and she quickly left. The pain in his head withdrew, chased away by the fizzing on his tongue. He wiped away the remains of the bloody tears, feeling defeated.

"Keep your head down."

The instructor's shoes clipped the polished floor with the same precision with which he spoke. He never took his eyes off Thaniel as he changed the bucket for a smaller one, then retreated back behind his light.

"Try again."

When he'd first arrived, Thaniel had been contumacious, answering back continuously and defying every command. He suspected there were even worse punishments than crystal cords and canings, but he was too broken now to risk finding out what they were. Defiance was still his constant companion, though now it flitted about him with no more substance than a wraith.

He lifted his head and concentrated. This time, the bucket lifted easily, and though it was full to the brim with water, not a single drop spilt over the sides. Thaniel was able to levitate it up, down, side to side, and even tip the contents into the larger bucket, all perfectly controlled.

"That will do for today." The instructor's voice rang out in the quiet room. "Obviously you are not quite ready for heavier weights yet, but it will come. I have a feeling there will be no limits to the things your mind can achieve when you are fully trained." There was a pause as the instructor tapped on his phone screen. "You have to earn everything here at Blackwell. Up until now, you have been on remand, and your behaviour has done you no favours. Today, however, you have finally shown yourself willing to start paying attention. As a result, you will be moving from your holding cell to a new room.

"Away from the heavily warded area you are currently in, it will allow you the freedom to work through the manual provided. I am sure I have no need to remind you that no magical communication can pass either in or out of Blackwell. This new room will be basic for now. How long it remains so is up to you."

Thaniel bit back his response. It would only get him thrown back into his usual cell, no doubt wrapped in yet another cord.

"Study the manual." The instructor got to his feet. Thaniel heard his chair scraping back and the slight shuffle of his shoes on the smooth floor. He didn't turn his face to look; he had been blinded by that spotlight too many times. "I expect you to be able to make that water move without the bucket tomorrow."

The door opened, and the same woman as before led Thaniel down the long corridor. At the end, she turned left and went up the stairs instead of down. Thaniel followed meekly. She was only slight, though he knew from experience that both chaperones carried a shortened version of the crystal cord and would not hesitate to use them on him should he step out of line.

They made it three flights up with no sound other than their feet on the steps and the occasional beep of the chaperone's phone. Why didn't they just use walkie-talkies to communicate? Could it be something to do with the slight sizzle of magic that Thaniel could feel all around him?

The decor of the building was the same throughout. The floors were painted blood-red, with the lower portion of the walls a deep forest green. The top half and ceilings were cream. It was institutional and depressing. For reasons Thaniel could not put his finger on, the colour scheme irked him. He was still trying to work out why when the chaperone stopped and gestured him into one of the rooms. He stepped past her, and the door closed behind him. There was a distinct click as the lock snicked into place.

The room was dimly lit by a small, barred window facing out over woodland. Thaniel's previous cell had offered no such luxury. He pressed his face against the glass, taking in as much of the view as possible. Were those the same trees he had been forced to walk through on his way here? He could see no sign of the impenetrable metal fence beyond, though maybe that was not so surprising, given the length of time that horrendous journey had taken.

Up here, under the eaves of the building, the magic in the air felt like static failing to discharge, almost as if it were trying to communicate. In the training room, the magic was fluid, ebbing and flowing around him as he used his powers, whereas down in the holding cell it had dropped away from him the moment he had approached, leaving only a faint frisson of awareness on his skin. When he had first arrived, not understanding what it was he had felt coming off the building in waves, he had found it disconcerting. Now the feeling was comforting, and he wore it like a weighted blanket.

With regret, he turned away from the window to look at his new room. The manual the instructor had mentioned lay on the small table. Thaniel flicked open the front cover with his forefinger:

Guide to the Practical Application of Magic

He scanned through the first few pages, his mouth getting drier by the minute. He had got it all wrong. They were not studying him—they were training him. Why? The oligarchy did not tolerate magicians; it was a fact as indisputable as spring following winter, and there could be no doubt that this was their facility; they had been right there, cast in stone along the front of the building.

Thaniel had assumed it to be a penitentiary, and these weeks of assessment simply the prelude to his sentence. His skin prickled as a strange feeling of dread settled over his shoulders. If they were training him, they must be wanting his powers for something, but what on earth could the people who had eliminated magicians possibly want him to do? His head darted up, scanning the walls for a camera. His last room had one, clearly visible with its blinking red light. It was only a partial relief not to find one. He had always hated the thought of being spied on, yet now he wasn't sure if he wanted to be the kind of person his captors trusted.

No one knew for sure if they still killed magicians. Thaniel had been clinging to the hope that as he hadn't really been one long enough to do anything about it, they would keep him for long enough to give him a good fright, then after doing something to remove his powers, let him go, a bit like a prolonged visit to the hospital to get a wart removed.

He longed to get outside, to breathe fresh air, and feel the wind on his face. Even more than that, he wanted to know what had happened to his mother. Was she safe? Did she still miss him? They were all each other had during those long, dreadful years after Dad and Jess were gone. Now he was gone too, and all his mother had left was that son-of-a-bitch who had betrayed them both.

Thaniel could still see her, distraught at the open gravesides as his sister's and father's coffins had been lowered, side by side, into the chalky earth. It had been a beautiful autumn day, the sun warming their backs as red/gold leaves fell around them like confetti. That was about all Thaniel could remember of their funerals—the perfect weather and his mother's keening cries. He hoped she was coping with his loss better; hoped even more that she had managed to get away from Paul. Thaniel rubbed his eyes; there were still bits of dried blood clinging to his lashes. The sight scared all thoughts of his mother away. What would have happened if he hadn't stopped the magic when he did?

There was a tap on his door, and the key turned. The nicer of the chaperones came in. This one at least had a smile for him, along with a tin meal tray and a cup of fruit juice. The staff's lack of words always left him feeling tainted, not worthy enough to be spoken to. Right now, that smile was all that stopped him from falling into complete despair.

The food was never very appetising, or warm for that matter, but Thaniel was too hungry to care. Before the chaperone had even left the room, he had picked up the flimsy wooden thing that served as a spoon and fork combined and started shovelling the orange mush he presumed was carrots into his mouth. Accompanying this mush was a lumpy brown meat offering and an off-white dollop of something that had once resembled potato. There was never enough, and as usual, the fork thing snapped before he had finished. He gulped down the juice and dropped the cup onto the tray, where it landed with a clatter.

Everything was designed to be harmless and demoralising. The food was just slop; there was no crockery, only thin and dented aluminium; even the cutlery was next to useless. He laid the broken fork thing out on his hand. A moment's concentration and the wood fibres knit back together, all trace of the damage vanishing. Thaniel sighed, dropping it back onto the tray. If only he could make this prison disappear so easily.

He looked at the manual. If he didn't study, he would be punished tomorrow. Still, he just couldn't bring himself to start. Today he'd been lucky, only one lash of the cane.

He eased his shoulders, and the wounds on his back pulled. Closing his eyes, he tried to imagine the state his skin must be in, but his mind could only think of how his back used to be. The cuts tingled, increasing to an almost unbearable itching, and then, as quickly as the sensation arrived, it was gone. Thaniel opened his eyes in surprise, twisting and stretching his spine. For the first time in weeks, there was no pain. He reached around as far as his fingers could go, finding only the slight ridges of scars where cuts had once been.

A bark of laughter erupted from him. Automatically, his glance shot to where the camera would have been in his last room. The blank wall stared impassively back at him, and he laughed again. The instructor had told him that he needed to be looking at something in order to perform magic on it. The instructor had been wrong.

For the first time since his capture, Thaniel felt a glimmer of something positive. It wasn't hope exactly, more the excitement that came from knowing a secret. He could perform magic no one else knew about. Thaniel had no idea how it could help him, but it was important; he was certain of that. He pulled the manual towards him and started reading.

****

Water splashed onto the floor, sending up sprays of droplets. Thaniel felt a couple hit his face. He braced himself, knowing that the cane would soon follow. He expected it, wanted it, and had even courted it. Still, he flinched when it came. Sometime in the early hours of the morning, he'd realised that he needed fresh wounds, and quickly. He couldn't risk anyone realising what he could do. Wrapping his new skill in a network of scars was by far the best way of keeping it hidden. Two short, sharp cracks came down across his back. He sucked in air and blinked quickly.

"Again."

The instructor's footsteps sounded on the floor. Thaniel turned his head towards them and received another crack for his trouble. "Eyes forward."

This time, Thaniel moved the water as requested. It would not do to be too antagonistic.

"Good, now see if you can pick up the spilt water."

Thaniel concentrated on the wet floor, a smile forming on his face as he watched the water rising up. He pulled the droplets from wherever they had landed and gathered them all back into the bucket.

"Excellent. Now, see what else you can do with it."

Thaniel focused. The water spouted up from the centre of the bucket like a fountain. He made it rise higher and lower, then he jumped some of it to the next bucket and made water from that one jump back. It flowed between the two in a never-ending stream. Thaniel grinned to himself. This was actually fun. He danced the water spouts until they formed loops in the air, always landing neatly in one or other of the buckets. Not a drop landed anywhere but where he intended.

The instructor clapped his hands for Thaniel to stop. "You seem to be good with liquids. They are more malleable than solids, though tricky to control fully." He got to his feet. "Eyes down."

As he looked to the floor, Thaniel caught sight of a pair of highly polished black shoes beneath neat, perfectly pressed, pinstriped black trousers; exactly the type of clothing Thaniel would have expected him to be wearing. He risked lifting his head a fraction more and saw one of the instructor's hands reach down and place an old-fashioned fountain pen on the floor.

Safely back behind the lights, the instructor said, "I want you to remove the ink from the pen."

Ever since Thaniel had first learnt of his magic, it had bound him, defeated him, and taken him away from everything he loved. Last night, when he'd realised what he could really do, the self-imposed chains of that incarceration had shattered. Yesterday, he had been an unwilling student. Today he wanted to be top of the class.

Thaniel imagined the liquid pigment flowing from the pen's chamber and out through the shining, gold nib. Sapphire ink cascaded from the pen. Thaniel had to think quickly to contain it into a hovering ball of blue. Behind him, the instructor took a step forward.

"What else can you do with it?"

With only a moment's hesitation, Thaniel looped the ink along the wall in foot-high letters. *Thaniel*, they said, in neat cursive writing. He finished the word off with a flourished line beneath and a tear-shaped dot above the *i*.

He heard the instructor's sharp intake of breath and knew he had done well.

"Can you put it back?" For the first time, there was something other than imperious scorn in the man's voice.

Within seconds, Thaniel had pulled the ink from the walls. It lifted into the air like ribbons waved by invisible hands. One by one, the letters stretched out and slid effortlessly back into the pen's nib, disappearing from sight.

A few moments later the door opened, and one of the chaperones appeared, bearing a drink for Thaniel.

"Thank you, Janson," the instructor said as she handed it over.

She was the one that Thaniel disliked the most. Still, he accepted the drink with thanks. It was the first time he had been offered anything in the training room, other than the pain-reducing sherbet. The juice was fresh pineapple, served in a glass. Thaniel savoured the taste. It was so much more refreshing than orange juice tainted by aluminium. Usually, using magic left him feeling sluggish and tired, but the juice acted like a shot of ultra-strong caffeine, racing through his bloodstream and making him feel more alive.

"This is a two-way thing, Nathaniel," the instructor said to him from behind the blinding light. "If you please me, you will be rewarded. Remember that the next time you think about being awkward. There are no limits to what we can achieve together if you set your mind to it. I would have thought that still being alive would have been motivation enough, but it appears, with you, that just isn't the case.

"Maybe now you will see that I am not the enemy? Sherbet and pineapple are not the only things that can help you; I can show you how to control the use of your powers so you are less likely to overexert yourself. And, if you prove yourself to me, I may even teach you how to boost them."

Lessons continued to improve, and each day Thaniel found he was able to do a little more before his head began to hurt and he needed the sherbet. Small drinks of the pineapple juice continued to be his reward every time he managed something more significant. It wasn't much, but in his deprived state, the drinks were like candy. After a week, Thaniel was able to command even the thickest of fluids to do his bidding.

He was enjoying himself now. Even out of the classroom, he spent long hours poring over his manual. Unbeknownst to the instructor, he was also practising his powers on things he could not see, as well as trying to expand his abilities in every way he could possibly think of. Meals improved; the thin foam on his bed was replaced by a thick, well-sprung mattress, and new, warmer clothes appeared in his room.

Thaniel found himself looking forward to his lessons. Soon, even working with solid objects no longer seemed such a daunting task. He could feel his powers strengthening and growing. It was a shock when he realised he could no longer remember what it had felt like not to have them.

The first snowflakes of the year were falling on the morning that Thaniel entered the training room to find a glazed window frame propped against the wall.

"Today we are going to do something a little different," the instructor said. "Instead of simply moving objects around, I want to see how well you can control a destructive act."

Thaniel's head jerked up, and the man gave a hollow laugh.

"Do not think I am being so foolish as to teach you how to escape. Even were there no bars outside the windows, all ways in and out of this building are warded against such magic. All you would achieve by trying to get out of your window would be to give yourself a very cold room."

Thaniel's heart was thudding in his chest. The thought of escape was like a carrot dangling in front of a starving donkey who had suddenly found himself in a field full of ripe oats. The instructor must have realised what he was thinking, because his tone took on a gentle air.

"Besides, where would you go? Who else would teach you all there is to know about your wonderful talents? You would be killed the moment you left here."

He spoke so matter-of-factly that at first Thaniel didn't register his words. When he did, he felt sick. In his eagerness to learn all he could about his talents, he had forgotten that he was balancing on the edge of something so dangerous he could not even begin to comprehend it.

"You are safe here, Nathaniel. Do not worry about outside. No one will harm you, so long as you stay with me."

The instructor's voice was calm and reassuring, with no sign of the usual sharp edge it wore. Thaniel gulped and blinked furiously. He was too old to cry. He wiped his sleeve across his flushed face and stared forward at the glass. Using his powers for destruction was bad. It was everything people expected of magicians. Yet Thaniel could not deny what the instructor had said. Apart from the whippings when he was being defiant or hadn't been concentrating, no one had harmed him here. This place could not be so bad—could it?

10

"Is there anything you wish to tell me?" Blain's cold look settled on Amelia. It had been a relief when only Gipton and Johns had been called up for questioning by the oligarchs on the night of the dinner party, but now, only two days later, Amelia found herself standing in Blain's sombre office, trying desperately to curb her growing anxiety.

"I am sorry I had my accident, sir, but it was Mrs Lee who insisted that I rested. I wouldn't have..." Her voice trailed off as nerves ate her words.

Blain rubbed the length of his finger down his neat moustache a number of times, his eyes never leaving Amelia's. "That is not what I was referring to. I am interested in *why* you had the accident in the first place."

Amelia could feel her face flushing. She felt pinned in place by those eyes, like a fly under a microscope. Could he read her mind? Would he know if she told a lie? Her hands knotting together would have given away her guilt, had it not been something she always did whenever she was in this office.

"Why?" She tried her best to look innocent. "I don't understand. The pan handle was hotter than I'd realised, and I dropped it. I didn't have the chance to move out of the way in time; it all happened so fast." Her words came out in a rush, galloping along with her heart.

Breathe, she told herself, counting to four as she inhaled. Omission was not the same as a lie. She held the breath for a second before letting it out just as slowly. Blain finally released her from his gaze. He looked down at the desk between them for a long moment, then back up to her. Like a cat, toying with a mouse.

"You have been here a long time. Am I supposed to believe you just forgot that pan handles get hot?"

"I should have been paying more attention."

"And why weren't you?"

The question was like a bullet aiming straight at her. Amelia's mind went blank. She was caught. A crashing noise outside made her jump. Blain's eyes flicked briefly towards the window, then, dismissing the sound, back to Amelia.

"Are you sure you didn't have any pains, something sudden that caused you to drop the pan?"

Downstairs, Mrs Lee screamed. A heartbeat later, the phone on Blain's desk rang with the single long tone of an internal call. Amelia jumped again, her heart thumping all the harder.

A flash of annoyance crossed Blain's face as he lifted the receiver. "I am with Amelia now."

"It's not her." Amelia heard Gipton shout down the line. "Out the back, come quickly."

Blain slammed the phone down into its cradle. "We are finished here."

Not waiting for her to leave, he snatched a strange, silver rope from his desk drawer and rushed from the room. She followed, keeping well back as he almost slipped on the stairs in his haste.

The rest of the household was already in the yard. Amelia was shocked by the scene of utter chaos that met her there. A fresh load of hay and straw had been delivered just before she had been called up to Blain's office, and, as usual, the boys had been tasked with storing it neatly in the barn. They hadn't got very far. Broken bales littered the ground, a whirlwind spinning half their contents high into the air. In the middle of all this, arms outstretched, stood Aarav, a look of wild fury on his face.

Mrs Lee grabbed at Blain. "Do something," she cried. "Before he kills us all."

Amelia rushed over to Jasper and Mark. "What's going on?"

Mark ignored her. He was staring at Aarav as if his closest friend for the last seven years was nothing more than a stranger.

"He's a magician," Jasper said, visibly upset. "Git-ton was freaking out about us getting the load stacked in the barn before the weather turns, and Aarav just flipped. You know how cross he's been getting lately? Only this time it was much worse; bales started flying through the air and crashing on the ground, then the wind started swirling. It was threatening to pick us all up and take us with it." His hands were flapping around as he spoke, his weight shifting from foot to foot.

"I don't think he realised he was doing it at first. Then I fell, and he seemed to snap out of it a bit." Jasper held out his arm. It was bleeding where he had grazed it on the gravel, and a small lump was forming on his temple. "He didn't mean to hurt me; I am sure of it. Mark and Johns grabbed me and pulled me back here, out of the way. I tried to get back to him, but then Mrs Lee came out and started screaming, and it all started up again." He frowned at Amelia. "I don't know what is going to happen now."

"They are going to take him away," Mark said, not taking his eyes off Aarav. His voice was oddly flat, his lip curling in disgust. "Get rid of him so he can never come back."

Amelia's mouth fell open, and Jasper's eyes widened in disbelief. Before either of them could think of anything to say, Blain took a step towards Aarav.

"Stop this at once," he shouted.

The wind increased, whipping up even more of the broken bales. Aarav stood in the centre, like the calm at the heart of a storm. His face was one of torment. Anger, hatred, and fear all mingled together, pulling his features tight. Amelia could feel her own body pulsing as her magic reacted to Aarav's, her fingers itching for release. She wrapped her arms around her body, gripping her hands into tight fists. Stones and other debris were being sucked up into the vortex Aarav was creating now. It spun faster, the wind buffeting them as it increased.

Blain called to Aarav again, louder this time. The wind snatched his words away, and they were lost. From behind his back he produced the shining cord. The small, polished balls of crystal on each end were now glowing with a cool, white light. He took a step forward. Sensing danger, Aarav flicked one of his hands, and a straw bale was pulled from the remains of the stack. It careered into Blain, knocking him to the ground, his grip still tight on the cord. Mrs Lee half gasped, half screamed in shock. She took a step towards Blain, but the swirling debris forced her back.

All the while, Gipton had been easing around the edge of the yard. Now he too began to close in behind Aarav, one arm held up for protection, the other brandishing a rake. He made no attempt to be quiet. Aarav swung to face him. The moment he was distracted, Blain jumped to his feet and threw the cord. It wrapped around Aarav's body like the chain and ball on a Devil Amongst the Tailors game, wrapping around its pole. Instantly, Aarav's magic was quelled, the whirlwind stilled, and detritus rained down, peppering them all with stones and straw.

"You have broken the bounds of your residency here," Blain called out, his voice pitched so that everyone in the yard could hear him easily. "We will suffer no magicians on these premises. You will be taken away and dealt with in the only way fit for your kind."

Mrs Lee's face was flushed with anger. "I almost wish they would kill you here, out in the open, instead of behind closed doors." Her voice was not merely laced with malice; it was pure hatred through and through. "You're an abomination."

Gipton nodded in agreement. "Always knew you were a bad 'un," he lied. "Could sense it a mile off. I've had my eye on you for a long time, lad. You can't hide a bad egg in amongst the good; they allus end up smelling."

Blain turned to look at Amelia, Jasper, and Mark. "Take note." He swung his free hand to encompass the yard. "This is what happens when people try to nurture magic. They lose control, and decent people get hurt. We will not stand for the problems of the past happening again. We honour the oligarchy here. Anyone harbouring possible magical tendencies must speak up the moment they feel anything strange. Only then can we help you to stay safe."

Beside her, Jasper's fingers closed around Amelia's wrist. Whether to offer her comfort or to take some for himself, she couldn't tell. She edged a little closer to him, unsure if her tears were for Aarav or herself.

"But," Blain continued, "if you ignore, or hide, any strange pains and let your... infestation... grow, you forgo the right to such help and will be turned over to the Guard without delay. As Aarav here will be." He leaned towards Aarav and lowered his voice only slightly. "Silly boy, why didn't you trust me to help you? There was no need for all this to happen."

Aarav ignored him. He stood, head hanging, the cord shining silver against his pale brown skin. Amelia took hold of Jasper's hand, unsurprised to feel it shaking just as much as her own. Aarav was loud and too cocksure of himself, but to kill him! He didn't deserve that. No one did.

For a brief moment, Aarav raised his head and looked over to them, his eyes searching out Mark's. They had been like brothers, despite their cultural differences. Born only months apart and raised here since losing their parents in the Purge, they had been inseparable for years. Mark lifted his chin and spat in Aarav's direction, then he spun on his heel and strode away. Aarav's neck reddened, the colour of shame leaching up into his cheeks. He lowered his head again, refusing to meet anyone else's eye.

Amelia never saw him leave. Blain ordered everyone into the house, and, reluctantly, she trudged inside with the others. She had rushed out with her heart racing. Now it was thumping with the overwhelming feeling that she was walking back into a trap. She headed straight for the basement stairs. Mark had disappeared up to his room, but Jasper chose to follow her.

"How long do you think he knew?"

Amelia shook her head. "I have no idea." She had been so taken up with her own problems that she had barely noticed the boys for the last few weeks. "I can't believe how Mark reacted. How can someone just turn on their best friend as if they meant nothing?"

Jasper's face had lost all its colour. He chewed at his bottom lip. "I've never seen him like that. He was, like, really pissed off."

Amelia pushed the door at the bottom of the stairs firmly shut behind them. "He's never said anything about magic before, has he?"

Jasper shrugged. "We've never talked about it."

As if by some unspoken mutual consent, they headed over to the cleaning room where, with its half-glass walls, they could be certain that no one could get close enough to overhear their conversation without being seen.

Jasper sat down, his voice thoughtful and quiet. "I don't believe Blain would really help if it happened to us."

He leaned back, putting his feet up on one of the other chairs. "I think he was just saying that to get us to confess. You saw how scared they all were." Jasper looked more than a little frightened himself. "Mrs Lee nearly had a baby when she came out of the house and saw what was happening."

"Don't forget, Mrs Lee's daughters were killed by magic." Amelia moved some rags from the remaining seat. The smell of polish floated around them for a moment before dissipating in the still air. "I suppose you can't blame her for being scared."

"Guess not." Jasper's voice trailed off to almost nothing as he turned to look up at the rear windows.

Amelia sat, dropping her head into her hands. *It's not her*, Gipton had shouted down the phone to Blain. The hairs on her neck prickled. They must have known someone had been doing magic at the house. But how? Did it leave some sort of trace? Her stomach churned at how easily it could have been her bound up in that strange silver rope.

"You're not listening to me, 'Melia." Jasper's face was drawn, and his frown had deepened. "What happens if we start to get magic? What do we do? I don't want to end up like Aarav. Whatever that rope thing was, it must have been powerful to make him stop like that. Do you think it hurt?"

"I don't know, Jasper." Amelia's skin crawled at the thought of that silver lasso tightening around her. "Morgan used to say that we should hide any pains or whatever if we start to get them. She said there was no way they could know if we don't tell them, but Blain knew magic was being done at the house."

Jasper's eyes went even wider. "How do you know that?"

"He was questioning me up in his office when Git-ton called him to the yard. They thought it was me." Her voice caught as she spoke. She shook it away with a shrug, put on a smile that was fooling no one, and in her bravest voice said, "If it happens, we'll just have to make sure never to do any magic and keep any strange pains a secret. Once we leave here, they can't do anything to us. We just have to hang on until then."

Jasper didn't look convinced. For a moment, Amelia thought she had given herself away, then Jasper spoke again. "So why didn't Aarav?"

Amelia sighed, half with relief and half with something that had been nagging at her ever since she had seen Aarav standing grim-faced in the centre of all that chaos. "Maybe he didn't want to, and that was why he's been so cranky lately? Maybe he wanted to hurt someone? Maybe magicians really are as nasty as everyone says?"

Jasper said nothing for a long time; finally, in a small voice, he said, "Do you really think that's true?"

Amelia raised her hands and let them fall. They sat in silence until they heard the slow, deliberate crunch of tyres rolling into the yard. They could see nothing of the yard from down here, though a shadow travelled deliberately across the far wall, melting into the recesses of the basement. There was no other sound until the vehicle drove out again, the shadow chasing after it like a forgotten thought. Moments later, Mark came thumping down the stairs. He spotted them straight away and jogged over.

"Well, that's him gone then. We can relax again." He leaned against the doorframe with studied nonchalance. "What are you two up to?"

Jasper frowned up at him. "Where do you think they'll take him?"

Mark shrugged, "Who cares? So long as they get rid of him, it doesn't matter where they do it."

It. The word hung in the air like a dagger waiting to fall. Amelia could feel the tip of it kissing the back of her neck.

"Anyway," Mark waved away the lack of response that had met his words. "Gipton wants us to go tidy up the yard." He pushed himself away from the wall and turned to go.

Jasper sloped off his chair. He sucked in a large breath of air, blowing it out with exaggerated force. His steps were heavier than usual as he made his way after Mark. Amelia watched them go, then headed over to her own work area. She picked up the tablet weave she had been working on before Blain had demanded to see her and settled herself down on her stool. The pattern was such that it needed all her attention to keep it running true. More than once she had to painstakingly undo her work until she finally managed to clear the day's events from her mind enough to concentrate fully on her task.

****

"Well, it has been some week." Mr Forth's eyes drifted to the seat Aarav usually occupied, as if pulled there by some invisible force. He blinked, cleared his throat, and smiled briefly at his three remaining pupils. "In the light of that, there has been a change of plan for this morning's class. Instead of our usual lesson, today I am going to be discussing social responsibilities."

Amelia, whose mind had been filled with thoughts of the boy she had dreamed about yet again last night, immediately brought all her attention back to the tutor. Jasper looked relieved; the work Mr Forth had set him to correct for today was still sitting upstairs in his bedroom, barely touched. Mark stopped doodling on his workbook, looking up with interest.

"A place for everyone and everyone in their place," the tutor began, echoing the famous oligarchy motto. "It is for this reason that once you turn fifteen, much of your time here at Marlborough House is spent on old-fashioned apprenticeships. These are in respectable, honest trades that many others nowadays eschew, yet there will never be a lack of necessity for such work." His beetle brow frowned down at them, and Amelia had the sense that he was holding himself back, biting off the words he really wanted to say, though his face remained as neutral as ever.

"As such, when you leave here, there will be a selection of jobs lined up for you, in which you will have the opportunity to excel. No one will be able to accuse you of jumping your place or using 'unnatural' methods. You will have a record of your hard work and commitment that no one will be able to deny."

He tapped his index finger on the desk in front of him. Once, twice. His brows almost touched one another over the bridge of his nose as he considered his next words carefully. "You are luckier than you might think. Had you been a generation older, you would have run the risk of having every single achievement scrutinised for malpractice and aberrant talents."

Mr Forth looked at each of them in turn, spending a fraction of a moment longer on Jasper than the other two. Outside, the air was unsettled, gusting erratically and sending smatterings of rain hurtling against the windows. In the classroom, no one noticed. For once, all their attention was on the lesson.

"But there are still some magicians out there," Mark said, raising his hand as an afterthought. He had begun speaking up a lot more now that Aarav was gone, as if he had shed his old, slightly shy skin for a new, more determined one.

Mr Forth responded with a thoughtful look on his face. "What do you think of that?" he asked after a few moments pause.

Mark curled his lip. "I think it's disgusting; they need to be rounded up."

"As of and in itself, the use of magic has never been a criminal offence." Mr Forth rubbed his chin, his face still carefully detached from his own feelings on the matter.

Jasper raised a hand. "If it isn't illegal, why are magicians taken away?"

"Ahhh!" Mr Forth raised his right forefinger and set his shoulders, something he always did when anyone asked a particularly thoughtful or clever question. "Why indeed? The answer, young man, is not an easy one. Magic these days is seen as immoral, though that was not always the case. Magicians have lived alongside us for as long as there have been people. In times long past, they were revered."

Amelia had never heard anyone speak of those who supported magicians without their words being smeared with scorn. Mark made a noise in the back of his throat, somewhere between a cough and a hiss. He rocked back on his chair as if trying to move himself as far away from the tutor's words as possible.

"But," Mr Forth went on, "this changed a decade or so ago, at the start of what is now referred to as the Purge." His gaze roamed backwards and forwards between them as he spoke. Whether he was watching for any signs of contention or merely wishing his words to sink in and settle, Amelia was not sure. Either way, his scrutiny was not unnerving. It felt to her more like he was delivering the most important words she would ever hear.

The stillness in the room seemed to take on a whole new identity. Jasper gasped in a breath. The pendant he always wore around his neck was clutched tightly in his hand as he slid it absently up and down its cord.

The rain hurled itself at the windows once again as yet another gust of wind battered at the building, blocking its way. Mr Forth cocked an eye at the weather but neglected to comment on how fitting the unsettled day was for the topic under discussion. He sucked in a deep breath and ploughed on.

"The first indication of anything amiss was when the oligarchy clamped down on the use of these so-called 'unnatural' powers in their own departments. In doing so, divisions were created where none had ever been before. Suddenly magicians were being seen as something other and undesirable." He paused for a moment, letting them ponder a world where that opinion was something new.

"Until then, they had been as much a part of society as the people who could turn paints and pigments into fabulous works of art; those who could take a chisel and turn wood or stone into lifelike creatures; or those who looked at numbers and could instantly solve any equation given to them. There are natural geniuses in all walks of life," his voice had been gradually rising as he spoke. Now it dropped, as suddenly as a stone, "but not all are welcomed."

He rose and came around the front of his desk. Perching on it, he folded his arms and looked down at them. It was obvious by the expressions on their faces that this was the most anyone had ever told any of them about magic. Even Mark had stopped pulling faces, sitting still on his chair as he listened.

"It was never demanded that others follow the oligarchy's lead. Though naturally, the business world was quick to follow suit and shed their magician employees: contracts with the ruling body were, and still are, much sought after and highly valuable. Chinese whispers followed. Running wild, they leapt easily from the business world into the rest of society. Those who coveted power and influence were instant advocates. And they made sure that the cleansing of their households was a public affair. They cared not for the reasons behind this targeting of a minority. Only for the advancement such behaviour could get them.

"Supported by the majority, the magicians stood their ground. They were not going to disappear just because they had been declared *persona non grata* by the upper classes. Over time, however, the rot of negativity set in, creeping through unsuspecting psyches like mould in a forgotten loaf of bread. People started talking of magicians in hushed tones, looking over their shoulders lest anyone hear and think less of them." Mr Forth's eyebrows rose, and his eyes grew wide. "Tensions grew."

He stood, though he did not keep still. His almost constant motion was followed closely by the class, like a hypnotist's pendulum putting his audience into a trance.

"Any work wrought with magic was deemed inferior and soon started to lose its value. People wanting to stay within the fashions of the day began to dispose of any such products, lowering their value even further. The magicians began to fight back. They marched against the oligarchy, demanding fair treatment and an end to the discrimination. Their public statements only highlighted who the magicians were and who people should no longer be seen associating with."

Outside the small classroom, the sky had brightened. A small patch of watery blue peered hopefully down through the scudding clouds. Almost as soon as it appeared, it was gone. The rain returned with a vengeance, hammering the ground until the wind picked up anew and sent it driving sideways, taking even more of the leaves spinning from the trees. Mr Forth paused for a moment as he once again eyed the gale. He shook his head as he gave up the last shred of hope that his roof slates would still be in place when he got home. "Some magicians hid their powers and tried to blend in. Witch hunts started, and numerous people were falsely accused. Others were dragged from their homes by vigilantes and subjected to abuse, whilst their neighbours looked on, too afraid to step in and help. It was inevitable that the magicians would eventually start to fight back in earnest. Over long years, the worst of the troubles raged. Good people were thrown into the fight on both sides. Many who originally had no problems with the magicians found themselves siding with the oligarchy when a member of their family or someone in their close friends' circle was hurt or killed."

Amelia remembered little of the Purge herself. For a good part of the unrest, she had been living with her aunt, who had protected her from most of what had been going on. She was only nine when that sheltered life had been brutally taken away. She had woken one morning to a blur of strange faces and the news that her precious Aunt T had been murdered in the night. The only place left for her had been at an orphanage, where the following weeks and months had coalesced into a miasma of grief and loneliness.

"Still the oligarchy seemed reluctant to officially declare magicians as outside the law," Mr Forth's voice pulled Amelia gratefully back to the present, "their official line remained 'a place for everyone and everyone in their place.' It did nothing to clarify matters. Just what was the magicians' place?" Mr Forth's eyebrows had taken on a life of their own now. "Behind the scenes, however, the oligarchy was developing the means with which to subdue magic. Only when life had become intolerable and everyone was crying out for something to be done did they step up and finally play their hand."

He returned to the desk and once again perched on the edge. "They had found a way to use crystals to bind a magician's power. These crystals were, and still are, used in numerous ways, but silver bolas are one of the most commonly used. Two crystals at each end of a silver rope, the bearer of which can subdue any magician the bolas are wrapped around. More commonly known nowadays as crystal cords, they are the equivalent of a straitjacket with the added benefit of extra control."

Mr Forth paused as he noticed the faces before him. "Yes," he said, shifting his feet uncomfortably, "I expect you have seen these in action very recently."

For a moment, Amelia thought he was going to stop the lesson there, but after another brief pause, he carried on. "After everything died down, the oligarchy reverted to their empathic spin on leadership. Those grateful for an end to the tyranny of the magicians failed to see the autocratic steel behind the seemingly caring exterior."

Amelia looked up sharply. Had he really just said that? Mr Forth flicked his eyes briefly to her surprised face and then carried on speaking, as if the slip had never occurred. He kept his focus on Jasper and Mark, neither of whom appeared to have noticed a thing. Amelia found herself wondering what his opinion of the oligarchy and the treatment of magicians really was. He had given no other indication of it throughout the lesson. Such careful neutrality was not something she had ever experienced before, and now that she came to think about it, it gave her pause to wonder. The hatred every other adult here had for magicians was palpable. They couldn't even say 'magic' without their mouths twisting around the word.

"The majority of people picked up their lives and moved on." Mr Forth looked her way again. "Any magicians remaining simply melted away." His gaze roamed back to the boys. "Those with magic in their families were left trying to blend in, either moving to new areas or starting again with new friends."

There was silence in the classroom as the air settled around them, heavy with the weight of assimilation. Amelia had the feeling of teetering on something as insubstantial as the surface tension of water.

Mr Forth gave them only a few moments before he waved a hand to indicate all three of them. "As you know, orphans such as yourselves are now given over to the protection of the Guardians to start their new lives afresh."

As if that had been a signal, the door opened, and Blain stepped in. This was the first time any of them had ever seen the Guardian enter this room, and they were immediately alert. Mr Forth gave him a small nod and retreated to his seat, though he continued to study Amelia and the boys' reactions from beneath his animated eyebrows.

"As you know," Blain said, coming over to the side of the tutor's desk, "we do not tolerate you bringing up your pasts. Arriving at Marlborough House is a fresh start, a clean slate where everything that went before is to be set aside. This rule has not changed. After the unfortunate incident you had to witness a few days ago, I have allowed you to be given a brief rundown of the turmoil that brought you to my door, but make no mistake, it is not an invitation for discussion." He smiled, making every attempt to look considerate and sincere. "Forwards is where your focus should always lie, now that you are here, in this place of safety and care."

****

"How are you coping without Aarav?" Amelia asked Mark as he shrugged into his coat.

He had not mentioned Aarav once since he'd been taken away, nor had he shown any signs that he was lonely or upset. She was hoping that after the lesson this morning, he might be ready to open up.

"I don't want friends like that," he answered in a flat voice, "so there's nothing to miss." He pulled a pair of almost clean black gloves from his pocket, gave them a quick shake, and pulled them on before walking away.

It was as if his close bond with Aarav had never existed. The staff were just the same; not a glimmer of sorrow from any of them, only a kind of subdued annoyance. It wrapped itself around everything they did, like a big dirty secret everyone had been forced to endure.

Jasper stepped aside to let him pass. "He's going into town with Johns to buy creosote for the barn," he said, giving Mark a filthy look over his shoulder. "Bet he's not so happy to be helpful when it comes to putting it on. That stuff stinks."

Amelia poked her head back out of the door to make sure no one else was in earshot. "I thought Johns fixed the damage as soon as Aarav had gone?"

"Yeah, but Gipton said the new wood stands out too much, and he wants no reminder of 'Aarav's betrayal.'" Jasper air-quoted the last two words and rolled his eyes. His back was uncharacteristically slumped, and his feet dragged as he moved. "Wouldn't surprise me if they sent me up the bleeding ladder to paint it on. It would make a change from sweeping bloody leaves, though."

Amelia couldn't help but feel for him. "How are you?"

Jasper hunched his shoulders and let them fall. He looked as if he wanted to say something, but then he just shook his head and turned away. He touched his pendant absently as he pushed his feet into his rubber boots. It was a habit he was doing a lot more of lately. Amelia wondered if it had been a gift from someone in his family. He noticed her looking, and a corner of his mouth crooked up. It wasn't quite a smile, more an acknowledgement of what she had been thinking.

She could have kicked herself. She needed a much better poker face if she was going to keep her powers hidden. The magic in her veins prickled, needing the release she could never again risk giving it. As a distraction, she toyed with her bottom lip, biting hard enough to wince. The air around them felt full of secrets, as if their lives were mere masquerades. The waifs and strays of the Purge wiped only surface clean when their old lives had been left behind.

She thought of Blain's words that morning. How insistent he was that they were in a safe place, looked after, and protected. Well, last week had proved that such care could be snuffed out in an instant. The gossamer threads of a spider's web, so beautiful in the morning mist, yet so deadly a trap to any unsuspecting victim getting caught up in its strands. Her thoughts ran straight to the memory of Aarav bound up in Blain's strange silver rope, and she shuddered at the similarity.

"There you are, missy. I've been looking for you all over." Dorothy stood in the cloakroom doorway, her hands folded and her face stern. She glanced at Jasper, who flashed one of his winning smiles at her, and she softened. He slipped out of the cloakroom before he could be dragged into any more unwanted jobs.

"Mrs Forth has telephoned. She won't be able to make it this afternoon, so you've to get on with the spinning instead."

Amelia felt a shiver of pleasure as she skipped down the basement stairs. There was only one person occupying her thoughts at the moment, and now she had a whole afternoon alone to spend with him. She would not need to prick her finger on the spindle of her spinning wheel to transport herself into a fairy tale. Since she no longer had to concentrate quite so hard on keeping the wheel at a consistent speed and the fleece twisting evenly through her finger and thumb, she often found herself slipping easily into a wonderland of her own imaginings as she worked.

She settled herself on her stool and pulled one of the bags of rolags closer, daydreaming forgotten for the moment as she went through the motions of setting up the new bobbin. From outside came the *swoosh* of a sweeping brush as Jasper made a start on the yard. Somewhere above her a door banged, but all else was quiet. With a flick of her wrist, she set the large wheel turning, her foot immediately picking up the rhythm on the treadle. The morning's lesson crept back to echo in her mind, and as she began to draft the wool, she found herself wondering again what Mr Forth's true opinion was. Running over the lesson in her mind, her thoughts caught on how he had looked right at her when he'd told them about the remaining magicians melting away. There had been something pointed in that. Had he been trying to tell her something?

Her mind was running free now, caught up in possibilities. What about his wife? Was that why she had not come in this afternoon? Were they both in it together, warning her and then giving her the chance to get away? Amelia shook her head at her own madness. Even if it were true, how on earth could she just disappear? She had no money, no family, and no idea who in the world she could really trust. She was suddenly struck with an overwhelming longing for her Aunt T.

The wheel continued to move steadily; the newly spun wool coiling neatly around the bobbin whilst her heart sank. There was so much she had not known, so much her oblivious mind had failed to recognise: Had her aunt been killed because she'd had magic? Had her parents? Was fear of discovery the reason Aunt T had given her such a sheltered upbringing? And if so, how much terror had that wonderful woman been living in when all Amelia had been bothered about was what game to play next?

She took her foot from the treadle, letting the spinning wheel come to a stop. These were all questions she was not ready to face. With considerable effort, she pushed the thoughts of her family away. She moved the thread a couple of hooks along on the flyer so that the next part of the bobbin could start to fill. After a deep breath, she focused her thoughts on the boy from her dreams. If anyone could give her hope, he could. Giving the wheel another flick with her hand, she began to treadle again.

11

THE GIRL WAS THERE AGAIN, HER DARK HAIR ALMOST black against the starlit sky. A half-moon shone down on the field, stroking the fallen leaves and washing out their glorious colours. The air felt crisp around Thaniel, fresh with the scent of promised frost. He felt such a need for this girl that it blotted out everything else. He hurried towards her. Before he could get near, the stillness was broken by a brisk wind. It whipped up the leaves around her feet, revealing water seeping up through the dormant earth to whirlpool around her in a deadly torrent.

Thaniel called out a warning, but in that strange, confused manner dreams have, she could not hear him. He strained forward, desperate to reach her before the autumnal vortex took her from him. The dream had other ideas. She turned her head just as the mass of water and leaves reached her chest. Her hand came out towards him, clawing for help.

It tore at Thaniel to see her so scared. He wanted nothing more than to be able to protect her, to wrap her in his arms and keep her safe forever. She was beautiful, that could not be denied, yet it was the beauty that came from deep within her soul that sang its siren call of recognition to him. He had considered himself complete until their eyes first met. Then he'd learnt what it really was to feel whole. There were parts of him that he'd had no idea

124

existed until that moment because they only existed in her. Without her, he was only a shadow of what he should be. He needed her; she was his lifeline, the only person who could save him, but she was dying herself.

He threw himself against the tide of water, feeling the static touch of her terror as it mingled with his own. All the times he had tried, yet failed, to save her flashed through his mind, urging him on. Their hands were a hair's breadth away from touching, and then the maelstrom was gone, taking her with it. The leaves settled back to the ground, once again covering the brook that trickled so silently underneath its seasonal cloak.

Thaniel woke, dripping in sweat. Consumed with grief and guilt, he swung his legs out of bed, needing to feel something solid beneath his feet. From the glass on his nightstand, he scooped out a handful of water, splashing it over his tear-soaked face. He should have known she would appear to him tonight. These dreams always came after bad days, and yesterday had been particularly bad. He let the girl's image filter back; a happier face this time, one that would hopefully help him get through the day to come.

He had never got over his reservations about the instructor and what the man was making him do. Still, he had applied himself. Since the lesson with the window, he had honed his power to such an extent that he could now shatter the glass into a thousand pieces and put them all back together again without a mark left to show the pane had ever been anything less than perfect.

That was all very well, only then he had been made to break the window into dagger-like shards. These, the instructor had Thaniel aim at a dartboard hung on the far wall, over and over again, until he could hit any segment the man named. Thaniel couldn't deny how pleased he was with his improved control, yet nothing could stop the constant rumblings of his conscience.

As he thought back to the previous day, when he had arrived in the training room to find a crate of live chickens clucking away in place of the window and dartboard, Thaniel's inner qualms vibrated their warning, just as strongly as they had done then.

"We have reached a milestone in your training," the instructor had told him. "Today you are going to prove to me that it has all been worth the effort." Even now, Thaniel could remember the slight scraping noise as the instructor pushed his chair back before getting to his feet. "You will open the cage, make one chicken leave, and then close the door behind it. You have not worked with living things yet; you will find it quite different from working with inanimate objects." The man had actually laughed before continuing, "Chickens don't have much of a mind of their own, but it will certainly be more challenging than anything you have done before. You will need to be strong and exert your will on the birds. You must force them to do your bidding, even though they will fight against you."

You must force them. Those words were toxic, droplets of dread that resonated throughout Thaniel's whole body. They weakened his resolve even further, so that although he tried to stop the memories from coming, it was no good. His head dropped to his hands, and before he could stop himself, he was right back there in the training room.

From behind the strong light, Thaniel could hear the tapping of the instructor's heels as he took slow, deliberate steps back and forth. It reminded Thaniel of drumbeats sounding out a death march to the scaffold. He drew his attention back to the chickens squashed into the crate in front of him and felt his skin go clammy.

"Do you hear what I am saying, Nathaniel?"

Thaniel had never harmed anything in his life; he didn't even kill spiders when he saw them. "I, I don't want to do anything to hurt them." He could smell the birds' fear, or maybe it was just their excrement. Either way, it was acrid and did nothing to calm his anxiety.

The instructor's voice whipped out, hard and cold, like the flexing of his cane. "You will do as you are told."

The scars across Thaniel's upper back prickled, reminding him just what would happen should he refuse. He would readily take a beating if it meant saving the birds, but he knew from previous experience that it was never an either-or option. Whatever the instructor wanted, he would get, eventually.

Willing the chickens to be compliant, he focused his mind on the cage latch, which sprang open easily enough. Immediately, the chickens surged forward. Thaniel had to stamp down on his determination to stop them from escaping. Needle-like pains stabbed at his temples as he juggled the wills of the five birds. When he was convinced he had full control of them, he released one, allowing it to dash to freedom. Slamming the cage door behind it, Thaniel sighed with relief as the pains eased.

"Again," the instructor demanded.

The free bird was pecking at the floor, its time in the cage already forgotten as it fruitlessly searched for food. Its ease helped Thaniel's resolve. And there were only four birds now; this time was bound to be easier. He took a deep, steadying breath and focused again.

If letting them out had been difficult, getting them back in was far harder. Twice, Thaniel received strokes of the cane across his back, both times for losing control and letting the birds escape behind the spotlight. The instructor cared nothing for the pain Thaniel was suffering or the stress inflicted on the birds. By the end of the session, Thaniel's nose was bleeding, and pink tears trickled from his eyes.

"Do you think I am being overly harsh on you all of a sudden?"

The instructor's question was more of a statement. Thaniel let the words fall unanswered around him as he did his best to wipe away the blood. He felt drained, as if all the energy had been sucked out of him, leaving him as limp and useless as a wet paper bag.

"Life is all about control, Nathaniel. Whether you realise it or not, each one of us is controlled by someone or something, just as each of us in turn controls who and what we can. Only the lowest of the low have no control at all. In order to be successful, you must learn these powers of manipulation. The more you are able to command, the more use you will be to me, and the greater the level of security your life will have."

Since he had been here, Thaniel had realised so many ways in which magic could be used for good, but forcing his control on another creature was not one of them. How could he possibly justify such actions? He bit the inside of his cheek to stop himself from saying something he shouldn't. Arguing back was futile.

As if sensing his continuing reluctance, the instructor said quietly, "I have enough magicians who can only control inanimate objects, Nathaniel; I have no need of any more. You, however, have so much more potential than that. It is the reason you are here." Hardening his voice, he added, "The only reason."

Thaniel shuddered at the words, the movement bringing him back to himself and his small room. The sickening reminder of the direction his lessons were taking had been enough to allow the dream-induced grief around his heart to gradually begin releasing its grip. It was stupid to be in love with a dream girl; he knew that, yet he couldn't help wondering if there was any chance his magic could actually bring her to life.

The stars were still shining outside his narrow window. He yawned, though he was too agitated now for sleep. Behind him lay a lesson he would far rather forget and a dream he could not let go of. Ahead lay the looming prospect of more tutoring in manipulation and control. He groaned and rubbed at his temples. There was a creaking sound in the roof above him. The constant static charge of the building felt almost as agitated as he did.

Holding his hand up, he willed a flame to spark from one of his fingertips. The bright glare was startling in the darkness. All he could do was practise: the better his control, the less likely he was to cause harm. Fire was not the same as a bird or animal, but should he let it drop as he danced it from fingertip to fingertip, it would soon become a living thing.

Of all the creatures to await him in the training room later that morning, the cage of tortoises was something of a shock. Thaniel looked at the sleepy-looking shells with pity and relief.

There was a cold laugh from behind the light. "Let us see how you fare with these creatures," the hated silhouette said. "They will not be as easy as you think."

With a stab of self-loathing, Thaniel resigned himself to his morning's work, soon finding that the instructor was right. The tortoises were far from pliant. Some were stubborn, refusing to budge when Thaniel urged them gently. Others raced at the cage door, their rigid shells, armoured legs, and long claws no hindrance when they decided to put on a burst of speed. Though they were surprisingly agile, their minds were as inflexible as their shells. Thaniel's head was throbbing with pain by the time he finished.

He was rewarded with a tall glass of pineapple juice. The first mouthful quickly eased his headache, though for once barely touched how tired he was feeling. Thaniel stifled a yawn; he would have to remember that the miracle juice only worked on magical exhaustion. If he was going to spend half his nights practising, he was going to have to find some other way to keep himself alert. A second yawn quickly followed the first. Thaniel covered it by rubbing his face with his hands. The instructor never let on if he noticed; he simply waited until Thaniel had finished his drink, then had someone bring in a cage of cats.

Their minds were far easier to access than the tortoises', and had they been tame animals, they would have proved no bother at all. These felines, however, were no pets, and their anger at being confined was all-consuming. Thaniel soon learnt, painfully, that unlike chickens and tortoises, he could not release control of them once they were out of the cage. Cornered feral cats were nothing short of hairy balls of mindless aggression. The bloody scratches down his right arm and hand were proof of that.

As soon as the terrors were back in their cage, it was quickly removed and the next one brought in. This time, the two men carrying it remained, long stun-gun batons in hand. The cage held only one animal, though it was a few minutes before Thaniel could tell what it was. The creature threw itself against the bars, snarling, all teeth and claws. Thaniel's adrenaline surged, his heart thumping wildly at the sight of the long, bloodied canines biting on the metal. The cage rocked, almost toppling as the enraged dog inside battled to free itself.

Thaniel took a few deep breaths, fighting his rising panic, and reached out with his mind. He hit a wall of scorching energy and recoiled, almost falling backwards with the shock.

"Steady," the instructor said. "Feel your way forwards."

Thaniel tried again, bracing himself this time. He grimaced as he felt the seismic activity of what he could only think of as mental magma. Gritting his teeth, he pushed slowly through it. Once inside, he could feel the full intensity of the dog's aggression. Even with the struggle it had taken to reach this point, it was shocking. Thaniel's own pulse began to race as it tried to match that of the dog's.

"Be careful now." The instructor's voice seemed to be coming from right beside him, though Thaniel had not heard him move. "The transference of emotions is something you must guard yourself against. If not, you will find yourself being overcome."

With a conscious effort, Thaniel slowed his breathing and let his shoulders relax. The instructor had no doubt been expecting him to increase his dominance, battling against the animal until he crushed its will beneath his own. Thaniel understood compliance through fear all too well, and that would never be his way. Instead, he chose to soothe—to meet the dog's antagonism with quiet yet unbending resolve.

Calm his actions may be, but they still took every ounce of his willpower. He blinked as his eyes pricked. His nose was tickling, and needles of pain were lancing through his temples. Just as he was beginning to think he could not hold on any longer, the dog whined, lowering his head in a sign of submission. Keeping firm control of the canine mind, Thaniel branched his power out to the cage lock. It sprang open, and the dog pushed out of the door.

Becalmed the beast might be, but it was still a highly energetic animal. The speed of its movement caught Thaniel by surprise. He felt something drip from his nose, and his concentration snapped. In an instant, the dog's ferocity was back. It leapt towards Thaniel, all teeth and saliva. The noise from its throat was terrifying. Thaniel could smell its breath, inches from his face. Then there was other movement; the dog yelped and collapsed to the floor at his feet.

Thaniel was on his back. He didn't remember falling. Everything had happened so fast. The two men were standing over the dog, stun batons in hand. There was also a tall, whip-thin man in an immaculate pinstriped suit looping the noose from a short catch pole around its neck. Thaniel watched as the snarling hound was forced back into the cage. He was so shaken that it took him a moment to realise just who the suited man was.

The instructor turned to look at him, and Thaniel was immediately reminded of a rook. He pushed himself up on his elbows and stared. Almost everything about the man was dark, from his clothes to his collar-length black hair. Even his cold, assessing eyes were dark as they glowered down at Thaniel from above a long, beaky nose. Only his skin was pale, with a bloodless tint that had nothing to do with what had just happened.

Thaniel gulped. After a moment, the instructor shook his shoulders as if smoothing down his ruffled feathers and held his hand out. Thaniel took it and was pulled to his feet.

"Well," the instructor said, dropping Thaniel's hand and brushing his own together as if to rid himself of any taint. "Now that you have seen me, we can drop the charade. You will call me Doyen. My real name is not important, and I am sure that Doyen is politer than anything you have previously called me." There was a slight snigger from one of the men as they hauled the crate out of the room. Doyen's mouth pulled into a brief, amused smile.

"I... I... didn't." Even in the middle of the room, Thaniel felt cornered.

Doyen raised an eyebrow but made no comment. He pulled a packet of tissues from his pocket and held it out. Thaniel took one and wiped his nose, unsurprised to see that it was bleeding. Doyen pointed to his eyes, and Thaniel dabbed at the blood-stained tears.

"As you are the first mind magician to be lucky enough to have found a place here, withholding my identity has given me the chance to watch your progression at a remove."

No, you think I can only perform magic on something I can see. Thaniel's thought came out of nowhere, and with it the realisation that the instructor had been scared of him. Something must have shown on his face because Doyen took an involuntary step backwards. He caught himself quickly, though, swallowed, and almost as if they were playing a subconscious game of chess, came straight back on the attack.

"I must say, you have fared far better than anyone else who has had the privilege to come to Blackwell. Some do not even get past the first week before I have to step in and save them. Though considering what happens to those who do not live up to my expectations, it hardly seems worth my effort."

Thaniel could feel the pulses in his neck and wrists throbbing. He had almost forgotten the fear of those first few weeks when Doyen's threats had been an everyday occurrence.

"Have you heard of the word doyen before?" The instructor continued, as if the killing of countless young magicians was of no concern.

Thaniel shook his head.

"It really means the most experienced and senior member of a body of people." Doyen waved a hand in the air in a dismissive gesture. "The word is seldom used these days, yet I find it rolls off the tongue quite nicely, wouldn't you agree?"

Thaniel's attention was caught by the brief flash of a heavy gold bracelet under the instructor's shirt cuff. He felt a frisson of something run over his skin and sucked in a breath.

"It also serves as a reminder to everyone of exactly who I am." Doyen's voice hardened at Thaniel's lack of response. "Leader of Sheldon Wing, and the person you will answer to for the rest of your time here. Follow the rules and serve me well, and you shall have a happy and rewarding life. Cross me," he leaned forward menacingly, "and your days will be numbered."

Checkmate!

Doyen leaned back and sighed dramatically. "But enough of this. We have reached another milestone, young Nathaniel, have we not? I feel as if we can now get to know one another and begin to really enjoy our time together."

Thaniel was not sure about that and wisely declined to say so. Behind him, the training room door opened.

"Tomorrow, we will start a new series of lessons." Doyen's half-smile was sickly. It sent shivers of dread up Thaniel's spine. "But first there is one final test you need to pass."

He turned Thaniel to face the wire crate one of the men had just brought in. A small speckled hen shifted its feathered feet as it nervously peered out through the bars. Standing just behind Thaniel's right shoulder, Doyen leaned forward and said quietly into his ear.

"Now, kill the bird."

12

THE CHANGING OF THE SEASON MEANT THERE WAS plenty of work to keep everyone busy at Marlborough House. It took almost constant tidying to keep the grounds clear of fallen leaves, while the remainder of the fruit had to be gathered, along with seeds for next year's sowing. Herbaceous perennials needed dividing, roses pruning, and frost-sensitive plants had to be removed to the large greenhouse for overwintering.

The interior of the house was undergoing the second of its biannual transformations. Heavy brocade curtains replaced the lightweight summer ones. Scatter cushions and throws were changed to match, and the cotton rugs rolled up to make way for warmer, woollen ones. Everything coming out of storage needed to be aired and pressed. The retiring items had to be beaten out in the yard to remove the dust before being folded in layers of tissue paper and taken back down to the cellar to be laid in great armoires, lined with cedar to deter the moths.

To combat the darkening effect of the heavier draperies, extra lamps were cleaned and placed around the formal rooms. The pale mint colour scheme that had accented the house throughout the summer was now replaced with rich reds. Next year's schemes would be different again, so the unwanted candles, potpourri, and other flourishes were taken away and shared amongst the staff's rooms. Marlborough House might be a rich, formal property, but it did not believe in waste.

"Why can't we live in the north?" Mark moaned after a long morning raking leaves. "They have nothing but pine trees there. No raking needed."

Johns shot him a scathing look. "The north has many fine trees other than pines. Besides, you've seen the mess that great Douglas fir creates by the front gates. Those dead needles are the devil to sweep, and the dropped cones cause havoc with the mower. Imagine hundreds of those buggers to clear up after."

"Have you ever seen one of those giant ant hills you get in pine litter?" Jasper said as he pulled off his boots. "I saw one on TV once. It was amazing, crawling with millions of ants."

Mark held up his hands in submission. "All right, all right. I'm sorry. Deciduous trees are brilliant."

Johns tucked his boots into their cubbyhole in the cloakroom and pushed his feet into his slippers. "Tell you what," he said, ruffling Mark's hair as he passed. "I'll change my plans. I won't do the gate area tomorrow whilst you're with Mr Forth; I will save it for you the day after." He almost caught the disgusted look on Mark's face as he ducked his head back into the cloakroom a minute later. "One of you go shout Amelia, will you? Mrs Lee needs her out front right away."

The large front door stood open. Mrs Lee and Dorothy were both waiting out on the steps, looking determined.

Amelia felt faint as she made her way towards them. She had been out in the orchard collecting cooking apples when Jasper had called her.

"It sounds urgent," he had told her. "Better hurry."

She closed her eyes and tried to still the growing panic that was filling her stomach with acid. Whatever was happening, she couldn't afford to lose control like Aarav. Already, she could feel the prickling in her arms as the magic within her began to flare. She rubbed her palms down her sides and willed herself to calm down.

"At last," Mrs Lee snapped. "Look at the state of your hair. Smarten yourself up; the car will be here any minute."

Oh God, they really were going to take her away. She hadn't even thought to say goodbye to Jasper. Trying to hide the shaking of her hands, she pulled the band from her hair and hurriedly ran her fingers through the released locks. Bunching them quickly together again, she looped the band back into place, just as Blain's car appeared through the gates. It crept slowly forwards, the intensity in Amelia's hands growing as it neared.

Blain was sitting in the passenger seat, Thomas Grange behind the wheel as usual. Amelia's heart gave a lurch as she noticed they were not alone. Behind them, two more heads were just visible, though it was impossible to make out who they were through the tinted windows. Gravel crunched under the wheels as Thomas swung the car around to park in front of the steps.

Blain was out of the car the second it stopped. Then the back doors swung slowly open, and two girls got out. Amelia's legs almost buckled in relief. Both girls had black hair, brown skin, and matching burgundy clothes, though that was where their similarities ended. The younger of the two had an open, friendly face and smiled eagerly back at Amelia. This contrasted firmly with the other girl, who had her hands fisted at her sides, her jaw set firm, and her head high. She glared at the welcoming party on the steps, everything about her screaming teenage defiance.

"Everyone, this is Tiffany," Blain held his hand over the youngest girl's head, "and Jalissa." The older girl flicked her head away from his hand. Blain gave no sign of noticing, though Amelia doubted he had missed it. "They will be living with us here at Marlborough House from now on. I trust you to see them settled and clothed in something a little less like a uniform."

Mrs Lee met Jalissa's unfriendly eye with one of equal distrust. She glanced at Blain as he passed, appearing satisfied at what she read on his features. Ignoring the two of them, Dorothy stepped forwards, fussing around the girls.

"Come away inside," she said, "and we'll get you sorted." She picked up Tiffany's bag and led the way.

Tiffany skipped after her, taking in her new surroundings with open-eyed interest. Amelia made to reach for Jalissa's bag, but Jalissa grabbed it, holding it tightly against herself as she trailed silently behind them. Amelia caught sight of Mr Grange shaking his head as he drove the car around to the garage. She bit her tongue, remembering how nervous she had been when she'd first arrived here.

"You will be sleeping downstairs with Amelia and Letty," Dorothy told the girls as she led them through the house. "You will meet Letty soon enough; she is just out on an errand." She noticed the look of alarm on both the girls' faces as she opened the door to reveal the basement steps.

"Now, it might seem like you are being shoved into the cellar," she said, flicking on the light, "but I can assure you, the rooms down here are just as nice as the ones up on the top floor."

There was still a lingering smell of laundry detergent wafting from the armoires as they passed. Above them, through the clerestory windows, the autumn sunlight streamed down. Dorothy led them to the room next to Amelia's. "I'm sorry the beds aren't already made up, but we had no idea you were arriving. It won't take a moment, though."

"We don't even get our own room?" Jalissa exclaimed when she saw the twin beds.

Tiffany looked hurt. "Don't you want to share with me?"

Dorothy picked up a pillow and pummelled it into submission. "Residents usually share rooms here," she told the girls in a no-nonsense but still friendly manner. Dropping the defeated and now perfectly shaped pillow, she started on a second.

Jalissa glared at Amelia. "Who do you share with?"

Amelia took a step back at the forcefulness of the demand. "I don't." She swallowed a wave of longing for her old friend. "I used to, but Morgan, the girl I shared with, died."

Jalissa paled a little, biting back whatever else she had been about to say. She folded her arms and sat herself down on one of the beds with as much force as she could muster.

"Come on, it'll be fun," Tiffany said, bouncing down on the other. "At least it's not another dormitory. It will be like being sisters; we can tell each other stories and share secrets."

Jalissa's head snapped up. "I don't have any secrets."

Tactfully, Dorothy made no comment as she went to get fresh bedding, leaving Amelia to try and defuse the tension by asking the girls their ages.

"I've just turned fourteen." Tiffany sounded as if that was something she had achieved through good behaviour alone. Going by her innocent face, Amelia could almost believe it. "Jalissa's fifteen," Tiffany added when her roommate failed to answer.

Jalissa rolled her eyes, saying nothing. When Dorothy reappeared with two piles of bedding, she took hers with a clenched jaw, though she set about making up her bed without complaint.

When they had finished, Dorothy patted Tiffany's hair, which was twisted into neat little Bantu knots. "I will be able to help look after your hair for you if you like. You too, Jalissa, even though I barely bother with my own." She ran a hand over her own low-maintenance hair. Tiffany giggled. It was cropped very short, the tight, greying curls hugging her head with perfect neatness.

Jalissa didn't bother to respond. She remained sullen, closed off behind a wall of attitude as Dorothy and Amelia sorted the girls out with something to wear before taking them on a tour of the house. Tiffany, on the other hand, was warm, friendly, and eager to meet everyone. She seemed to have a natural bounce to her step, and Marlborough House already felt lighter with her presence.

It had started to rain sometime during the afternoon. When the boys came in, they were soaked to the skin yet surprisingly chipper as they met the new arrivals. Jalissa took one look at Mark, and for the first time since arriving, Amelia saw a spark of interest on her face. Letty bustled in moments later, almost slipping on the wet floor in her haste to get the door closed behind her.

"Damn, that weather has turned nasty," she moaned to no one in particular. "I need to get a new brolly; this one turned inside out on me." She threw the offending article into the bin, where it landed with a resounding clatter.

"Girls, this is Letty," Dorothy said, handing the cleaner a towel. "Letty, this is Jalissa and Tiffany; they will be living with us from now on."

Letty stopped her muttered curses and raised her brows at the girls. "I hope you two are going to liven things up around here. It's been far too stuffy lately."

****

"And so here this bright orange van pulls up, right into the puddle, spraying me head to foot with water." Letty dropped her knife and fork into her half-eaten dinner and began gesticulating as she spoke. "The delivery driver hops out and only starts wiping me down with a dirty, great rag."

Everyone but Mrs Lee laughed; the last thing she wanted to do was listen to yet another one of Letty's no-doubt tall tales.

"Hands all over the place, he had." Letty was well into her stride now. She gave Jalissa a knowing wink, and the girl responded with laughter.

Mrs Lee hated the air of attitude that always seemed to swim around Letty, even on her better days. Was it any surprise that it was an attraction for Jalissa? The cook pursed her lips as it dawned on her that the woman might actually be their greatest asset where the young delinquent was concerned.

"When it all came to it, the shop he was trying to find was right behind us. That new antique place with the huge globe in the window, Ernest's Antiques. He was complaining that there was nothing to identify it," Letty paused to brandish her hands in the air, "when he was the one delivering their new sign." She wiped a tear of laughter from the corner of her eye and picked up her cutlery.

Whilst Jalissa had warmed to Letty, it had not escaped Mrs Lee's attention that she was far more interested in speaking to Mark. She made a mental note to make sure those two were never left alone together. You could never trust teenagers not to follow their hormonal urges. Mrs Lee wouldn't be at all surprised if that madam hadn't already fooled around far more than was good for her. The girl was clearly trouble, besides which, Blain had warned her earlier to keep a close eye on her; apparently, she had been exhibiting some strange behaviour at her last home, so there was a good chance she would not be with them for very long.

There were no such qualms about Tiffany, however, and Mrs Lee already found herself warming to her. She was old enough to be useful yet still young enough to easily keep in line. She'd had a hard life, always moving from home to home, though it didn't seem to have affected her nature. That was probably a good indicator that the girl had come from a decent family.

Mrs Lee knew that it was unwise to try and predict which children would turn out to be magical and which would not; far easier to keep them all at arm's length. Sometimes, though, she just couldn't help herself. It was the same with Jasper. From the minute he'd arrived, she'd had a soft spot for him. He was a little mischief-maker if ever there was one. His cute smile and innocent eyes did not fool her for a moment, but there was a clean, wholesome kindness about him that couldn't possibly be there if he were harbouring powers.

Jasper and Tiffany were the same age. It was good that they would grow up together. Mrs Lee had always thought it hard on those orphans who ended up surrounded by magicians during their early years. They lacked the healthy social interactions only peers of their own quality could provide. Of course, children and teenagers growing up at Marlborough House would always benefit from the rigorous discipline and practical learning that Blain insisted they all received. Mrs Lee could only hope that the other guardians were as considerate, though she worried that with their focus on weeding out the undesirable magicians, some places may well forget their responsibilities to those who were pure.

****

"How on earth did you find that piece?" Amelia glared at Jasper. "I've been looking for that for ages."

Jasper grinned. "I'm just brilliant."

"You're not that good," Tiffany laughed. "This is our fifth day here, and you were working on this jigsaw for days before we arrived." She slipped a small, irregularly shaped piece into place.

"And how many 10,000-piece jigsaws have you done in under two weeks?" Jasper's mock indignance only served to make her laugh even more.

"I've never done one," she told him, slipping another piece into place.

At the sound of Aarav's name, Amelia looked up to see Jalissa and Mark coming into the room. They had been almost inseparable in their free time since the girls had arrived.

"To think, I was sharing a room with him," Mark was saying. "Obviously he must have put some kind of spell on me to make me like him; there's no way anyone would want to be friends with one of his sort."

Jalissa's face changed from flirtatious to disgusted in an instant. "His sort!" Her foot stamped in fury. "Magicians are not a *sort*. Just because the oligarchy don't like them, don't make them monsters. I've known some wonderful magicians." Her wide eyes flashed. "And they were far nicer than hypocrites like you." She jabbed a finger at Mark, stopping just short of his chest; then she swung on her heels and marched out.

Mark jerked his head back in surprise before rounding on Amelia. "Did you hear that?" he demanded, his face flushed with embarrassed anger. "You'd better talk some sense into her or I'm telling Git-ton. We don't want magic lovers here."

Seconds later, the lower basement door slammed with such force that Amelia felt the vibrations through her feet. The light fitting was still swinging as Amelia hurried down the stairs. She opened the door and stopped dead. Jalissa stood in the centre of the open space, her arms outstretched in front of her, palms up. On them sat a flame, not much bigger than that of a candle, but there was no wax, no wick, just a solitary flame burning on its own.

"Stop," Amelia called, hurrying forward. Jalissa looked up, and the flame rose higher.

"Jalissa, you will burn," Amelia cried.

The other girl just shook her head. "I knew it was a mistake coming here. Back at Dawnsend I was doing alright, but here you're all haters. I don't want to live with haters."

Amelia threw a panicked look over her shoulder. One of the adults was bound to have heard that door slamming. It was a miracle no one had appeared yet. "No, Jalissa, it isn't like that. You must listen to me. Mark is just an idiot. Please, you have to stop."

"They'll take me away now." Jalissa's lip curled in what might have been fear, though it could just as easily have been disdain. "You're gonna to tell them." She looked scared, angry, hurt, and confused all at once.

Amelia recognised that feeling. She looked back to the cellar stairs again. They were still clear. "I won't, I promise. Look, you've only just arrived; don't spoil it now. Let me help you."

"How?" the other girl yelled back. "How can you possibly help me?"

"Shh, you'll bring the whole house down here. They'll call the Guard."

"Mark." The flame in Jalissa's hand was trembling. "He told me that the last boy here was nothing but a filthy magician. A devil who should have been killed at birth. All my life I've had people look at me as if I were summat wrong. Just because my family were magicians." She sniffed angrily. She would not cry. "Well, I will *not* be a devil."

Amelia never got to answer. At that moment, footsteps came pounding down the cellar steps. It was Gipton, closely followed by Blain, his dreaded silver whip in hand.

"Put the flame out," Blain ordered, his voice like cold metal.

Jalissa had her feet planted on the ground, firm and defiant. She had been expecting this. Her flame flickered slightly but otherwise remained steady on her hands.

"Don't be a fool, girl." Gipton was trying to edge around behind her, just as he had done with Aarav. "You are just making things worse for yourself."

"Worse?" Jalissa almost screamed the word. "How can anything be worse?"

"Things can always be worse," Gipton growled back menacingly.

Blain shot him a silencing look.

"I know what you're going to do." There was a tremble in Jalissa's voice now. "You're going to send me away so they can kill me."

Blain tucked the handle of the silver rope into the back of his belt and held his hands out in a placatory gesture. Amelia could only watch in mute horror as Blain turned on the charm.

"I gave you a home, a safe place to live. Can't you trust me?" He risked a step forward.

Too wound up to listen, Jalissa threw a bolt of fire at his feet. He danced safely out of the way, then stamped down on the flame before it could do anything more than scorch the floor. Whilst the girl's attention was taken with Blain, Gipton moved. He was almost behind her when his foot caught on something. Hearing the noise, Jalissa swung around and threw more fire. It missed and landed by the loom.

"No! Jalissa, stop it," Amelia screamed as the flames began to lick up the side of the tinder-dry wood.

"Get water!" Gipton yelled at her. "And help, before all this burns."

Amelia fled up the stairs. She had barely reached the kitchen when Dorothy, Johns, and Mr Grange came rushing in, Mark close behind them. There was no time to wonder whether it was Mark, Blain, or the noise that had alerted them. Amelia held her hands up, blocking their way. "We need water. She is burning down the house."

She couldn't have said if it was concern for her precious loom or the lure of the magic that drew her straight back down the stairs, leaving the others to bring the water. The shouting from the basement was becoming louder. Amelia's heart was in her mouth as she plunged through the lower doorway just in time to see Jalissa fill her cupped hands with flames, then plunge them down over her body. Amelia screamed as the girl's clothes began to burn.

"Mark is getting the hose and..." Johns' words cut off behind her at the sight of the pillar of flames that had once been Jalissa. A second later, he was darting forwards, the only one of them making an attempt to reach Jalissa and smother the flames. Tongues of fire licked out at him, driving him back.

The inferno only lasted a few minutes, then the flames died away, leaving an unharmed but completely naked girl behind. Jalissa looked as shocked as everyone else.

Blain started to laugh. "You stupid girl!" he said, all signs of his previous nicety now stripped away. "Fire magicians do not burn, not even their hair. You can't get out of what is coming for you so easily." From behind his back he produced the silver rope. Flicking it almost casually, he wrapped its length around Jalissa.

Gipton coughed. Smoke from the forgotten fire was starting to thicken. He began beating at the flames that were spreading quickly from the loom to the spinning wheel and nearby storage area. The wool just shrivelled, but the cotton reels and materials stored on the shelves flared instantly. Dorothy appeared with two buckets of water. Snapping out of his shock, Johns took them from her and hurried to douse the smaller pockets of fire. Dorothy grabbed a broom and began to beat industriously at the flames. Amelia gave Jalissa one last hurt look and hurried to help them. There was a loud pop as a bottle on one of the shelves broke.

"Quick, get everything you can reach onto that rug," Johns called to her, running back to swap his empty buckets with the full ones Thomas had just brought down.

"I've got Letty keeping the others out of the way," Thomas called over to Blain, who was trying to stamp out flames whilst still keeping a firm hold of Jalissa. "Elsie's on the phone to the fire brigade." He didn't wait for an answer, plunging back up the stairs with the empty buckets.

Amelia set to work dragging as much as she could from the shelves whilst the others fought the fire. When the flames got too close, Johns came and hauled the rug across the floor to safety, just as Mark arrived, dragging a long hose. The fire did not take long to extinguish after that. Though it had been intense and produced lots of thick black smoke, the damage had been contained to Amelia's favourite corner.

Everyone gathered outside in the yard, gulping down mouthfuls of fresh, clean air. Gipton was in a bad way, coughing and retching. Even Blain looked the worse for wear. He stood with Jalissa, a little way away from them all. Subdued in the crystal cord, with her arms bound tightly to her sides, she showed no signs of smoke inhalation. Her face, however, was aflame with anger and humiliation.

The rest of the household joined them. Letty had her arm around Tiffany, who was sobbing quietly. Thomas Grange handed around cups of water to everyone apart from Jalissa. He never so much as looked at her. Mark and Jasper, on the other hand, both had flushed faces at the sight of the naked girl.

Mrs Lee finally appeared, red-eyed yet determined. Gipton rested a reassuring hand on her shoulder and was relieved when the cook did not shrug it off. She had relived her nightmares whilst they were dealing with the fire. Now she was filled with nothing but cold, hard hatred for the girl before them.

"Shouldn't we get her a blanket?" Amelia suggested as mortification for Jalissa's state of undress clouded her anguish at what the girl had just destroyed.

"She brought it on herself," Mrs Lee snapped. "She was the one who burnt her own clothes off. Girls like that will do anything for attention."

Jalissa opened her mouth to make a retort. At the same time, Mark let out a bark of laughter. Whatever Jalissa had been going to say was eaten up with shame.

"Oh for goodness' sake." Dorothy turned and marched into the stable, returning with an old coat. "We can't send her away like that. I won't be party to the sexual exploitation of a minor, however she came to be naked." She threw the coat over Jalissa's shoulders and fastened as many buttons as the cord would allow. It covered the girl down to mid-thigh. Dorothy gave a nod of satisfaction.

Mrs Lee snorted her derision just as a fire engine belatedly pulled into the yard, closely followed by a black transit van. Unable to contain herself any longer, she took a step towards Jalissa, her eyes narrowed almost to slits. "Magicians who play with fire deserve everything they get." Her lip was curled up, and she looked as if she were about to spit at Jalissa's feet. "There is a special place in hell for those of you who walk away from the flames unscathed."

No one commented on the film of tears in her eyes as she spun on her heel and began ushering everyone else indoors, leaving only Dorothy to bring in the firemen and Blain to deal with the Guard.

13

DOYEN TOYED WITH A SMALL REMOTE CONTROL AS HE looked down over Blackwell's gardens. In his other hand, he held a small transceiver up to his mouth. "Are you in position?"

A figure crouching behind one of the tall privet hedges raised his hand.

"Can you see the fountain?"

The hand raised again.

"Good. Now wait for my instructions, and do not hesitate to do whatever you are told."

From his vantage point at the window of one of the meeting rooms on the second floor, Doyen could see almost all of the formal gardens laid out to the south of the building. There were not many people strolling in them today. Aside from the recent heavy downpour, it was midweek, and most people were busy preparing for the weekend's Halloween celebrations.

Down in the gardens, Thaniel waited. Doyen's voice sounded clear in his earpiece, but the communication was only one way, so there was no chance for him to complain that the ground was wet or to ask how long he would have to stay like this. He shifted one of his feet to a more comfortable position, his shoulder catching on the hedge as he did so. Gaspingly cold raindrops pattered down on

154

him. In his effort not to make a noise, he accidentally bit his tongue and cursed silently under his breath.

He had been excited when the excursion outside had first been mentioned. How stupid to have forgotten that at Blackwell nothing good ever came without consequences. First of which had been a quick trip to the hospital wing, where Thaniel had found himself face-down on a padded bench whilst a small device was implanted under the skin between his shoulder blades. When triggered, it caused varying levels of pain to radiate out into Thaniel's spine, ranging from a slight vibration to instant incapacitation.

Now, as Thaniel shook the droplets from his hair, he felt a small tingle in the centre of his back: Doyen's warning to obey. Thaniel's stomach gave a nervous flip. The instructor had not told him what they were waiting for, but Thaniel doubted it would be good. Ever since he had been forced to end the chicken's life, he had begun to really fear what Doyen had in store for him.

The fountain made a cheerful noise with its three tiers of water hissing out of long copper spouts and raining down musically into the knee-deep pool below. Thaniel could just see it through the small hole he had woven for himself in the branches. It had been fun working with the hedge, linking with the spirit of the plant to ease the greenery aside instead of simply forcing a way through. He breathed deeply, taking in the smell of petrichor and privet. There was another vibration in his back, stronger this time.

"Get ready."

Thaniel's heart beat a tattoo in his chest as he heard three people approaching. From his vantage point, he watched as an instantly recognisable woman came into view. She laughed as the group paused near the pool. She was tall, with a straight posture and extremely dark skin. Her black, plaited hair was twisted into a high bun, making her appear even more formidable. Even in the chill autumn air, the sun caught on her cheekbones and illuminated her regal face. Thaniel held his breath. Surely he shouldn't be here? He glanced over his shoulder towards the looming edifice of Blackwell, only to receive another, fainter shock to his spine.

Pazia took a step back from the pool to avoid getting splashes on her immaculate coat. The movement brought into view another person that Thaniel had no trouble identifying. Short and squat, with hair beginning to thin on top, the man had round cheeks, bright eyes, and a friendly, approachable face. His jolly appearance always reminded Thaniel of the man who had owned the corner shop near his old home, though with his smart suit and mirror-polished shoes, Baxter Carswell was clearly far more than a common worker.

The third person was talking avidly. Unlike the other two, he was not an oligarch, nor anyone Thaniel recognised. He was blond-haired, with a pompous tilt to his head, and clearly thought himself someone worth listening to. He clapped the shorter man on the shoulder, then perched on the low wall that surrounded the pool.

"The water in the fountain; make it dance."

The relief that he had not been ordered to hurt anyone made Thaniel slow to obey. A low rumble of static grated on his vertebrae, urging him to action. Without giving himself chance to think about anything else, he concentrated on the pool.

"Baxter!" Pazia shrieked, her eyes wide with shock. "He is a magician!" The words rang out clear and unmistakable, shattering the calm atmosphere of the damp gardens.

"No, that wasn't me. I had nothing to do with it." The man had already jumped to his feet, casting his head around in search of the real culprit. He looked angry and more than a little confused.

Baxter, his face now flushed with anger, pointed an accusing finger at him. "So this is how you have achieved your successes, is it? You have tried to pull the wool over our eyes, sir, but we will not have it."

"Move back out of the way." Doyen's order sounded in Thaniel's ear. "Do not be seen. Make your way back to the building. I will be watching your every move." Thaniel's implant buzzed again, just a short burst this time to enforce Doyen's command. Thaniel needed no such reminder; he could not wait to get away. He had seen the disgust in Baxter's eyes, and it echoed deep in his own conscience.

His nerves felt shredded as he jogged along the shaded paths. There were no sounds of pursuit, but at any moment he expected to hear someone cry out and reveal him. He desperately wanted to get back to his room and search for the girl. He felt sick and unclean, needing her purity to cleanse the stain of his actions. Yet she only appeared in his dreams, and how could he possibly relax enough to sleep after what he had just done?

That poor man had been set up to be accused and found guilty of magic, and Thaniel had been the one to spring the trap. He really was no better than the monster his stepfather had accused him of being. He stumbled, going down onto one knee before he could right himself. Grass and mud smeared his trouser leg, but what did it matter? He already felt sullied, sickened to the core.

Because of his actions, that man would be tarnished for life. If he even had a life now. The oligarchs had looked just as surprised as the victim, so they couldn't have known what was about to happen. They had been angry and, if Thaniel wasn't mistaken, a little scared. He felt more confused than ever. Reaching the shabby red door that led into Sheldon Wing, he allowed himself a quick look over his shoulder. The path behind him was clear.

Chaperone Janson let him in without question. She walked him through the long corridors and up the stairs, though not to his room as he had hoped. For the first time ever, he was taken to the third floor. Thaniel was not ready to consider what that might mean. Instead, he focused his attention on the short hallway leading from the stairwell. It had the same basic decor as everywhere else, though here, just above the wainscoting, someone had painted an intricate frieze of animals and leaves, interwoven with vines.

He ran a finger along its base, intrigued by the unexpected artwork. Janson gave him no time to stop and admire it; already she was at the end of the hallway. Turning her back on the left-hand corridor, she led Thaniel along to the right, past numerous numbered doors until she reached the one marked twenty-seven. This one she opened.

"In here." She stepped aside to let him enter the bedroom, then she closed the door behind him and left.

It was bigger than his attic room, with a much larger, though still barred, window. Obviously someone had been busy because his own clothes had been stored neatly in the cupboard, his manual, pens, and paper placed on the small table, and his indoor shoes tucked just under the foot of the bed. Thaniel didn't need to double-check to know that his toothbrush and wash things would be waiting for him in the adjoining bathroom. Evidently, life in this prison was to be made more comfortable now that he was an abomination.

The door to the room burst open, and Doyen strode in, looking taller and even more foreboding than usual. "Well done, Nathaniel. You have done us a great service today."

Well done. Well done! Thaniel could barely believe his ears. "That man had done nothing wrong, and now he is being called a magician."

Doyen raised an eyebrow as if to say, 'And your point is?'

"It's... entrapment."

"Correct." Doyen looked anything but abashed. "That man was a magician hiding in plain sight. He needed to be caught red-handed, and now, thanks to you, he has."

Thaniel did not know what was worse: to have condemned an innocent man or to have helped with the capture of a fellow magician.

"Would you like to meet everyone else? I think you have finally earned it."

For a moment, Doyen's words did not register. When they did, they knocked the wind right out of Thaniel's sails. In the five weeks he'd been here, he had not seen or heard another soul, apart from the staff, but he hardly thought they were who Doyen was referring to.

"It is lunchtime, and everyone is gathered in the refectory. Come on." With that, Doyen turned and left the room, leaving the door open for Thaniel to follow.

"You will find that each one of them has power of one sort or another," Doyen told him as they made their way back down a floor. "All are helpful in their own ways."

Thaniel could feel his nerves rising, like a sparkle of fireflies had suddenly taken up residency in his stomach. He was going to meet other magicians.

"You can join them from now on, though you will still have your one-to-one sessions with me."

Speechless, Thaniel simply nodded. Just how many more surprises, good or bad, was this man going to spring on him? He could hear voices now, the noise getting louder as they neared a pair of open double doors. Standing just outside them was a guard in a dark navy uniform. Thaniel suppressed a shiver. These magicians might be together, but they were still prisoners.

Doyen paused just before the door. "Like I told you, Nathaniel, do as I ask and you will be rewarded."

Even with the noise, Thaniel was surprised at how many young people were in the dining room. Most of the large, round tables had at least two occupants, some as many as six. Their ages ranged from about twelve to twenty, with just as many girls as boys. Doyen walked them to the centre of the room, then clapped his hands for attention.

"Everybody, this is Nathaniel. He is very special; I expect you to be nice to him." He ran his gaze over the room, one hand resting none too lightly on Thaniel's shoulder. The silence was even more intimidating than the man. For all his eagerness to meet more people here, Thaniel wished the floor would open up and swallow him whole. Doyen waited for a minute, then, with no more ado, he turned on his heel, threw a pointed look at one of the older boys sitting at the nearest table, and left, leaving Thaniel standing like an idiot.

"Don't be fooled," the boy said quietly. "They're still watching us. They're always watching us." His smile was calculating, with a hint of condescension glinting in his eyes. "It can be a little daunting when you're new, but you'll soon get used to it." He stood up and held a hand out. "I am Jarrett, by the way."

Thaniel shook his hand a little warily. "I'm not really new. I've been here for weeks."

Jarrett's frown was instant, then his face lit with understanding. "Oh, so you're the mental one?"

"I am not mental, thanks very much." Thaniel snatched his hand back. He'd had his fill of insults and smears from the bullies who had daubed their filthy lies in bright spray paint all over their home in Harforth.

"No." Jarrett shook his head and laughed. "I mean mental magician, or mind magician, to be exact. We're all physical magicians here."

Everyone in the room was staring at them. Thaniel could feel his face starting to flush. He had no idea what Jarrett was on about and did not appreciate being made to look like an idiot in front of everyone. He caught a sympathetic look from a couple of boys and a girl sitting at a table not too far away. The boys looked about his age.

"I take it no one has ever explained it to you before?" Jarrett blazed on. "Our powers come from our physical energy, so we need our hands to guide it."

Thaniel felt an overwhelming urge to be back up in his attic room, where the magic buzzing about him was friendly and welcoming, instead of here, where once again he was being made to feel like the odd one out.

Jarrett finally seemed to realise that he was not coming across in the way he had intended. "So we have limitations," he added quickly, "but mind magicians don't need anything other than their thoughts to use their powers. That means you're strong." He gave Thaniel a light, friendly punch on the shoulder. "No wonder Doyen said you were special."

There was still that slight arrogance in Jarrett's features and something else Thaniel couldn't put his finger on. "Mind magicians are very rare; no one has seen one since before the Purge. Everyone was starting to think that they had been wiped out." He took a predatory step towards

Thaniel, "You should come and sit with us. We're the best here; we can help you find your way."

Thaniel glanced at Jarrett's friends, with their matching imperious faces. He gave them a nod in greeting, then turned away. "Thanks, I might do that later, but I better get to know some of the others first."

Used to getting his own way, Jarrett's eyes darkened dangerously as he stepped back. "Suit yourself."

Thaniel cast his eyes around the rest of the room. Most of those still looking at him were smiling now, and he got the feeling he had just done something they approved of. Someone waved at him—the friendly-looking girl sitting with the two boys. She pushed out the chair next to her. He hurried over and sat down, eager to be out of the limelight.

"Doyen is such a shit doing that to you." The girl looked furious on his behalf. "It was so unfair. What's your name?"

Thaniel found himself starting to relax. There was a strong sense of solidarity at this table, and for the first time in weeks, he felt the stigma of being different start to fall away.

"I'm Thaniel," he said, then, unable to help himself, he added, "apparently I'm mental."

The girl giggled, "I'm Tisha. This is Toby and Stephen."

"You've probably just made an enemy out of Jarrett," Stephen said. "Good on you for that, but you'd better watch your back." His dark hair flopped over his forehead. He looked worried and impressed at the same time.

Thaniel pulled a face. "I was right not to trust him then?"

Toby nodded. Pulling up his sleeve to show Thaniel a nasty scar. "He gave me this not long after I got here. We arrived two days apart, but he didn't like the fact that I got on with everyone and he didn't."

"You should just heal it." Stephen sounded like this wasn't the first time he had made the suggestion.

Toby shrugged, "Nah, I keep it as a reminder to always be careful who I trust." He grinned at Thaniel, open and honest. Thaniel found himself relaxing even more. Stephen just smiled and tucked into his dessert.

"You can't trust everyone here. Some will do anything to suck up to the tutors," Tisha said, throwing a look over to Jarrett's table. "It's not just him and his mates you have to watch, though he's the worst cos he's Doyen's favourite."

"You hungry?" Toby asked, pushing his chair back. "I've finished now. So I'll show you where the food is."

Most people were too busy eating to notice them making their way over to the food counters, but a few stared, keen to get a good look at their first mind magician. Thaniel tried to look friendly and harmless. He'd already pissed off Jarrett and his mates; he didn't want any bother with anyone else.

"How old are you?" Toby asked while Thaniel loaded a burger and chips onto his tray.

"19. You?"

"Same, so is Stephen. Tisha's a bit younger. She's okay; she usually hangs around with Jade, but she's away just now."

Thaniel shoved a chip into his mouth as he slid his tray along to the dessert counter. He nodded to the serving lady as she spooned treacle sponge into a dish and topped it with custard. It seemed so long since he'd seen decent food, let alone eaten it.

The noise in the refectory was back up to the level it had been when Thaniel had first heard it. "I can't believe you lot were here all this time," he said as he unloaded his tray at the table. "Doyen said he had other magicians, but I didn't imagine this."

The others watched as he picked up his burger and looked at it with wonder. He took a huge bite and groaned with delight. "All I ever got to eat before was some kind of prison slop on a metal tray," he managed when his mouth was almost empty.

Toby, Stephen, and Tisha exchanged surprised looks. "How long have you been here then?" Toby asked him.

Thaniel swallowed the last of his mouthful and picked up a chip, dipping it in ketchup. "About five weeks, I think; I've lost count."

Stephen's mouth fell open. "Bloody hell! Five weeks in solitary? That's harsh."

"So what is this place?" Thaniel looked around him. "I mean, I know it's called Blackwell, but that's about it." He took another bite of his burger, swallowing it almost before he'd had a chance to taste it. It felt so good to have texture to the food he was eating.

"This place is a training school for young magicians," Toby explained. "The oligarchy has something to do with it. They keep out of sight, though they're definitely behind it." He paused as if trying to read something in Thaniel's expression. "They're using us for their own ends, to make sure that no one can ever be more powerful than them," he shrugged, "but it's probably treason or something to say so, so you'd better not repeat that." He rolled his eyes. "Cos, you know, we're not all living on a song and a prayer here anyway."

"Doyen keeps telling me that he's the only reason I'm still alive," Thaniel said, "That if I do as I'm told, he can teach me all this great stuff. He keeps making out that he's this great guy when he's not beating me or forcing me to do magic until my eyes bleed." He shuddered. "I don't want to be some kind of magical pawn for a twat like that." A ripple of something Thaniel couldn't help but notice ran through the others at the table. They seemed to visibly let go of a tension he had not realised they were holding. Tisha was smiling. It was a sad smile, though, filled with understanding and regret. Thaniel shook his head. "I thought magicians were killed when they were caught. I don't get it."

"The oligarchy never actually banned people from being magicians." Toby pulled a face. "They just made it look as if they had because they want us all under their control."

"They kill the adults, though," Stephen's voice was heavy. "They killed my dad when they caught him, and he hadn't done anything wrong."

Tisha leaned over and gave Stephen's hand a quick squeeze before turning back to Thaniel. "My parents were killed too," she said. "The Purge was pretty much over. We were all out on the lake having a picnic. Someone complained 'cause no one was rowing the boat. I mean, how can magic like that be dangerous?" Her blue eyes misted over, like clouds reflecting in the sea, and her voice dropped. "When we reached the jetty, there were lots of men in blue uniforms. One of them shot my mum. Dad screamed and jumped out of the boat to try to calm everyone down, but they shouted that he was trying to attack them and shot him too. Mum died in my arms."

She sniffed, then took a deep breath, flicking her blonde hair back over her shoulder. "That was five years ago. I was taken to some house where they said they were going to look after me. Then that night I started with these awful pains in my legs. I couldn't even stand. More men in blue uniforms came and brought me here. They said the shock must have triggered my powers early."

Thaniel didn't know what to say. At least he hadn't been there to witness what had happened to his father and sister. He hoped someone else would speak up, but it was Tisha herself who broke the silence. "How did they get you? Were you taken to a watch house too?"

He frowned, "What's a watch house?"

"It's a place where orphans of the Purge are taken," Stephen said. He pulled a packet of fruit gums out of his pocket and handed them around. "They call them guardian houses to make them sound caring, but it's really just so they can filter out those of us who develop powers. That's how a lot of us came here. I was at Fordon's House along with Patty and Niall. It's the same one they took Tisha to. Toby was at the Devonshire, where Tracy, Evan, and Callum are from. The biggest one is Dawnsend. Quite a few come in from there."

Toby leaned over and took another of Stephen's fruit gums. "Some, like Jarrett, already had their powers when their parents were killed, so they came straight here, though hardly anyone ever comes from home now."

In between mouthfuls of pudding, Thaniel told them all about his dad and Jess being killed at the start of the Purge and everything that had happened since.

"That sucks," Tisha said. "Your stepfather sounds like a real shit."

"He sure does," Toby agreed.

Stephen nodded, offering his packet of fruit gums to Thaniel. He knew there were no words to make up for having your father killed by the Guard. He gave Thaniel a thoughtful smile as he took one of the sweets. For the first time in weeks, Thaniel felt as if he was amongst friends. He glanced back over to Jarrett's table and saw the older boy studying him. He didn't care if he had just made an enemy. Snubbing him had definitely been the right decision.

14

THE NEATLY CLIPPED HEDGES LOOMED LIKE SENTINELS, each one more unlikely than the last. Atop them, huge birds and animals prowled the mist-drowned landscape, looking for survivors. Only the featureless faces showed that they were nothing more sinister than topiary. Still, each time another appeared, Thaniel's heart leapt into his mouth. He had been trying to find his way through the maze for what seemed like hours. Doyen had told him to make haste; he had only until the sun rose to make the kill.

Everything had started out easily enough. He'd had no trouble remembering the way to the maze; it was, after all, only a short walk from the fountain. As he passed the water feature, he wondered about the man they had entrapped. Had he been killed, or was he, like Thaniel, locked away in some secret magical establishment? Pushing the thoughts away, he'd crept on; that was yesterday's job; now he must concentrate on tonight's.

"You will know your target," Doyen had said. Thaniel hadn't stopped to think about that, but now, with his heart thumping in his chest and the clipped hedge creatures rearing up at him through the fog, he began to question the instruction. How would he know his target? Doyen had not been specific. Fingers of fear crawled up his throat. What would happen if he killed the wrong person? Feeling a warning spasm of pain in his spine, he inched forwards. Whatever happened, Doyen had been clear. He must not get caught in the maze. There would be no help for him if he were seen.

A shriek overhead made him jump, the noise cutting through the air like a bayonet reaching for his heart. It felt as if his body was going to shatter into a thousand pieces, even as he recognised the call. The white shape of the barn owl swooped overhead, screeching again. Ignoring it, Thaniel edged forwards. Seconds later he was shying back as a lion, rampant, clawed out its front paws. He had reached the junction of three paths. To his left, he thought he heard a slight noise. He took a cautious step towards it. Tendrils of white mist closed in behind him, urging him on. Thaniel could feel its icy cold fingers tickling the back of his neck. Overhead, the sky seemed to be lightening. *Oh god!* he thought. *Dawn.*

Rounding another corner, he finally found himself at the centre of the maze. In the small enclosed space stood a low stone bench. Upon it, he could make out a figure wrapped in a long, flowing cloak as red as freshly drawn blood. The colour stood out stark against the monochrome landscape. The noise came again, a tiny whimper from beneath the cloak. He reached a tentative hand forward and pulled back the hood. The girl, his girl, lay there, flat on her back, looking straight up at him.

"Please," she whispered. "Don't hurt me anymore."

The edges of the cloak had slipped from her body. Beneath it she wore what had once been a simple white dress. Now it was ruined, torn, and bloody from countless small stab wounds that pierced deep into her flesh. The only part of her body unscathed was the area over her heart. She lay unmoving, as if trapped on a stone altar. In a panic, Thaniel looked around, half expecting a knife-wielding madman to launch at him. He realised with yet more panic that Doyen had not told him how he was supposed to make the kill. He carried no weapons.

The dense hedging was becoming more visible as cool light bleached the sky overhead, each needle-like leaf becoming more defined. Thaniel threw another look around him, realising for the first time that the maze was made of yew. A cold hand clutched at his heart. Yew was well known for its associations with death.

He dropped to his knees beside the bench. The girl's face was even more beautiful than he remembered. Her skin like porcelain, her lips red and full, and her eyes... her eyes were the palest green, flecked with slivers of burnished bronze. They looked at him now with such hurt, as though she loved him more than life itself but knew he had betrayed her.

"I haven't done this to you." Thaniel's insistent voice was smothered almost to a whisper in the moisture-filled air. "It wasn't me."

A tear slid from one of her eyes, rolling over her temple and down to the bench, where it landed and formed a tiny diamond that twinkled at him like an accusation. Thaniel knew then, somehow, that each of her wounds had indeed been caused by him. He had tried so many times in his dreams to save her, and every failure had cut her like a knife. The cold hand around his heart squeezed tighter, no longer willing to be ignored.

You will know your victim when you find them.

No! It couldn't be her. Thaniel was frantic. He loved her. He realised it now. It didn't matter that he'd never really known her; that he'd only ever seen her die over and over again. He wanted to reach out and touch her, to run his fingers through her long, dark hair, to lean over and press his lips to hers. In his hand, where there had been nothing a breath ago, a dagger appeared. Its pommel glowing like the terminating crystals on a set of silver bolas. He had a moment to look at it with horror, then his other hand came up, and together they were holding the blade above the girl's chest, the tip just touching her dress.

"Please," she begged. "Please, save me."

Thaniel's heart contracted again. The air was too thick to breathe. He could feel invisible pressure on his hands, trying to force them down. A droplet of blood formed around the blade, and the girl gasped. Thaniel fought the urge to press harder with everything he had. The sun was over the horizon now, the daylight strengthening. His arms weakened.

He woke with a lurch, heart beating heavily in his chest, his face wet with tears. Had he done it? Had he killed her? He couldn't remember. He was out of bed and pacing the room before he knew it. Around him, the residual magic seemed to flare. Thaniel welcomed its unseen embrace. It was good to have a room amongst all the other boys, but he did miss the charged atmosphere of his old attic room. His palms prickled. Thaniel dashed them against his thighs to rid himself of the ghost of the dagger and shuddered. That had been no ordinary dream. Something had been in there with him, taking over his movements and forcing him when he'd tried to resist.

Doyen. Could he have done this to him? Thaniel had been dreaming of the girl ever since he had arrived at Blackwell, so why now? He stopped dead in his tracks. What if Doyen had put the girl into his mind right from the start, to torment his nights just as he tormented his days? The thought was like stepping into a shower of icy rain, shocking every cell in his body. His knees gave way, and he dropped to the floor.

Idiot. He threw his head back against the wall. Of course there was magic involved; he'd always known that the dreams were somehow different from the norm. He was just too desperate, too needy of someone to care for him, that he hadn't been able to see the truth. He headbutted the wall again, the pain nothing compared with the aching loss he felt in his heart.

****

Amelia awoke screaming. Frantically, she pulled at the neckline of her nightshirt, her fingers not dexterous enough in that moment to handle the buttons. First one, then a second, pinged off to reveal the unmarked skin of her chest. Her fingers pressed where the blade had pierced, and she sucked in a great gulp of air. He hadn't wanted to kill her; she'd seen that in his eyes, seen how much effort it was taking him to try and stop the blade from plunging into her. He had been mouthing the words. *It wasn't me* over and over again. She brushed a hand over her cheek, almost expecting to feel the tears that had dripped from his face onto hers.

"Are you alright?" Tiffany burst into her bedroom, looking alarmed. "You were screaming so much."

The mattress dipped as Tiffany sat on the bed by her knees. Hurriedly, Amelia clutched her nightshirt together and tried to still her panicked heart. For a second, she felt pulled in two directions as the dream refused to release its grip on her.

"Here, have a drink." Tiffany grabbed the water from the nightstand and thrust it at Amelia. "The nurse at one of my old homes always used to give us water if we'd had a nightmare."

Obediently, Amelia reached for the glass of water she kept at her bedside, each sip helping to chase the gossamer-thin strands of her dream away.

"You're crying," Tiffany said. "Was it the fire?"

"Ughh," Amelia rubbed her face. "Maybe." She looked at the clock, relieved to see that it was almost time for her alarm. "Sorry I woke you."

Tiffany shook her head. "You didn't. I sometimes wake up early, so I sit and read until it's time to get up." She looked wide awake, and though she had been quick to mention the fire, she did not look upset about it herself.

Amelia felt a pang of sorrow for her. "Are you missing Jalissa?"

Tiffany shrugged. "No one stays around for long, and I don't think Jalissa liked me very much."

It was surprising that she hadn't mentioned the magic. Just how many young magicians had Tiffany known?

Amelia was about to ask her when Tiffany jumped off the bed. "I completely forgot. I was s'posed to go and get my hair done early this morning. Dorothy said she wouldn't have time if not."

In an effort to distract her the previous evening, the housekeeper had spent quite a while combing through Tiffany's freshly washed curls before oiling them, adding a touch of shea butter, and then working them into twists. Dorothy had always been the most motherly of all the staff at Marlborough. It was hard to associate that care with someone who would stand back and see her charges handed over to the Guard without a word.

The clerestory windows had been left open all night. The air was chilly, and by the time Amelia was washed and dressed, goosebumps pricked at her skin. She looked around at the destruction of the basement and sighed. Johns had carried away the remnants of her precious loom and spinning wheel, but the walls and ceiling still bore the evidence of where they had once been. While the others set about washing the mountain of things that had been cleared out to the barn last night, Amelia had chosen to remain down here and wash all the surfaces. It suited her to get on with something that would keep her away from the staff she no longer trusted.

She got to work, mixing white vinegar and a small amount of shampoo into a bucket of water, then started on the big empty armoires and the shelving. One of the firemen had assured them that it was the best way to remove the smell of char from the room. Amelia hoped he was right, because just now it felt like a thankless task.

"Phewee." Dorothy appeared at the bottom of the stairs. "No wonder you're too busy to come and eat. It smells bad enough up in the kitchen, but down here it's cloying. I think you should come upstairs, eat your breakfast, and take a few minutes for some fresh air." She rolled her large brown eyes as she turned to go. "Letty picked a fine old time to spend a few days away visiting her family, I must say. We could have done with her help to get this place back to normal."

It was a bright autumn day outside. The air was crisp, with a slight hint of frost on the way. The trees were still putting on a glorious display of yellows, oranges, and deepest reds. Leaves pattered down around Amelia like summer rain, catching in her hair and crunching underfoot. She breathed deeply, ignoring the sharp bite of cold at the back of her throat. The events of yesterday evening had thrown her more than she cared to admit. She wondered again how long Jalissa had been hiding her powers. Like Aarav, had she lost the will to keep them hidden, or had they just grown too powerful to be kept inside? Amelia turned her face into the breeze, hoping that it would blow away her rising dread. How much longer before she reached that point herself?

She could feel bile rising in her throat. Jalissa had chosen to burn to death rather than be taken. What had she known that Amelia didn't? She pushed the image of the burning girl away. Almost immediately it was replaced with one of Jalissa naked and bound in Blain's silver cord, those strange crystal balls glowing like shining jewels against her dark skin. Amelia could not think what must have been worse, the terror of her magic or the humiliation of her nakedness.

Amelia had seen the looks on the boys' faces, and it made her insides squirm. To have a boy look at her unclothed like that; heat rose in her cheeks at the thought. Before she could recover, the dream boy's ice-blue eyes were in her mind. She couldn't help but wonder what it would be like to have him look at her body. She thought of him reaching out and touching her as gently as he had touched her hair last night.

"What are you looking so guilty about?"

Jasper's voice made her jump. She spun around to face him, mortified that she had been caught thinking such things.

"And how come you get to wander about without doing any jobs?" He indicated to the leaves with the rake in his hand. "It's not fair. I've got all this yard to clear this morning."

"Trust me, you've got the better job." Amelia held out her arms to show the grimy soot stains streaking right up to her elbows. "I've been washing down the surfaces in the basement; it reeks in there. Dorothy told me to take a walk outside and get some fresh air, so I'm not skiving."

Jasper's frown melted away. "I don't know how you slept down there last night."

"The bedrooms were kind of okay." Amelia had been surprised at how well the closed doors had kept out the smoke. "It wasn't nice, though. I kept thinking about Jalissa going up in flames; it was so horrible."

"What do you think will happen to her?" Jasper lowered his voice, even though there was no one else around to hear him. "Do you think she will go where Aarav went?" Unlike Mark, Jasper still worried about Aarav. He was too old not to face the truth, yet no matter how many times Mark had told them that Aarav would be dead by now, Jasper refused to believe it.

Part of Amelia wished she could pretend as well; the rest of her knew all too well that hope was not always the lifeline people wanted it to be. She sighed. "I don't know, Jasper. If there were still magicians around, wouldn't we have heard about them? It's Halloween this weekend..." Her voice trailed off. She hated Halloween.

Years ago, when she'd had a home and the closest thing to a mum any orphan could wish for, it had been something fun. She had been encouraged to make costumes, wearing them whilst they ducked for apples and carved faces into hollowed swedes. Extra places had been set at the dinner table for Amelia's parents and Aunt T's mother; their spirits welcomed in to join them for the meal. Then, when it was dusk, they'd light the Jack-o-Lanterns and place them on the front step to guard the house all night.

Now, Halloween was a very different affair. No one honoured the dead anymore or celebrated the final harvest before the cold, dark days of the coming winter. Instead, the focus was on celebrating the routing of magic from the nation. People placed crystals in their windows to mimic the glowing magic-quelling crystals used by the Guard. They held Halloween parties and dances where they told tales of strange and unusual goings-on. Many a person had been named a magician at such events, though the number of actual magicians being caught dwindled each year. Amelia was dreading it, and, by the look on Jasper's face, he was too.

"Do you think they'll still insist we make a guy for the bonfire?" Jasper looked over to the pile of leaves that was slowly building into a substantial mound.

An effigy of a magician was placed on top of their bonfire every year. Amelia couldn't bring herself to even think about it. She had seen the real thing last night. She would never again look at a bonfire without seeing Jalissa engulfed in flames.

15

"RIGHT, STACY, TOBY, JAYDEN, AND TRACY, STAY behind please. The rest of you, leave."

Farle, the tutor who had been taking Thaniel's first class, was almost as bad as Doyen. Nevertheless, Thaniel had enjoyed every minute of it. Just the fact he had not been alone in the lesson meant that even her uncompromising and blunt manner had failed to penetrate his buoyant mood. They had been focusing on using the element of Air, and he had been fascinated to see the way everyone else had to use their hands to direct their energy. They had been equally intrigued by the fact Thaniel didn't.

"Why do you have to stay behind?" Thaniel whispered to Toby as everyone began filing out of the room.

"Halloween Watch." Toby's voice sounded flat.

Stephen nudged Thaniel towards the door. "Come on, I'll explain over lunch." He gave Toby a look that was hard for Thaniel to read. "See ya later."

The training rooms were on the first floor, along with the kitchens. Enticing smells floated up the stairs behind them as they made their way to the refectory on the floor above. Thaniel's stomach growled. It hardly seemed possible that the slop he had been given up until yesterday had come from the same kitchens.

180

"You've heard of the Halloween Watch?" Stephen asked him as they set their full trays down on an empty table.

"Yeah, of course, but that's a Guard thing. Isn't it?"

Stephen shook his head, hooking a foot around a chair leg and dragging it neatly behind him. "Everyone thinks it is, but most of it is us. Half the bloody chaos put down to magicians that haven't been caught yet is just us. They make us go out and do things to stir people up."

"Doyen made me do something." Thaniel kept his voice low. He was ashamed of what he had done, but Stephen didn't seem the type of person who would judge. "He made me trick someone into looking like they had done magic. The guy didn't stand a chance."

"Yeah, that happens a lot." Stephen rubbed the flats of his hands together as if he could erase the memory of some of the things he had been made to do.

"Bastards." Thaniel didn't swear very often, but the word was out of his lips before he'd even realised he was going to utter it.

Stephen gave him a considering look. Not everyone thought that what they did here was bad. Many of the kids were so grateful to have found somewhere they were accepted that they were happy to believe all the lies they were constantly fed.

"That's why Doyen finally let me meet you all," Thaniel said between mouthfuls of food. "He said I'd proved myself."

Stephen lowered his voice to not much more than a whisper. "I bet it's also so Jarrett and his mates can spy on you. They will do anything to keep in favour."

Thaniel followed his gaze over to where the older magicians were sitting. Sure enough, one of them was looking their way. She leaned towards Jarrett, whispering something in his ear.

"Look, just don't go telling anyone else what you really think." Stephen paused to check who had just sat down at the next table. "I mean, Toby's alright, and probably one or two others, but you've got to be careful in here. Like Tisha said yesterday, not everyone's got your back."

Thaniel suppressed a shudder. "So will I have to go out on one of these vans too?"

"Dunno. They don't usually take newbies out. Then again, they don't usually keep them in solitary so long either. Most of us only got a day or two in the holding cells." Stephen took a forkful of food, chewed, swallowed, and then added, "I guess being a mind magician makes a big difference."

"Am I really the only one?"

Stephen laughed, "You're myth made real. It's no wonder Doyen is treating you like a special case."

It was good to see him laugh, Thaniel thought. Stephen always seemed so serious and worried. He felt more than a little concerned himself right now. Every new thing he learnt about this place only made his life weigh more heavily on his shoulders. His grin faded. "Do you all have a thing in your back?"

"You meant the implant?" Stephen's laughter had dissolved too. "Yeah. Doyen might say he trusts us, but he doesn't really. The tutors all carry a controller, so don't go thinking it's only Doyen that can hurt you. They just say your name into it, and bam! You're on the floor, writhing like a snake. They don't even have to be able to see you for it to work."

Wriggling his shoulders, as if to settle the unfelt implant into a more comfortable position, Thaniel swallowed his last mouthful of food. "How long will Toby be gone?"

Stephen shrugged. "Dunno. Sometimes it's only a day, but it can be longer. Depends where they're going or if they're after anyone in particular. Halloween is a really good time for them to clear out more of the unwanteds."

"Unwanteds?"

"Yeah, you know, people who've been annoying the oligarchy, or who they just need out of the way." Stephen poked at the food on his plate. Unlike Thaniel, he wasn't really hungry. "We get sent out to deal with them all year round, but more so at this time of year when we can use the Halloween Watch as cover." He watched as Thaniel's face paled even further. There was a lost, panicked look about him that Stephen recognised well.

The noise in the refectory was loud. As usual, one guard was standing at the door, a second wandering around the room. Stephen waited until that one was far enough away before leaning towards Thaniel, "Look, the oligarchy never wanted to eliminate magic from the world; they just wanted to keep it all for themselves. Obviously, magicians would never have agreed to that, so they got rid of everyone they could and kept us. Now we're locked up in here where we can't do anything for ourselves. They have complete control, and I don't think anyone has any idea.

"All people see is them providing homes for all the orphans of the Purge and think how kind that is. But half the kids in the watch houses still had parents alive when they were grabbed. Everyone judges them on how well-treated those who get to grow up and leave are. They have no idea that the rest of us are syphoned off into here so we can be trained to use our powers in whatever way the oligarchy wants. We're not allowed to ask too many questions, and there are no illusions as to how fragile our lives are if we don't comply."

The hunted look had gone from Thaniel's eyes, replaced instead by a fierce anger. "Doyen's threatened me loads of times."

"He's not bluffing." Stephen leaned even closer. "The rumour is there's a graveyard at the far side of the maze; that's where the ones that disappear end up. The staff have never bothered to deny it." He pushed his half-eaten food away. "I doubt they bother with gravestones; they won't want anyone knowing who's really in there."

Thaniel shuddered. What was it about mazes and death? Going by his first impression of Blackwell, the graveyard could almost be expected, yet during his mission for Doyen, he had been surprised by the grounds at the rear of the building. Set back from public view by the extensive woodland, these gardens were a showpiece of historic design, at the bottom of which stood the maze. Crowned in fantastical topiary, it did nothing to hide its existence. It drew the eye so entirely that Thaniel had never even wondered what lay beyond it. Just like the rest of Blackwell, the garden knew how to keep its secrets.

Approached by car along a sweeping gravel drive, visitors were met with the imposing facade of the building, complete with carved depictions of the oligarchs set in their niches above the doorway. There was no grand portico or ornamental staircase; instead, a wide double door under a plain archway formed the entrance. Whilst Blackwell was dark and rather foreboding, with its blackened stone and plethora of gargoyles and grotesques, there was nothing to indicate that anyone was being held here against their will.

The front part of the building was given over to the reception, offices, and meeting areas. Few ever proceeded further than these barrier rooms. The interior of what masqueraded as the oligarchy's top science facility was not a place for idle wandering. It benefitted from the strictest of security. Even those lucky enough to be given access to the hidden rear courtyard and gardens would learn nothing further about the building, for here all the windows from the ground right up to the top floor were silvered as well as barred. Prying eyes would see only their own reflection, should they choose to risk a peek.

Situated above the reception rooms was Barrett Wing, and together these two sections, along with the courtyard, formed the brace that kept Sheldon Wing and the greatly feared, but rarely mentioned, Jacob Wing apart. Barrett Wing was always a hive of activity. It was here that the letters and parcels of people of concern were secretly routed for untraceable screening; here also, where anything magical was examined and tested; and here where a great deal of effort went into designing items that the young magicians of Sheldon Wing could then imbue with magical powers for the oligarchs' secret use. It was no wonder that the oligarchy, a group that currently consisted of only seven people, plus three spouses, remained so powerful and untouchable.

***

The Halloween Watch vans came and went over the next few days. Thaniel was relieved that he was never called to go out on one. Toby had been back by the following morning, but both he and Stephen had gone out again the next day, staying away for two nights before returning.

"I can't deny that haunting graveyards can be fun," Toby told Thaniel on the way into class one morning, "but I'd prefer it if we were scaring the shit out of someone who actually deserved it."

"Who, someone like Doyen?" Tisha said, half under her breath.

Toby's face lit up. "Exactly!"

"Your friend Jade still not back?" Thaniel asked Tisha when they'd stopped laughing.

She shook her head. None of the other vans had been gone more than three days. A number of people were whispering that there had been some trouble. Tisha was adamant that her friend was okay.

"I can hear her," she confided quietly to Thaniel. "They think I can just hear through walls, but it's more than that." She flicked her eyes to the front of the class where the tutor had just walked in and lowered her voice until it was barely more than breath. "Don't tell anyone I told you that though. Only Stephen and Toby know, and Jade, of course. Most of us have powers that we keep to ourselves. It makes living here that bit more bearable."

Thaniel was saved from replying by Farle clapping her hands for attention. He wasn't yet ready to confide about his own secret power, but it was heartening to know that he wasn't the only one keeping valuable information out of Doyen's grasp.

***

The wind whipped the fallen leaves around in a swirl, blowing Jade's wiry dark hair across her face. Not for the first time, she regretted not getting it braided. A low whistle sounded. Quickly, she stepped back behind a tree where the shadows hid her perfectly. A second whistle came, and she relaxed again. Two figures appeared on the path, hand in hand, oblivious of the magicians hiding nearby. By the looks of them, all bundled up in hats and scarves, eyes only for each other, they wouldn't have noticed anyone else even if they had been standing right in front of them.

Jade pulled a face. She wished she could have such a relationship. So far the only person to show any interest in her was Niall, but he was only fourteen, so he didn't

187

count. She was beginning to wonder if anyone would ever be able to see past the fact that her left arm ended just below the elbow joint. It wasn't as if that missing hand and forearm was what made her who she was. She looked down at the stump, all bloody with her sleeve torn to rags around it. As much as she loved this kind of job, she was starting to worry that all she was good for in other people's eyes was pulling pranks.

The couple disappeared down the path. Jade stepped back into the light and tried to convince herself it was slightly warmer out of the shadows. She put her hand into her pocket again, reassuring herself that the small gold box was still there. If she were to lose that, she would end up in the graveyard for sure; then there would be no need to worry about boys and love and... The whistle sounded again. Jade ducked back into the shadows, ready. This time, there was no follow-up call. Her target was on his way.

He was not alone; a second man was walking with him—perfect. Jade paused only long enough to ruffle up her hair, then she staggered forwards. "Help," she cried, tripping over her feet and almost falling, "please, help me."

"Oh God!" Don Brook cried as both men rushed forwards. He reached out to steady her, recoiling as he connected with something wet and sticky. He looked down in horror, the old-fashioned streetlamp up ahead emitting just enough dim light to make out the blood now covering his hand.

She really should have been an actress, Jade thought as her knees buckled and she fell to the floor at his feet. She was crying now, tears streaking her dirty face. "There was a man," her trembling voice got out, "he attacked me."

"Where?"

Jade reached for Don, grabbing at his outstretched arm. "He ran back into the trees when he heard you coming. Please don't leave me."

With his friend incapacitated, the second man darted off. They could hear him charging through the trees. There was a shout and a cry. Don, on his knees now beside Jade, turned to look. The second his attention left her, Jade lifted her fingers. The gold box rose from her jacket and dropped unseen into the pocket of Don's knee-length woollen coat. He must have felt something because he turned swiftly back to her. Before he had a chance to speak, Jade shrieked.

"My arm. Oh god, my arm's gone. He hit me with an axe." She held out her seemingly severed limb.

"Hell!" Don cursed. "It's alright, love, I'll call an ambulance." He was trembling himself as he went to grab for his phone.

Jade clutched surprisingly tightly to his arm, stopping him. "Please," her voice was desperate, teetering on the edge of hysteria. "Just get me out of here. He'll come back to get me."

She lay limply in his arms, enjoying the feeling of strength around her. It had been a long time since anyone had held her. She thought briefly of her father and the way he used to hold her on his knee when she was young and hurt. She let out a groan as genuine tears mingled with her false ones. Assuming she was in pain, Don hurried his steps even more. The light of the road was clearly visible up ahead now, an illusion of safety on such a shocking evening. Moments after they emerged from the path, a dark van pulled up alongside them. For a second, Don thought it was a Guard van, but the occupant was a woman in a green and turquoise hooded jacket.

"Are you alright?" she called out of the driver's window. "Do you need help?" She jumped out of the van. "Oh my god," she cried, seeing Jade's missing arm. "Quick, put her in the front; I'll get her straight to hospital."

"I was going to call an ambulance," Don said, suddenly all too aware of how precarious his position was, alone with a vulnerable teenage girl who was bound to be in shock. "I just needed to get her out of the wood. She was too scared to stay in there."

The woman all but ignored what he said as she opened the passenger door and helped to bundle the injured girl inside. The interior light was harshly bright. For the first time, Don could see the full horror of Jade's ragged stump. His own hands and that of the woman's were covered in bright, fresh blood. It was smeared down his coat and on the front of his shirt.

"It's ok now," the woman told him, easing him out of the way and shutting the door. "I'll see that she is taken care of. It will be quicker than phoning the ambulance."

Don nodded, taking one last look at Jade before the driver's door shut and the interior light blinked out. The van set off so quickly that he had to jump back as it pulled away, its red tail lights gleaming like eyes. There was a moment of dislocated calm as Don tried to take in what had just happened. It had been so quick, yet so shocking. He took an involuntary step after the van, wanting suddenly to regain his connection with the injured girl and give reason to the adrenaline still pumping through his body.

Footsteps sounded to his right, making him jump, pulling him back to reality with a resounding start. His friend staggered back onto the path, one hand holding the side of his head. Don took in a deep breath of relief. They threw themselves onto the nearby bench, and for a few minutes the pair of them sat in stunned silence.

"That's not your blood, is it?"

Don looked down at the drying blood covering his coat and hands. Under the yellow glow of the streetlight, it looked almost black. He smelled like raw meat, and it made his stomach clench again. "No. It's not mine."

He wasn't ready to voice what had happened just yet, so he reached into his pocket for a handkerchief. His hand closed around a small box. He pulled it out, the gold gleaming as the embossed filigree pattern caught the light. Curious, he pressed the minute catch on the front, and the lid sprang open. Both men gasped in unison as the will-o'-the-wisp trapped inside floated up. A thin gold thread tethered it an inch or so above the box. Don Brook closed his eyes. Every curse word he knew, and there were many, streamed through his mind.

It had been a risk, he knew, printing anything less than complimentary about the oligarchy, but he hadn't become the editor of the country's leading newspaper, the one all others emulated, by taking the easy route. Journalism was all about exposing the truth, not taking backhanded pay-outs from the political elite to keep a story quiet. Clearly, his downfall was to be a lesson no one would miss. It would be splashed across every headline and banner, held up as the shining example of how far someone could fall if they dared to put a foot out of line.

His companion slid as far down the bench as he could go, a look of sheer incredulity on his face; still too woozy to trust his ability to stand, he opened his mouth to speak, but nothing came out. Finally, with one last pained look at his now ex-friend, he pulled out his phone and punched three numbers into it. Before the operator could even answer, another dark van screeched to a halt beside them. There was no mistaking the Guard this time.

"We've had a report that someone is doing magic here," the passenger said, getting out and fixing his hat firmly on his head. His colleague came around the van with her handcuffs at the ready. There was no need to say any more; the evidence was right there before them in the shape of a misty blue-white orb floating over its precious metal prison.

Jade and the woman were laughing. They drove around the quiet suburban streets until they came to the other end of the wooded path. Two more dark-clad figures were waiting to be picked up. The rear side door was opened by Niall, who had been hiding in the back, and they tumbled in. Jade slipped out of the passenger seat and joined them. The driver, Robertson, called through the small interconnecting window. "Everything ok?"

Staff at Blackwell were always known by their surnames. Doyen liked to keep a certain amount of anonymity around his workers.

"Yup," Brown said with a grin. "Managed to get the friend away, no problem. Clobbered him when he got too close, and Evan did his mind trick on him."

Unlike the others, Evan's face showed no sign of enjoyment. "He won't remember anything other than having a headache."

"Have you heard from 'eather yet?" Brown's voice was heavily accented, and he had a tendency to drop his Hs.

At the same moment, Robertson's phone pinged. "That's her now." She hauled on the steering wheel. The van did a neat U-turn in the road and headed back the way they had come.

Heather was sitting on a wall at the end of the road. Like everyone except Robertson, she wore dark unisex clothing with her hood pulled right down over her forehead. She jumped into the passenger seat and pulled off her hood, revealing a shock of long blonde hair.

"Well?" Robertson asked.

"It was brilliant. The Guard arrived just after he'd opened the box. The wisp was just floating there, and his mate was glaring at him like he'd grown a second head."

"Red-handed." Niall, who had so far remained quiet, laughed.

Evan gave him a withering look. It didn't matter that the boy was young; he should still realise that everything about what they had just done was morally wrong. Heather, who never liked to mix with the younger kids, just ignored him. Niall didn't care. This was all a big game to him. He never gave a thought to the victims of their trickery or the creatures he tethered in their makeshift prisons. His lack of conscience and eagerness to please had made him one of the youngest magicians ever to be favoured by Doyen.

Evan ran a hand over his tight-cropped hair and tried to look as if he didn't care about what they were doing either. He picked at a scratch on the back of his hand until blood began to appear, gems of ruby against his dark skin. They had waited just over a week after Halloween to target the newspaper mogul. All so that his downfall would be headline news and not blurred in amongst the rest of the Halloween detritus. The others might be proud to be associated with such a catch, but Evan was sickened by it.

"Have we any more pep juice?" he asked Brown as Robertson sped off down the road. He had used his powers far more than usual today, and it was taking its toll.

Brown tossed a bottle over to him. "We're done now. You can have a good rest when we get back. You've certainly earned it today."

They had spent a number of hours at Brook's home whilst the man himself had been out with his former friend. Heather, a bloodhound when it came to finding hidden magical items, had scoured the house just in case Don actually did have some magic working for him. Finding nothing, they planted their own incriminating evidence whilst Robertson had Evan alter the memories of Don's family and house staff. There were now plenty of people who could testify to say that they had witnessed Don doing various magical acts, none of which were anything other than Evan's manipulations.

In the front, Heather was reading a magazine. Next to Evan, Niall, Jade, and Brown were playing a noisy game of cards. Evan leaned back in his seat and closed his eyes, blocking everyone out as the pineapple juice worked its way into his bloodstream. He would never understand how anyone could take this work so lightly.

16

Amelia glanced at her clock. 4.30 am. She'd been awake since two and knew from her heavy eyes that she couldn't hold out much longer. She stared up through the shallow clerestory window that ran the length of her room. Two stars shone down on her. Curious, she forced her exhausted body out of bed and padded closer until Orion came into view. Its proximity to the brightest of the two stars confirmed it as Sirius. She had learnt that as a child, lying in the garden looking up at the night sky with her Aunt T. The other star remained a mystery. It looked down on her nonetheless, its welcoming glow like a smile in the night.

Thoughts of her aunt made her wonder, would both of her mums be looking down on her? The one she knew and the one she didn't. Aunt T had faded in her mind over the years, but she was still there when she looked, laughing as they had toasted marshmallows over a small fire in the garden, wrapping her up in lavender-scented hugs, and singing made-up songs as she'd twirled about the house with a feather duster in her hand. Every memory a happy one, filled with love and affection. Of her birth mother, Amelia had no recollection at all; not even the faintest glimmer of a memory.

She shivered, feeling goosebumps creeping up her flesh. Back in bed, she snuggled down under the covers, tucking

196

them tightly in around her neck. The thought of her mums watching over her made her feel a little more secure. She knew that was silly. Then again, so was being afraid of falling back to sleep in case the dream person you'd fallen in love with was forced to try and kill you again.

Maybe if she focused her mind on something good, her dreams would stay kind? Closing her eyes, she took a deep breath and let it out as slowly as possible. It made her yawn. She let her mind drift to thoughts of standing alone amongst peaceful trees, the warming sun reaching through the branches overhead, forming a pool of light around her. With every inhale, she thought of sleep creeping in, filling her body, letting it relax into the mattress just like the orange leaves that fell from the trees around her and floated, softly, slowly, to the ground.

The sand was damp under her bare feet. She could wriggle her toes and make firm indentations that stayed when she stepped away. The sea was shallow and calm, sending low, white-tipped waves rippling up the beach in wide, curving arcs. Laughing, she hitched up her dress and skipped into the shallow water. Sun-warmed and clear, it lapped over her feet, tickling at her ankles. Overhead, seagulls whirled on the breeze, their joyous cries ringing out in the clear, still air.

Amelia had never felt so peaceful. To each side of her, the beach stretched out, deserted but for a couple of figures walking away from her far in the distance. She threw back her head and let the sun fall on her face. Further out to sea, the waves were darker; a green-blue that spoke of boat rides and fishes, mermaids basking on rocks, and dolphins leaping from the depths. Amelia had never been to the seaside before and had never realised that up close the water would be so transparent. She saw a small crab scuttling away from her, its shell almost white in colour, so different from the large brown crabs she'd seen lined up in the fishmonger's window. She ventured further out, holding her dress higher until the water was almost to her knees. It cooled as it got deeper. The waves were higher too; one splashed right up to mid-thigh, making her gasp.

"Stop."

She would know that voice anywhere. Spinning around, she saw him standing on the dry sand, a look of sheer panic on his face. Amelia could not think why.

"It's not safe," he yelled, frantic now. He started running, splashing through the water, heedless of his clothes. Almost in slow motion, Amelia turned and looked over her shoulder to see a huge wall of water heading towards her.

"Run!" She heard him cry.

The sea held onto her, dragging at her legs. In the shallower water, the boy had been faring better, but even his movements were slowing now. They were almost in reach of each other when she heard the roaring, as if a great monster had reared up out of the sea and was charging down on them. She saw fear paint across the boy's face. He surged forward, and then his outstretched arms were wrapping around her, pulling her close.

Oh, it felt so good. All the nights, she had longed to feel his arms around her, wanting so much to be able to touch him, to hold him, and now he was here. Finally, he had reached her in time. Heart clamouring in her chest, she tucked her head into his shoulder just as the tidal wave broke over them. If the noise had been bad before, now it was deafening. Amelia tightened her grip, holding on for dear life. Still, the force of the water tore her arms away, buffeting her downwards so that she hit hard on the seabed.

Flailing and disoriented, she had no idea which way was up. Her throat began tightening, the muscles of her diaphragm contracting, urging her to take a breath. Bubbles of air broke from her mouth, only to be lost in the surrounding turbulence. Familiar terror gripped her. Then, fingers grabbed at her clothing. She was yanked upwards. Her face broke the surface, and she gasped in precious air. Her hair was clinging to her face. She brushed it away, taking in the devastation of the beach and the drenched, smiling boy beside her. She felt shy all of a sudden. This was not a position they had been in before. He took a step towards her and then stopped, as if he too was suddenly unsure.

The seagulls whirled above them, their calls raucous now as they laughed at the two figures standing thigh-deep in the swirling water. The air had taken on a chilly edge, the wisps of white cloud chasing together, darkening as they went. Thaniel didn't notice; he was too enthralled by the girl in front of him. Her white dress clung transparently to her skin; he was sure she hadn't realised. The sight stole his breath as efficiently as the sea had stolen hers only moments before. Another step and he was close enough. He reached out and took hold of the flimsy clothing, pulling it gently.

Amelia felt the cold waft of air hit her skin as the boy plucked the sodden material away from her body, only now realising that she wore nothing at all underneath. Heat radiated up her face; he must have seen everything, yet, even in her innocence, the thought was as exhilarating as it was terrifying.

"Thank you," she whispered, not sure if it was for protecting her modesty or for saving her life. His face was close to hers; she could feel his breath, warm on her cheek. As she tilted her head up to look into his eyes, he leaned in and kissed her. It was feather-light, his lips just grazing hers.

Thaniel had never wanted to hold her as much as he did now; to gather her in his arms, pull her tight against him, and feel her heart beating next to his. Pressing his body up against hers, though, would reveal far more about how he was feeling than was wise. He caressed the side of her face with one hand, the other tucking a wayward strand of hair behind her ear. As his lips brushed hers a second time, he felt her intake of breath, then her hands were on him. They slid up his arms, over his shoulders, and he was lost.

His breath caught in his throat, then he was melting into her lips. He touched them with the tip of his tongue, and they parted, giving him access. His tongue found hers, and he tasted coffee, dark and sweet. One of her hands was in his hair now, the other tracing skin-tingling circles on his neck. Every nerve in his body was alive, electrified by her touch.

Amelia could feel herself smiling even as they were kissing. Her first kiss with the boy in her dreams, and her first kiss ever. It was so much more than she had thought it would be; who could have known that a boy's lips could be so sensuous? A tiny part of her was amazed at how brazen she was being, standing here in a transparent dress, pressed up against a boy, willing the kiss not to end. His hands were around her back now, firm and protective. She forgot about her wet clothing, the sea frothing about their legs, and the gulls crying overhead. Nothing else mattered but that they were here together, kissing at last.

Gently, Thaniel caressed her body. Amelia's insides lurched with the thrill of it. She was pulling at his shirt, suddenly desperate to feel his bare skin under her hands, when something bumped against her leg, wrapping around it like the arms of a hidden creature. She screamed, pulling away and kicking her leg out, frantically trying to dislodge whatever had hold of her. She saw the shadow of dark green tentacles in the murky water and shrieked again.

"It's alright." Thaniel held his hands out, as if to steady her. His face was flushed, his breathing heavy. "It's seaweed; it's just seaweed." He tugged at it, and Amelia felt it slide away. "Come on," he took her hand, "let's get out of here."

As their hands touched, the feeling of 'oneness' returned, driving away the cold chasm that had opened up when their bodies had parted. Thaniel began leading the way back to the beach, taking it slowly as they realised just how much debris was swirling around them. The wave had fled far inland now, obliterating any sign of the high tide line and scattering its leavings right up and over the dunes.

They had thought the danger was over as they made their way up the beach. When big, fat, warning raindrops began to fall from the increasingly leaden sky, they realised they were wrong.

"We can shelter there." Thaniel pointed to a small wooden café with a covered veranda. "Come on."

They raced across the sand, heedless of the debris now as they tried to outrun the approaching deluge. For a few hopeful moments, they thought they might make it. Then the monsoon hit, and once again Amelia's dress was stuck to her skin, the skirt wrapping around her legs. She stumbled, hearing the boy yell for her as their hands tore apart. Just at that moment, the return flow of the giant wave came crashing back over the dunes. Amelia screamed, frantically reaching for Thaniel as she was caught up in the seaward torrent. This time, there would be no chance of rescue. The waves would have their victim; they would not be foiled again.

As the briny water closed over her head, Amelia screamed one last time, and then everything went dark. She had no idea where Thaniel had gone, though she knew he was no longer with her. That sense of unity she had felt when she was with him had vanished, leaving a cold, empty void in its place. Time and space lost all meaning. There was no pain, no feeling of water in her lungs, or waves buffeting her as she floated in the inky blackness.

It took a long time for her to realise that the darkness surrounding her was no longer that of the sea. At some point she had woken, not suddenly as she usually did when she dreamt of drowning but incrementally, sense by sense, her mind taking its time to bring her back to full awareness. Her bedside clock told her less than an hour had passed since she'd last looked at it, such a short space of time to have her last thread of hope snatched away.

The floor was cold on her feet as she eased open her bedroom door and fled, careful to skip over the steps that could give her away. Up in the kitchen, the Aga's heat was comforting. She poured some milk into a pan, added a milk-saver ring, and placed it on one of the hot plates. Inevitability hung heavy in the air, and she huddled down underneath it to wait.

For weeks now her life had felt like a tightrope of fear, her only escape the boy who had walked into her nightmares and offered her salvation. When she had watched first Aarav and then Jalissa lose control, part of her had felt like a traitor. Despite knowing what a foolish thing it would have been, she couldn't help thinking that she should have had the courage to stand up for them instead of saying nothing whilst Blain lassoed them in his rope of light and metal. It had been her own wild fears keeping her rooted to the spot with her words trapped inside her. Fears that she might have overcome had she not been selfishly clinging to the hope that somehow her dream boy would sweep into her life and save her, just as he'd tried to do over and over in her nighttime terrors. Common sense told her that no matter how tangible he seemed, such a rescue was completely impossible. She had always known it was. Still, she'd clung to the hope because it had been her only escape from the day-to-day reality of her all-too-dangerous situation. She could not pretend any longer, because now she knew that it didn't matter if he rescued her. There would always be another danger coming for her just around the corner. She had misunderstood her dreams entirely. They had not been giving her a saviour; they had been a warning, telling her that, no matter what happened, she could never survive.

Her heart skipped a beat as she thought back over the dream. She had read the desire in his eyes and known instantly that he loved her, just as she loved him. She brushed her fingers along her lips, cheeks flushing as she remembered the passion that had ignited between them, scandalised that even subconsciously she could have thought up such a thing, thrilled that she had.

The glass saver ring made its first tentative noises. Amelia dived for the stove, pulling the pan from the heat before it could begin rattling in earnest. She poured the milk into an old mug and carefully cleared every sign of her nocturnal visit away. Back down in her room, she sat on her bed, sipping her drink, the boy's touch ghosting around her as she thought back to their embrace.

Where was he now? Did he live in her mind, just waiting until she slept—or was he, like her, a real person sitting in the cold darkness of the pre-dawn, bereft and alone once again? It came to her then that she didn't even know his name. Why hadn't she thought to ask?

17

HE WAS JUST CLOSING HIS EYES AFTER ANOTHER LONG day when Thaniel suddenly realised that, had she lived, today would have been his sister's 24th birthday. Instead of respecting her memory, something he had done without fail every year since she had been killed, he had been cooped up in a sickeningly bad private lesson with Doyen. His mother had always made such a big fuss over her children's birthdays. Even losing Jess had not stopped them celebrating each year. He wondered, with a wrench, how she had coped with today.

I love you, Nathaniel.

The last words he'd heard her speak echoed in his mind. It shook him to realise that, after today's lesson, he could have choked off those words as easily as blinking. Thaniel's skin crawled at the thought: a thousand fire ants marching over his body. Part of him wished that he could stop his mind from constantly going over everything Doyen made him do, but that would only lead to him becoming immune to the reality of it all, and that, Thaniel thought, would be even worse.

Toby and Stephen understood. They hated this life just as much as he did. Even so, Thaniel saw kids every day, like Jade and Niall, who didn't seem to realise that what they were being asked to do was wrong. They revelled in the mischief and destruction, their consciences never pricking for a moment. Then there was Evan. He was one of the oldest magicians at Blackwell and tended to keep to himself. Thaniel's suspicions were growing by the day that underneath his cold, quiet demeanour, Evan still retained his sense of honour. Thaniel wanted to stay like that, to keep his humanity and not be drawn into this life of covert deceit. If that meant keeping Doyen's lessons raw in his mind so that the shame of them never dulled, then that was what he would do.

The wind whispered against his window, taunting him with accusations he knew damn well that he deserved. Swallowing back nausea, he forced himself to go over the horror of today's lesson, to see again the white rabbit whose heart he had stopped, its velvet nose giving one last twitch just before it collapsed dead at his feet; the way the black rabbit had convulsed as he stopped its lungs from pulling in oxygen; the brown lop with its huge ears, that had dragged its back end along the floor after he had frayed the nerves in its spine. Thaniel hated himself for every second those animals had suffered. It didn't matter that Doyen used the implant in his back to punish him every time he was slow to obey; that taking the time to secretly ensure each animal had felt nothing of the cruelty he was being made to inflict meant that he had endured far more pain and suffering by the time they had finished. Each time the light of life had dimmed in their eyes, it felt as if part of Thaniel was dying too.

No doubt Evan would understand. Thaniel had heard the story about Don Brooks, editor of the Inquirer newspaper, and his downfall, numerous times now. How

Niall had 'cunningly' trapped the innocent will-o'-the-wisp inside a gold box and how Jade, her arm made up to look freshly severed, had 'brilliantly' played the victim to get close enough to levitate the box into his pocket. Of course, they'd also had to admit that the whole ruse had only worked because Evan had used his magic to creep inside the minds of numerous people connected to Don and place false memories to twist and destroy any relationship they might have had with the press magnate.

The closed expression on Evan's face as the story was told over and over again had not been missed by Thaniel. The older boy did not join in with either the bragging or the laughter, nor would he be drawn into discussing his part in the proceedings, no matter how much the others pestered and cajoled. He never spoke out against what had been done, though; instead, he bore every congratulatory clap on the back like a condemned man hearing his sentence read out.

Thaniel sighed, the sound fading away into the silence of the room. "Happy birthday, sis," he whispered, her grinning face a little more faint in his memory than it had been last year. There was another face now that seemed to take over most of his thoughts. It came into his mind again, driving away all thoughts of his family. When he had seen that wall of water coming towards her last night, his heart had contracted. Nothing in him could have stood by and just watched her die.

At first, when he'd surfaced after the torrent overcame them, he'd thought she was gone. Then, he'd turned, and it was as if someone had stolen away his breath. It caught again now as he thought of her in that drenched, white dress, clinging so provocatively to her body that she might as well have been wearing nothing at all. He had done it; he had finally saved her, and she was more beautiful than he could ever have imagined. He'd been scared to touch her at first, lest she disappear in a cloud of water droplets. She hadn't, though, and he'd taken her in his arms, and she'd looked at him as though he was everything. Then he was kissing her, and she was responding. Even now, his pulse increased as he tried to remember exactly how it had felt. It was like clasping a snowflake and hoping to keep it intact on your palm. There was only one way to get it back, but that was to watch her die over and over again. Could he bear it? It wasn't as if he had any choice; he couldn't exactly stop himself from sleeping.

He could feel it coming now, weighing the lids of his eyes heavy and sinking his body further into the thin mattress. He found that he didn't want to fight it. Even knowing that he would see her die again, he couldn't stop the longing to have just one more moment with her.

****

Clive Greckham dropped the newspaper on the desk and sat back in his chair. The headline could have been written in neon lights rather than thick black ink, and it would not have made more impact.

Don Brooks: Tyrant, Liar... Magician!

The write-up was not much better. Clive had already read it once. It was no less shocking the second time. He'd always read the Inquirer and had become quite friendly with Don in the last few years. He admired the man, who had risen from nowhere to become one of the biggest names in media, all down to his no-frills method of reporting. If Don Brooks were a magician, Clive would eat his hat. He lifted the phone and started to dial, then thought better of it and slammed the old-fashioned receiver back into its cradle. He ran a hand over his face. Did he really want to poke the beast? Again, he scanned the words he already knew so well. One phrase stood out. *Masquerade of the Magician.* He dropped the paper. Masquerade indeed, but just who was the one wearing the mask?

Pushing his chair back, he went to the dark wood cabinet in the corner of the room. The cupboard at the bottom held a single bottle. He removed it and poured a finger of cognac into a snifter glass. This was certainly not the first time he'd suspected the oligarchy of framing someone they'd wanted to get rid of. Anyone who got under the skin of the ruling body, it seemed, was liable to meet a very shameful demise. Clive downed the brandy in one go, almost breaking the glass as he thumped it back down. He must keep his cool. Pazia had asked to meet up for an impromptu coffee in half an hour, and she could ferret out a weasel in a room full of rats with her eyes closed.

He moved over to the dragon carving mounted on the wall, its body curved around a small, circular mirror. Frowning, Clive ran a finger over one of his eyebrows, smoothing the hair back into place. He could feel the drink warming his insides, easing his tension. Satisfied with his appearance, he patted the small pendant that hung beneath his shirt and headed for the door.

****

The Conservatory Tea Room was one of the best places to be seen. Pazia smiled at the waiter as he held a chair out for her, casually running her eyes over the crowd as she did so. She tucked her long legs under the table and took an idle glance at the menu. Both the action and the words printed there were irrelevant, she always had the same thing.

"I'll order when my companion gets here," she waved the waiter away. "I'm a little early."

The buzz of conversation around her was tempered by the music of a classical harpist in the centre of the huge glass room. Pazia recognised strains of *Smetana's Vltava* drifting delicately through the air. A little too intense a piece for such a setting, but of such complexity that no doubt the harpist was using the opportunity to practice where there was plenty of distraction. Judging by the amount of talk in the room, no one was really paying that much attention to her anyway. Pazia had overheard numerous references to Don Brooks as she'd wound her way between the tables behind the waiter. Only one conversation had given her any cause for concern.

"It was clearly a setup," a red-haired woman had said. "Don was no more a magician than I'm a mouse."

210

Oh no, my dear, I'd call you more of a shrew, Pazia had thought as she'd breezed past the table, not even glancing at its occupants. Now though, as she carefully angled her chair, she was able to see the two women easily. They were almost identical in appearance, even down to their twinsets, pearls, and neat chignons; the type of women who never got so much as a second glance in a room full of people wanting to be seen.

She herself was always conspicuous, which she used to full advantage. Six feet tall without shoes on, she rarely left the house in anything lower than a three-inch heel. Her natural poise and deportment, which in her youth had been taken as defiance, were now seen as nothing short of regal, and the amber undertones in her darker-than-dark skin glowed with a radiance most women could spend thousands failing to achieve.

Her beauty drew admiring glances wherever she went, yet it was a veneer that hid a core of steel. Once Pazia had her hooks into something, she never gave up. Oligarch Baxter Carswell had once jokingly called her Elon Kelby's personal sniffer dog. He'd not made that mistake again. Pazia was no one's puppet. Her talents might be the best-kept secret of the oligarchy, but it was a role she had carved out all by herself.

From a very young age, she had learnt to use her incredible mind to her advantage. A photographic memory, people called it, yet hyperthymesia was so much more than recalling images. Every little detail of everything she had said, heard, and done was indelibly imprinted on her memory. So, she'd begun collecting tidbits of seemingly useless information on people and soon found that more often than not they created a far more revealing and useful picture. Teachers, lecturers, and anyone else who gave her cause soon realised that they had underestimated her to their peril.

She had landed her role as a junior employee at the Chambers building twelve years ago. Though she'd had no political interests at the time, the government's centre of operations had been hiring, and she had been desperately in need of a job. Two years later, she had marched uninvited into the Master Oligarch's office one quiet Monday morning and dropped a plain manila file onto his desk. Elon had opened it with an air of impatience only to look up a second later, mouth opening and closing like a badly worked marionette. Within days, Pazia had been installed as an official member of the oligarchy, much to the shock of her former colleagues.

The harpist had reached a series of mesmerising runs in the music. Pazia closed her eyes for a moment. She opened a new mental dossier and stamped the words *Ginger Twins* on the cover. Not the most original name she'd ever thought of, but she'd just noticed her companion approaching.

Clive made his way across the tea room, wondering who it was that Pazia had been considering. Surely not the Narosh Sisters? The calculated look on her face evaporated into smiles the moment she noticed him. She leaned forward as he bent and kissed her cheek, the smell of her spicy perfume wafting over him. It matched her orange-tipped nails and the autumnal colours of her tailored suit.

She was the very epitome of this time of year, he thought: the beauty that hides the bite of the coming winter. The stronger the colours, the brighter and more abundant the rich berries on the bushes and trees, and the worse the dangers that lay ahead. Clive took his seat, smoothing down his chequered tie. The waiter appeared like a ghost at his shoulder.

"Rosemary tea..." Clive inclined an enquiring head at Pazia, who nodded. "for the lady, and a cinnamon latte for myself. And I think we will have a plate of those lovely-looking macaroons." He glanced over to a passing waitress carrying a tiered plate of the pastel-coloured fancies.

Pazia raised her eyebrows. "Feeling decadent today?"

Clive clapped his hands together. "I find myself in an excellent mood. I have no idea why. So, I have decided to just go with the flow."

She laughed; Clive was always fun to be around. He had a lightness to him that not many men could carry off without appearing contrite or effeminate. Clive was neither. What was more, he was every bit the respectable and trustworthy man he appeared to be. Pazia should know; for years she had tried to dig something up on him, but the man was so open about his unfortunate past that she had failed to find anything untoward at all.

"I must say, this smell is heavenly." Clive gestured to the huge bouquet of flowers sitting atop a short, mock-stone pillar behind Pazia. It was one of a row of such arrangements reaching right across the tearoom and effectively screening off a more secluded area where those not inclined to 'see and be seen' could enjoy a modicum of privacy in cosy, high, lattice-backed booths. "I had wondered why you chose to be seated right back here, but now I see the wisdom in your choice."

Pazia lost her smile for a brief moment, then her face lit once more with amusement. "You've got me." She flicked her eyes to the flowers. "I had a tip-off from the manager that they'd had a fresh batch of gardenia in this morning."

Clive raised a quizzical eyebrow at her. "They do that?"

"It seems they do." She fluttered her lashes at him and grinned. "Of course, my complaints the last time I was here had nothing at all to do with it. Jasmine is far too overpowering when you are trying to enjoy your afternoon tea, don't you think?"

Deadpan, Clive answered, "Can't think why so many people rave about it."

Pazia couldn't decide if he was teasing her or not. She let it pass. "I thought it only courteous to show my appreciation for the gesture by requesting to sit here."

The waiter returned with their order, and in the few moments it took to set everything down, three people had been seated at the table on the other side of the screen. Their voices drifted through the flowers, mingling with the scents of gardenia, rose, and freshly brewed coffee. Pazia tuned out their chatter, concentrating on her companion.

Clive was on his third macaroon when she dropped her bombshell.

18

"So, have you heard about Elon Kelby and Lorena Hunter?" Pazia's eyes glinted behind her long, false lashes.

For half a second, Clive was stunned. Up until now, her conversation had all been minor, irrelevant stuff, which had lulled him into a dangerous state of complacency. Exactly the time when the Queen of Spiders pounces. His heart was beating a little faster. Only a fool gossiped about one oligarch to another. It just wasn't safe; but how could he lie when the whole world had heard about their unfortunate encounter? "I did hear the odd whisper," he admitted.

Pazia lowered her voice. "There were pictures."

There was nothing else for it. Clive raised his eyebrows and played along. "Have you seen them?"

"Of course." Smugly, she helped herself to a pale, peachy-orange macaron that wouldn't clash with the colour of her jacket. She bit into it, holding her other hand underneath to catch the falling crumbs.

"And...?"

Pazia gave a malicious chuckle. "Never has a woman looked so...ravished." She took a sip of her tea and watched his reaction over the top of her cup. His shocked grin did not disappoint, so she pressed on. "One frame even had Elon standing in the doorway looking... well... let's just say that red lipstick does not suit his complexion."

Clive was surprised that she actually seemed to believe this nonsense about an affair. There had been rumours, back when Pazia had first been elevated to the oligarchy ranks, that something was going on between her and Elon. Clive hadn't believed that either. Everyone knew that Elon had still been mourning his dead wife at the time, something that still hadn't changed all these years later. The thought of Jane Kelby made Clive's grip tighten, and the remains of his macaroon shattered into a lemon-coloured shower of crumbs. He wiped them away with a feigned nonchalance he was certainly not feeling, almost jumping as the waiter reappeared to ask if they required anything else.

"Not just now, my dear, but thank you for your attention." Pazia patted his arm and winked, slipping a banknote into his hand as she did so.

Though discreet, Clive caught the move and had to force himself to blink. It would be so like Pazia to bring him somewhere public to throw him under the proverbial bus, and looking like a deer in headlights would make it so obvious he was expecting it. This kind of approach was something he had known her to use numerous times before. She would land a shocking statement about someone else entirely, lulling her victim into a false state of security, before firing out a perfectly timed accusation to which they had no possible chance of deflection.

The waiter moved away, and the glint in Pazia's eye sharpened to a pinpoint. For the space of two breaths, the air coalesced around them. Clive could feel it pressing in on him. He loosened his tie, ever so slightly, hoping that

the move appeared relaxed. His hands were not shaking—
yet.

"He paid off the press, you know." Pazia leaned
forward, lowering her voice even further. "Tried to get the
whole thing shoved under the carpet."

Clive reached into his pocket and pulled out a packet of
mints, offering one to Pazia. He swirled the tube in his
fingers and took one himself. "Have you spoken to them
about it?"

"Oh, I will." Pazia popped the mint into her mouth and
leaned back again. "Now, tell me what you have been up
to. I hear you have a new commission on the go?"

The surrounding noise rushed back at Clive, with it a
sense of relief that almost bowled him over. Whatever was
going on here, it wasn't about him. He tucked the tube of
mints away, pleased to see that his hands had still not
betrayed him.

****

Sylvie Cartright sipped her Earl Grey as she listened to
her sister and their friend describe the musical they had
seen the week before. She had been unable to join them,
due to the dinner at Blain's. It sounded like they'd had a
great evening, whereas hers had been a complete disaster.
Blain had barely paid her any attention at all. She'd been
ousted to the other end of the table and could still hear
that desperate, grabbing Isabel Branwell and Blain
laughing together. Even when the meal ended, he'd been

no better company, shutting himself away in his office with the oligarchs as if none of the rest of his guests existed.

Was he being advanced into their ranks? No other guests had been invited to join them, and she couldn't think of any other reason why they would need to closet themselves together like that. It had eaten away at her the whole evening. If Blain was about to be honoured by the ruling class, then she needed to know. He was the most eligible catch in the area; others would soon be trying to muscle in on him. Sylvie could not afford to let him slip through her fingers now that his star was on the rise.

She had tried poking a few gentle questions to Lillian Lanford, whose husband had also been shuttered away in Blain's office, but it had been like talking to a closed book. Marlon Hunter hadn't been forthcoming either. Sylvie couldn't blame him for being distracted. It couldn't be easy keeping up appearances when the whole world knew his wife was cuckolding him with her boss.

All in all, it had been a very unsatisfactory night. The oligarchs had left almost immediately after their meeting was over. Peyton Lanford had looked angry, Elon and Lorena thoughtful; only Pazia had emerged looking her usual, collected self. Beyond doubt, there was something going on. Blain had been vague when she'd asked him what it was, dismissing her questions with a wave of his hand. Even his goodnight kiss on the cheek had been barely more than perfunctory. She would have enjoyed herself much more had she been with Sarah and Lesley at the theatre.

"You don't look very happy," her sister said, pulling her face into a moue. "Is it Blain again?"

"He was such a pig the other night, Sarah. Honestly, I was so annoyed." Sylvie pulled a corner off her crustless cucumber sandwich and tossed it into her mouth. "He all but ignored me all night."

"Bugger." Lesley visibly drooped. "I was hoping with that many oligarchs at the dinner, you would have at least found out something useful. Clinton was hoping for another investment tip; he made quite a killing on that last one."

Sylvie shook her head. "I think Blain might be getting more involved with the oligarchy. He was holed up with them in his office for ages after the meal."

"Oooh, do tell." Sarah's voice was eager. The ladies of the oligarchy were the leaders of fashion, and she always wanted to be up there with the best.

"Well..."

****

On the other side of the floral screen, Pazia was listening to her companion with only half an ear. Clive was busy rattling on about the stone sculpture of a gryphon he was working on. She had no doubt that when finished it would be marvellous. Clive was an outstanding craftsman. He could talk for hours about his work, the perfect cover when one wanted to surreptitiously listen to someone else.

Blain's little sidekick was not someone she had ever bothered about before, presuming her to be just another typical social climber, out to get her clutches on anyone who could give her a better life. Something that had been said at the dinner party the other night, though, had intrigued Pazia. A bit of subsequent delving had turned up a number of interesting facts.

Sylvie Cartright, it turned out, was no poor little wannabe rich girl. She was the daughter of business tycoon David Statton and a very wealthy woman in her own right. Her heavily insured husband had conveniently died of a brain tumour after ten years of childless marriage. That alone had given Sylvie enough money to be comfortable for the rest of her life. Then, a few years later, on the death of their father, Sylvie and her surviving sister, Sarah Cornwell, had become the joint beneficiaries of his vast estate.

Proving that she was cast in her father's mould, Sylvie had proceeded to make a number of extremely clever investments over the intervening years, which had more than doubled her net worth. Her interest in Blain, therefore, was something other than money. Pazia did not think it was love. Women like Sylvie were ruled by their heads, not their hearts. She'd possibly married for love the first time, but the second was definitely going to be a calculated move. The sister, Sarah, was also a shrewd woman, using her inheritance to turn her husband's second-rate building firm into one that now held a staggeringly impressive property portfolio.

Though they had chosen to sit at a private table, the women seemed oblivious to the fact that they could still be overheard. Pazia listened in to everything Sylvie had to say about Blain's dinner party. The details of the information she had picked up on were impressive, though, as the other two women were quick to point out, not very lucrative. So, that was their game, was it? Mine the elite for information, which they could then use to keep up with the latest trends and swell their individual bank accounts. Whilst it wasn't exactly insider trading, the ethical lines on such practices were very blurred. Whether Blain was in on the ruse was as yet unclear. Something Pazia definitely intended to rectify.

"... So only that one foot and the tail will be attached to the base. The balance has to be spot-on." Clive's cheeks were glowing now that he was talking about something he loved. Pazia wasn't really listening to him, he knew, but in his relief, he didn't care. If her devious mind was concentrating on someone else, then it couldn't be ferreting about in his own secrets. He kept up his babble until he saw the glaze clear from her eyes.

She glanced at her watch. "Goodness, is that the time? I really must be going. I have a meeting to attend at three."

She rubbed her fingertips together, shedding imaginary crumbs onto her plate before rising. She leaned into Clive for a kiss on each cheek before winding her way majestically through the tearoom, her heels clicking on the polished floor like the ticking of a doomed clock.

****

"Are you still awake?"

"Hmmm." Pazia stroked the arm that lay casually abandoned across her chest. Skin so pale against her own dark tones. Soft lips kissed her neck, tracing a fine line from just beneath her ear down to her collarbone.

"Who is it this time? Anyone I might know?"

Pazia smiled in the dark. She could smell the red wine on her partner's breath and see the shape of their entwined bodies beneath the covers, just visible in the starlight from the window. She pushed her overactive thoughts to the side and turned her head. "It's no one to worry about."

"You always get like this when you know the person involved."

Pazia couldn't deny it. Although it was Sylvie that she'd set her eyes on, it dragged in the possibility that Blain was not the squeaky-clean, safe person they'd always believed him to be, given the enormity of the find in his woodland, that could prove to be a very big problem indeed. She blew out her breath in a huge sigh. "I'm sorry. I shouldn't bring my work home with me."

She leaned forward, and their lips met. It wasn't a gentle kiss; hungry and searching, it was met with a fervour that more than matched her own. Eleena was Pazia's saviour, her refuge in a cold, hard world. She knew just when to be firm, when to push, and when to back off. She kept herself in the shadows of Pazia's life, not because Pazia was ashamed of their relationship, but because that was what Eleena needed. She had not always been reclusive. When she was young and fresh on the scene, she had been a sought-after model, rising high. But that was then... before everything changed for the both of them.

They drew apart, breathless. Eleena laughed. "You can bring your work home any day if I get that." There was a clatter as something fell to the floor. "Damn it, that was your phone. Watch your eyes." Eleena flicked on the light.

Pazia watched her, shamelessly enjoying the sight of Eleena's naked body reaching down over the side of the bed, her white-blonde hair spilling forward onto the floor. It was moments like this when Pazia forgot, just for a fraction of a second, expecting to see Eleena's beautiful face, whole and perfect, when she turned back.

She recovered herself just in time. Eleena settled herself back down beside her but wasn't still for long. With a wicked gleam in her eye, she began to slide further down the bed. "Get the light, would you?"

The sound of rain hammering down on the porch roof almost drowned out their voices. Eleena pulled the door closed and turned back into the kitchen. "Better leave your hair down today. I can catch it back in a wide band to match your outfit."

Pazia nodded her agreement, though Eleena was already reaching for her accessories box. She sipped her morning tea, trying to keep her mind off Blain. He couldn't be the one, could he?

"I should have redone this last night." Eleena tutted to herself as her nimble fingers ran over the braids.

All those hours that people presumed Pazia must spend in a salon were really her evenings at home being pampered by the woman she loved. Self-taught and determined, Eleena had refused to listen to any of Pazia's initial qualms.

"There is so much else you could set your mind to. It's not right that you focus all your attention on my appearance."

"Why, just because I can't look in the mirror anymore without grimacing? I adore beauty; why the hell should I stop just because I can never be it again?"

Pazia could agree with most things Eleena said but never, ever, with that. To her, Eleena had never stopped being beautiful. She was the only person who mattered in this world, and what Eleena wanted, Pazia would move heaven and earth to make sure she got.

"We had better things to do last night," Pazia said, clasping the hand resting on her shoulder and letting her head brush up along Eleena's arm.

"I should still have found time." Eleena placed a kiss on the top of Pazia's head. "Who is going to be scared of you if you go to work with rats' tails as hair?"

Pazia laughed. Eleena could be just as fierce as her, in her own way. The coward who'd taken her spirit would never understand the strength he had given her in return. They had been in the very early days of their relationship then and were still finding their feet with one another. Both had risen from poor backgrounds, albeit on totally different paths. Eleena had been snapped up by a talent scout at the age of seventeen. Her short, silver-blonde bob, pale skin, and fragile frame had made her an instant sensation with photographers and fashion designers alike. She had been thrown into a world of money and power and for the next six years had been utterly lost within it. Pazia, however, had clawed her way out of poverty. No one was giving her a hand up. At twenty-five, she had just landed a job working for the oligarchy. It was only a basic admin role in the security department, but the perfect place for someone with her unique skills.

"Oh, hello, I am calling from the Grand Hotel. I have a message from Ylva Portune. She needs Penelope to bring the Rogini file over to her straight away."

Pazia looked around at the empty office. "I'm sorry, there is only me here at the moment; everyone else is out on lunch."

The receptionist gave an apologetic cough. "I'm afraid Ms Portune was quite insistent."

Well, that was typical of the oligarch wasn't it? Snapping her fingers and expecting everyone to jump. Pazia could easily imagine the woman's temper if she had to wait another forty-five minutes for her PA to return. Snatching up the file, she headed for the door.

The Grand Hotel was an elaborate setting for a charity luncheon. Needless to say, this was no run-of-the-mill fundraiser. It would be full of rich and famous stars, politicians, and businessmen flaunting their wealth and self-gratifying philanthropy. She patted the two simple puff buns on her head as she walked and then coiled her fingers through her fringe sections, pulling them out so they hung tidily against her forehead. There wasn't much more she could do to neaten her appearance.

Typically, Ylva Portune was sitting at the far side of the room. Pazia took a deep breath, straightened her shoulders, and refused to be cowed by the glamorous crowd. Halfway across the room, Ylva looked up. By the look on her face, Pazia knew she had made a mistake. She should have kept to the edges of the room and made her way as unobtrusively as possible. She faltered for a second, and then her resilience kicked in. She was doing the woman a damn favour; it wasn't her fault she didn't know the correct etiquette. These people were no better than her. Richer, yes. Better? Definitely not. She kept walking.

At Ylva's table, the oligarch snatched the file from Pazia and turned her shoulder. Dismissed without even so much as a curt acknowledgement, Pazia's first instinct was to stride back the way she had come, and to hell with Ylva and her fucking rudeness. Her second, and the one she listened to, was to meekly follow the wall until she could escape through the door. This job was too important to throw away.

She tried to imagine herself sitting here amongst the hoi polloi, someone to be noticed instead of doing the noticing. She would make the likes of Ylva bloody Portune pay then. Pausing to let a waitress pass, she turned her head a little more and saw a pair of stunning water-washed blue eyes watching her from across the room. They belonged to the most beautiful woman Pazia had ever seen. A thrilling bolt of static shot through her as the woman rose to her feet.

The model waited for her just outside the door. They stood not speaking for half a minute, and then Eleena grabbed Pazia's arm. "Come with me."

In the hotel's plush toilets she turned, and they were kissing. Just like that; no words needed, just raw passion, urgent and electric. Lips still locked firmly together, Eleena walked Pazia backwards until she fetched up hard against the flocked wallpaper. The toilet attendant had seen many things in her time, yet even she was forced to turn away.

From that moment on, they had met whenever the chance arose. Eleena's work often involved travel, taking her all over the world. Without fail, she would seek out Pazia as soon as she returned home. Then, one day, she didn't.

"I'm sorry, that number is no longer operational," the bored-sounding operator had said. "Is there anything else I can help you with today?"

Pazia put the phone down without replying and glanced at the clock again. It was now almost twenty-four hours since Eleena's plane had landed, and she still hadn't heard a thing from her. At first, she'd told herself to be patient; Eleena would get in touch when she could. As the hours passed, though, her nagging concern grew. When her texts started bouncing back, she really began to worry.

She did a quick search and dialled again, this time to the airport. "I just want to check if my friend was on the six pm inbound Airoots flight yesterday, please?"

"I am very sorry, madam; due to a system error, all passenger list data for that flight has been lost." The woman's voice was slightly distant, as if she had her mouthpiece set too far away from her mouth.

"Surely you must have some records? The sales logs, passport control?"

"I am very sorry, madam, but due to the system error, all data for that flight has been lost. There is nothing I can help you with."

Pazia cut the call and flung her phone on the bed. "FUCKKKK!"

The rest of her Sunday followed in much the same way. How hard was it to find someone as famous as Eleena? Even those who didn't know her would surely remember a woman with albinism; it wasn't exactly a common condition. Yet no one was able to tell her anything. Eleena Marr had, by all accounts, ceased to exist.

Lunch hour, the next day, was spent ploughing through records Pazia did not really have the authority to be looking at. She did not care to ask permission. Her diligence paid off when she found a single reference to a chauffeur taking three models from Prince Bastion Airport to a party held at the home of Oligarch Baxter Carswell. Another two days later, and she had finally tracked down someone who was willing to talk to her.

The woman worked for a catering agency and had been temping at the oligarch's on the evening of the party. She and Pazia met that evening in one of the city parks.

"I remember Eleena Marr. She is so beautiful; who wouldn't? She left the party early. There were chauffeur-driven cars put on for the guests, and when I was on my break, I saw her getting into one with a man."

"What man?"

The woman backed away a little at the sharpness of her tone.

"Sorry." Pazia rubbed a hand over her forehead. "Forgive me, it's been a long few days."

With a sad smile, the woman took a step back towards her. "I can't tell you who he was; I'd never seen him before, but," she paused for a fortifying breath, and Pazia's insides clamped together, "the party didn't go on as long as some of Baxter's others. We got away about two in the morning. We passed the remains of an accident on the way home, and it looked like one of the party's limos. It could have been them, and that's why you haven't been able to find her."

"Thank you." Pazia handed two twenties she couldn't afford to the woman and ran.

There was a twenty-four-hour office unit nearby, offering hot desks by the hour. With what she had learnt working in the security department, it would be a simple enough task to hack into the emergency services' incident logs. Her hands were shaking, and it was taking every ounce of willpower not to crumble under the weight of everything her mind was trying to envisage. It wasn't a heavily secure website, and she soon found a redacted report of the accident. Her heart leapt. The only surviving occupant had been recorded as one Jane Doe.

By the time Pazia got to the hospital, Eleena had already undergone three operations and was barely recognisable. The left-hand side of her face had suffered the worst; third-degree burns covered it from scalp to jawline. More burns covered her left arm, side, and leg, while her right leg had been lacerated almost down to the bone. Three of her ribs were cracked, she had a dislocated finger, and she had enough bruises to lose count of. But she was alive.

Pazia sat with her for three days and nights until eventually Eleena was strong enough to recount her terrible story.

"I wanted to come straight to you when we landed, but two of the other girls dragged me off to Baxter's party. My phone had died on the plane, so I couldn't send you a message. I would have borrowed someone else's, but you know how bad I am at remembering numbers. I left as soon as I could. I'd grabbed a limo and was just getting in when this man insisted we share the ride. He was drunk and wouldn't take no for an answer." Eleena's voice wavered away to nothing. Tears welled in her eyes, and she looked away in shame.

"Hey," Pazia took hold of her right hand and squeezed. "It's ok; it was only a ride home."

Eleena visibly winced. "No, you don't understand. He wouldn't take no for an answer."

Again, Pazia shook her head. "It's fine; it's not your fault."

"He raped me." Eleena almost shouted before dissolving into tears. "I feel so dirty, Paz."

Helpless to do anything other than hold her hand, Pazia brought it to her lips, kissing her fingers. "You're NOT dirty. You're here, you're alive, and you are still my beautiful girl." She was fighting back her own tears now. "Nothing will ever change that."

Inside, she wanted to scream. When she got her hands on that bastard, she was going to tear him limb from limb.

Then she remembered that Eleena had been the only one to survive the crash, and she felt anger all over again. How many times was she going to be denied the opportunity to vent her anger on the people who deserved it?

"The driver saw what was happening. He lowered the partition window more and shouted at the man to stop." The words were flowing from Eleena now. If she halted, she might never find the courage to speak them again. "But the man punched him. I don't know if he actually hit him; I couldn't see. Then the car swerved. The next thing I knew, there was a really loud tearing sound, and we were tipping. I must have passed out. When I woke up, I was kind of laid on him, the man, I mean, and he was dead. I could still smell him." She hiccoughed back a sob, "But I could smell blood and fuel too. I tried to move, but my leg was trapped." Her right leg moved reflexively, and she made a sound of discomfort.

"I could hear the driver; he was cursing in the front. Then I saw him out of the car; he was talking on his phone. I screamed at him to help, begged him, but he just pulled out a packet of cigarettes and put one in his mouth. I must have passed out again then because the next thing I knew, he was gone and there were flames everywhere. I could feel the heat." She sobbed, "I've never been so frightened, Paz. I was sure I was going to die."

"Hey, hey, come here." Frustrated by the bandages, Pazia pressed her cheek to the uninjured side of Eleena's face. "You're alright now. I'm going to look after you."

Everything Pazia had done since that day had been driven by those events. Whilst everyone thought she was riding high on her own personal quest for power, Pazia was a woman on a very different mission. Someone highly influential had ordered that cover-up. No one else would have had the authority to pull personal records so completely from the system. She was going to find them and the chauffeur, and when she did, she would make them pay a hundredfold for what they had done.

19

THE TWO HORSES THUNDERED DOWN THE BRIDLEWAY, each one straining to nose ahead of the other. For half a mile they galloped before they were reined in to a sedate walk. Blain laughed, reaching over and wiping a smear of mud from Isabel's face. She flicked out her riding crop, catching him lightly on the arm.

"Look at the state of me." She cried, a mock frown on her face. She wasn't bothered about the dirt, only that initially, Blain had managed to get in front of her. She patted Thorenteen on his damp neck. He had accounted well for himself after that. Realising he did not like to be behind, he had put on an exhilarating burst of speed and been neck and neck with Blain's mount in only a few strides.

Blain pulled off his hat with a flourish and bowed his head, still laughing. "You're welcome." It had been far too long since he'd taken Duke out for a good hack, and even longer since he'd had company on a ride. These woods were private; there was no chance of meeting anyone else on the quiet bridleways, which was a good job considering how recklessly they had just ridden.

"So what happened to bringing The Lady Rain?"

"I would have, last week." Isabel patted her new gelding on his neck. "But this one's had plenty of time to rest now. I started him off lightly a few days ago, just a little lunging and a couple of short rides out. His foot is perfect. I had the vet check him over again yesterday, and he declared him fully sound."

Blain eyed the horse appreciatively. "He's certainly a lovely beast."

The beast in question snorted, shaking his head and flicking foam into the air. Isabel patted him again. "He's great, isn't he? And so different from the madam."

The Lady Rain was a dapple grey, with a high head carriage and the demeanour of a haughty snob. Isabel loved her to bits but was in no doubt about her behaviour. Thorenteen, on the other hand, showed all the promise of a calm countenance and easy-going nature. They rode in silence for a while, dropping the reins and letting the horses stretch their necks. They were getting along unusually well together. Duke could be a little antsy with some horses, especially highly strung ones like The Lady Rain. He would have been flattening his ears and swinging out to nip at her neck whenever he felt her trying to edge past. Isabel hadn't appeared to have noticed yet, a sure sign that her thoughts were far away.

"Is everything alright, Izzy?"

"What?" She looked at Blain, confused for a minute, then sighed. "I'm sorry. Am I being awful company?"

"Not at all, you just seem a little... absent."

Isabel snapped a twig from an overhanging branch. The bough whipped back into place, making Thorenteen jump. She rested her other hand just above his withers to steady him, took a deep breath, and blurted out, "I'm not sure that I am happy with Armitage anymore."

Shit. Blain closed his eyes. This was not good news. Isabel had no idea that her marriage was a sham, set up years ago, to legitimise her husband. In fact, barely anything she knew about Armitage was the truth, even his name. His work did take him all over the country, but he was most certainly not a workplace efficiency consultant. Smoke-screen lives and dual personas were essential to all workers involved in the shadier aspects of the oligarchy's work. Blain was one of the few who knew what Armitage's role really entailed; after all, he had been to Marlborough House in the course of that work a number of times now. Even the staff were unaware that it was not, in fact, one of the Guard who came and took away their unwanted young magicians.

Oligarch Nirim Elex had been the one who found Isabel and introduced her to Armitage. He should have chosen better, or rather, he should have picked someone else to arrange the match. Nirim was a single man who would never be anything other than a single man. He dallied with both men and women, but no one would ever gain a foothold in his heart. It simply wasn't possible. Nirim's heart was his and his alone; cold, lifeless, and might as well have been made of steel. A man like that could never understand the sentimental needs of someone like Isabel.

Isabel looked guilty. She shredded the last of the brown leaves from the twig and let it fall. "I've been noticing myself getting more and more picky lately. Everything seems to annoy me. I thought maybe it was the change." She flushed a little; menopause was not something she wanted to be speaking to anyone about, let alone to Blain. "But the doctor said I am still too young for that." She threw the twig onto the ground. "It isn't as if it matters; Armitage will never let me have a baby."

Blain shuddered. Armitage did far more than just transport children with powers. It was no wonder that he had no intentions of ever becoming a father himself. Isabel wiped the corner of her eye. Oh god, she was going to cry. Whilst Blain could handle a woman in tears, Isabel's fell on his conscience like acid.

Blain gritted his teeth. She didn't deserve any of this. He wished he could tell her to leave Armitage, to find someone who would appreciate her and give her the babies she so desperately wanted, but he couldn't. His hands were well and truly tied. Now, he had to betray her all over again. Each time he had to do it, he felt even more wretched than the time before. He pulled a clean paper tissue from the small packet in his pocket and held it out to her.

"Tell me what's happened, Izzy. You weren't like this the other week."

She shook her head at the tissue, opening her eyes wide and staring up at the sky. After a moment or two, she looked at Blain, bright-eyed but tear-free. "I don't know why Armitage married me. He really isn't interested in me at all. I have tried to tell myself that it's his job, the pressures of work and all that, but..." Her voice petered out.

Bollocks. He felt like a heel, but nevertheless, Blain had to press her for more. "But?"

"This last week he was at home; I thought we'd have a great time: days out, meals together, cosy nights in front of the fire, you know."

Blain nodded. It was everything a wife should expect.

"He didn't even spend one whole day with me. When he wasn't buried in his office or on the phone, he had his head in the paper or was watching bloody damn sports on the TV. For four days he wasn't even there; he was out catching up with friends, and I wasn't invited."

Thorenteen twitched his ears, sensitive to the tension in Isabel's voice. "He managed to sit down to dinner each night with me, though he didn't have much to say. His phone was going off all the time, so he was busy looking at that. He could have been eating anything for all the attention he was paying."

If Armitage had been standing in front of Blain at that moment, he thought he would have punched him. Surely it wasn't too much to expect that the man take care of his wife on the few days he spent at home? After all she was doing for him, even though she didn't know it. Blain tightened his hands on the reins, and Duke threw his head up in complaint. Both horses were beginning to get skittish now.

"Maybe he is going through a tough time at work?" Blain tried to reason with her, knowing all the while that even if he did manage to convince her everything was fine, he would still have to notify Nirim. He wasn't quite sure what Nirim did to put things right each time, but he had his suspicions, and they made him very edgy indeed.

"I asked him about his work; he told me everything was fine. That doesn't mean a lot, though; he never says very much about it." She snorted in a most unladylike manner. "Apparently the fact that I am a woman means I couldn't possibly understand the complexities of a production line."

More like Armitage hasn't got the first clue about it, Blain thought. Isabel was certainly smart enough to understand most things.

"Oh god, sorry." Isabel sniffed. "I think I'm going to need that tissue after all." She dabbed at her eyes, thankful that she had thought to use her waterproof mascara this morning. At least she wouldn't have ugly black streaks down her face, though her foundation was no doubt ruined. It was embarrassing enough crying in front of Blain without looking like a panda while she was at it. "Do you realise that he has never even been to your house?" she sniffed. "All the times we have been invited, and every time his damn work has got in the way."

Blain shook his head. What could he say? He was sick of having to lie to her and even sicker that he would have to report on her again.

"Come on," Isabel said, gathering up her reins and nudging her heels into Thorenteen's sides. The gelding was more than happy to oblige. Though she had never jumped him before, Isabel headed for a fallen tree trunk jutting out into the path ahead, a reckless need to chase away her sadness urging her on. She counted his strides as they approached, then, lifting the reins, she gave him his head. Up they went, sailing well clear. He stumbled a little on the landing. Isabel was thrown forward onto his neck. She clenched tight with her knees, pushing deep into her heels to keep her seat. Laughing, she threw a glance over her shoulder to see Duke touch down perfectly. It had been unfair that she had given Blain so little warning before the jump, but he was an excellent rider, and Duke was a good, sound horse.

They said no more about her marriage, keeping the tone purposely light. Overhead, the clouds were beginning to thicken. Fenton Wood was a good size, though with Stanton's curse choking so much of it, only the outer edges were suitable for hacking. They were right over the far side now, with no chance of taking a shortcut. Trotting side by side, they tried to beat the weather home. Luck was not riding with them. By the time they clattered into the yard, both horses and riders were soaked to the skin. Johns hurried from the barn.

"Would you mind sorting him for me? I need to get out of these wet things." Blain handed Duke's reins over and turned to Isabel. "Do you need any help?"

"I'm okay, thanks," Isabel said, flicking her leg over the front of her saddle and sliding neatly down.

"Just shout one of the boys if you do," Blain said, already walking away. "Come into the house when you're done. We'll have coffee."

In her horsebox, Isabel untacked Thorenteen and rubbed him down with handfuls of straw. Changing over to towels, she removed as much of the moisture from his coat as possible and then threw a rug over his steaming back, tucking more straw underneath. She left him munching at his hay net whilst she ducked into the living quarters and took a quick shower. There was not much room, but it served well enough for her needs.

She was still slightly embarrassed about getting upset earlier. It was just as well that Blain was a gentleman and wouldn't hold it against her. She just hoped he would remain her friend after she'd put all her plans into motion and left Armitage. There was a lot for her to do. She needed a new home, for a start. Although she had her own money, she would need to downsize considerably. That didn't matter, though; who needed all that space when they were alone?

She had already checked out the market and had her eye on a nice three-bedroom property with stabling for five horses and enough land to satisfy all their needs. Not that she would be telling anyone about it, at least not until everything was done and she was settled. There probably wasn't enough time to get it all sorted and be moved in before Christmas, but certainly early in the new year. She seriously doubted that Armitage would even notice she was gone. He would notice when the divorce papers arrived and his bank balance was affected, though. Isabel smiled at the thought; she would be far better off in every way imaginable, and it would serve Armitage right.

Fifteen minutes later, in a dry change of clothes, she braved the rain again for the short dash to the kitchen door. The cook led her upstairs and into the drawing room. "I'm afraid you have been rather quicker than Blain.

Make yourself comfortable; I'm sure he won't be long. I'll send up some coffee and refreshments while you wait."

Isabel thanked her, wondering how she would manage without staff of her own. She enjoyed cooking at least, so she wouldn't starve, and surely a cleaner once a week wouldn't be beyond her meagre budget? No one would know where she was at first, so she wouldn't be having any visitors. It would be like going on her own private retreat.

Blain put down the phone, dropped his head into his hands, and groaned. It was a bastard thing to do, prising Isabel's story from her, just so that he could pass it on to Nirim. Still, at least this time, he had tried his best to convince the oligarch that a baby would be the best thing to keep Isabel content.

Blain had his suspicions about how Isabel would be brought into line again, but would the oligarchy really stoop so low as to employ mind control on someone? He'd thought better of asking Nirim. Then again, who knew— maybe they had already used it on him? The thought jolted him from his chair. He shook himself thoroughly and headed out of the door so quickly that he made Amelia jump. Did she look guilty? There was a flush to her cheeks that was not usually there.

"I take it Mrs Branwell is comfortable?"

Amelia nodded. "Mrs Lee showed her up. I've just taken in the tray."

Isabel was sitting in a low chair near the large picture window, looking out over the manicured front gardens.

Her nut-brown hair hung in loose, wet waves over her shoulders, making her look vulnerable somehow. The knot in his stomach tightened.

"Isabel, did you get sorted alright? Did Johns or one of the boys help you?"

"One of them offered." She turned from the window. "But I managed fine. The box is well set up, and I know where everything is, so it was quicker to do it myself. Besides, Thorenteen is still new enough that it's a novelty to do anything with him. He is such a calm boy; nothing much fazes him." She smiled at Blain, her face open and trusting.

The knot tightened even more.

They'd only been talking for half an hour when Isabel's phone pinged. She pulled it from her pocket and looked at the screen. "Seems like I'm having visitors tonight. Ylva Portune wants to come over and discuss arrangements for Carisburgh's winter lights. Apparently there is a problem with some of the fittings."

Blain had forgotten Isabel was on the committee that dealt with all the city's celebrations.

"They were due to be set up this week," Isabel continued. "I was assured only last Tuesday that everything was going ahead as planned." She shrugged. "Oh well, I am sure the mystery will be solved soon enough." She put her side plate down on the table and rose. "I had better make my move if I am to be ready for Ylva."

Pausing on the step, she held her cheek out for Blain to kiss. "It was a fun ride, apart from the rain. Let's not leave it so long next time."

"We should get in as many rides as we can before the weather turns," Blain agreed. "I'll give you a ring next week, if you like."

"Perfect." Isabel skipped over to her horsebox. After peering in to check Thorenteen, she climbed into the driver's seat. The lorry roared into life, a plume of black smoke exhaling from the exhaust. Blain watched as she drove away; his only easing thought was that at least Isabel would be feeling happier again soon. However fake the foundations for that happiness may be, at least she was not about to get hurt.

20

As Thaniel entered the training room, he was surprised to see Evan already there. These sessions with Doyen had always been private, the atrocities hidden behind closed doors and all the more shameful for it. His relief soon dissolved into apprehension, as the usual wall of remoteness Evan wore like a shield against the world seemed to thicken noticeably. Thaniel smiled at him, allowing a careful questioning look to show briefly in his eyes. Before Evan had the chance to either ignore it or respond, the door opened.

"Stand against the wall. Hands behind your back," Doyen told the girl who entered.

Her eyes flicked to Thaniel, widening as they passed on to Evan. She gulped a little as she took her place.

"You are an ungrateful, disobedient, wicked girl, and such girls get punished." Doyen did not raise his voice. His fury was contained in words that were edged in steel. "Did you like disobeying your tutor yesterday?"

Thaniel looked from Doyen to the girl in disbelief. She was only about twelve, with pale blonde hair and innocent eyes, the colour of a blackbird's egg. He couldn't imagine her doing anything to warrant this. Her lips were clamped into a tight line as her head shook in answer. She was trying to be brave, to convince herself that she was strong enough to endure whatever was about to happen. That much was clear in the firm set of her jaw and the upright tilt of her head. Her eyes, however—big and wide—betrayed her.

"You will not disobey me." Doyen folded his arms, done with the questions. "You will go stand in the corner, Krystal, facing the wall. No matter what happens, what you hear or feel, you will not turn around, and you will not move."

Her legs were already trembling. She tried to speak. Fear stole the word, and the sound that came out was indistinguishable. She nodded, not risking her voice again.

"If you do leave that corner, you will find yourself taking a one-way trip to the graveyard."

Krystal's legs dipped as she turned. Thaniel thought she might fall. He was ready to shoot forwards and grab her, but she managed to keep herself upright, just. Evan willed them both to be smart. Everyone he had ever seen stand up to Doyen either suffered or disappeared. There was no choice when it came to obeying.

Of course there is a choice, the tiny voice at the back of his mind said yet again. *There is always a choice.* Evan hated that voice. Hated it because he was too afraid to acknowledge it; too afraid of what it was saying. He had listened to it once; it had not ended well. His face pinched as he pushed it aside and tried to focus on keeping his internal walls up. *Coward.* The word resonated throughout his body.

"Bring the girl over here, Nathaniel, in front of Evan." The edge of steel in Doyen's voice was honed to perfection.

Thaniel's blood felt like molten metal in his veins, though his skin was icy-cold. The combination was alarming, but no less so than the thought of making Krystal do something that would get her killed. Doyen was looking at him, a faint smile on his face. The bastard was enjoying himself. The instructor took a careful step towards Thaniel and, in a voice so low that only the boys could hear, said, "It is her own volition that will end her life, not anything you make her do. See to it that she doesn't do anything stupid. The child is valuable to me; I would hate to lose her."

Even knowing that he had the power to keep her alive, it was with a leaden heart that Thaniel reached into Krystal's mind. She didn't want to move, fighting him every step of the way as he forced her out of the corner. He had expected it to be easy. Doyen had, after all, trained him on the most recalcitrant animals he could find, but he had never used his powers on a person before and so was totally unprepared for the feelings that assaulted him. It was as if he were a ghost, hovering inside Krystal's mind, feeling everything she was feeling: the fear, the hate, the anger. With the animals, this had all been on a different level, at such a remove from his own that he had never envisaged it could ever be anything different. He could feel her body trembling as if it were his own. He even knew what she had done to earn this punishment, because it was right there at the front of her mind.

Refusing to do as she was told in her lesson, she had turned her power on Farle instead. With just a single thought and a flick of her hand, every bone in Farle's hand had broken. What was more, she was not sorry. Not one little bit. Thaniel was shocked. For a moment, he wondered if this punishment might actually be justified. Then another thought rose in the girl's mind. Thaniel saw a tiny marmalade kitten, watery blue eyes wide and searching. It wobbled a little on its legs, mewling for comfort. He heard Farle's cold words: "Break its legs." Suddenly Krystal's actions were thrown into perspective.

Thaniel felt sick, and for a second he lost control of Krystal. She took a hurried step back towards the corner before he was able to stop her. He could both see and feel her fighting him, refusing to give in; her emotions running like liquid through fissures in his own body. She hated everything to do with this place, the 'wrongness' of what they were expected to do. She intended to fight it for as long as she had breath in her body, which would not be very long at all if she kept going like this. The strength of her will was impressive, and it put Thaniel to shame. He hadn't fought this much, and he was years older.

Thaniel wanted to tell her it was okay, that he understood and even admired her bravery. He would never have dared turn his magic on Doyen. He wanted to tell her to calm down, to not throw everything she had at defying the tutors. Sometimes it was better to be subtle; to play the long game and not burn out before you'd had the chance to make a difference. He wanted to tell her, and then, to his amazement, he realised that he could. He could talk to her without anyone else in the room hearing.

He paused. She would be bound to react. No matter what way he phrased it, she would give the game away somehow. Doyen was watching them like a hawk; he would latch on to any flicker of awareness, any lightening of her terror, and then he would know that Thaniel's power had grown. Hating himself, Thaniel kept quiet. Holding the trembling girl in front of Evan, all he dared risk was a slight smile of sympathy. Krystal glared back at him, as angry as any of the creatures he had honed this power on.

Doyen gave a brief nod of approval. "Now Evan, make her forget that she has the power to heal bones."

"Nooo." The cry tore from Krystal before Thaniel could stop it.

Doyen laughed, the satisfaction at her distress almost more chilling than his words. "She wants to break them, so let that be the only power she thinks she has from now on." There was a controller in his hand now, a presage to what would happen should any of them disobey. "After we are done here, you will be making sure all her friends forget what she once was, too."

The heat in Thaniel's veins turned to ice. This was cruelty beyond belief. She was just a little girl. How could anyone even consider expecting her to torture and maim? He felt all the strength and defiance in her gutter and die. She would have collapsed to the floor had his control been any weaker. Instead, feeling soiled by what they were having to do, he kept her upright and steady, facing Evan. The last thing he wanted was for Doyen to trigger any of their implants while he was inside her mind.

He felt the precise moment Evan reached in and pulled the knowledge from Krystal. For a second their three minds touched, though if Krystal was aware of it, she would never remember. Beside him, Evan tensed almost imperceptibly as he realised what had happened. Then he was gone, pulling back out of Krystal's mind, taking the knowledge of her treasured, healing gift with him.

The hurt vanished from Krystal's eyes, leaving her bewildered and frightened to find herself away from the corner.

"Release her." Doyen's face showed no trace of the smile that corrupted his voice.

Thaniel freed her from his control, and she shot back to face the corner. He and Evan glanced at each other. There was a question in Evan's eyes, but he made no attempt to ask it. Doyen was glaring at Krystal's back. He took a step towards her.

"What is your power?"

"To break bones."

Krystal swallowed, unsure why he was asking yet not daring to turn around and look. Thanks to Thaniel, she had not stayed in her corner; she had been over in front of Evan, and everyone knew what he could do to people. She didn't think he had taken anything from her, but she still felt violated. Had he sifted through her private thoughts? Would he relay what he had seen to Doyen? Had he done that already and made her forget?

Doyen clicked his arachnodactyly fingers, and the tension in the room went up a notch. He took another step towards her, the grim reaper without his cloak and scythe.

"Turn around."

Krystal turned, craning her neck back to look up at his face. Thaniel saw her gulp. He was about to reconnect with her mind, to try and offer her some support so that she didn't have to face the tall menace of a man alone, when he felt Evan's hand on his arm. The older boy shook his head. Taking a risk, Thaniel sent out a tiny telepathic feeler. It found its way into Evan's mind and met him there, ready and waiting. *Don't.* Evan relayed to him. *Whatever you were thinking of doing, don't risk it. Trust me, you can't help her now.*

Shock pulled Thaniel back. Evan's face showed no trace of their communication. He stood now with his hands clasped behind his back, shuttered eyes staring straight ahead, looking every inch the obedient student. Only a slight tightening of the muscles in his shoulders showed any sign that he was uncomfortable. After a moment, a flash of something too quick to identify hit Thaniel. He couldn't say if it had been an image or simply a feeling, but Evan had sent him enough to make it clear that he too had tried to interfere once. The memory was like a scar across his mind.

Thaniel shuddered just as Doyen's voice cut through the air, rough-iced and deadly. "Put out your hands. Palms facing each other."

Krystal hesitated. It was not defiance; all signs of that were long gone now; this was fear, pure and simple. Tears tracked down her cheeks as she realised what was about to happen.

"Put out your hands." Doyen enunciated the words, emphasising the last letter of each.

Krystal held out her trembling hands. Thaniel understood the positioning of them then, just as…

"Break them." The words rang out like hail on glass, clear and shocking.

Thaniel's heart contracted. He opened his mouth to say something, but again Evan stopped him.

He will only make her do it to you too. Don't put her through that.

Thaniel could almost feel the shackles he'd been wearing the last time he had felt so powerless and defeated. He bit his lips together, remembering back to his stepfather's storeroom. There was nothing he could do then, and there was nothing he could do now. Not without making matters a whole lot worse.

Krystal was shaking her head, "I don't want to." The words escaped in a whispered sob.

"Would you rather I did it, then?" Doyen made a sudden grab for her hands. Krystal yelped and pulled them away. She squeezed her eyes tight shut and screamed in pain as she snapped the bones. Though she had done it in a rush, she had still managed to make the breaks clean, far cleaner than Doyen would have made them. She didn't know how she knew it, but, with care, they would heal well and with no lasting damage. Doyen clicked his long fingers again and spun away from her.

"Anyone who turns their power on one of the tutors will receive punishment in kind. That goes for all of you."

Thaniel barely heard Krystal crying as she tried to cradle her shattered hands in her arms. The sound of her scream was echoing through his head. He felt sick. Evan shifted one of his feet ever so slightly until the tip of his shoe connected with Thaniel's. Thaniel pressed back. That slight reassurance, the knowledge that for once he was not in this alone, gave him the strength to keep standing there looking compliant under Doyen's corvid glare.

"I will be saying all this in an announcement tonight in the dining hall when everyone is present, but there is no reason you cannot hear it first. I will not tolerate attacks on my staff. You are all here under sufferance; make no mistake about that. It is only by my kindness and tolerance of your abilities that you, lucky few, have been allowed to keep your lives. Do not throw my kindness back in my face. I will not permit it." Doyen took his phone from his pocket and typed a quick message before turning back to Krystal. "If I hear of any more defiance from you, girl, you will mete out the same punishment to one of your friends. What is more, I will make you stand in front of everyone and choose who it is to be."

The door opened, saving her from responding. "Take her to the hospital wing, please," Doyen told Barker. "She is to heal naturally, not with magic."

Barker was the kinder of the two chaperones. At least Krystal would be in good hands. She ushered the girl firmly but gently from the room, and the door closed behind them. The atmosphere did not lighten as Doyen swung back to Evan and Thaniel.

"I must confess, I did not know how you would perform today, Nathaniel. There was a moment when I thought you might try to defend the girl, despite the despicable cruelty she showed Farle."

Thaniel swallowed, his mouth dry as ash. Did the man honestly not see where the true cruelty lay? He saw again the tiny kitten from Krystal's memory, the rabbits he had been forced to maim from his own. It was an effort to stand there and keep his face bland.

"It is good that you did not," Doyen continued, "that you proved yourself as useful as Evan in such situations."

The pressure against Thaniel's foot eased a little as Evan stiffened. It was only for a second, just long enough for Thaniel to realise how hard the other boy had to brace himself to cope with what Doyen put him through. He pushed out a feeler of understanding, still too new to this ability to know if Evan would be able to feel it. A wave of gratitude flowed back at him.

"That said," a cold smile played at the corners of Doyen's mouth, "if either of you ever repeat what was done to her today, I will make her break every bone in your body, one by one, saving the last fatal break of your neck until the very end."

21

ALISTAIR CALVINGTON TAPPED HIS FOOT IN TIME TO the music. The atmosphere in the large ballroom was electric, with barely an empty seat to be found at the tables surrounding the sprung dance floor. On the stage, the orchestra was playing *Festive Overture,* building up the excitement in the room to even higher levels. As the final crescendo grew, the crowd fell quiet in hushed expectation, all eyes facing the stage.

Nirim Elex, in full top hat and tails, walked to the podium. A formidable-looking man: six foot three with a broad chest and stern face, his skin was a rich, dark brown, his eyes sharp, and his jaw firm. Liquid authority ran through his veins, commanding the room's attention. He had no real need for the walking cane, which tapped firmly on the floor as he stepped forward. Alistair caught a glimpse of the silver pommel just peeking out through the oligarch's fingers. Nirim had carried this particular cane for as long as Alistair could remember. The pommel was supposedly shaped in the likeness of the First Master, founder of the oligarchy, whose name had been enshrined in mystery for many years, left behind and allowed to wither into obscurity by those who would rather all the limelight fell on their own legacies. Nirim scanned the faces of the crowd. Satisfied that he had everyone's full attention, he opened the gathering.

"Welcome to the oligarchy's annual winter ball. To start off the evening, can we all put our hands together for the world-renowned Orchestra Animarum, who will be playing for us throughout the evening?"

The conductor stepped forward and took a bow. Nirim gave him a generous smile, waiting until the applause faded. "If I am not mistaken, we have just heard Dmitri Shostakovich?"

The conductor dipped his head, and Nirim returned the gesture. "A brilliantly inventive composer and one of my personal favourites, though I am sure we will be hearing from many of the Greats during the course of the evening. I might even tinkle the old ivories myself." He mimed his long fingers skimming across a piano keyboard.

The conductor smiled, holding an arm out to indicate that the oligarch was welcome to join them. It was quite the accolade. Then again, Nirim was an accomplished pianist. He could have had a successful career as a musician had he not chosen to become a politician.

Once the formalities were over, Nirim took his seat, and strains of Beethoven's *Moonlight Sonata* drifted in the background. Waitresses came into the room to clear away the remains of the hors d'oeuvres. Waiters poured wine, and the buzz of conversation picked up again.

At the table with Alistair sat Marcus and Lucy Blatt, Isabel and Armitage Branwell, Blain Cordright, Sylvie Cartright, and Clive Greckham. They had barely touched the tiny morsels of appetisers, too aware of the remaining seven courses still to come. Sylvie was looking much more relaxed than when Alistair had last seen her at Blain's dinner party. Seated in between Blain and Clive, she was elegant in a sea green dress of sheer silk organza. Tonight, Blain was paying her much more attention, and her face was animated and alight. She did not seem to catch the odd, suspicious glances he kept paying to the Branwells across the table.

As the soup course arrived, Isabel reached across and smoothed down Armitage's tie. "Can't do with getting it in the soup," she laughed. "It's bad enough that it blends so well with the tablecloth."

"I should have known." Armitage rolled his eyes towards the huge banner forming the backdrop of the stage. On it, the oligarchy's seal, an intricate gold Celtic knot, was set on its usual red background. Their official colours of gold and red had been used extensively around the hall. If Armitage's tie had not matched the tablecloths, it would have matched the serviettes.

Alistair watched him with interest. Armitage was so different in a social setting. Only a handful of people were aware that the two men's paths ever crossed at work. Who could possibly expect that the eminent head of the Sheldon Scientific Research Establishment would ever require the services of a factory specialist? Armitage managed his soup without incident, and the waitresses whisked away the bowls ready for the fish course. The waiters topped up the Sauvignon Blanc and placed fresh iced water on each table.

"I hear that you're going on holiday, Isabel?" Lucy asked, filling her water glass. "Anywhere nice?"

Clive Greckham took a sip of wine to hide his grin. As if anyone would choose to go somewhere *not* nice! Lucy, he always found, had a habit of asking such banal and pointless questions.

Isabel did not seem to notice. She grinned at Lucy. "We're going on a cruise. I've always wanted to see the ice floes and the northern lights."

Blain's head snapped up. He looked curiously at Armitage, who appeared to be very happy at the prospect. Whatever Ylva had done the other week had certainly borne results. Isabel was glowing with happiness, and even Armitage seemed more content than usual. Whilst Blain was happy to see that she was no longer distressed, part of him still baulked at the idea of anyone being so blatantly manipulated.

He had received a 60-year-old bottle of malt and a pair of gold and lapis cufflinks two days after he'd reported to Nirim. He had kept up with expectations and was wearing the cufflinks now, but they were rough sandpaper to his guilt whenever he caught sight of them. Still, at least Izzy had not been hurt, he told himself, knowing deep down that was hardly the point.

"Brrrrr. Won't that be cold?" Lucy really was outdoing herself tonight.

"Of course," Armitage said, deadpan, "that's why we are going. The ice floes are terribly disappointing in the warmer regions."

Clive couldn't hide his reaction this time. He wasn't the only one. Lucy took it all in good spirits, even Sylvie's look of contempt. She knew she was a tad gormless. So what? Life was for enjoying, and if she made some people laugh, then all the better.

The roast and game courses followed, the wine changed from white to red, and the music became a little more energetic to lift the spirits of those who were starting to flag. Clive and Alistair got onto the topic of work. Clive's *Griffin in Flight* sculpture was still an ongoing project, which he spoke about with his usual enthusiasm. Alistair, as ever, was elusive with his answers, using long Latin names and discussing intricate procedures that soon bored most people into changing the subject. Not Clive.

He had a strong suspicion that Alistair was not telling the full truth. He had seen a picture of Blackwell a number of years ago. The Gothic revival building with its spires, gargoyles, and lancet windows was hardly the type of place one would expect to house the latest in scientific research. It piqued his interest. The dessert course was served, and Clive let the subject move on to other topics. It would have been crass to push the subject any further.

There was an interlude in the music as tables were cleared, and the musicians took a well-earned break. Guests took the chance to stretch their legs and mingle. Clive nodded across to Pazia. She had a strange man on her arm to whom ordinarily Clive would have loved to be introduced, but he was still wary after their drink the other week. He took his mints from his pocket and offered one to Alistair, who declined with a curt shake of his head.

Pazia flicked her hair over her shoulder. She had given in and finally let Eleena straighten it, though with hair irons, not a relaxer. The effect was transformative and so much longer than she'd expected. She would enjoy it for now, though she preferred her curls.

"It really suits you." Niles, her partner for the evening, crooned in her ear. A nice man, smart, and confident. If he was feeling at all out of place amongst the well-to-do crowd, he was showing no sign of it. She had slept with him two days earlier and would again before she was done with him. Given enough persuasion, she had no doubt that she would get the information she needed out of him. She did not enjoy sleeping with other people and would never have stooped to such an act if Eleena had not convinced her what a useful tool it could be.

Paz, my love, sex only matters if your heart is in it. Screw anyone you need to; just make sure that you only make love to me.

Pazia had to admit that Niles looked good tonight. He'd chosen not to wear a tux, instead matching a three-piece mohair suit in shimmering two-tone burgundy with a black silk shirt. He was drawing a number of admiring glances from both women and men. Even Ylva had commented on how suitable a match he was for her. No doubt she had thought she was being so tactful, not mentioning Niles' skin tone outright. As if her disapproval of the fact Pazia did not care one jot about skin colour, race, religion, or any other characteristic that could be used to create division wasn't obvious. She choked back a laugh at the thought of Ylva seeing her with Eleena—wrong colour and sex! The woman would have a heart attack.

She watched as Ylva strode away from their table, her limp very pronounced tonight. Maybe it was as well there was no sign of the walking stick she occasionally used. She was just as likely to rap someone else about the legs with it as she was to use it for support. An overbearing woman, Ylva was also a formidable presence and brilliant at her job. Pazia had always thought of her as a role model, even back in the days when Ylva treated her little better than a louse.

The older oligarch, in her russet trouser suit, was momentarily blocked from view, as someone Pazia wanted to speak to walked past. Pazia followed, leaving Niles in the company of Peyton and Lillian Lanford.

The ladies' cloakroom was almost as elegant as the ballroom. Behind marbled counters inset with white basins, huge mirrors covered the walls. Soaps and hand cream were provided in glass dispensers, along with packets of nail files, miniature shoe polishing kits, hair grips, and spray. All this was overseen by the restroom attendant, a short, dumpy woman with feathered grey hair and a permanent smile. Pazia rested one hand on a gold-effect tap and leaned towards the mirror, making a pretence of checking her eye make-up. She already knew it was perfect; Eleena would never have let her leave the house if it was not. Next to her, Sylvie Cartright was applying a fresh coat of lipstick.

"You seem very happy tonight, Sylvie. Last time I saw you, you seemed a little... distracted."

The remark hit home, just as Pazia had known it would. Sylvie's hand froze, halfway to her mouth. A frown played on her brow as she realised, with dread, that perhaps Pazia had seen her at the Conservatory Tea Room after all. The lack of any comment from Blain in the following weeks had led Sylvie to assume that Pazia had been too engrossed with listening to Clive to have heard her unguarded talk. Now, however, she felt the creeping sensation of hairs rising on the back of her neck.

Seemingly oblivious, Pazia pressed on, "At Blain's dinner party. You seemed very quiet. I know I was right down at the other end of the table, but you know me; I don't miss a thing."

Sylvie gave up on her lipstick, dropping it back into her clutch bag. "Of course, I was forgetting." Needing a moment to collect herself, she took one final look at herself in the mirror, pressed her lips together, then wiped away an imaginary smudge before continuing, "I had a splitting headache that night. I ended up leaving early."

The lie was not important enough to acknowledge. Pazia merely nodded her head in feigned sympathy. "I was so relieved to see you and Blain looking happy together tonight. I had thought that his news must have upset you."

Sylvie's smile faltered. "News?"

Pressing the plunger on a bottle of hand cream, Pazia caught up a generous amount in the palm of her hand, the scent of high-quality lavender filling the air. "Such a shock for everyone concerned," she continued, as if Sylvie hadn't spoken. "I wouldn't have blamed you if you'd run a mile." She rubbed her hands slowly together, the quintessential baddie in an old black-and-white movie. "Not many women would have stayed around after hearing about that." Her smile was genuine as, hand cream not quite absorbed, she hovered a consoling hand just above Sylvie's arm. "Most women would hate him now; I am so glad you can see past it."

Leaving Sylvie open-mouthed, Pazia left the cloakroom, sashaying back into the ballroom, where the dancing was just about to start. She held her hands up to her face and took a deep breath, enjoying the calming smell. *You would have liked that one, Eleena.*

Unable to turn up anything conclusive on Sylvie since overhearing her at the tearoom, Pazia's doubts had still not been allayed. Why, when the woman had so much money of her own, did she persist in chasing after a man who clearly had no real interest in having an intimate relationship with her, let alone any intention of ever taking her down the aisle? The almost-but-not-quite insider trading was a bonus, a skill Sylvie had undoubtedly learnt from her father, but that was just side play, not the main lure.

Had Sylvie been trying to get herself closer to the oligarchy, then Elon, Nirim, or Baxter would have been far more obvious targets for her attention. Whilst it would be very unlikely that any of them would ever entertain ideas of a serious relationship, there were still a number of other single men more closely associated with the ruling class. Quite a few would have jumped at the chance to wed such a rich, good-looking woman, especially one with no awkward family commitments to contend with. Sylvie's parents were both dead, and she'd never had any children. There had been a younger sister who had been killed in a tragic incident years earlier. That left Sarah Cornwell as her only living relative, and she was happily married with a fortune of her own.

No, money and influence were definitely not the drivers. Sylvie must have another reason, something unique to Blain. Was it too much to suspect that it might be the woodland, with its hidden cottages? Pazia needed to tread carefully; Elon had not given the okay to talk about the findings. The head was still unidentified, and, despite sending men to comb over every inch of the area, nothing else had been found. It was interesting that the boy she'd asked the gardener about had very quickly turned out to be a budding magician. Pazia had suspected as much. Often when their powers were emerging, young magicians felt themselves drawn to places of power. Of course, the boy had since been questioned thoroughly. His naivety, while frustrating, was not altogether surprising.

There had also been a girl taken from the house not long after, this one newly arrived and unable to control herself. Something in those woods was definitely making its presence felt. Could it be that Sylvie knew all about it? If she did, now Pazia had planted that kernel of suspicion, how long would it take Sylvie to make a move that would expose herself? How long would it take Blain? In her searchings, Pazia had found, to her surprise, that Blain Cordright appeared to have popped into existence shortly before he took on Marlborough House. The scant records covering his time prior to that had all been forgeries; excellent forgeries, but false all the same. A man with a hidden past was not something Pazia was going to let go. Especially when that man had been given control of one of the most important searches the oligarchy had ever undertaken.

Blain might not know the reality of what was hidden in the woods behind his house, but he knew all about the orphan program and the sham marriage between Armitage and his pathetic excuse of a wife. If he wanted, he could cause much and more trouble for them all. Nirim Elex was not a stupid man; he would never have sponsored Blain to such a position and no doubt engineered his new identity if he didn't have some sort of hold over him.

Pazia loved a good mystery. She excelled in uncovering the secrets people wanted to remain buried. It was like a game to her, and when one of the targets was a man who could have been anyone or done anything in his past life, that game took on a completely different flavour. Pazia stretched out her fingers, her long red nails shining like blood-tipped talons. She spotted Niles dancing with Lillian and made her way over to Peyton. "Care to take a turn?" she asked, guiding him onto the dance floor before he could muster suitable resistance.

22

THE KITCHEN DOOR SLAMMED SHUT BEHIND BLAIN, rattling the walls. Dislodged by the force, the key fell from the lock, landing with a chink on the cold floor tiles.

"Goodness, what's got his dander up?" Dorothy cried, rubbing her shoulder.

"No idea." Mrs Lee glared at the door as if expecting an apology from it. "He will be off to the stable, no doubt. Let's hope he works it all out of his system before he comes back."

They heard the sound of hoofbeats a few minutes later. Mrs Lee gave Dorothy a knowing smile. "I think I'll just pop the kettle on. You get yourself settled, and I'll make us a brew."

Slowly, Blain's anger dissipated into frustration and then finally crossed over into puzzlement. The air puffed in small white clouds as horse and rider breathed, and with the heat of annoyance out of his veins, he began to wish that he'd brought his scarf and gloves. He pulled his collar high around his neck, tucked his hands up inside his sleeves, and buried his face into his coat, where the warm air soothed his frost-burnt throat. He pushed Duke back into another trot, the ground too hard for anything faster, and stifled a yawn. It had been almost two in the morning when he'd returned home, nearer to three before he'd unwound enough to climb into bed.

All in all, the winter ball had been a great success, apart from Sylvie's behaviour. She had been fine throughout the meal; any lingering annoyance over the seating plan at his own dinner party had obviously faded into obscurity. She'd not even made one of her usual snippy remarks about Isabel. Then, just as the dancing started, she'd changed. It was as if someone had lit a slow-burning fuse and just left her to smoulder. There was nothing he could put his finger on that could have started it. She had simply stopped being happy and started to steam.

She'd kept up appearances. Sylvie was not the type of woman who caused a scene, but her guard had gone up, locked into place by that particular set of her head. Luckily, very few people were still sober enough by that time to notice anything amiss. Blain had tried taking her out onto the dance floor, hoping the music would soothe her mood. She'd held herself like a waxwork doll in his arms, eyes fixed on a point just over his left shoulder, the smile on her face as fake as her eyelashes.

"Oh dear," Pazia had commented, as she and Sylvie swapped partners for the next dance. "Do I detect trouble in paradise?"

Blain, relieved to be free of the suffocating tension, had rolled his eyes but said nothing. The dance had continued in silence, right until the last few bars of the music. "Maybe you shouldn't keep secrets," Pazia had said, one eyebrow raised in accusation. "Secrets are weaknesses. People always find out, you know."

She'd whirled away, leaving him standing like a puppet with its strings cut. Only after someone bumped into him had he shaken himself free from the web her words had entrapped him in. He had bee-lined straight for the bar. A neat brandy, downed in one, had done nothing to alleviate the shock. Sylvie, he'd noticed with relief, had moved on to waltz with Marcus Blatt. Blain could see her tight smile as he whirled her around. She had been no more forthcoming in the taxi home. Blain hadn't pushed it. He might be a committed bachelor, but even he knew better than that. Besides, Sylvie was not the real problem. It was Pazia who had set his nerves jangling.

He'd snapped at Thomas Grange that morning, shouted at Letty in the corridor, and almost barged poor Dorothy off her feet when he'd left. A groan escaped him; he owed them all an apology. Around him the woods were quiet, the heavy layer of frost giving everything an eerie coating of white. Cobwebs glinted between low-lying branches, occasionally stretching right across the path to catch on his face.

The empty wood set a further tremor of anxiety dancing along his flesh. Its stillness framed his movements, as countless unseen eyes noted his passing. For some reason Pazia was playing with him, letting poison whispers forth and sitting back to watch the drama unfold. Just as she'd done with Gipton when she'd pressed him about Aarav. Not once had she voiced what, in hindsight, she had clearly realised to be fact. After that night, Gipton had watched the boy like a hawk, a new suspicion in his gaze that had never been there before.

Duke's foot slipped on a patch of ice, the sudden movement jarring up Blain's spine. At the same moment, like a frozen hand taking hold of the scruff of his neck, a single word drove everything else from his mind.

Magic!

He shook his head, not wanting to entertain the thought, but it had him now, and it wasn't going to let go unacknowledged. It called out to him, teasing him with guilt-ridden memories. He had done so many bad things in his past, thinking himself safe from retaliation. His hand reached automatically for where the pendant used to rest, just above his heart. He had not thought about its loss in months, not even when they had uncovered the cottage.

Oh, how easy it was to be lulled into a false sense of security. To wrap it around oneself like a blanket and forget to worry about that which could not be seen. Twice before he had let himself succumb: once when he'd had the pendant and again after he had lost it and Nirim had offered him his chance at redemption. He rubbed a hand over his face, as if to wipe away the taint of his past actions. Was this what Pazia had meant, the truth she had accused him of concealing? But how could she and Sylvie know? No. He shook his head again; it was not possible. Only Nirim knew who he had been before, and the oligarch would not be telling anyone. The invisible hand slackened its grip slightly but remained in place, dripping icicles of dread down through his body to pool in the pit of his stomach.

Sylvie's actions last night had not been some flippant mood swing. There had been no hurt in her eyes, only anger. For the life of him, he could not think of anything else that could have caused it. Neither could he see any link between the two women. They knew each other, of course, but were far from friends. Sylvie, Blain suspected, was one of those people who still held on to the slender threads of racism that refused to completely die away. There were no people of colour in her close circle of friends, and she only ever bought the clothes that were modelled by white models at the frequent fashion shows she attended. She had dragged Blain to a few. Dull, boring affairs that sent his mind wandering to details no one else would probably pick up on.

Duke slipped again, and Blain eased him back to a walk. This frozen ground was unforgiving, and the horse's legs were too precious to risk. Blain shivered, and it wasn't just from the cold. If only he could take away the fiery, prickling sensation that had invaded his body when Pazia had thrown those final words at him, each one piercing his cognisance like sharp little elf shot. Even in sleep he had not been free of it. The few hours he had managed to get had been peppered with nightmares, throwing him awake again with cold sweat chilling on his bare skin.

He was really starting to feel that lack of sleep now. His body felt heavy and slow, his eyelids wanting to stay closed every time he blinked. As soon as he was able, he turned Duke onto a smaller path where the protection of the trees might mean softer ground. It had once been an unmetalled lane, now reduced to a narrow track. He would likely end up knocked out of the saddle by the overhanging branches if he wasn't careful. He was past caring. Tightening his legs on the horse's sides, he pushed Duke back into a trot. His knees felt as if they were cracking as he started to post. He ducked another section of overhanging branches, his head almost down to his calf. Still, he felt the scrape of them across his back. Duke slowed a little but remained trotting; he could sense he was going home. Blain's thighs began to burn with the workout. He doubted that his hands and feet would ever feel warm again, but at least the rest of him was now casting off its icy gibbet.

The area began to open up as they got to where all the recent clearance work had been done. Duke's head was high and alert, his ears pricked forwards. They were getting close to where the magician's cottage had been found. If Blain stood in his stirrups and peered into the undergrowth, he could just make out a heap of blackened stone. The scorched earth around it was still holding back the undergrowth; soon it would have all grown back and even the stones would be hidden beneath shoots of bramble and nettle. The cottage would, thankfully, just be a forgotten memory, lost to time and the magician's spell that kept the plant life thriving.

There was no way Pazia would have told Sylvie about the find. Far more likely she had just hinted about something going on that Sylvie was not party to. That was definitely the Queen of Spiders' style—drop a few hints and let her targets ensnare themselves with their reactions. It was probably her way of testing him, to make sure his silence could be assured. It would certainly be enough to set Sylvie's mind overworking itself, especially after her annoyance at his dinner party. She would probably accuse

Blain of having an affair with Isabel and, in defending Isabel's untarnished honour, maybe Pazia thought he would let slip about the findings. She was wasting her time with that idea.

He turned his face away from the remains of the ruin. Of all the things in Blain's past that should never know the light of day again, this came too close. Anything connected with Stanton Meads' world needed to be stamped, crushed, burnt, and annihilated in every conceivable way. Not that Blain was connected to the magician himself; it was Stanton's notoriety that concerned him. Such infamy created interest, which in turn created gossip, and as people talked, others would also be remembered for their egregious actions.

Many years ago, Blain would have laughed at such talk; revelled in it, no less. Many years ago, he had been a young, idealistic man who had stepped on the path to darkness and almost made it all the way. He was ashamed now, finding it hard to believe that he could ever have been such a person. Over the years, it had become easier to forget, but now, as it all came rushing back, Blain found that the mantle of shame was even heavier. It was as if, packed away in a neat little compartment in his mind, it had grown a lead lining, ready to weigh him down the instant he let it out again. How much longer would he have to bear it? Would he ever be free? Ever feel that he had finally made amends for all the wrong he had done?

With the reduction in ground cover, the earth was concrete-hard again. Blain slowed Duke to a walk, not wanting to return and face anyone just yet but unable to cope with his tiredness and the bitter cold any longer. He took a deep breath, wincing as the frigid air hit the back of his dry throat. He had learnt long ago that the only way forward was to face the truth and deal with it. If he wanted to be the man everyone now thought he was, then he was going to have to meet what was coming head-on.

Still, it would not hurt to set some defences in order, and for that, he needed a phone.

****

"Damn that woman!"

Nirim swore in frustration, kicking out at the wastepaper basket beneath his desk. He picked up the phone, replacing the batteries that had fallen out when he'd slammed it down a few minutes earlier. One of the clips on the plastic cover was broken, and it wouldn't stay on. He ground his teeth together and swore again. That was all he needed, a new phone on top of everything else.

He had never found out exactly why Elon had raised Pazia into the oligarchy ranks. "We need her skills," was all the Master would say when questioned. Nirim had always wondered what it was she must have over him. She knew about his wife; all the oligarchs did. They would not be where they were today without Jane Kelby and her untimely demise. No, it had to be something else, though Nirim was at a loss as to what on earth it could be. He would dearly love to know, though; it would have to be something really gritty to get that wily old goat on the back foot.

There was a chance, of course, that Elon genuinely just believed in Pazia's abilities. He would not be wrong in that. The woman was inordinately good at her job, and it was nice to have another person of colour on the board. Nirim stamped his cane down. It made an unsatisfying lack of noise on the deep-pile carpet. The face of the silver head atop the cane seemed to look at him with disdain. Nirim stroked his thumb over it, as if to reassure the figure that he had everything under control.

Most people thought he was deranged, claiming that the head was a depiction of the First Master, the man who had founded the oligarchy and overseen its rise to power. They were wrong. They were also wrong to doubt his claim that the man was a distant relation. Gilbert Elex had commissioned the small bust of himself when he had first come to power. It had then been passed down through the subsequent members of the family who had followed tradition and joined the ruling party. When Nirim's father had passed away, the bust had come to Nirim.

He had been only a young boy then, three years old and far too young to remember. His mother had died on his birthing bed, and having no other family to take him in, he had been sent to a private orphanage. Whilst a far better class of establishment than the usual places, it had still been a cold and heartless place. Nirim had found himself one of just seven children. He might have been young, but he'd been old enough to know that this life was not for him. He had been born with a golden spoon in his mouth and did not take kindly to being reduced to wanting and doing without. What little he had been allowed, he'd had to share with the other children. He had hated it, withdrawing into himself and building walls so impenetrable that even now he could not let them fall. No one had ever got close to Nirim, and no one ever would.

The orphanage might have had its faults, but it did protect the belongings of its residents. When Nirim was eighteen and making ready to leave the home for good, he was handed a sealed envelope with his name on it. Inside were the details of the solicitor acting as trustee of his impressive inheritance and a small brass key. The key belonged to a large wooden trunk that had sat in the attic for the fifteen long years Nirim had lived there. The contents of that trunk had reopened his eyes to the world he had been missing out on. What really caught his eye, though, was a faded pen-and-ink depiction of his family tree, complete with his own name at the very bottom, and the small silver bust of the First Master.

Within four years, Nirim had put himself through university. Twelve years later, he had been made an official member of the oligarchy. Only after he had achieved that hallowed rank did he admit whose son he was. It had been 103 years since Gilbert Elex had founded the oligarchy. Times had moved on, and most people had forgotten. The preceding generation, where no Elex had sat on the board, had diluted the name even further. Though annoyed by this lack of respect, Nirim was not disheartened. He had suffered greater hardships in his life. People may wish to deny him, but the Master's spirit had lived on down the line. Nirim felt it strongly. He'd had the small silver bust made into a pommel and mounted on the cane that he'd carried ever since. When the time was right, he would take what was his, and the Elex name would rule once more.

<h1 style="text-align: center;">23</h1>

NIRIM SAT ACROSS THE TABLE FROM PAZIA, SWITCHING between surreptitiously watching her and biting back the urge to ask her why she had set her snooping sights on Blain. He had thought long and hard after Blain's phone call. The man was immensely useful to him and to the oligarchy in general. It would be hard to find someone to fill his shoes should there be a need to do away with him. Nirim did not want to take such drastic action; his hold over Blain was such that it could never be replicated with anyone else. Until now, they had been the only two to know of it; he hoped that was still the case.

Each of the oligarchs had their individual secrets, as was their given right as leaders of the nation, but the secrets of the oligarchy itself must never, ever be allowed to escape. They tied the members together, uniting them no matter what grievances they may have amongst themselves. It was one of the reasons why these weekly meetings were so important. There was more to lose here than just power. Only by staying united would the board stand firm. They all understood that. It was for this reason that none of them were ever cut loose. Once a member, always a member, until their very last breath. Pazia had better think very carefully before rocking the boat.

Just now, their numbers were the lowest they had been for many years. Their secrets had become too shocking and too complex to trust anyone new to the board. They would have to take on new blood eventually; this current level was simply not sustainable for long. They all knew what needed to happen first, and Blain was key to that. He was their best shot at future stability, if he only knew it.

The buzz of the meeting carried on around Nirim. He was barely listening. It was the same argument they had been having for the last couple of months: whose head had been in the barrel, and why would Stanton Meads have put it there?

Elon tapped the paper in front of him. "They have been able to say without doubt that the missing teeth were removed post-death..."

"What about the DNA?" Baxter Carswell interrupted.

"I was just getting to that," Elon barked back at him. "The little they found was corrupted, though not naturally." A slight tremor had begun to haunt the edges of his voice. It had been there off and on since the final worthless report had arrived on his desk that morning.

"The best forensic scientists in the country, and not one of them can find a single identifying marker?" Ylva Portune's tone was incredulous.

Elon shook his head.

"Clearly, we're dealing with a very knowledgeable and skilful magician," Lorena Hunter said quietly.

Ylva was not the only one to shoot her a scathing glance. Stanton Meads had bested them again, and it left a very sour taste in all their mouths. Just how much more was this search at Fenton Woods going to throw at them? Disembodied heads aside, the discovery of the cottage had raised all their hopes. Raised them, then crushed them asunder like nothing more than paper ashes under a sodden boot.

They had expected to find a book—the most important book on magic that had ever been written. The majority of magical works had been destroyed during the Purge, and whilst the oligarchy had their own extensive secret library, this one book, the one they really needed, still eluded them. The fabled Totar, or Tome of Time and Reason, to give it its full name, was a highly advanced book of magical theory and, as such, had always been a very rare specimen. Whether through magical means or sheer ill fortune, the oligarchy had failed to obtain a copy.

The only version known for certain to be in existence had been owned by Stanton Meads, along with an enviable library of rare magical texts. With such information at his fingertips, Stanton might have remained under their radar for the majority of his life, but in the years before her death, Elon's wife had somehow found out about the collection. The oligarchy couldn't just neutralise him. With their newfound neurosis about magicians, they wanted to know everything he had been getting up to at his peaceful retreat in Fenton Woods.

Baxter Carswell had tried to befriend him, hoping to lull the magician into giving away his secrets. The plan had failed—dramatically. Baxter had not taken kindly to this insult to his charms. Judging by the animosity in his tone now, he was still harbouring the grudge.

Never a gregarious man, Stanton had withdrawn to a near-reclusive state. Forced to change tack, the oligarchs had managed to get Stanton another way, though a hollow achievement that had turned out to be. The implementation of his curse meant that despite all their efforts, they had been unable to get anywhere near his home, let alone get their hands on the Totar. Countless magicians had been driven to Fenton Woods under cover of darkness and forced, with increasing brutality, to find a way through the defences. All had failed. They had brought in machinery, again with no success. Engines stalled, electrics fried, and fuel lines fractured. Only painstakingly slow, manual clearance had any impact. It was lucky, therefore, that Marlborough House provided the perfect cover for such a lengthy task.

The Guardians had been Nirim's own plan. Growing up in the orphanage, he had experienced firsthand the secrets such institutions could keep. He'd learnt well the lessons his upbringing had thrust upon him: the power that was open to adults who forced children away from their birth environment, their ability to manipulate, to mould, and to control. The Guardians had served the oligarchy well over the years, and even though their wards were dwindling in number now, many of the retained children were still proving to have powers.

Using the potential magicians in Blain's care to unsuspectingly claw through Stanton's barricade might take longer than having a team of men working night and day, but it was by far the most inconspicuous and controllable way. The wait had not been easy because the

Totar, for those who knew how to read the magical text, held the knowledge of all things: how they came to be and how everything interlinked. In short, it was the ultimate manual of life itself. When the oligarchy got their hands on it, they would be unstoppable.

Baxter leaned forward, his forearms flat on the table in front of him. "And you can assure me that the fire those pillocks set at the place won't have burnt the damn thing?"

"As I've already told you," Elon's forbearance was starting to wane, "fire might cleanse, but books of the Totar's magnitude need an intricate combination of all five elements in order to destroy them. The flames of a fire, however intense, would be like water off a duck's back."

"So, what do we do now?" Baxter Carswell threw a hand up in frustration. "The book was not there, and this unidentifiable head is not going to tell us where it is. Stanton has seen through our plans once again."

Elon closed his eyes. For the length of time it took him to take a long, deep breath, he fought to keep his temper under control. It was a fight he lost. Slamming his hands down on the table, he rose to his feet, his chair tipping backwards with the force of the movement. "That damnable man will still be laughing at us from the grave." It was not a shout, nor was it quiet. "That head is a message, mocking us. Mocking me."

He swallowed hard, his Adam's apple bobbing beneath his shirt collar. He glared down at the table, not seeing the carefully polished mahogany but the face of his dead wife looking back at him with pleading eyes. *Save me,* she was saying, just as she always did whenever he saw her shade.

Because he hadn't saved her, he had failed to listen to her warnings, to all the concerns she'd started having. He had been a stupid, arrogant fool, and they had all paid the price. Jane Kelby was Elon's one true failing, and his only way of making amends was by getting his hands on that Totar. Had Stanton Meads known that? There was no telling.

Well, it just would not do. Elon could feel his blood pressure rising. He blinked away the image of Jane and looked around the table. Not everyone met his eye. "I will not be mocked." The embarrassment he noted in both Peyton's and Lorena's eyes stung. "I say we have had enough of tiptoeing around this issue. There is no telling what that bastard did with it, but one thing is for sure—we will find it." He retrieved his chair and sat back down, his body filled with the cold, hard iron of renewed determination.

"Well, they just have to hurry up and find the other house," Ylva said after a beat of silence. "After all, we don't actually know if the one found was even Meads'. The other was home to a magician, was it not?" Around the boardroom table, two or three heads were nodding slowly. "It might even be his head. Didn't folk say that he had disappeared?"

The simplicity of her statement brought even Nirim out of his reverie. How stupid they had all been, forgetting about the other cottage. "That is probably the most sensible thing anyone has said in ages."

Elon slapped a hand on the table in front of him again, his face at once more animated than it had been in days.

"Blain must be told to push on with the searches with all haste." He could feel new sparks of hope germinating. They were enough to override the rising memories of things he would rather keep shrouded in the dregs of his mind. "There was a murder at the other house, now I come to think about it. The wife..." he shook his head. "Her killer was never caught. The husband disappeared, and everyone assumed him guilty. Stanton must have killed them both." Having blackened Stanton's reputation so much over the years, even they were starting to believe their own hype. "He was probably in the process of getting rid of the body when we got to him."

"Well, that is certainly the official story we should be releasing," Baxter said, bouncing a little on his seat in eagerness to finally be moving forwards again. "I know we said we would keep all this under wraps, but someone is bound to notice all the activity over there sooner or later. We have enough now to make this a plausible investigation." He raised his eyebrows. "And you never know what rat the news might shake out of the closet."

Around the table, heads began to nod in earnest.

"It never hurts to remind everyone how much danger those with magic pose." Ylva's smile was thoughtful, "Or how much work we are doing to keep everyone safe."

Baxter was scribbling notes on the pad in front of him. "I'll get started on it right away."

Elon rapped the table with one hand, twice in short succession, using the tips of his three longest fingers before pointing at no one in particular. "I think we should also include a warning that there is still residual magic in the area, hidden from view and all the more dangerous for it. We don't want people becoming blasé after we've worked so hard."

"Is that wise?" Lorena asked, her forehead creased in a deep frown. "Won't it just get vigilantes crawling over the woods, hoping to find the rest of the body?"

Peyton looked at his watch. He needed to be elsewhere. The important work was done here; he could trust the others to sort out the nitty-gritty. He pushed his chair back, "If there is nothing further on the agenda?"

"We haven't finished discussing the statement yet," Lorena snapped. She hated it when the others ignored her concerns. Why was it so hard to accept her opinion on anything outside of financial matters?

"Yes, yes," Peyton answered, waving a dismissive hand, "But I think you're forgetting that the wood has been cordoned off for years. The public knows better than to trespass on our private land." He thrust his paperwork into his briefcase and snapped shut the clasps. "I'm sure you can sort the rest out between you, so if you will excuse me, I have a rather important appointment to get to." He nodded first at Elon and then to the rest of the board. Ignoring the furious look from Lorena, he picked up the briefcase and left the room.

Elon waited until the door closed before continuing, his earlier loss of self-control now nothing more than a distant memory. "Baxter, can you word the press release so as not to antagonise the local Hooray Henrys, treasure hunters, and any other wannabe heroes out there?"

He looked pointedly at Lorena, who smiled unconvincingly back at him. She had been a little preoccupied this morning, and Elon was feeling a tad concerned. Whilst his timely intervention had stopped the incriminating photographs of the two of them being published, it hadn't stopped the news of their rendezvous from appearing in the gossip columns. Don Brook had been sailing far too close to the wind over the last few months with his aggressive journalism. They couldn't have allowed it to continue. He had been dealt with now, but was it possible someone else had started causing problems?

"I am concerned," Pazia said.

Nirim sat a little straighter. Was she about to bring up something about Blain?

"There have been a number of happenings in that area of late. First the cottage was found and, shortly after, the cellar with the head. The boy who found both came into his powers not long afterwards, then a second child almost burnt Marlborough House to the ground within hours of her arrival. Is there a chance the area around the cottage could be a nexus of some sort?"

Nirim narrowed his eyes thoughtfully. If this was why she was suddenly so interested in Blain, maybe he could start to relax a little? His thumb rubbed subconsciously over the silver face of the First Master, as if he could draw advice from his spirit.

Ylva turned to Elon. "Is that possible?"

"I'll put a call through to Alistair Calvington; he would be the one to ask."

"This could work to our advantage." Lorena pushed her annoyance at Peyton to the side. "What spare capacity do they have? If it's drawing out any localised magic, we should transfer as many children there as possible."

"Too risky; it could be making powers unstable, which is why both youngsters lost control so dramatically." There was a pause as everyone pondered Baxter's words. The man might look like someone's harmless, bumbling uncle, but he was as sharp as a diamond-edged blade and just as dangerous when he wanted to be. The oligarchs' public relations man always had his eye on the less obvious outcomes, the things others failed to plan for or expect anyone else to notice. "I would hazard a guess that Meads did leave more magic behind than just an overgrowing woodland. If there's a chance that something has been disturbed in those trees, then we need to get to it before anyone else can take advantage."

The oligarchy was all-powerful, but should the Totar get into the hands of a magician able to read it, that person could easily bring them to their knees. The air in the room seemed to grow colder. Lorena visibly shivered and pulled the corners of her angora jacket closer. Elon coughed, and Nirim tapped his cane subconsciously against the side of his foot.

"We need Blain to crack on with his searching and find this other house." Ylva's curt tone had tightened even further. "Surely it's easier to search in the winter when most of the greenery has died back?"

"You are forgetting the ground conditions." Nirim was finding it hard to keep his own frustrations at bay. He'd had this same argument with Blain two years earlier. "Either the ground is hard as rock or else it's so boggy that any evidence would be trampled into the ground without even realising it, and that is without snow hampering everything."

Ylva was not a nature lover; she preferred her landscapes to be made of concrete and glass. She curled her nose in distaste. "Why anyone would want to live outside the city is beyond me."

"I think I'll pay our friend a visit." Elon pulled a small diary out of his pocket and began leafing through the pages. He gave an exasperated snort as he saw how full his commitments were. "Nirim, perhaps you would go in my stead? I am sure you'll have no trouble thinking up some reason why he needs to make this search his priority."

"Better still," Pazia's skin prickled with anticipation; things were taking a turn in her favour, "why not just go in and take control of the situation? As Baxter said, this is surely enough to warrant a full-on official investigation. With the possibility of a nexus, we're going to need our own people on it anyway." Not to mention that with all eyes on Fenton Woods, Blain would be distracted. She forced herself not to smile. It was not often that loose ends like this arranged themselves so neatly or so quickly. "I will go as your eyes; Nirim will be too busy coordinating things."

Elon hung back as the meeting ended, grasping Lorena by the arm as she moved past him. "Ten minutes?" he hissed quietly before releasing her. At her nod, he too left the room, heading straight to his office. Pausing only to grab his jacket and umbrella, he was soon taking the elevator to the ground floor. Stepping out of the Chambers and into the pouring rain, he was unsurprised to find Carisburgh's streets almost deserted. Those unfortunate enough to be out in the deluge kept their heads down as they scurried along the sodden pavements, trying in vain to avoid the puddles.

Not far away, a side alley led to a number of expensive-looking doorways—quality office space for those able to afford the exorbitant leases. Elon made his way to number four, pressed his forefinger onto a pad reader, and tilted his head so that the camera hidden within the brickwork could get a clear view of his face. A second later there was a click, and the lock released. He pushed the heavy door, collapsing his umbrella with the other hand and giving it a firm shake. A quick check back up the alley showed that no one had followed him.

Ignoring the first two internal doors, Elon unlocked the final one and let himself into the tiny, windowless office. Locking himself in, he then moved over to the wall cupboard on the far side of the room and slipped inside, shutting the door firmly behind him. A soft green glow shone down from the ceiling, barely illuminating the space. Elon needed no light to find the catch hidden behind a small panel in the wall. He had been using this place for the last few years and never had the security system shone red. A simple flick of his finger on the catch, and a hidden door popped open. Dim light flooded into the dark cupboard. Elon stepped out into the chilly office beyond.

He was sitting with a glass of whisky in his hand when three warning taps sounded on the main door. Lorena entered, dropping the key into her pocket. She sighed, shook out her wet hair, and accepted the proffered glass. For a few minutes, neither of them spoke.

24

"ARE YOU GOING TO TELL ME WHAT'S WRONG?" ELON asked when the silence was beginning to get annoying. The whisky was light and fruity, slipping down his throat and hitting his stomach with a pleasing warmth. Still, he could sense Lorena was not relaxing.

"Pamela is rambling again."

"How is that news?"

"This time it's different." Lorena sighed. "I think you're going to need a better whisky." She tossed the drink back and held out her empty glass.

Elon looked up at that. He had served them a single malt with an excellent reputation. He eyed the glass, then shrugged. The next malt was dark and spicy. It crawled down their throats on wings of fire, leaving behind gasps of appreciation.

"She is claiming that two of her children have poisoned her and are keeping her locked up against her will."

Elon slugged back another mouthful of whisky. Lorena had been right when she'd suggested the change. He swirled the glass in his hand, almost too afraid to ask, "Has anyone believed her?"

"It is a common enough statement from patients, apparently. Nothing her nurses pay any heed to, but it's a little too close to the mark for comfort, don't you think?"

Elon closed his eyes, feeling the heat of the whisky chill to ice in his stomach. Family members were not allowed to sit on the board together. Whilst it was an idiotic rule as far as Elon was concerned, it came from the First Master himself and thus was set in stone. Consecutive generations had served, of course, but never concurrently. It made no difference that their relationship had come as a complete shock to both of them, nor that they had each achieved their positions without any awareness of their true parentage.

When members became problematic, sentiment did not come into it. It was a role for life, and lives could easily be cut short. With so few members at the present time, losing two would mean the board could not feasibly hold on to power unless they took on new blood. With everything that was going on behind the scenes right now, the risks of such a move were not something Elon could even begin to contemplate. Nirim had been biting at his heels for long enough as it was, with that self-grandiose belief of his that it was his familial right. The remains of his whisky glinted like liquid amber in his glass. Water of Life, it had been called in one of the old languages. What secrets life could hold.

Pamela had been a high-class surrogate specialising in covertly providing well-to-do families with the babies they so desperately wanted. It was all snobbery, of course: rich families wanting to maintain a perfect reputation, free from the stigma of infertility and the inability to perform one's hereditary duties. Whilst most families would turn to adoption to continue the family name, for others an unbroken lineage going back generation after generation was considered too important. Bloodlines could never be retrieved; the male DNA had to endure wherever possible.

The contracts were locked in secrecy, with dire retributions should any of the signatories divulge so much as a single detail. Yet Lorena's mother had kept a diary. It had shattered the oligarch's world when she'd found it. Suddenly the sealed paperwork her father had bequeathed to his solicitors became clear. Within the week, Lorena had used her influence to retrieve the devastating file and track Pamela down to a neat little house, half home, half art studio, on the outskirts of a small town called Beackott.

That first meeting had been amiable yet strained. Lorena, still feeling angry and betrayed, had found herself strangely defensive, whilst Pamela, fiercely proud of the help she had provided to those desperately in need, had never expected to come face to face with any of the four children she had borne. Neither of them had been at their best, so it was probably not surprising that their conversation had become so confused. Somehow, Pamela had mistaken Lorena's husband for one of her other surrogates. It was only when she'd called him Elon for a second time that the penny well and truly dropped. Until that moment, Lorena had been merely wallowing in the shock of finding herself at the centre of her parents' deception. If only her life could have remained that simple.

Elon poured himself another whisky. For eight years he had dreaded this moment. How Lorena had managed it all on her own for the first two years, he would never know. She wouldn't have divulged the information at all had

Pamela not been rushed to hospital with a mini-stroke. Signs of forgetfulness had begun to emerge, frightening Lorena into letting Elon into yet another secret the world could not be allowed to uncover.

Things had moved swiftly once Elon had taken control. He'd never met Pamela and never intended to. Back then, he'd considered her nothing more than a malignant presence, so he'd had no qualms at all in having her medical records altered to show a history of violent outbursts before putting her into Tainmoor Lodge. No one had cared enough to challenge it. She had no other family, and the three-hour drive from Beackott to the small, private sanatorium had ensured that her few close friends soon lost interest.

The closest Elon had been to his birth mother was to help Lorena and her husband, Marlon, search her house. It was a good job they had. Pamela had kept all her paperwork for the four surrogacies, along with newspaper clippings and handwritten notes. Elon now had everything locked away in his safe. It would have been wiser to burn it, but something had stayed his hand.

He threw back his head, downing the whisky in one, then pushed both bottle and glass away. Befuddling himself with alcohol when he needed a clear head would only make matters worse. Lorena was watching him, tapping her fingertips nervously on the wooden arms of her chair. It made barely a sound. Her nails were ruined, bitten to the quick from worry.

"Don't look at me like that," Elon growled. "I'm not going to suggest we get rid of her."

There was a tangible feeling of relief in the small room. Lorena closed her eyes and swallowed. That was exactly what she'd been afraid of. Elon had threatened as much back when she'd first told him of Pamela's existence. It made sense, and had it been anyone other than her blood mother, Lorena would have agreed to it at once. Luckily, once sedated, Pamela had taken to life in the facility quite well. In the last few years, however, dementia had set in, and Pamela was becoming increasingly obstinate.

"Do you know what has unsettled her this time?" Elon watched the colour return slightly to his sister's face. She was not a soft woman, despite her troubles coping with Pamela. Nothing less than a redoubtable nature would have enabled her to gain her place as Chancellor of the Oligarchy. Still, everyone had their weakness, and Lorena's was dealing with Pamela. Elon thought momentarily of the chink in his own armour and quickly pushed the thought away.

Lorena took only a moment to gather herself. "Apparently she wanted to go out and paint the ducks on the local pond."

"Is that all?" Bloody painting; that was all the woman bothered about. Elon forgot his earlier resolve and poured them both another whisky. "If she wants to go paint, I say let her."

"They don't have enough staff to send someone with her." Lorena moved to bite one of her nails, realised there was nothing left to get her teeth onto, and reached for her glass instead.

Somewhere in the building, a door banged. Their eyes shot to the adjoining cupboard. Elon had left the door open for just this reason. The light inside was still green. No one had managed to get into the other room. They both relaxed.

"Should we get them to increase the tranquillisers?"

Elon shook his head. "Better leave that for now. Don't want it to look like there could be any truth in what she is saying, do we?"

Lorena sighed and took a mouthful of whisky, rolling it around in her mouth before swallowing. "I've told them to distract her with fresh things to draw when she starts. Seems it is happening more often these days. She's restless and impatient, getting cross very easily."

"Then we need to sort that." Elon smiled, relieved. If only everything was so easy. "We pay for a private carer to go in once or twice a week and accompany Pamela on her painting trips."

"Mike isn't going to like that idea."

"He doesn't have to like it, but if he wants to keep his most lucrative resident, he's going to have to accept it." Elon rubbed his thumb against his fingers. "Mike is a greedy bastard; he'll agree to anything if the money's right."

His sister sighed again. "Do we really want to risk pissing him off? He could start piecing things together?"

Elon almost snapped at her. She was just looking for problems. One look at the strain on her face and he relented. She was the one who bore the brunt of all this. The face of their little charade. He stayed in the background, out of sight, and so long as they kept their wits about them, unconnectable to Pamela in any way. It kept both him and Lorena much safer, though it put an enormous pressure on her shoulders. He knew that she'd started to feel more about Pamela than she cared to admit. Truth be told, so had he. The woman was their birth mother, after all.

Sentiment was one thing, but at the end of the day, their positions within the oligarchy came above all else; on that, they were both resolute. He reached into one of the drawers and took hold of a shining gold orb mounted onto an ebony base. He placed it pointedly on the desk in front of him. Lorena's shoulders relaxed. Without another word, she pulled out her phone and tapped on the contact list. As she moved away, Elon poked a long pin into a tiny hole on the underside of the orb. There was an inaudible click, and an almost imperceptible throb vibrated once through the metal. He held the orb up to his mouth. "Mike Bradshaw, Tainmoor Lodge." Elon gave another prod of the pin and immediately the shining metal tarnished.

"He will see me at four," Lorena told Elon a few minutes later. She tucked the phone into her bag along with the now-active paperweight. It rested reassuringly heavy underneath her glasses and purse.

****

Mike Bradshaw rubbed a hand over his head as he watched the door close. His eyes tracked back to his desk, where the shining gold paperweight sat. He let out a slow breath, clamping down on the urge to whoop with joy. Mrs Hunter would be going to visit her aunt; she wouldn't be out of the building for a while yet. It would never do for her to hear him. He wondered again about the strange relationship between the two women. Pamela always said she was her daughter, but Mrs Hunter was insistent she was her niece. Still, he shrugged to himself; what did he care? So long as he got his money, they could be anything they wanted.

He rubbed his hands together at the thought. Little did Mrs Hunter know that the basic rate he charged for Pamela was almost twice that of any other resident. He was no fool where the rich were concerned. On top of that, she paid him extra for his discretion and gave him a generous bonus every year. A car started up outside. Mike looked up just in time to see Mrs Hunter sweep out of the car park. She hadn't stopped to see Pamela then. A grin spread across his face as the engine noise died away.

He had not been happy to start with about her insistence on hiring a private carer. It was bad enough having to pander to the district nurses coming in at all hours. Still, at least this time he was not the one footing the bill. There were hurdles to put up with in any business, and where Pamela Carrson was concerned, they always proved lucrative. He picked up the paperweight, weighing it in his palm. It was a thing of beauty. There was no doubt it was expensive. Maybe it would look better on his mantelpiece at home?

As he sat it carefully on the passenger seat of his car, he noticed how dull it looked. Frowning, he picked it up, turning it over in his hands, remembering Mrs Hunter's words as she had placed it on his desk. *There, it looks perfect. The light just catches it right. It's as if it knows where it wants to be.* Almost without thinking, he got back out of the car. Once more in his office, the paperweight shone just as brightly as it had before. On second thoughts, it would be better to keep it here on the desk. It made him look much more professional.

In his own office, Elon smiled as he watched the small screen on his phone. He had a full 360-degree view of Mike's office, along with crystal-clear audio. He should have thought of using one of these at Tainmoor Lodge long ago. He typed a few trigger words into the app, words that if heard would start his phone recording. Elon could relax now; Nirim would have to wait a good while longer before he got the chance to fill his shoes.

****

From the top-floor flat in the city's southern corner, just at the edge of the affluent Liscombe district, laughter rang out. A cat, startled by the sudden noise, gave a brief hiss and fled. No one else heard.

The flat had been well chosen both for its privacy and its location. It was near enough to Liscombe to be impressive, yet not quite close enough to warrant that area's exorbitant prices, nosy gossiping neighbours, and prowling paparazzi. Clive Greckham had lived here for fifteen years, and in all that time, the small, downstairs flat beneath him in the modest three-storey townhouse had remained uninhabited. The neighbours to his left spent the better part of each year at their overseas property, and to his right the old widow was as deaf as a post. The only sound she ever heard was the tinnitus that squealed incessantly in her ears. She claimed that the sound kept her company, always with her, protecting her from the perpetual silence she would otherwise be forced to live with. Clive was not sure he would be able to think of it in such a positive light, but Enid Blackshaw was a rare sort of woman. Clive made a point of visiting her most days, checking on her welfare, and making sure that she had everything she needed.

His impromptu laughter trailed away as the kettle clicked off. He poured the boiling water into the teapot, took a couple of croissants from the oven, and sat down to eat his breakfast. The woman on the radio had moved on through the headlines and was just coming to the start of the main article. Clive pushed his plate away and gave the newsreader his full attention.

Details of a grisly find uncovered back in the autumn, close to the small town of Fenton, have just been released. Workers clearing an area of contaminated private woodland unearthed a broken-down secret room. The cellar, which appeared to have been connected to a nearby cottage, was initially thought to be empty. Upon closer examination, the remains of a badly decomposed head were discovered inside a water-filled barrel. The rest of the body has yet to be found.

It is not the first time that the area has been used for nefarious purposes. Notorious magician Stanton Meads, who killed thirty-seven people when he turned his power on the innocent residents of Fenton, called the woods his home. We can only guess at the extent of the atrocities that took place there.

Clive's grin faded a little.

Meads' last act when captured by the Guard was to curse the woodland surrounding his property and that of fellow magician, Drake Pennywell, sealing off the two houses within an impenetrable barrier of forest. The land, which was immediately seized by the oligarchy, has been subject to rigorous investigations ever since. There have been a number of accidents affecting those involved in the dangerous work. The magical contamination choking the area is the worst ever discovered. It is now clear why Meads went to all that trouble.

Clive leaned forward, tense now to hear what conclusion they had come to.

Investigations have been complicated by the poor condition of the head, but the oligarchy can now confirm that it has been identified as the remains of Drake Pennywell. Pennywell had been reported missing shortly after the horrific killing of his wife, twenty-five-year-old Florence Pennywell, a number of years before the Purge began. Pennywell had been the chief suspect in his wife's murder. Now the oligarchy is in no doubt that both Mr Pennywell and his wife had fallen foul of the deranged and power-hungry madman.

It has long been suspected that Meads had also turned on his fellow magicians, as many were apt to do. We will never know the full death toll of his victims and can only give thanks that the oligarchy stepped in when they did to end his reign of terror...

Clive closed his eyes, letting the voice fade into the background for a moment. His initial mirth at the dramatic headline now scattered at his feet like unwanted confetti. The newsreader continued to praise the oligarchy's handling of Stanton Meads for some minutes. Clive snorted in disgust.

...no cause for panic. Investigations into the dangerous plot of land are still ongoing. The area remains completely sealed off and inaccessible to anyone without full security clearance.

"Unbelievable." Clive's voice sounded hollow in the empty room. Stanton Meads was the scapegoat yet again. Whilst the head had been assigned to the one person Clive had both hoped for and yet dreaded, he knew full well there had been no positive identification. When he had left it in the barrel, years before, he had made sure that no one would ever be able to identify it. Still, he consoled himself; the oligarchy had their cover story, and it was about as far from the truth as they could possibly get.

The true owner of the head did not deserve to be remembered. He was no victim as the news story had suggested. He had been a cold-blooded killer, who had got nothing less than he deserved. Clive was damn sure the man would not benefit in any way from the notoriety of being 'the head in the barrel'. Far better that Drake took that spot for the time being, and whilst it was hard hearing Stanton accused of yet another crime he had not committed, at least they had not regurgitated the rubbish about Drake that had once filled the news.

Twenty years ago, the Pennywells had lived in their little whitewashed cottage in the woods. Clive could still see it now. Florence had painted pink roses over the doors and window frames, and Drake had surrounded the garden with a neat picket fence, inside which they had planted a vegetable plot, herb garden, and lots and lots of roses. Florence had loved roses, from wild climbers to heritage blooms, and anything in between.

They had lived quite a reclusive lifestyle for people so young, keeping mainly to themselves and bothering no one. When Florence had told Drake she was pregnant, it had been almost as thrilling as the day she had agreed to marry him. Clive closed his eyes tight. He could not think of the baby—would not allow himself to. He pressed his hand against his chest, feeling the reassuring pressure of his pendant pushing against his skin. It was not enough. The pain of Florence's death was still raw, but the baby—that was something else entirely. The memories didn't just surround him; they cut through him like a thousand hot needles.

A gasp of raw emotion tore from him, shocking him back to awareness. In his small bathroom, he threw handfuls of water onto his face. When that did no good, he thrust the plug into the drain hole and let the water fill the basin, then he plunged his head beneath the surface. The shock of the cold water helped temper his grief, pulling him back from the edge of despair. Clive sat heavily on the side of the bathtub, feeling as wrung out as his old, tatty facecloth. He picked it up and smoothed it out. Florence had bought him this; it was long past its best, but Clive would not be parted from it. He saw again Drake and Florence standing in their garden, the sun shining down through the clearing in the trees. He could almost feel the heat of it on his skin. With a sob, he crushed the cloth back into a ball and hurled it across the room.

Downstairs, the door slammed behind him. There was a slight thud to his right as something unseen fell. Clive ignored it, knowing full well what it would be. The lobby separating the two flats was only small. Four strides and he was out of the main front door and into fresh air. He would go into the other flat and hang the picture back later. It was about time he moved some things about and made the place look like someone used it. Property in this area was highly sought after, and people would not be happy to know that the place was being kept purposefully empty. He could, of course, just knock the property back into one, but he didn't need so much space. Besides, he didn't want people knowing that he owned the whole building. The less people knew about his business, the better.

25

"I HOPE THE WIND DOESN'T CHANGE DIRECTION," LETTY said, critically eyeing the slight sway of the bare branches on the nearby trees.

Amelia wrestled another bed sheet onto the washing line, clipped on the first peg, and then pulled the next one from her mouth. "It seems such a drastic thing to do, setting fire to the woodland. It was bad enough last time when they just burnt the old cottage. I feel sorry for the wildlife." She jabbed the peg onto the corner of the sheet.

"Well, they've got to do something. You never know what else could be lurking about in there." Letty shook herself with no small amount of exaggeration. "Better to burn the whole damn lot down, if you ask me."

Through the trees, they could just make out the back of Armitage Branwell. He had arrived a couple of days ago, along with Nirim and Alistair Calvington. The three men unnerved Amelia. She longed for the peace of Mr Forth's classroom, or the sanctuary of her newly refurbished weaving corner, but the presence of the visitors had turned everything on its head. The Forths had been given leave, lessons had been postponed, and it was all hands on deck to help with the increased workload.

There was something satisfying about sheets blowing on a washing line. Amelia allowed herself a smile as she secured the final peg. Letty scooped up the basket as if she had been the one to do all the work, though she had barely managed to hang more than a couple of pillowcases. Dorothy met them at the back door, a slightly harassed look on her face. "We have another visitor for tonight."

Behind her, Mrs Lee's grousing could be heard floating down the passageway from the kitchen. There was the sound of something banging down on the table, followed by more chuntering.

Dorothy forbore rolling her eyes. "Can you make up the green bedroom, please, and make sure to place some fresh flowers on the mantelpiece?"

Before Amelia had a chance to speak, Letty thrust the empty washing basket into her hands and made a grab for the secateurs hanging just inside the cloakroom doorway. "I'll get some right now." She spun around and sashayed down the back step.

This time, Dorothy did roll her eyes. She patted a warm hand on Amelia's arm. "It would be better if you made up the room, my dear. It's that overbearing woman from the oligarchy, Ms Olvalroyd." She overemphasised the Ms, raising one eyebrow as she did so. "She always seems so above herself, that one. I don't want to give her any reason to complain. We're all on tenterhooks as it is." She tucked a stray strand of Amelia's hair back behind her ear, cupped her cheek in one hand as if she would say more, and then reluctantly turned away. "I'd better get on; I left Tiffany taking firewood up to the formal rooms; she's bound to try and carry more than she can manage, and if she drops it down the stairs again, Mr Grange will not be happy."

Upstairs in Blain's study, Nirim was working his way through his morning emails. There was the usual amount of dross, which he quickly deleted. The various messages regarding policy matters had taken him the better part of an hour to sort, then there were a couple of enquiries about public spending, which he transferred to Lorena, and half a dozen requests for his personal endorsement. He sent most of them his standard cut-and-paste 'thank you but no thank you' reply and requested more information from the only one to interest him. Then he closed his laptop with a click and looked towards the window.

From here he could just see the tops of the trees, and in the distance, a plume of dark smoke rising. He felt a flutter of anticipation in his stomach at the sight of it. This fire was more than just a way of finding that second property. It was the means of pinpointing the Totar's location once and for all. According to Alistair, the pulse of a nexus's magic would strengthen significantly in response to danger, allowing them to identify its exact location as the protection intensified. Such a strong pulse would also draw out any hidden magic nearby, whether it be located in places or in people. With two young magicians losing control of their powers here already, it was clear that the recent work in the woods had already begun this process.

It had been a smart idea of Alistair's to bring in Armitage from the start. He would be perfectly positioned to contain any emerging magicians and transport them swiftly away to Blackwell for assessment, leaving Alistair free to concentrate on the woodland and anything that might emanate from the flames. Once the fire had done its work, it would then be a simple case of clearing the area before bringing in a select few of Alistair's magicians to get to work dismantling the defences Stanton had so carefully constructed.

They would take over Marlborough House for the duration, with Blain and his household temporarily located elsewhere. As soon as they were finished, the young magicians helping with the work would have their memories suitably 'corrected,' and Blain could resume occupancy. Only Alistair and the oligarchs would ever know what they were really looking for and what had been found. Nirim leaned back and stretched, feeling his spine pop as he eased the tension out of it. He liked it when plans were neat and compact. It could end up being such a juggling act when everyone had different levels of knowledge about what was really going on.

The smoke was thicker now, billowing up from a much wider area. Nirim looked at his watch. Pazia would be arriving any minute. Her presence was annoying, but he couldn't very well deny her attendance when she was the one who had recognised the probability of a nexus. On the bright side, her bloodhound tendencies would be just the thing for sniffing out anyone acting suspiciously. Between her, Alistair, and Armitage, no one was going to keep their magic hidden for much longer. Nirim's mouth quirked into a smile. Elon might be a good figurehead for the oligarchy, able to formulate ideas and visualise the direction the organisation needed to go in, but unlike himself, he lacked the sophisticated cunning to actually get the work done. When the time came for Nirim to challenge for the leadership, that is what would be Elon's undoing.

All day, the light breeze had continued to blow away from the house, but now there was something else in the air. The atmosphere felt charged, as if a large electrical storm was brewing, though the watery blue of the winter sky was still calm and clear. Amelia could feel all the little hairs along her arms standing on end as she gathered in the washing. The bedding was slightly damp, though nicely aired and with no trace of smoke. It would not take long to finish drying inside. Just as she was putting the last pillowcase into the basket, a fresh wave of tingling pain shot through her cold fingers. She crunched them into her palms, dismissing the feeling. It had been weeks now since her magic had awoken. There was no reason for it to start hurting again.

Down in the basement, she rehung everything on the airers before raising the frames high up to the ceiling, where the warmer air would soon have them ready for Dorothy to iron. Her fingers were still a little cold, so she tucked them under her arms and headed back upstairs. There was a clatter of footsteps from the back door as the men returned from the woodland. Johns and Jasper came into the kitchen, bringing with them the strong odour of smoke and sweat.

"Blain says, can you give him and Mr Calvington about half an hour before serving dinner?" Johns told Mrs Lee.

"Gipton, Mr Branwell, and Mark have stayed behind to tend the fire. If we can grab something to eat now, we'll go back out and relieve them as soon as we're done."

"You can take those stinking coats off and wash your hands and faces first," the cook told them, turning back to the pans steaming on the range.

Two heaped plates of stew were waiting for them when they returned, quickly joined by a pile of thickly sliced fresh bread, some pats of butter, and a jug of hot, liberally spiced fruit punch.

"Just the thing to warm us back up," Johns said with a grin. "You are an angel, Mrs Lee."

She tutted at him as she began serving everyone else but couldn't help the brief smile that flickered beneath her stern expression. "Is it going well?"

She wasn't really sure if she wanted to know the answer. All this talk of magic in the woods was too unsettling by far. Ever since that first cottage had been found, her grief had been brought sharply back into focus. She saw the faces of her beautiful twin daughters numerous times throughout each day, and then when she closed her eyes at night, they were waiting for her in her dreams. Sometimes they were young, just toddlers running around the neat little lawn they'd had at the back of their Fenton house, giggling their infectious laughter. Other times they were older; the adults they had never lived to be. Whatever their age, they taunted her with their absence.

It was not just the girls who haunted her. In that barely lucid realm between wakefulness and dreaming, she had begun once again to feel her husband's firm presence beside her. She cherished the familiarity, only to wake each morning to find herself alone in her narrow, single bed. The years may have buried the pain, but they had not dulled it. Unearthed as they were now, the constant memories, combined with the dread of what else might happen, were doing nothing to soften her fractious nature. Still, this was a job that needed doing, and she had every sympathy for the men out there undertaking all the work. They were the ones who had to suffer those claustrophobic trees and the malignancy they were hiding. She held her breath, waiting whilst Johns swallowed his mouthful of food.

"We have just over half the area burnt now," he told her, reaching for another piece of bread.

"All those poor trees and all the wildlife," Amelia couldn't help saying as she set about laying the rest of the table. It was usually Tiffany's job, but Dorothy had commandeered her for another task elsewhere, and Letty was busy in the scullery.

Mrs Lee let out a scathing snort. "As if a few trees and squirrels matter, girl."

Johns looked up and laughed. "The trees are alright. It would take more than that little fire to make them burn." He smirked at their surprised faces. "Got no resin in them, see? If they was pine, they'd have gone up, but we ain't got none of them in there. You don't need to worry; tis only the undergrowth that's burning. That's the stuff we need rid of. It's so thick, it's going to take hours to burn. The wildlife have plenty of time to get away."

"I hope so." Amelia was not really convinced. Even if they managed to get to safety, those who lived above ground would have nothing to come back to. "Will you keep the fire going through the night then?"

"Got to," Johns said through a mouthful of bread. Mrs Lee looked as if she were about to remind him of his manners, then resigned herself to a shake of her head.

Amelia just shuddered. The thought of being out there in the dead of night set the hairs on the back of her neck standing on end.

"The wind is set to change tomorrow," Jasper put in. He was pouring himself a second glass of punch, his plate of stew already half empty. "Besides, it would be too hard to stop the fire now it's going so well, and we might end up missing bits when it's restarted. We've already cut the breaks, so it will just burn itself out when all the area has been covered."

Though he seemed a little less anxious than he had been lately, Amelia certainly didn't envy him working with Armitage Branwell every day. At least she only had to put up with the man occasionally. The other one, Alistair Calvington, was only a little better. He reminded Amelia of the tall raven costumes people in the village wore at the harvest festival parade: narrow cones of wire, covered in black tatters and topped off with papier-mâché raven heads. They were worn over the head and shoulders, covering right down to the knees. The result was tall, looming black figures with staring eyes and pointed beaks. Not that Alistair Calvington had a beak, but he did have a rather large hooked nose, which was just as alarming.

Amelia was just about to ask if he was going to be staying out there as well when something she could only describe as a flash of static shattered inside her. She had to grip the table hard in an effort not to cry out. It left her cells fizzing in its wake, each one more alive than it had ever been before.

"Fetch me another loaf, girl. A sliced one." Mrs Lee's voice cut through to her. She blinked back sudden tears, relieved that the cook was too busy reaching for the butter to take any notice of her. "I'd best make up some sandwiches for you then, Johns, and you can take some flasks of this hot punch out with you."

"I'm sure we'll all appreciate that, Mrs Lee." Johns gave her a cheeky smirk. "Though to be honest, a hot toddy would do more good. It is going to be a long, cold night."

Not daring to look at anyone else, Amelia almost ran to the pantry. Only Jasper seemed aware that anything might be amiss. She gulped down large mouthfuls of air, hoping to quell the surging magic in her veins. She could get through this. She had before, even though this was a thousand times worse than when her powers had first begun. Grabbing the bread, she forced herself back into the kitchen. She just had to keep her head down and not draw attention to herself. Jasper gave her a small smile. For some reason, it made her feel better. That little bit of normality settled her, and the trembling in her hands eased.

The sandwiches were ready, wrapped in foil and tucked into a canvas bag, along with two large flasks of punch and a small one of boiling water. Mrs Lee was just coming back into the kitchen with a small bottle of whisky when Jasper turned suddenly, looking towards the doorway. Even though there had been no warning sound, he was the only one who didn't jump when Mark burst into the house, blood dripping from a cut on his temple. "Something's happened in the woods, a kind of explosion."

26

Amelia took the stairs two at a time, her heart doing some kind of ferocious off-beat tap dance in her chest. She banged on Blain's study door, urgency making the knock far harder than was polite. The door swung open with a force that surprised her. She could feel herself shaking, nausea churning in her stomach, though whether it was from fear or adrenaline she couldn't say.

"What the hell are you playing at?" Blain ground out. Behind him, Amelia could see Nirim and Pazia glaring in her direction.

"I... I'm sorry, sir, but there's been an explosion in the woods. Mr Gipton and Mr Branwell have been hurt."

"What about the boy?"

Amelia had not heard Alistair approaching behind her. She jumped around to find him leaning over her. "H-h-he came running for help."

Alistair's eyes bore into her, demanding more. Amelia wasn't even aware of taking a breath. "He said it blew them all off their feet. H-h-he was the only one to get back up. He didn't know what to do, so he came for help. He's taken J-Johns and Jasper back with him." She knew she was gabbling, but it was taking all her effort not to lean back away from his scrutiny.

Alistair, remarkably calm considering the news, raised an eyebrow at Blain. Inside the study, Nirim had already picked up the phone. They all turned to the window, waiting.

"Look." Pazia gasped, pointing towards the tree line as a shower of red sparks suddenly lit the night sky like a giant Roman candle. Downstairs, Mrs Lee screamed.

Amelia edged away, not sure what was happening. She could see the sparks outside over the woodland, but it felt as if they were exploding inside her. Was this how it started when a magician was about to lose control? Footsteps on the stairs heralded Dorothy, looking as anxious as Amelia felt. Her voice tremored a little as she spoke. "Mr Grange has phoned the emergency services. Will you want us to send them into the woods when they arrive, or will you meet them back here?"

Her voice seemed to snap Blain into action. "Tell Grange to bring them to the edge of the wood; someone will meet them there." He turned back to Nirim with a pointed look, "Bottom drawer on the right."

The oligarch nodded, his eyes flicking briefly to Amelia; he closed his phone with a snap. "The vans are on their way."

Blain didn't answer as he charged out of the door, heading for the stairs. Alistair took one last look at the dwindling sparks. His eyes were shining with something other than reflected light as he hurried after Blain. Dorothy and Amelia followed, leaving Pazia and Nirim alone in the study.

Nirim took a long, deep breath, then he bent and took Blain's silver cord from the drawer. Pazia's mouth had already twitched into a smile. Things were about to get very interesting indeed.

****

Amelia and Dorothy watched as Blain and Alistair rushed into the woods, leaving Letty to follow on behind with her arms full of blankets. Mrs Lee was fussing in the kitchen, shakily plating up meals for Pazia and Nirim. "No sense in everyone going hungry," she said to no one in particular, not seeming to notice how much she was spilling.

Thomas Grange rested a hand on her shoulder. "It will be alright, Elsie. Once all this is over with, there will be no more magic to worry about." His voice resonated down the short hall to the back door, anxiousness making the timbre slightly higher than usual.

Amelia heard the words, though they didn't register. She felt as if she were made from the finest porcelain and could shatter at any moment. There was no sign of the red sparks in the sky anymore, but they were still exploding inside her body. She could taste the copper-laced tang of blood on her tongue, and she realised she was biting her bottom lip. She needed to get away from everyone. Her magic was swelling. It was out of control. Filling her up and taking her over. A tap on her shoulder nearly sent her running. She jumped around in alarm.

Dorothy's own face was grey with shock. "I'm sure everyone will be safe enough so long as they keep their heads." She brushed a tear from Amelia's cheek. "Why don't you go wait at the gate and guide in the emergency services? Tiffany can manage the food." She held out a long red scarf.

Amelia didn't notice Dorothy's hand trembling or that the housekeeper's vision was blurred with unshed tears. She grabbed the scarf and took off running towards the gate, hoping that if she pounded the ground hard enough, she could shake out the feelings that were overwhelming her. Up at the dining room window, Nirim watched her go. His fingers rapped thoughtfully on his cane pommel. The door opened, and Thomas Grange entered with two bottles of wine. A minute later Tiffany appeared, carrying a large tray.

In three strides, Nirim was at the head of the table. "I will sit here today. That way I can see when lights come up the driveway."

Pazia ducked her head to hide a smile. She pointedly avoided the seat at his right hand, walking round the table to take the one to his left.

"What happened to the usual girl?" Nirim asked when Tiffany had carefully set their plates down and left the room.

"She is a little shaken up by the fire." Thomas tried his best not to bristle. "The last girl here set herself alight right in front of her. We didn't want her spilling your meal, so she's been sent to wait for the ambulance." He had always liked Amelia, and the way Nirim was narrowing his eyes unnerved him. "She is a good girl," he added, "hard-working and considerate. She herself was burnt in an accident a few months ago; it is understandable that she would be upset."

The instant the words were out of his mouth, he knew he had made a big mistake. Pazia looked at him like a hawk spying a mouse. "The girl seems to be quite attracted to fire, don't you think? You're sure you haven't overlooked something?"

"Amelia's accident had nothing to do with fire." Thomas straightened his back indignantly. "She was scalded trying to stop a pan boiling over. Besides which, she has been thoroughly screened; she is no danger to anyone. Mr Cordright questioned her himself after the incident."

Only then did he remember that Amelia's interrogation had been interrupted by the events with Aarav. For the first time, a seed of doubt crept into his mind. He stepped back, nodding at the guests. "If you will excuse me, I must be downstairs ready when the emergency services arrive. If you need anything at all, please ring the bell, and someone will attend to you."

****

Flames licked up the trunks of the trees, engulfing the smaller branches like strange giant candles. The fire was out of all control, blazing like a furnace. The noise was incredible as it consumed everything it touched. Armitage had recovered his wits enough to stumble away from the flames. He was shaken and sore, though not badly hurt. The fire cast an eerie orange gloom about itself, through

317

which he could just make out Ted Gipton's crumpled form not too far away. The boy, however, was gone. Armitage bent double and coughed, longing for some cooler air to soothe his rasping throat. Blurred shouts reached him, and he looked out into the black void looming just outside the reach of the fire's glow. The intense darkness was broken only by three beams of light bobbing closer.

Armitage tried to shout back, but the sound was snatched by the roaring of the inferno and swallowed whole. Still unsteady on his feet, he wobbled a little, almost going over on the uneven ground. He was saved by the crownless trunk of a tree, snapped just above head height by the force of the blast. It was no small sapling, the bole being far too wide for his arms to reach around.

"Fuck." He pushed himself away from the tree and looked at the devastation around him. That had been no small explosion. Its focus must have been upwards, or this whole area would have been levelled. The calluses on his hands scratched at his face as he rubbed it, trying to clear the fuzziness that still remained. "Fuck." He swore again as he looked back over to Gipton. Flames were licking dangerously close to where he lay.

It was no easy task, negotiating the way back to him. Armitage almost fell twice before he got there. Gipton still had not moved. Dead most likely, Armitage thought as he dropped to the ground beside him. He could make out Mark picking his way through the trees now, Johns and Jasper close on his heels. So, the boy hadn't fled; he'd gone to get help and returned with it. Armitage let out a sigh of relief. He was in no state right now to go tearing through the woods after an absconder. He waved an arm to get their attention, and the trio changed course towards him.

Gipton had fallen face-down amongst the remains of a blasted-apart oak, the back of his head dark and damp, where some flying debris must have caught him on the way past. Armitage tugged off his gloves and slid two fingers under the man's collar. He was surprised when almost at once he detected signs of life.

"We need to get him back to the firebreak," he told the others when they were near enough to hear. "His pulse is weak but steady."

They had to stop a couple of times on the way. Once when Armitage began coughing again, and then when Mark, who was lighting their way with one of the torches, stumbled into a rabbit hole and twisted an ankle. On the rough-cut ground of the break, they laid Gipton into as near the recovery position as was possible. They had managed to get him as far as their equipment stash, where a few bottles of water and a number of rubber firebeaters had been left ready for use. Even splashing the gardener's face with cold water brought about no response. Mark dropped to the ground beside him.

"Don't take off that boot." Johns prodded a telling finger towards him. "If your ankle swells, you'll never get it back on again. Try and prop your foot up and keep it raised until the others get here. They won't be long." He looked at Jasper and then nodded his head in the direction of the beaters. "You grab us some of them."

Armitage sat as well, pushing down the urge to cough again. He just needed a few minutes out of the smoky air. Johns and Jasper left them to it, heading back to the fire. The intensity of the heat increased with every step. The sound was phenomenal, nothing like the conflagration they had left less than an hour before.

"You start over there," Johns yelled over the noise, pointing to where a finger of flames was steadily working its way out from the perimeter. "I'll take these spots here."

Jasper nodded. He shoved his torch into his pocket, pulled his scarf up over his mouth, and eagerly attacked the flames. Everything else vanished into the background as he worked, adrenaline and panic fuelling his arms. Embers fell like early snowfall, floating down from the burning canopy. Here and there, sparks burst out from fracturing wood, like partying fire sprites celebrating their victory.

Around them, the fire roared like a beast, refusing to be tamed. As fast as one small area of flames was extinguished, three more sparked up around it. After a few useless minutes, the sweat was pouring down Johns' face, stinging his eyes as much as the smoke. This must be what it feels like to be trapped in hell, he thought as he paused to swipe the cuff of his jacket over his forehead. There was a sharp crack in the branches above him. He was already flinching backwards when the falling limb missed him by a hair's breadth. His heel caught, and he went down with a thump, his crown taking the brunt of the fall. Johns blinked hard, hearing a shout behind him. He gave his head a shake and blinked again. His focus cleared, and he made a shaky attempt at rising.

"Give it up." Armitage pulled at his arm, heaving him back to his feet. "It's too dangerous. We need to get out of here." He pointed upwards, towards the flaming canopy overhead, so much worse than it had been only minutes before.

"Shit." Johns' eyes rounded in alarm.

Armitage had never been a curious man. Some may say that was a fault, but, as far as Armitage was concerned, it kept him safe. He got on with his job and was trusted simply because he did not seek to know any more than was strictly necessary. That didn't mean he was blinkered. Over the years, he had witnessed many things he was not expected to understand. Today, it seemed, was to be another one of those times. He had sat at the break while the fire hissed and roared, tree trunks glowing red-hot like flaming sentinels. Magic was the only thing that could have caused grown trees to succumb to the flames in such a way. Armitage had felt it in the air ever since he had regained consciousness. He had thought it was coming from one of the boys, but neither of them were displaying any signs of losing control.

Maybe no one thought he would understand the significance of the spiky, dark leaves that were still defiantly green amidst the onslaught? Yet Armitage needed no other sign to know that this was a protection blaze. He peered through the holly to where the fiery eruption had come from and saw the unmistakable lick of bright, nexus-green flames. So this was why Alistair had wanted him here; why he had been so adamant that he would be needed. Armitage smiled. There was no way any of the children would be able to contain their burgeoning powers now.

"We need to leave," he told Johns. The girls would be just as affected back at the house; it made sense to have them all in one place.

Johns needed no encouragement. "Jasper, stop," he shouted, backing up a few more steps. "It's time to go."

Jasper ignored him, slapping his beater down over and over in a frenzy of uncoordinated effort.

"Jasper!" Johns called him again.

This time, Jasper paused long enough to look at him. Their eyes connected through the smoke, and the words Johns had intended to say died on his lips. "You're doing a great job," he said instead, holding up his thumb.

Armitage's skin prickled, and a smile crept slowly over his face. "Pull back to the others at the firebreak. I'll get him."

Another branch fell, much smaller this time, and further away. Johns threw his arms over his head, though there was no need. He cursed under his breath, then bobbed his head towards Armitage. "Don't be long."

They parted ways, Armitage stopping a few feet short from where Jasper still flailed ineffectually at the flames. Unlike Johns, there was no friendliness in his tone as he called out. When things got to this stage, only brusque efficiency would do.

Jasper wanted to ignore his command to stop, but open defiance was not something he had ever been capable of.

He broke off his fixation with the flames and looked at Armitage, though he didn't move towards him.

The hairs on Armitage's arms and neck rose in a static dance across his skin. His smile grew into a grin, which spread across his smoke-blackened face. "That won't work with me." Armitage didn't bother to hide his amusement.

Jasper had always been able to convince people to do what he wanted. A handy knack and a winning smile, or so he had thought. That was until recently, when he'd begun to realise that it was much more than that. Before he'd had time to settle to the notion, Aarav had shocked them all with his loss of control. The household's reaction had terrified Jasper. The prospect of being so hated frightened him even more than the thought of being taken away to the unknown. He brushed away Armitage's words, sending out even stronger thoughts. He was good, trustworthy, and should be allowed to remain here tending to the fire.

Another wave of prickling ran across Armitage's skin. The boy stood dangerously close to the flames, his face marred with fear and frustration.

"You cannot escape it." Armitage's voice was raw from the smoke. "That feeling, as if you're about to burst out of your own skin. There is nothing you can do." Despite the intense danger they were in, he stepped closer, raising his left hand and pulling back his sleeve to show a gold band fitting snugly around his wrist. Armitage's grin widened. "No matter what it is you are willing me to do, it won't work. I am protected from whatever filth runs through your cursed veins."

Jasper made to step backwards, but the fire was already licking at his heels. He had beaten his path forwards, with no thought of retracing his steps. Now he was trapped on a spit of blackened ground with only one way to run. Armitage stepped directly into his path, sliding one of his hidden crystal cords from an oversized pocket. Panicking and unable to think straight, Jasper leapt sideways over the flames, hoping to reach safety. Armitage had anticipated the move. He shot forward, and with an expert flick of his wrist, the silver metal flashed out, wrapping itself around Jasper's body. Giving him no time to react, Armitage pulled the cord sharply towards him, hauling Jasper from the burning scrub.

It was all Jasper could do to keep his feet underneath him as he felt the compounding pressure of the rope smother the cacophony of feelings, flaring throughout his body, into silence. For a moment, relief, mixed with crushing loss, blotted out the realisation that his trousers were aflame. He flinched as Armitage lunged forward to beat at his legs with his free hand.

Gipton was still unconscious when Alistair and Blain arrived. His pulse was weak, and blood oozed from a deep gash at the back of his head. Armitage stood a little to the side with Jasper, still confined in the crystal cord. Mark had only looked at them once, then pointedly turned his back and ignored them. Jasper felt a stab of anger as he watched the older boy fawning over Git-ton as if the man were some kind of precious guardian. Yet that old bastard had turned Aarav in without a second's thought. He would turn in Mark as well, given half a chance.

Jasper hissed breath out through his teeth to stop himself from saying something he would no doubt be punished for as he watched Mark help get the man onto a makeshift stretcher formed from one of Letty's blankets. Sycophant; did he really think that by sticking so close to the adults, he would be protected from magic? All but Letty looked shocked at the sight of the cord around Jasper. She was far too busy trying to look important to notice anything other than whose eyes were on her.

As the small group began to make their way past them back to the edge of the wood, Alistair hung back. "You've got one then."

Armitage gave the rope a slight tug. "He's a good 'un; would have taken quite a while to be caught without all this."

Alistair ran a critical eye over Jasper. The boy didn't look like anything special. He was weedy and could easily be mistaken for someone far younger. Just now, he was filthy, coated in grime with a red, blotchy face and wet, scared eyes.

"Mind control," Armitage explained, giving the rope another tug. "Probably been running rings around the household for months." He rubbed the protection band around his wrist ruefully. He would have cottoned on sooner had he not put the almost imperceptible vibrations he had felt ever since arriving down to the magic emanating from the woodland. Presumably, that was how the boy had managed to slip under Alistair's and Blain's careful detection too. "He certainly knew what he was doing; just couldn't control it once the fire touched the nexus."

"Hmmmm." Alistair's face was shuttered and cold, though there was a glint in his eye that even the darkness of the woodland could not hide. "I'm almost certain that we have the eldest girl too. Nirim is keeping a close eye on her."

Dread crawled an icy path over Jasper's skin. He had been right about Amelia then. He willed her to hear his thoughts and run, but even without the magic-quenching silver rope around him, that was not how his powers worked.

"What about the other boy?" Alistair nodded to where the lights were slowly dwindling down the track.

"I couldn't sense anything off him. He seems like a good lad. We can check again before I leave."

Jasper seethed, exhaling an almost silent pffft of disgust under his breath.

Armitage gave him a scathing look. He opened his mouth to say something, coughing instead. Even this far from the seat of the fire, his chest was still burning, and his lungs felt as if they would never taste fresh air again.

"You need to see a paramedic." Alistair took the cord's handle from Armitage. "Go get yourself checked out; I'll take the boy the other way and meet you back at the house." He turned away, dragging Jasper with him like a dog on a lead. Away from the eerie glow of the flames, darkness closed in around them. Like a living entity, it pushed at the unwelcome illumination from Alistair's torch and the dim glow from the cord's terminating crystals. Armitage was left to follow in their wake. For a short distance, his torchlight protected their rear, then their paths separated, and even that small comfort was gone.

The wide path had not been too hard to navigate. Once they turned off that, however, the ground became more uneven. The trees were closer to them now, their clutching branches creating uncanny shadows on the ground. Jasper staggered, unable to balance properly with his arms pinioned to his sides. Before he could steady himself, he tripped over a root and slammed into the ground. The cord was yanked out of Alistair's hand and, for a second, began to loosen around Jasper's body.

He only had time to suck in a single, welcome breath before the cord re-tightened and the bright light of Alistair's torch shone in his eyes. Jasper struggled to his feet. His knees were smarting, and he was sure he could feel blood seeping through his trousers.

"Where is your torch?" Alistair asked him. Unlike Armitage, he did not sound angry or cross.

It puzzled Jasper, but he was too frightened to ask why. Instead, he patted his hand as close to the torch as he could reach. "My pocket."

Alistair pulled the torch out for him, flicking the switch and pushing it into Jasper's hand before setting off again, a little slower this time.

****

Amelia stood at the gateway, every molecule in her body grating violently against the rest. The dark that usually lingered behind her closed eyelids was flecked with brilliant specks of colour, like a fluorescent glitter bomb had been detonated somewhere out of sight. What was happening to her? She thought of Jalissa burning up in flames and of Aarav, angry and afraid inside his vortex of wind. Was this how they had been feeling? Out here, the air was still and calm, as if waiting for her to unleash. A small part of her wanted to. The pressure inside her had built to an almost intolerable level; it felt as if powerful streams of magic would erupt from her palms if she didn't keep her fists tightly clenched together. Her fingers twitched. How good would it feel to just... let... go?

Somewhere, a fox screamed in the dark; a vixen calling out for a male. Amelia froze and then sighed as the eerie sound faded away. Fight, flight, or freeze. She had subconsciously chosen the right one. She let out a long, slow breath. Aarav and Jalissa had fought, and look where that had got them. Another breath. The road ahead lay black and forbidding, though even that seemed like a sanctum compared to what she would face behind her. She couldn't run away yet, though; she had to warn Jasper. She had seen his face just before Mark had burst into the kitchen. He had felt whatever had happened, just as she had. Maybe they could run together? All she had to do was hang in there long enough to grab him.

Before she had come to Marlborough, she used to pretend to be someone else whenever things got tough, or she needed more confidence. She had fallen out of the habit once she'd met Morgan. Now Johns came to mind. Strong, capable Johns who never flapped or panicked when things went wrong. Just the kind of person she needed to be right now. Surely he would be able to handle magic and not get caught? She took another deep breath and focused. Like an actress preparing to go on stage. If she could convince herself that she was just like capable Johns, then she would manage. She had to.

Suddenly, sirens were screaming in the distance. She could make out blue lights reflecting off the trees lining the road. The noise intensified as the vehicles came closer, jangling with the chaos inside her. Amelia jumped up and down, waving her hands, relieved when she saw the right indicators coming on. This gateway was easily missed in the dark.

"Down there," she said as the lead ambulance paused beside her, the driver leaning out of the window. She pointed along the drive. "Ignore the first turning and keep going past the house. Someone will meet you in the yard at the back."

"Right you are, mate," the paramedic called out over the din, holding up a thumb in thanks.

Behind them came another ambulance and three fire engines. She followed on behind, watching the mesmerising number of lights shattering the darkness. She had the distinct feeling that she was heading back into a maelstrom. She clung to Johns' persona and kept her breathing slow and controlled, just like a meditation. Amelia couldn't handle this, but Johns could.

27

NIRIM STOOD AT THE DINING ROOM WINDOW, LOOKING down. The driveway was lit with small solar-powered lights. From here he could see almost all the way down to the gateway. There was no sign of Amelia. With an exasperated sigh, he left Pazia and went downstairs. The first person he saw outside was Mark.

"Have you seen the girl, Amelia? Did she return from the gate?"

"I don't know, sir; I haven't seen her. I've been with the paramedics."

Biting back a curse, Nirim was about to order him to start searching when Johns came around the side of the house. He was walking slower than usual, looking shaken and afraid.

"Johns," Mark hurried over, "are you alright?"

Johns took a step back and rubbed a hand over his forehead. He looked at it for a second; it was trembling.

"Johns," Mark's voice was raised now; he sounded concerned. "What's the matter, is it your head?" He turned to Nirim, who had come up behind them, "He fell, sir, and hit it in the woods when a branch fell on..."

"Have you seen Amelia?" Nirim had no patience for such time-wasting.

"I..." Johns shook himself, seeming to recover a little. "She was here, but I don't know where she went."

Nirim tutted his annoyance. "If you see her, send her to me." He gave Johns a less than favourable look, "And get yourself seen to." He nodded in the direction of the ambulances before turning back to Mark. "You go search the house." Without waiting for any response, he strode away. The girl could not hide forever.

"I think you're okay." The paramedic removed the oximeter from Armitage's finger. "But your saturation level is a tad low; I want you to come to the hospital for a full check-up."

Armitage shook his head; there was no time for that. He eased the oxygen mask away from his mouth. "I have somewhere urgent I need to be," he said, a little hoarsely. "I can check into A&E later if need be."

The paramedic didn't look pleased, though he made no attempt to persuade him. "If you won't come back with us, at least make sure you drink lots of water, and I mean lots, for the next couple of days."

Armitage nodded. Blue lights reflected across his face as the other ambulance rolled past, taking Gipton away to the hospital. The feeling of pure oxygen going down into his chest was wonderful. It had lessened the irritation that had been causing him to cough, but he couldn't sit here any longer. He pulled the mask off, handing it over.

The paramedic took it with practised disappointment. "See if you can get someone at the house to make you a drink of hot water and ginger root. The ginger will help your lungs, as well as your blood circulation, and the hot drink will help your body get rid of anything that the smoke brought in."

Armitage raised an eyebrow in disbelief—as if a drink could help clear his lungs.

"It will get something called your cilia moving again," the paramedic explained, beginning to pack away his equipment, "a bit like tiny hairs on your cells. That in turn will help your saliva and mucus to flow, which will carry out any contaminants."

He had dealt with plenty of people like this, those who thought they were too important to stop what they were doing and get the medical attention they needed. *Horses,* he called them. *You can bring them to water, but you can't make them drink.* It used to frustrate him; now he was resigned to it. All he could do was advise them; the rest was up to them.

The firemen couldn't get near enough to the fire with their equipment from the yard. They had assessed the situation, and already specialist vehicles were on their way. Meanwhile, their engines needed to move to the emergency access gates closest to the seat of the fire. They began turning around in the limited space, wheels crunching on the tarmac, before heading back down the drive. The remaining ambulance followed a few minutes later. Without the flashing lights, the night seemed darker than ever.

Alistair had timed his longer route back well. As he led Jasper across the yard, they met Blain striding from the house.

"Nirim tells me that Amelia has gone missing. Have you seen her?"

"I have not." Alistair toyed with the end of the crystal cord. Unpleasant waves of something verging on pain wove through Jasper, setting his teeth on edge and detracting his attention away from the joy he felt knowing that Amelia might have got away.

"She was seen heading to the gate." Blain's voice was tight with anger. "I've questioned the staff. They say she was very upset at the news of the fire, so they sent her to guide in the emergency services. Johns saw her briefly after that, near the house, but then nothing."

Shadows hid Alistair's face. He sounded more interested than annoyed. "Where is he now?"

Blain looked taken aback for a moment, then shrugged, "I've no idea; I haven't seen him since we brought back Gipton. It was Nirim who spoke to him."

"Has the girl ever absconded before?" Alistair's hand stilled on the cord.

Jasper's face broke into a grin as soon as the sickening waves stopped. He hoped Amelia was running as fast as possible.

"Do you think this is all we have, boy?" Alistair had not raised his voice, but there was a steel edge to it that his words only served to sharpen. "These ropes are child's play compared to the other methods we can employ. Do you want me to show you what else we have?" He put a hand in his pocket and began pulling out something small that glinted as it caught the light from one of the house windows. Jasper's face reddened. What he had mistaken for almost kindness now looked far more like unnervingly calculated calm. He shook his head, desperately hoping that the man would change his mind.

He looked towards Blain, but there was no help to be had for him there. Of all the children taken in at Marlborough House, Jasper had fooled Blain the most. He would have put money on the boy being an innocent, had even said so to Alistair and Armitage only that morning. He didn't like to be wrong, to be made to look like a fool. He glared back at Jasper with such hatred in his eyes.

Just then, there was a cry from the house. Mrs Lee, standing on the step, bathed in light from the kitchen hallway, had just noticed the cord wrapped around Jasper. Her sweet boy, the one who could always make her smile. A tear swelled in her eye, dripping onto her cheek. Dorothy appeared beside her, mouth gaping open in shock. Jasper saw their faces and dropped his eyes in shame.

Alistair continued to search the boy's face for a few moments longer, then, as if he had read the answer he was looking for, pushed his hand back into his pocket and turned his attention back to Blain. "Where is Armitage?"

"Here," a croaky voice called from behind them. Armitage opened the back door of his van. "Bring him over here, and I'll get him loaded up and out of your way."

There was a small hole in the solid bulkhead that shut the front seats off from the rear compartment through which the handle of the crystal cord was threaded. Even in transit, Jasper was not going to be given any release. He sat on the seat looking at his feet, thinking that the mud on his soles was the last mud he was ever going to see. The doors slammed shut, and what little light there had been evaporated. Seconds later, Jasper felt a tug on the rope as Armitage fastened the handle to a hook inside the cab. He felt the sudden urge to urinate. He shouted out, but the front door banged shut, and he was left alone in the cold van with nothing but his full bladder and whirring mind for company.

****

Amelia had walked slowly back from the gate, relieved and disturbed to have been left alone in the dark. The way that paramedic had spoken to her had made her uneasy. Then she had walked into Nirim and Mark, and what had happened there had thrown her even more. She looked down at her hands, hoping to see her slim fingers and long, narrow palms. Instead, she saw the large, square hands with short, stubby fingers that she had seen before. Man's hands. Her breath caught in her throat.

The barn loomed silently at the other side of the yard. No one was paying any attention as she slipped past one of the retreating fire engines and made her way over to it. The door closed quietly behind her. She collapsed back against it. *Oh god! What am I going to do?* Duke moved to look expectantly out of his stall, his breath ghosting into the cold air. Amelia didn't even notice. Her head was spinning with the craziness of it all. She had willed herself to become Johns—had wanted his calm, controlled manner—and somehow it had happened. She couldn't recall feeling the change come over her. Then again, the cacophony of things she was feeling just now was enough to mask anything. She turned away and fell to her knees, pressing her forehead down onto the dry, earthen floor. She didn't want to be a man; she wanted to be herself.

Outside, she heard the final ambulance pull away, then voices. Blain, talking with Alistair. She heard her name mentioned; already they knew she was missing. A new wave of fear spiked through her, dancing with the magic that still fizzled and burned for release. Judging by the anger in Blain's voice, she wouldn't stand a chance if they found her. Changing back to herself would have to wait; she had to get away. But how? She felt a stab of guilt at the thought of Jasper. She had given up her best chance at escape to come back and search for him, all for nothing. She couldn't hang about to warn him now. She had to get away the moment the yard was clear.

Not waiting to listen to the rest of what the men were saying, she crept away from the doors. Even if they thought she was already away and running, they were bound to look in the outbuildings sooner or later. The barn was not completely dark; chinks of light speared through the walls and under the doors. They picked out the hulking shapes of the small tractor, the ride-on mower, and the three wheelbarrows, up-tipped onto their front ends and stacked like hugging friends, but not much more. She knew there was an array of old ropes and disused harnesses hanging on the rear wall that no one ever used. There hadn't been any carriages at Marlborough House in decades. If she could get in amongst them, hopefully, they would be enough to cover even Johns' form.

They were reassuringly heavy as she eased her way through them. She tasted cobwebs and bit back an urge to shriek. She couldn't think of spiders just now. Bracing herself, she arranged the harnesses around her. She was right back against the wall when she felt something hard and round pressing into her back. It felt distinctly like a doorknob. More magic? Amelia neither knew nor cared. She reached behind her and twisted. The knob turned easily enough, though the door it was attached to did not move. After a little more groping around, Amelia's fingers closed on the curling handle of an iron bolt. She gave it a tentative tug. With a piercing grating of rusted metal, it gave a little. She froze. Blain wasn't stupid; he would know such a noise could not possibly have come from Duke.

Even her breath sounded loud as she waited for the door to burst open. She inhaled as slowly as she could. The harnesses smelled of dust, with the faintest hint of Neatsfoot oil. It had been a very long time since that had last been applied, and the leather felt hard and cracked beneath Amelia's fingers. She clung to one of the straps, her chest hurting with anxiety and the frantic pounding of her heart. In complete contrast, the air around her felt tomb-like and calm. Then Duke shifted his weight and pawed through the shavings on the floor of his stall. His hoof thumped lightly onto the rubber matting beneath.

Amelia let out her breath; there was no one coming. A vehicle moved in the yard, the rumble of the engine sounding loud in the quiet night. Amelia took her chance, yanked the rusted bolt back, and shoved the door open just wide enough to slip through. It was immediately obvious why it had been forgotten. The tennis court on the other side was almost completely destroyed by the encroaching woodland. It hadn't been magic at all, just pure luck that she had found it.

She ran, not stopping until she was deep amongst the trees. Here the thickness of the undergrowth forced her to slow her pace. She caught the occasional smell of smoke and heard the odd shout coming from the men busy fighting the distant fire. It did nothing to calm her nerves. She was a mess of cuts and scratches. Her clothing was torn, her throat burning from gulping at the frigidly cold air. She staggered on a little further until a pheasant broke screaming from the undergrowth almost underfoot. Her nerves couldn't take any more. She fell to the ground, shaking and terrified, and let the tears come at last.

****

Rain was dripping from his collar, trickling uncomfortably down between his shoulder blades. It was soaking through his clothing, finding easiest passage at the seams. It was that fine, incessant kind of rain that seemed quite light at first but just never let up. The biting wind was the real problem, though. It had a Siberian edge to it that cut through Thaniel's wet clothes. Ahead of him, the path lay wide and open, a straight line through the flat, unending landscape. It appeared to be bare and empty. That was as misleading as the rain.

You could not see fear, nor aggression, anxiety, or dread. Yet the air was choked full of them. It should have looked like a pea-soup fog, so thick was the malice surrounding him. Thaniel imagined lurid greens, dark ambers, and poisonous mauves, but those colours only existed in his mind.

A number of times he had stepped off the path, trying to find another way. Without fail, after only a few steps, his path had become blocked. At first, thorny bushes had sprouted up, with vicious barbs that tore his thin clothing, forcing him back to the path. The second time, it had been a flock of birds with razor-edged talons and long, sharp beaks. They had swirled overhead like red kites at a feeding station, taking turns to swoop down and attack. His third attempt found the ground peppered with shards of glass, growing up like clear-bladed stalagmites, barring his way.

He had lost track of how long he'd been trudging this suffocating road. There was nothing else, had been nothing else at all in his life, but this. He had faint memories of a pair of loving arms and his mother's voice crying out his name. Nothing more. How long did it take to drown in despair?

All of a sudden, something caught his attention. The tiniest orb of light, like a far-off star. It spoke of freedom and release. As he watched, it grew larger, and he realised that it was drawing closer. A spark of hope ignited within him, like a cigarette lighter's flame spurting into life. He knew this presence, knew her for the love he bore her, even though he had always been on this lonely, isolated road.

They were connected in a way that Thaniel could not explain. She was a star now because he had failed to save her. He had watched her die, over and over. The last time he had dreamt of her, something had changed. He had felt it within, like the snapping of a tendon. Then the joy of her appearance caught in his throat. It sat there like a scream waiting to unfurl because he knew, with the certainty of his heartbeat, that if she reached the road, she would be just as trapped as he was. He wanted to shout out to her, to warn her not to come any closer, but his longing for her chained his tongue. *Selfish, you're so selfish,* he berated himself even as he watched the other half of his heart draw inexorably closer.

When the orb was only feet away, he realised that it was not perfect. If a star could limp, it was doing so now. Her edges were ragged and her glow dimming. Thaniel could feel her misery, her need for him reaching out through the invisible oppression. He knew then, without a shadow of a doubt, that this time he really was her last and only hope.

28

"Get up."

Amelia startled at the voice. She was further dragged out of sleep by the sound of a whistle blaring in the distance. For a brief second, she had no idea where she was. Then it all came flooding back: the fire, the tumultuous feelings of uncontrollable magic exploding through her. Johns. She gasped, opening her eyes to find Blain standing over her.

"I said, Get up," he hissed through gritted teeth. He had a crystal cord coiled around his hand and a look of utter fury on his face.

Fear gripped her insides with fingers of molten iron. She could feel their heat as they squeezed away her last remnants of hope. It surprised her to find that the cord didn't hurt. After what she had witnessed with Aarav and Jalissa, she had expected it to feel like a lasso of electricity. Even Blain looked surprised at her lack of reaction. It took him a minute to realise that she was the first young magician he had caught who was not out of control. Amelia was frightened, but he didn't think she was using magic. She would soon learn what the device was capable of the second she tried. Blain hoped she would. It would give him satisfaction to see her suffer.

He pulled the cord unnecessarily tight. She could have cost him his home with her stupid actions. Pazia had already ordered his staff to pack their bags and leave. They had been relocated to a hotel far out of the way. How much they would be allowed to remember had not yet been divulged to him. A frisson of annoyance crawled over his skin when he thought of how impotent he now was in his own home. Vehicles had come and gone all night, and by first light, Marlborough House had been in total lockdown, its usual residents replaced by people from Blackwell.

Nothing had been said to Blain, yet he sensed disapproving looks from all angles. That a ward of his should be putting them all to such trouble was not only a reflection of his levels of discipline but, he worried, could also give serious doubts to his future usefulness to the oligarchy. He had worked too hard to be bested by a filthy magician girl. So when the search parties had left at dawn, he had headed straight for the barn. It had been searched the night before, but Blain wouldn't put it past Amelia to come creeping back when all was quiet. She would be scared and alone and looking for somewhere familiar to hunker down.

It had been the broken cobwebs that had given her away. Thick layers of yellowing dust coated everything at the back of the barn, including the old webs. Obvious only to someone who knew the barn well, they'd swayed in the breeze from the newly found door like flags marking the way. The little bitch had almost outsmarted him again. Whilst the evidence of her headlong crash through the undergrowth had been easy enough to follow, once he was through the door, had she closed it properly, he doubted he would have ever remembered it was there.

Amelia stood dejected. He would get no fight out of her to satisfy his sense of injustice. "Have you used up your magic already?" he jibed. "Or could you not get that right either?"

A whistle sounded in the distance. One of the search parties was getting closer. A few more minutes and he'd have been too late. Blain gave up his goading.

"Move," he snapped.

****

"How did you get past everyone?" Nirim stood in front of Amelia, his eyes narrowed. The girl did not look like much of a menace and certainly not someone with the wit to outsmart the likes of them. There was a leaf still stuck in her hair, and he could smell the earthy scents of the woodland wafting from her. It annoyed him almost as much as her disappearance had.

Amelia felt the hairs on the back of her neck rise as she looked up at the tall, dark man. The last remnants of doubt that she had really turned into Johns floated away like gossamer on the breeze. In the dark confusion of the previous evening, she'd had no need to lift her eyes to meet Nirim's. At six foot three, willow-thin Johns looked down on most people, a detail she had failed to grasp at the time.

"Answer me, girl." Nirim nodded at Blain, who flicked the crystal cord still wrapped tightly about her. Amelia braced herself, though no pain followed.

Alistair looked pointedly at the smoothly polished terminating crystals. "That cord will only work when she's using her powers," he said, resisting the urge to roll his eyes at Nirim's ignorance; the oligarch really should have known they would never give an unrestricted cord to just anyone. Alistair looked at Amelia with a coldly assessing gaze. "But you are fully in control of your powers, aren't you? I suspect you've had them for quite a while, or you would never have been able to withstand the nexus so well."

A fresh wave of fear bloomed inside Amelia. Acting like this, Alistair was more terrifying than Nirim and Blain put together. How had she not seen that before? "I... I can heal myself a little." Her voice came out thin and quavering. "I don't know about anything else."

"You're lying."

Amelia blinked. Somewhere deep inside her, she felt a flutter of something completely unexpected. Wrapped deep within the crippling fear she had felt ever since Blain had jarred her awake... was a spark of hope. Not the desperate feeling she'd had when trying to escape; this was different, joyous, as if something wonderful had just come within her reach. Alistair tilted his head to one side, like a jackdaw listening. Could he sense it? His eyes bored into hers as if they could draw out the answers he sought through sheer will alone. Amelia had no idea where the feeling was coming from, but she hung on to it with everything she had.

"I didn't want any magic. I... I was scared to use it; I just wanted to be normal." She turned desperately to Blain,

"You'd have known, wouldn't you, if I'd been using it? It would have left some sort of trace, and you'd have known. Isn't that how you catch everyone?"

Blain's lip curled in disgust as she addressed him. As if it wasn't bad enough that she had almost evaded them, now she was clarifying his failings for everyone else to hear. Beside him, Nirim bristled.

"You know I haven't been using any magic," Amelia insisted.

Behind the men, a dark grey van crawled ominously into the yard. None of them turned to look at it.

Alistair's voice held a note of triumph. "So, you know enough to be able to evade detection. Clever girl. It is no matter; I will get to the bottom of what you can do soon enough. You will not be so smug then."

Smug? She was pleading for her life; how could he not see that?

The van pulled to a halt alongside them. Armitage jumped from the driver's seat, and Amelia's fear went up another notch. With it went the grain of hope, still nestling inside her like an incubating egg.

"Any problems with the boy?" Alistair asked, without turning from Amelia.

Armitage shook his head. "Quiet as a mouse by the time I left him." He reached back into the van and pulled out his own, far longer cord with its multi-faceted crystals. He looped it three times around Amelia, then let Blain's drop to the floor.

Alistair continued to hover over her for a few more moments, then with a flick of his head, she was dismissed.

Armitage pulled on the cord, and Amelia felt a jolt of shocking pain run through her body.

****

Music drifted from the front of the van. Armitage was singing along, his voice following a tune no musician had ever made. He carried on regardless, in between bouts of coughing. How could he be so happy when he was taking her to her death? Amelia was so scared she felt sick, but even as it threatened to overwhelm her, that thread of hope flared again. Was she going mad? The only thing she should be feeling was paralysing terror, yet for some reason a tiny part of her felt as if she were being pulled, inexorably, towards something wonderful.

For the second time in twelve hours, Armitage pulled up outside Blackwell. He was suffering more than he cared to admit after the incident with the fire and was relieved to finally be able to get some rest. It was unusual to bring new arrivals in this way. Normally they were walked the last mile through the surrounding woodland, arriving thoroughly demoralised and with all hopes of escape driven out of them. If he could have brought both the little fiends in together, he would have walked them, but that stupid girl had forced him to make two rushed trips. Ordinarily he would have been impressed at her tenacity, but he had no energy now for anything other than impatience.

A face appeared at the small, barred window in Sheldon Wing's unobtrusive red door. Armitage waved a friendly hand as he walked to the back of the van and pulled open the doors.

"Welcome to your new abode."

Fear crept like vomit up Amelia's throat, giving her no time to take in the actual meaning of his words. She was pushed up a handful of steps and in through the now-open door. Inside, she found herself face-to-face with a sullen-looking man.

"They found her then," Coates said, giving Amelia a cursory glance. "She don't look like much. Then again, most of 'em don't. You look like shit, though. Get her stowed, and I'll have a coffee ready for you."

Amelia was too afraid to even cry. She was pulled after Armitage down a chilly corridor. It was brighter than she'd expected, though. The floor was tiled in red, the lower walls in deep green, and the rest in cream. They walked in silence until they came to a heavy, reinforced steel door set into the wall. Lights flickered on as it opened, illuminating a short hallway containing four ominous-looking holding cells. Almost immediately, a voice began shouting from behind the only closed door.

"Jasper!" Amelia yelled, pulling forward in an attempt to reach the small viewing window.

"Oh no you don't, missy." Armitage grabbed her arm, letting the restraining cord fall to the floor. He shoved her into the cell diagonally across from Jasper's and slammed the door behind her. Jasper's desperate voice was no match for both heavy doors; it cut off into a muted, incoherent sound.

"Shut up, you." Armitage banged against Jasper's cell on his way past, then the heavy outer security door thudded closed and the hall light went out.

Amelia pressed her face to the tiny window in her door, imagining Jasper doing the same. All she could see was the band of light from his cell reaching out into the unattainable void between them. She didn't want him to be here, yet she couldn't help being grateful that neither of them was completely alone. A shadow moved through the light as Jasper backed away from his door. Amelia closed her eyes and swallowed back a sob before turning.

The cell itself was clean and warm, with painted walls instead of old-fashioned tiles, but that was about all that could be said for it. The furniture consisted of an uninviting bed, a hard chair, and a small table by the door. Behind a flimsy curtain, in barely enough space to contain them, was a small toilet and sink. A thin green towel hung from a rail on the wall. High up on the opposite corner, a small camera with its tiny red flashing light observed the room in silence.

Amelia sat on the bed, wrapped her arms around herself, and tried not to think of who could be watching. Did they think she was stupid enough to sit here and do magic? She thought of Aarav and Jalissa and the two other empty cells. How long had they been kept here before the end? Tipping sideways onto the unforgiving mattress, she curled up into as tight a ball as she could and let the tears fall. She must have dozed off for a while because she awoke with a start when the security door clanged. Her cell door opened seconds later, and the man called Coates stepped in, carrying a tray.

"Amelia," Jasper's voice followed him in.

She jumped to her feet. "Yes, I'm here."

The table was right by the door. Coates plonked the tray down with one hand, held the other out as if to ward her off, and backed out of the cell without saying a word. The door closed behind him with a resounding thud, turning Jasper's reply into muffled incoherence. Amelia reached the small window just in time to see Coates opening Jasper's door.

"Are you okay?" she yelled, frantic to get the words in before they were cut off again.

"Yeah," Jasper shouted back. "Do you think Aarav is…"

Coates slammed the door, making the rest of the sentence unintelligible. A moment later the main door closed, and the hallway went dark. Amelia wanted to thump her door in frustration. Judging from the odd noises she heard coming from outside, Jasper was not so restrained. She turned and leaned back against the door, closing her puffy eyes. She swallowed hard, determined not to cry again.

Coates had brought her a cafeteria tray, each section containing a portion of equally unappealing food. Liquidised shepherd's pie, faded marrowfat peas, and what looked like some kind of watery tapioca. The final section held a small, dry cereal bar in a shiny wrapper. There was no drink.

As unappetising as it all looked, Amelia's stomach was quick to remind her how long it had been since she had last eaten. She remembered seeing a cup sitting by the sink in the tiny bathroom and helped herself to water from the tap. A wayward tear rolled down her face as she picked up the strange-looking wooden utensil and began to eat, unable to decide if she was grateful to be still alive or terrified of staying here too long.

****

They came and took Jasper away later that day. Amelia hadn't been able to see what had been used on him, but his terrified shouts had cut off abruptly before he was led from his cell. For the next three days, Amelia was left alone. Her only company was the ominously watching camera on the wall and the ever-present fear that had travelled with her from Marlborough House. Her meals were brought in silence. Any questions she dared to ask the brooding Coates went unanswered. She was so frightened that her body shook constantly. Barely anything she ate stayed down, her stomach muscles hurt from retching, and her jaw was so tight that even her teeth seemed to ache.

The strange spark of hope she had felt at her capture reignited inside her every so often throughout the first day, like a spirit calling out to her to stay strong. It stopped after that. Whatever it had been had deserted her, and she was left feeling hollow and terrified once more. She pretended it had been the dream boy calling out to her. In the moments between tears and sleep, she would fill her mind with memories of their encounter on the beach: the touch of his hands on her body, the pressure of his lips on hers.

350

Yet no matter how hard she tried to cling to the thoughts, sooner or later that final wave would break over them, and with it the stark reality of her situation would come crashing back.

29

CLIVE GRECKHAM FOLDED HIS ARMS AROUND HIMSELF and rested his head back on his chair. The pain that had incapacitated him for almost twenty-four hours had finally abated, leaving him feeling like week-old, wet paper. He closed his eyes and let out a long, slow breath. He had always known that the magical kickback would be bad, but he had grossly underestimated just how intense it would be. When the room stopped spinning and his trembling lessened, he would try to make it the rest of the way to the kitchen.

Outside, the day was dull, the winter sun struggling to burn through the light covering of cloud. He smiled to himself, imagining the escalating tempers and angry voices over the coming weeks as the oligarchy eventually realised that what they were looking for was not, in fact, there at all. Staggering back to his feet, he wove through the doorway and into the kitchen. The pineapple juice was cold, hitting his throat like a shock of energy.

There was a loud ringing as someone downstairs pressed the doorbell. Clive ignored it. Even over the intercom, he was not himself enough to risk speaking to anyone. He rubbed a hand over his face, needing no mirror to know who he looked like just now. Ordinarily it would have taken him mere moments to set his features back in order, but after the pummelling his mind and body had just taken, that was not going to be possible just yet.

He felt sad for the destruction of Stanton Mead's cottage. The smaller of the two in the wood, it had been packed full of character. The magician had never been overly house-proud, and the garden had run mainly to weeds, but there had been a charm about the place that even Stanton's peculiarities had not been able to eradicate.

Stanton had been a scholar, his mind able to store and retrieve information most people would need a library to hold. He had spent many years working at the university until his cantankerous nature and increasing temper had forced his early retirement. Clive knew that beneath it all there was a genius who wanted nothing more than to be left alone to collate and protect everything he could about the history of magic.

Despite his encyclopaedic knowledge, he'd owned a great number of books, including numerous rare editions, some not even recorded. Clive could remember many a time when he had found Stanton with his nose buried deep in a dusty tome, a cup of stone-cold coffee by his arm, and what had once been intended as his dinner reduced to carbon in the oven. It had been hard watching his old friend's descent into something akin to madness, and Clive had missed him terribly since his death.

The pineapple juice was working its way through his system. He sat for a few more minutes as the weakness and trembling gradually left him, then, almost without thought, he pushed himself to his feet, grabbed a set of keys, and headed unsteadily downstairs. He paused in the lobby. There was a missed delivery note pushed through the right-hand letterbox. The courier was still outside in his van. Clive made no attempt to catch him. Instead, he turned to the door of the ground-floor flat and let himself in.

His bare feet padded on the parquet floor as he crossed the empty sitting room. There was no other sound, not even the ticking of a clock. He made his way to an ordinary-looking door in the back hall. The top corner had been cut off to allow for the slope formed by the stairs up to his own flat. It was locked. He inserted a brass key into the rusty keyhole. The barrel of the lock turned smoothly, and the door swung outward, revealing a set of stone steps leading down to a large cellar.

Enormous wooden bookcases lined one wall, overflowing with books, many of which were ancient and in various stages of decay. In the centre of the room stood a hefty oak table, on which sat a sloped bookstand, numerous pots of ink, stacks of thick paper, and a collection of calligraphy pens. Clive had lost count of the hours he had spent down here, laboriously copying out the worst of the books, for no amount of magic could stabilise the decay forever, and the contents were far too valuable to be lost.

Once the duplication work was completed, each new volume had to be carefully bound. He finished them with hard leather covers, glamoured to appear plain and uninteresting. Clive inhaled the rich smells of parchment, ink, and leather and smiled. The deception, the keeping of such highly coveted, magical texts out of the hands of the oligarchy, was more than just rebellion. Someone had to protect the knowledge when their rulers seemed so hell-bent on eradicating it all.

The stairs had been too much too soon. Pineapple juice was great stuff, but when the damage was this deep, it needed time to work. He perched on the edge of the table and ran a light hand over the book on the stand. It was one of those he had rescued from Stanton's house after his friend had been taken. It had been easy for Clive to pass through the thickening undergrowth, noticing, each time he did so, the increasing signs that others had tried, and failed, to do the same. It had taken him many trips until he was satisfied that he had acquired everything of literary and magical value. The current book on the stand was not in such bad condition compared to some of the others he had saved. One or two had crumbled to dust before he could finish reproducing the contents. In others, the ink had faded so much that the words could no longer be deciphered; knowledge now lost forever unless another copy existed elsewhere.

At the base of one of the bookshelves sat a small, locked trunk bound in leather and iron. Clive crouched before it. He pressed his right forefinger to a small indentation beneath the fake keyhole. The clasps sprung open, and he pulled back the lid to reveal his three most important books, the largest of which bore the gilded words: The Tome of Time and Reason. Beneath it, at the bottom of the trunk, was a photograph. Clive picked it up. "They will never get the book," he told the woman pictured, "but they have finally found the nexus I set up inside Stanton's defences." He grimaced, his eyes tightly shut. "Those poor children at Marlborough."

Florence smiled benignly at him, one hand placed protectively over her swelling stomach. Clive Greckham, the harmless stone carver he was masquerading as, had no reason to think much of children. He was a confirmed bachelor, enjoying the auspices his successful career brought him, and he was as settled as he was ever going to get. It was a useful façade that served him well. Closing his eyes could not stop images of his old life and the family he had lost many years ago flooding his mind. The hurt was still there, carved so deeply into his soul that he would never take on another. It had been finding out that their deaths were closely linked to Jane Kelby, wife of the Master Oligarch that had set him on his current path: to do whatever it took to stop the oligarchy.

As Clive, he had learnt enough over the years to know that, despite their assurances, the ruling body was not, in fact, trying to eliminate magic. Instead, they were hoarding it, sealing it off, and keeping it solely for their own use. Many magicians had died over the years, especially during the Purge, but Clive was now convinced that the oligarchy only ever disposed of those who were of no use to them. After all, what was the point in hoarding magic if you had no one to perform it for you? Whether that use was willingly given was something that had Clive regularly waking up in the middle of the night, a cold sheen of sweat soaking his body.

It was the children who were the key to their plans; he was sure of it. The slightest hint of any child developing powers and the Guard would sweep in and drag them from their homes. As if that wasn't bad enough, those damn guardian houses had been set up to rake out emerging magicians from all those unfortunate enough to have lost their families. Clive had been watching them for years and had grave concerns for anyone placed in them. He had his suspicions as to where they were all taken, though he had yet to confirm it.

At least there was one pocket of free magicians hidden away at the very edge of the oligarchy's reach. Etherea Forest was a place where magic ran through every root and leaf. Clive had spent a good deal of time there, nursing his grief and formulating his plans. He had been back a number of times since, and each time, the population had grown. With a shake of his head, he brought his attention back to the present. His legs were starting to hurt; even without needing more pineapple juice, he was long past the age where crouching for any length of time was comfortable. Giving Florence one last smile, he placed the photograph back in the trunk and closed the lid, hearing the satisfactory click as the locks set back in place. Stiffly, he got to his feet, stretching out his limbs and stamping away the pins and needles.

The picture of Florence had reminded him of his neighbour. He hadn't been able to see her for a few days, and though the unfinished copy of the open book on the table called to him, he ignored the inkwell and the old-fashioned pen he preferred to use and made his way back upstairs. He paused briefly to check himself in the mirror.

Almost satisfied, he helped himself to one of his mints and took his time to dress.

****

Enid Blackshaw was sitting in her conservatory, making the most of the emerging winter sunshine through the glass. Her knitting needles worked so fast that the ends blurred, even though her eyes remained fixed on a coal tit pecking away at the peanut feeder hanging from her bird table. Clive had his own key, but he pressed the doorbell anyway before letting himself in. Lights flashed from the chime unit, and the pager Enid kept with her vibrated. Her needles stilled. She made to get up, smiling as she realised who it was.

Clive mimed drinking and disappeared into the kitchen to put the kettle on. A quick scan in the fridge and cupboards showed that Enid was getting low on essentials. He grabbed one of the notepads she kept lying around the place and scribbled a note offering to take her shopping. He placed it on the tray with their cups and the teapot.

Back in the conservatory, Enid nodded at the note then eyed him shrewdly. "You look tired," she said, a little too loudly.

Clive poured out the drinks, tore off the top note, and wrote a new one. *I've had a migraine, but ok now.*

She continued to study him for a few more moments and then nodded. She'd never been one to fuss. "I was hoping you would pop round today." She gave him a nod of thanks as he poured her tea and placed the cup in front of her. "I think the offer on toilet roll is still on at the supermarket. I can't manage them all in my shopping trolley."

Enid had no need to keep an eye on her money, but she had been raised to be frugal, and the habit was deeply ingrained. Clive was used to it. He stuck his thumb up to indicate he would take her, then pointed to the knitting with a quizzical look.

"It's a doll's dress for the retirement club's coffee morning," she told him, stroking the wool on her knee. Beside her in a small, grey craft bag, a pattern book was folded open to reveal a blue and white sailor dress with matching bootees and hat. "Minnie is going to take me so I can help on the stall."

Clive picked up the pencil again. *When is it?*

"A week on Saturday." Enid pushed a couple of pink rubber end caps onto her needles, rolled the loose wool back around the ball, and packed it all neatly away in the craft bag. She picked up her cup and sipped carefully at the steaming tea. No matter how many times Clive advised her to wait until it cooled a little, she refused to listen. She drank her tea scalding hot, her water ice-cold, and woe betide anyone who offered her a scone with the cream on before the jam.

Clive had known Enid for over twenty years, though she had no idea of that. She thought they'd met just before her husband, Frank, had passed away. Many things were foggy in her memory now. She could remember Frank as if he had just walked out of the room, but what he had done for a living was a mystery to her. She couldn't even remember moving to this house, though she knew deep down that most of her life had been spent somewhere far away from the city.

Further back, her memories were much clearer. She'd had a daughter, Florence. A happy, carefree girl, who had been a joy to both her and Frank. The man her Florence had married had been everything she could have ever wanted in a son-in-law. She hadn't been able to remember his name for a long time now, but he'd been kind, thoughtful, and very protective of his wife. Whenever Enid thought of them together, it filled her with happiness.

The pain of Florence's death had dulled over time, and though she envied the grandchildren of her friend, Minnie, she had stopped shedding tears over the loss of her own. It had hurt that she'd never seen her son-in-law again, not even at Florence's funeral. Frank had tried his best to find him, to let him know that they didn't believe the rumours, but there had been no trace of him anywhere. It had made them so angry that people who had never known the man could consider him a killer. Whoever it was that had murdered their darling daughter, it had not been her husband.

Clive watched her as she drank her tea. She'd had a good life since moving here, a far cry from the one she would have had to endure had he not stepped in when he did. She had no recollection of the magic her family had been capable of; no idea even that she herself had hidden powers. Clive had taken all that knowledge from her when her memory began to fail. It had been one of the most painful things he had ever done. To deny her the essence of who she was seemed a cruel act of care, but there could be no room for slip-ups. As far as all her friends at the retirement club were concerned, Enid was a safe, non-threatening old woman with no links whatsoever to anything they could possibly be afraid of.

Clive had good reason to be so protective, having seen the way people had turned on her and Frank when the early troubles of the Purge began. The couple had lived in the same small village all their married lives, with never a moment of bother. When the outcry about the dangers of magicians erupted, their good deeds and friendships had counted for nothing. As with countless other magical families, their lives had become untenable; no longer safe to leave their home and no longer safe to stay within its walls.

Clive had been there for them then, spiriting the couple and what few belongings they could carry away from the village and setting them up in this new home, where the residents of the street were far more interested in their own lives than that of anyone living nearby. This new life took its toll on Frank. He was no coward, so to deny his magic and do nothing to support others like himself, who were constantly targeted and abused, wore him down. Six months after coming to the city, Frank suffered a massive coronary and passed away.

Enid was a strong woman. She had weathered the changes in her life with fortitude. Grief, though, has a way of hollowing out a person, silently stripping away the parts that others cannot see. Slowly, she began to falter, and with the loss of her hearing came the failing of her memory. She began to forget that her magic had to be kept secret. It was too easy to simply call an object that was out of reach, especially when doing so came as naturally to her as blinking. It was sheer luck that when she had done it one day in the supermarket, Clive had been the only one to witness it. He had known then that it was time to act, however heavy it made his heart feel.

I'll try and make it, he scribbled on the notepad. He was not a coffee morning sort of person, yet every so often, he liked to keep an eye on how well Enid was interacting with her friends. The threat of her using magic might be gone, but there was always the chance of her suddenly remembering something that could, unknowingly, reveal more about her background than was wise.

30

THE GREEN RING OF PROTECTIVE HOLLY TREES WAS obvious now that the surrounding area lay so devastatingly blackened. With most of the canopy gone, the other remaining tree trunks stood out like gnarled, black sentinels. A little heat still radiated off them, though the risk of the fire reigniting was over. The last of the firemen had wound up their hoses and cleared out of the area, leaving nothing but tyre tracks in the water-soaked ground. With their large engines being unable to enter the wood, they had relied on specialist wildfire vehicles, which had no trouble negotiating the rough conditions. One by one, they had pulled away, taking the story of the huge, magical blaze back to their respective fire stations.

Alistair and his team of magicians had spent the last few hours taking down every last vestige of the nexus that had protected Stanton's home so well. It had been a long and tedious process. Thankfully, it was now complete, and they were ready to finally move on to the stage Alistair and the oligarchs had been so desperate to get to. Nirim stood beside Pazia in the wet ashes and looked around with distaste. Along with everyone else, he had forgone his usual footwear, tucking his suit trousers into a pair of dark green wellingtons and trying to ignore how absurd he looked. A good few feet in front of them, Alistair, looking slightly more comfortable in pristine cargo trousers, was quietly talking to two of his older magicians.

"They don't seem to be doing much now," Pazia grumbled, subdued today in a dark navy trouser suit that matched her mood. Her only nods to colour were the bright, floral wellingtons she wore and the rainbow tips of her French manicure.

Nirim gave her a sidelong glance but refrained from answering. For someone who looked so out of place in the countryside, she had been quick to volunteer to come and witness the searching of Stanton Meads' property. If Nirim hadn't already known about Elon's unbreakable prior commitment, he would have suspected her of orchestrating his timetable somehow. If she had indeed been rooting around Marlborough House, she had been very discreet. Not that her antics would do her any good; there was no trace left of the person Blain had once been. He pulled his thoughts back to the low murmuring of conversation ahead, wishing he could hear what was going on.

Pazia rubbed her thumb over her fingernails, trying not to wince at the chip she felt in the polish. Marlborough House had proved very easy to search. Blain kept the property in excellent condition, with not a squeaky hinge or creaking floorboard in the whole place. Even before the staff had been moved out to the hotel, she had covered most of the formal rooms. The hunt for the missing girl had then provided the perfect distraction for her to cover the rest of the house.

At the back of Blain's wardrobe, tucked away in a jacket pocket, she had found the acorn she had been looking for. She knew better than to let her good fortune show; Nirim was already suspicious of her motives. Copies of the bundle of photos she had uncovered were now safely stored on the memory card, zipped inside the hair scrunchie, which she had used to form the filler of her full, high bun. It was a fail-safe method of concealing small items, and one she had used ever since she was at school.

Up ahead, Jarrett and Heather had begun to move forward, leaving Alistair standing like a lone shield between the oligarchs and any possible danger. In the centre of the ring of holly, the chimney stack of the now-exposed ruin still stood upright, the remains of the roof hanging precariously from smoke-blackened walls. The two magicians split and went their separate ways around the remains, stepping slowly as they sensed for anything magical concealed in the rubble. They took their time, each spiralling around the area, covering every inch.

Finally, a shout went up, and they beckoned Alistair. There was a lot of shaking of heads and arm-waving, but no further movement. Nirim grumbled something inaudible, and no doubt offensive, under his breath and started forward.

"Finally," Pazia muttered, catching up to him just as he reached the heated discussion.

"Well?" he interrupted without preamble.

Unfazed by the presence of the oligarchs Jarrett shrugged. "There is nothing here."

Heather, looking slightly intimidated but trying her best to imitate Jarrett, shook her head in agreement.

Nirim visibly bristled. "What do you mean there's nothing?"

For once, Alistair's demeanour had slipped, and he appeared agitated. "The place is clear... empty. Everything is gone."

Pazia stepped closer, fixing her eyes on Jarrett. "Are you certain?"

"Yes," Jarrett said. "Positive. There is nothing here. No magic of any sort; I can't even tell if there ever was any."

Pazia turned to Heather as if expecting her to contradict him.

"It's not like the rest of the wood," Heather hurriedly explained. "The bit that hasn't been burnt, you can feel the magic there, but here," she raised her hands to indicate the ruins, "there is nothing. It's just... normal. Isn't that what you wanted?"

"What we want is none of your concern." Nirim's curt voice brought a flush to Heather's cheeks. "You are here to do what we instruct, not to ask questions."

She dropped her gaze to the ground, waiting for Alistair's reprimand to follow, but it was Pazia who spoke. "Is there any way anything could be cloaked, hidden inside a lead box or something?" Eyeing the ruins with suspicion, she kicked a stone with her muddy boots, sending it skittering across the ground. Small puffs of ash billowed up at each bounce.

"I was brought here because I am the best at tracing magic." Jarrett's tone was respectful, though a touch of pride did not go unnoticed by the oligarchs. "And Heather's gift is cloaking. If there was anything here, we would have found it."

Nirim raised his eyebrows. "Even if it was buried?"

Seeming to recover himself at last, Alistair pulled his phone from his pocket. "I'm going to send for a couple more magicians to help us, and we have diggers on their way. If there is anything here, it will be found."

Nirim nodded brusquely to him, "Keep me updated. I will be back at the house."

****

The outer security door opened. Amelia jumped to her feet. Seconds later, her cell door was flung wide, and she found herself face-to-face with Alistair. It was the first time in the three days she had been here that she had seen anyone other than Coates.

"It appears there is something missing from Fenton Woods. Would you like to tell me where you have put it?"

Though he remained in the doorway, he seemed to loom over her, sucking the air out of her lungs with his presence. She would have taken a step backwards had his stare not pinned her in place.

"I don't know what you mean?" Her voice came out thin and reedy from lack of use.

Alistair's features settled into their usual poker mask, contrasting with the annoyance still evident in his tone. "You might think me a fool, girl. I can assure you I am no such thing. You were missing for several hours before your

367

capture, giving you more than enough time to evade the firefighters, take the item we are looking for, and hide it away somewhere else in the wood. I have my people searching for it, but it would be far better for you if you were to tell me where it is, saving us all a lot of valuable time."

Amelia shook her head. What he was saying didn't make any sense. "I didn't take anything."

In one large stride, he was across the room. Before she could as much as blink, he had her by the throat. "I will not be lied to."

She could feel his hand shaking with anger, so unlike the perfectly controlled man he had been at Marlborough House. She flinched as the spittle from his forced words spattered her face. There had never been any talk of looking for something during his visit. At least, she frowned, they had been looking for the second cottage, but there was no way he could have expected her to take that, could he?

As if he could read her thoughts, his grip tightened, pulling her right up onto her tiptoes. "What?"

His grip was so tight it was beginning to cut off her airways. The edges of her vision started to cloud. Her heart hammered in her chest as if trying to pound the threat away from her. She pulled at his hand, frantic for air, and the pressure eased slightly. Still, she had to strain to get her words out. "Y... you were looking for a cottage. I couldn't have taken that. I can't... do things like that." It seemed ludicrous that she was even having to say the words.

Alistair's face hardened even more, and for a moment, Amelia thought he was going to drive it straight down onto hers. He checked himself and, with a slight shake of his head, thrust her onto the floor. It took him only the space of one breath to get himself back under control. His voice, when he spoke again, held a note of humour.

"You would have me believe you cannot do much, even though we both know that is not the case. Though I have to admit, even I did not think you could move a whole house."

Amelia barely heard him. Her throat was bruised, and she had landed hard on her hands and knees.

Alistair took a step back towards the door and crossed his arms, his long fingers tapping on his sleeves. "I told you I would get to the bottom of what you can do, and that is about to start now. Heal yourself, and then you will follow me to one of our assessment rooms. I am looking forward to seeing exactly what it is you can do."

There was no getting out of it; she was going to have to use her magic in front of him. She closed her eyes and raised her hand to her throat. Even as the pain eased, her fear pulled tighter around her. She opened her eyes to see him watching her as if she were a puzzle to be studied.

"One last thing before we go. Up until now, you have known me by the name Alistair. Here at Blackwell, you will refer to me only as Doyen. Do you understand?"

She didn't, but even had she the courage to admit it, he was not about to let her speak.

"If you fail to do so, I will have my name removed from your memory by force. You will not enjoy the process."

Hours later, Amelia was tired, hungry, and sick of the endless questions and constant demands. Tests designed to show the range of her powers covered the tables surrounding her. They ranged from basic tasks like moving an object to more complex requirements such as attempting to read someone's mind. She had failed a good number of them, yet surprised herself on many more. Doyen might think she was lying when she said she had never practised her magic, but she was not. His face went from downright hostile to one of more considered appraisal as the morning wore on.

"You probably think that all magicians are equal," Doyen said when they finally stopped. "They are not." He waved a hand to dismiss her surprised look. "It is a common misconception. Magic is elemental, and the range of abilities a magician has depends on which of the five elements he or she has an affinity with. I presume you know what the elements are?"

"Fire, Water, Earth, and Air," Amelia heard the tremble of fear in her voice and tried to make it stronger. "I don't know what the other one is."

"The fifth one is Ether." Doyen lifted a sardonic eyebrow. "You have already shown some skills in that area."

Amelia frowned; wasn't that something to do with anaesthetic? Doyen didn't wait for her to ask. This was clearly a lesson he had given many times before.

"Ether deals with all things connected with the spirit and life; you would not be able to heal without it." For a second the fingers of his hand drifted out as if he were about to demonstrate. Instead, they closed around fresh air, and he pulled his arm back. He carried on, oblivious. "Each element governs much more than their names initially suggest. A water magician, for example, may range from someone only able to manipulate that element in its purest form, when no other pressure is exerted on it, right through to someone able to fetch every water molecule out of a living person's body."

Amelia shuddered, both at the words and his indifference to them. If Doyen noticed, he chose to ignore it.

"If, however, they also had control over Ether, they could, to a greater or lesser degree, be able to manipulate a person's emotions. So you see, the different blends and scopes of abilities a magician can have are as individual as their personalities. Most will only have two, or possibly three, elements they can work with, though there are two rare types of magician who can work with all five." Doyen's voice took on a note of reverence. "Rounded magicians may not necessarily have the strongest control over each element, but the combination of all five working together gives them abilities most others could not even begin to dream of. It is a great shame that I have not been able to find one yet, although I am sure it is just a matter of time. Then there are mind magicians, the most coveted of them all. Unlike the rest of you, they need only their thoughts to let their powers flow." A smile threatened to fracture his carefully controlled features. "I was fortunate enough to obtain one of these not so long ago." He paused to take in a self-satisfied breath. "Every magician I have here is powerful." He spoke as if he were a proud collector. "There is no place in Blackwell for any other. Think about that and what it will mean for you if you continue to hide your abilities from me."

After a long, pointed look, he stepped away and swung open the door. Amelia was surprised when a slight woman with auburn hair walked in. She deposited a tray on the corner of the nearest table.

"Thank you, Janson."

Janson nodded and left. Doyen followed her out, and the door closed with barely a sound. Amelia took in a shaky breath. Nothing made any sense.

She longed for the peaceful hours she had spent at her loom or the spinning wheel, back at Marlborough House. Aarav had mocked her for it, calling her dull and boring. She hadn't cared. She had loved the escape of it, the chance to switch off and let the world melt away. She was not an orphan when she worked; she hadn't lost her aunt and her home, her freedom, and her friend. It was just her and the meditative rattle of the loom or tiny squeak of the wheel. She had assumed her future would be much the same. There had been talk of setting her up with a coveted studio workshop at the Greendale Heritage Centre when she was of age to leave. Now, as far as her guardians at Marlborough House were concerned, she was already as good as dead.

Expecting the usual bland meal she was always given, it was a surprise to find a drink of fruit juice along with an overfilled sandwich and a granola bar. Her head ached, and her hands were shaking as she raised the cup to her mouth. Her first sip of the pineapple juice was like drinking heaven. She could feel her tiredness falling away, her headache easing, and the tingling she associated with her magic reviving in her veins. She devoured the food without really tasting it and downed the rest of the drink.

Doyen's last words still rang in her mind. She didn't want to think about what would happen to her if he decided she was not powerful enough to keep; still, she shied away from divulging her ability to steal someone else's identity. She didn't know if self-preservation or shame was behind her compulsion to keep it secret, but it didn't matter; she would not tell. She began to wander around the room. How many of these tests had she already failed?

From high up on one of the walls, she heard a tiny whirring noise and realised, without looking, that a camera must be following her movements. Ignoring it, she held her hand up towards an unlit match at one of the tables. No matter how hard she concentrated, it remained stubbornly unlit. She moved on. Clay wasn't easily malleable for her, but she spent a few minutes moulding a lump of it into the rough form of a person. Then, realising that might be a little too close to changing her own features, she quickly crumpled the form and moved on. She could not predict what the cards, lying face down on a board, were or see anything in the dark obsidian orb, though she could create a small whirlpool in a bowl of water and cause a withering plant to flourish.

At the table containing needles, scalpels, sterile wipes, and scissors, she stopped and sat down. Earlier, she had pricked her finger on a small needle, healing the resulting injury with ease. Now that Doyen was not hovering over her, she took one of the scalpels out of its sealed packet and held it over her palm. Did she have the courage to cut herself?

"You will be needing a bathroom break before we start again."

She had not heard the door open. She jumped and yelped in pain as the blade cut deep into the fleshy mound at the base of her thumb. All thoughts of her healing abilities fled as blood spilt into her cupped hand, dripping down onto the table. It was only the sound of Doyen coming closer that jolted her mind into action. She dropped the scalpel and hovered her palm over the cut, willing it closed. There was a slight prickle, starting deep in the muscle, spreading outwards as the sides of the wound knit together. Only a faint scar remained when she was done.

"Well, that's one test we won't need to bother with now." Doyen waved a dismissive hand. "So far you have shown you can work with Water, Earth, and Ether, but these are just the basic tests. Next, we will move on to the more interesting rooms, where we can begin to assess your strength and potential."

Amelia shuddered at the inflection he placed on the word 'interesting.' She didn't need seer abilities to know she would not like what was coming. Should she mention her nightmares? It could be important that water was constantly trying to kill her. The words were almost out of her mouth when she realised she would then have to mention the boy, and that she was not prepared to do. He was private, even though he had failed to come to her at all since she had been here. It seemed the good things in her life were peeling away, leaving her raw and alone to face whatever this man had in store for her.

As Janson led her away to the toilets, she tried her best to find the spark of hope that had saved her on her journey here. Apart from those few flickers that first day, it had remained obstinately absent. Try as she might, she could not bring it to life. Was it some form of her magic too, one she hadn't yet learnt to control?

"Defensive magic is more instinctive." Doyen tossed a cricket ball up in the air, catching it easily in his large hand. They had relocated to a room across the hall. Here, the tables had been pushed to one side and piled with crates and boxes. Amelia wasn't eager to find out what was inside them. "You have less time to think about what you must do before reacting."

She soon found out what he meant. Slow to rely on her powers when something careered towards her head or startled her from behind, she found herself calling on her healing skills numerous times before Doyen finally called a halt. Janson returned with another pineapple juice. Shakily, Amelia gulped it down.

"Well, you certainly have powers, but so far I have not seen anything that could account for how you managed to pull off your little disappearing trick."

Doyen had remained impassive throughout the testing. Now he was building up to yet another threat. Amelia could see it by the glint in his eye. The fruit juice might be reviving her flagging magical energy, but her anxiety continued to drain her.

When he spoke again, his voice was lighter, surprising her. "It is a great honour being accepted into Blackwell. The sooner you realise that and start working with me, the sooner your life will become more bearable."

For the space of a heartbeat, Amelia thought she had been wrong; that whatever Doyen intended for her might actually be a lifeline. It was only one heartbeat, and then he was speaking again.

"You have seen how well equipped we are to support and train young magicians, though as yet I am not sure your power is such that it will be worth our while keeping you. I was serious earlier when I said that only those who prove themselves useful to us are retained here. This is either the start of a new life for you or the end of it all."

He was watching her intently, studying her face as if he could read her every thought. She could not stop the cold shiver that rippled through her body.

Back in her cell, Amelia curled up on her bed and cried as if her heart would break. Thoughts of Morgan and what her old friend would have done in her situation started to encroach. Quickly, she pushed the girl from her mind. It was too risky. She didn't dare even think of Jasper and what had happened to him. Not knowing how her transformation into Johns had worked, she was scared to let her mind run on. Frightened and alone, cutting herself off from the memory of her friends made her feel even more isolated.

Wrung out from all the tears, tiredness began to weigh on her limbs. Morgan's face smiled at her from behind her eyelids. She never had been one to do as she was bid. The thought brought a flicker of a smile to Amelia's face. Maybe Morgan was in a far better place dead than stuck here? Even Amelia's dream boy had deserted her. If she still had his touch to look forward to every night, life here would not be so bad. But there was nothing to hope for at Blackwell. There was only bleakness and despair.

31

AMELIA WAS WOKEN ABRUPTLY BY THE SOUND OF HER breakfast arriving. She hurried to wash and dress, hardly having time to finish before Janson came for her. The last few days had been monotonous. Hours spent up in the testing rooms with Doyen followed by even more solitary hours spent in her cell. He, at least, had never appeared at her door again, instead sending the silent chaperones, with crystal cords at their belts, to escort her.

This time, she was led to a room she had never been in before. Inside, a large pedestal desk stood to the left of the door. The woman sitting there looked up as they entered. She was dressed in a smart teal-green suit with a crisp, white blouse showing beneath. It was nothing like the grey uniform dress Janson always wore. Without smiling, she dismissed the chaperone, who backed quietly out of the room. Amelia thought she saw a flash of concern on Janson's face, and her stomach knotted.

The woman turned her attention back to the paperwork in front of her, leaving Amelia standing awkwardly in the middle of the room. After a few minutes of staring at the woman's inclined head, her gaze began to wander. The office was far different from anything else Amelia had seen at Blackwell. Wood panelling lined the walls, and beneath her feet lay a rich red carpet. Behind her stood two high-backed leather chairs facing each other over an ornate hearth rug. The fireplace was carved stone, topped with a heavy mantel, its freshly laid grate as cold as the woman at the desk. It was a homely room, quite a surprise in an institution as big and oppressive as Blackwell.

After a few minutes, the woman put down her pen, shuffled the papers together, and tapped their edges on the desk. She placed them in a neat pile and had just risen from her seat when Doyen walked in.

"Thank you, Farle. How is your hand?"

"It seems to have healed well." She flexed her right hand, stretching out each finger in turn.

"Farle is one of the instructors here at Blackwell," Doyen said to Amelia. "She recently had one of our young magicians turn on her in an outrageous attack."

Beside him, Farle glowered at Amelia, as if she had been the one to maim her.

"Of course, the girl in question is no longer capable of either being pleased with or regretting her actions." Doyen did not trouble himself to elaborate any further. Instead, he nodded to Farle, who left the room, closing the door quietly behind her. He greeted Amelia with a smile, not his usual cold thinning of the lips, but a genuine full-faced expression that even reached his eyes. Amelia's unease rose to new levels.

"Take a seat." He indicated to the chairs in front of the hearth, though he himself took the one at the desk, swinging it sideways to face her. "You will have to excuse the slight chill in the room; the fire was only lit a short while ago, and it seems to be taking a while to catch. Still, it should not take long to get going now."

Amelia looked again at the fireplace. Sure enough, there was a thread of smoke pouring up from the kindling. Even as she watched, a flame appeared, quickly followed by another.

"Relax for a few minutes whilst we wait for my other guest."

A lump formed in Amelia's throat. Was Blain coming? He was nowhere near as scary as Doyen, but to face the two of them together...

"You look worried, my girl." Doyen leaned forward, elbows on the chair's arms, his fingers slowly steepling together. "And so you should be. This farcical refusal to admit how you managed to escape from your former place of abode has gone on long enough. I warned you, did I not, that I had ways and means to get what I wanted? But you would not listen."

Despite the initial chill, Amelia could feel the air in the room cloying against her skin as her unease turned to panic. Against her leg, the slight heat beginning to radiate out from the fire felt ominous rather than comforting. The office, which had seemed quite cosy a few minutes ago, now felt even more foreboding than her cell.

"Of course, I have not had the misfortune of undergoing what you are about to endure." Doyen was enjoying her obvious distress. "I imagine having one's mind forcibly invaded is a very unpleasant experience. You can keep on trying to hide what I want to know, but the more you do that, the deeper he is going to have to go."

Amelia snatched her hands from the arms of the chair, half expecting chains and cuffs to appear, ready to clamp her in place. The urge to run was almost overwhelming, but she would never make it to the door before Doyen grabbed her. The fire hissed as a pocket of moisture in one of the logs evaporated. To Amelia, it sounded like laughter. There was a light tap at the door. Doyen moved to open it, his body blocking Amelia's view of whoever had arrived. She had never felt so scared. Tears filled her eyes, blurring her sight. She felt bile rising, the acid burning her throat. She tried to swallow it back down, but its way was blocked by a growing tide of... elation.

Oh god, what was happening? No longer hyperventilating, she blinked her eyes, furiously trying to clear them. As she did, she heard the minutest gasp of shock. Doyen, closing the door and turning the key, didn't hear it, but for Amelia it was as loud as a siren. Her eyes finally cleared, and she looked up, straight into the face of the boy from her dreams.

An explosion of emotions erupted inside her: joy, incomprehension, and concern, all polluted by the realisation that he was Doyen's torturer. A flicker of shock crossed his face, then it was gone, clamped down by the tightening of his jaw. She shook her head. This was all wrong. It was too cruel. They had taken everything from her, even the one thing she had thought was hers and hers alone.

Thaniel saw the recognition as it lit up her terrified face, chased along by the multitude of questions that no doubt mirrored his own. Judging by the whiteness of her pallor and the tear-stained lines on her face, she was also here under duress. His heart was galloping as he took the seat facing hers, willing her not to speak up and admit their prior connection. He was not going to hurt her, no matter what Doyen ordered him to do. The dream where Doyen had sent him to kill Amelia jumped into his mind; how the tip of his bejewelled dagger had pressed down into her heart. Opposite him, Amelia rubbed her chest. She could still feel the blade piercing her flesh. She looked at his pale, blank face. He had been crying then. Would he cry this time?

"Amelia, meet Nathaniel." The metallic rasp of Doyen's voice made Amelia jump.

"Thaniel," the boy, whose name made her heart leap traitorously to hear, added.

As usual, Doyen ignored the correction. "Nathaniel, Amelia here is refusing to co-operate with me."

Thaniel could not bear to see the accusation in her eyes. He wanted to look away; he also wanted to kiss her until the world stopped turning. He dropped his eyes, looking instead at the way her fingers wove nervous patterns around one another. He almost reached out to take hold of them, checking the movement at the very last moment. Doyen was no fool. As he spoke, he was watching them carefully with his beady, crow eyes. Thaniel dragged a hand through his perpetually messy hair instead, wishing he had taken a little more time with his appearance this morning.

"She believes she can withhold information and is under the foolish notion that I cannot gain access to her mind. Whilst it is true that I personally cannot," Doyen could barely keep the disappointment from his voice, "you most certainly can."

Thaniel sucked in a breath.

"I want you to tell me what power she has been holding back and what it was that she took from the fire where you and your friends have just been searching."

Looking up in surprise, Thaniel forgot all pretence of disinterest. In his first ever assignment away from Blackwell, he had just spent three days at Marlborough House. He'd heard how the nexus had shattered, sending two of the residents' powers crazy. Amelia must have been the one who had run away, the one that Doyen had returned early to deal with.

"Nathaniel is my mind magician. He has the ability to control other living things." Doyen leaned back in his chair, making a show of getting comfortable. "He can make you do whatever he wants. You will not be able to withhold anything from him."

It was Amelia's turn to look startled. Had he been weaving his magic on her all this time? She saw the edge of a smile on his face and misread it. Had he made her fall in love? More tears welled up, hotter now, ripping her heart as they fell. It had all been an illusion, and she was nothing but a fool.

"You do not have to be gentle," Doyen said, after a pause to let his words sink in. "In fact, I would prefer it if you were not."

The horror on Amelia's face was as satisfying as he had expected it to be. She had been clever up until now, outwitting him at every turn, but he could not allow her games to continue any longer. To say that the oligarchy was unhappy at the turn of events at Marlborough House would be a gross understatement. Alistair had been involved in several highly charged conversations with Nirim, both in person and, since he had returned to Blackwell, on the telephone. He could only imagine what Elon's attitude about it would be. Alistair himself was overeager to take a look at the fabled Totar. It would be the pinnacle of his life's work. Just the thought of having such power at his fingertips made every synapse in his body vibrate with anticipation.

Thaniel edged forward in his seat, grinding his teeth as Amelia flinched in expectation of his touch. He could not afford to let down his guard when Doyen was still watching them so intently. Amelia saw his jaw clench; she tensed, ready for whatever onslaught he was about to unleash on her. She had no idea what it would feel like to have him inside her mind, but the glee in Doyen's voice prepared her for the worst.

I am sorry.

The voice she knew so well spoke in her mind, the suddenness of it making her jump noticeably. At his desk, Doyen saw the movement and smiled.

I have to do as he asks. At least, he has to think I am doing it. Whatever you do, you must not let on that I can talk to you like this. He has no idea I have that power. He thinks I can just enter your mind and find out what I will. Don't worry, I will not hurt you.

Amelia's tears turned to those of relief. She closed her eyes, offering up no resistance as she felt him cautiously invading her mind. She had expected pain, and at his first few tentative forays, she flinched despite herself. Doyen took this as a good sign. He imagined hot slices of pain stabbing into her head, like tiny crochet needles looping each memory with their hooks and ripping them out. He could almost feel sorry for the girl; almost, but not quite. He jumped as his phone vibrated in his pocket. The message was from Pazia, furious that she was still stuck out at Marlborough House and insisting on being told the second he had any news from the probing. Alistair looked back at Amelia. Her lies had caused so much trouble for them all. He stabbed out a quick reply, hoping that Nathaniel was using similar force.

Amelia could not have described the sensation of having someone else burrow into her thoughts. It should have been invasive, but Thaniel tiptoed where Doyen expected him to march. The intensity of their connection surprised her. It was almost as if she were being caressed from the inside out. When he found the memories of their shared dreams, she almost felt him twitch. She opened her eyes then, staring deep into his. This time, she saw past the vague frown on his face to the immeasurable depths of his icy-blue irises. Her stomach flipped, and she knew without having to be told that his had done exactly the same thing.

Quickly, Thaniel closed his eyelids, shuttering his emotions before the distracted Doyen could notice. He moved on until finally he found what he had been sent to retrieve. His eyes shot open again, and this time the frown on his face was real.

"Is this going to take much longer?"

Thaniel pulled back. Amelia felt him go with an ache in her heart. He shook his head, looking at Doyen. "You're right. She's had her powers for some months."

Amelia gave a sob. After all this, all they had felt together, he was going to tell Doyen everything.

"Go on," Doyen said, turning a triumphant look in her direction.

Thaniel swallowed, using the slight pause to steady his voice. "She only used it once, to heal herself. She didn't want to be a magician, so she refused to do any more, afraid the magic would be traced back to her. Then the fire happened..." Thaniel could feel Amelia's tension coming off her in waves. It beat its rocky hands at him, but he could not stop. Doyen expected his answer, and he knew better than to deny him. "Her power started raging; she was shaking and in pain, not knowing what was happening and terrified someone would notice. She couldn't control it. When one of the fire engines was turning to drive out of the yard, she saw her chance."

Doyen sat straighter, his eyes flipping back to Thaniel. "Go on."

"The blue lights were dazzling, and she saw people shielding their eyes. While they were distracted, she managed to slip out of the yard and into the big barn where the stables are. There is another door at the back, leading out into the wood. She ran as far as she could. It was dark; she was scared and kept falling. In the end, she had to stop. She fell asleep and was caught."

The sound of Doyen's hand slamming down on the desk made both Amelia and Thaniel jump. "What about the fire? How did she manage to get past the flames? She has shown no affinity with fire whilst she has been here."

Thaniel shrugged, "She never went near the fire."

"She must have!" Doyen was dangerously close to losing control.

Amelia found that she was gripping the arms of her chair, her nails digging deep into the leather. Thaniel had kept her secret. More tears rolled down her cheeks. She could only hope that in the real world his attempts at saving her would be more successful than his dream ones.

Doyen pushed himself to his feet, glaring at them in turn. "What about before the fire? Has she ever been into the woods and taken anything that was hidden there?"

Thaniel chewed at the inside of his lip before answering, "I didn't have chance to get that far."

Doyen waved an arm theatrically, raising his eyebrows and looking pointedly at Thaniel. "Well, go on, then."

This time, Amelia did not flinch. She dropped her eyes to the row of wooden beads Thaniel wore around his neck, feeling heat rise up her face. She was not alone anymore.

I hoped you were real. Amelia heard Thaniel's voice in her head again.

Me too, she thought, not knowing how to make him hear her.

A smile flowered on his face, quickly quashed. Doyen moved forward a little, hopeful of news.

How...? The question cut off even as Amelia began to think it. There were so many words she could follow that simple one with, yet none of the sentences they would create would be anything like simple.

She felt Thaniel's understanding of what she was trying to ask. This wasn't like any conversation she had ever had before; it was almost as if their minds were connected as one. *I have no idea. It isn't uncommon for magicians to be able to use telepathy, but I have never heard of anyone dream meeting before.*

"Well, Nathaniel?" Doyen demanded, his patience wearing thin.

"She has not taken anything."

"You are sure?"

"I am." Thaniel's eyes met Doyen's. He held the contact, safe in the knowledge that this time, he was concealing nothing.

For a brief moment his leg moved, resting against Amelia's. She could feel her heart thumping in her chest, and alongside it, the echo of another beat. She didn't need to be told that the second heartbeat was Thaniel's; neither did she need to ask to know that he, in turn, was feeling hers. Like two halves of a chocolate egg, coming together and fusing at the join, to become one pure and perfect form. It was like the heat of the sun on bare flesh, the sinking, glorious feeling of laying your exhausted body in a feather bed, the safety of strong arms wrapping themselves around you and holding you tight. She almost sighed, but the tension in the air captured her breath and suspended it

just out of reach. Between her shoulder blades, a nagging
sensation flared.

32

THE CONNECTION BETWEEN AMELIA AND THANIEL VIBRATED in warning a fraction of a second before Doyen swept his arm across his desk, sending the contents flying through the air. His inkwell hit the wall with a resounding crack, splattering navy-blue ink all over the panelling and carpet. Amelia ducked reflexively, arms over her head. Thaniel shot back in his chair, Doyen's diary stroking his cheek as it sailed past, leaving a livid white scratch that quickly spotted with minuscule drops of scarlet blood.

Doyen slammed his hands down on the empty desk. He had been fixated on the fact that Amelia had been lying, unwilling to even contemplate what it would mean if she were not. He shot a look at the clock on the mantelpiece. In another hour it would be noon, and he would be making his promised call to Nirim. He did not relish the thought of breaking the bad news. Still, at least he wouldn't be the one informing Elon.

He glared at Amelia cowering in her seat and at Nathaniel, pale-faced and wary, leaning back in his chair. Instantly, he was regretful that his outburst had witnesses. With considerable effort, he regained control of himself, pulled his chair back into place, straightened the edges of his waistcoat, and sat down, thinking fast.

Nathaniel was too important to get rid of, not so the girl. She was wilful and had made a fool of them all. She had no special powers and was not hiding any information that would save them from the diabolical failure finding Stanton Mead's house had turned out to be. There was only one place she was going now, and it was not to the comfortable room waiting for her up on the third floor where all the other young magicians resided.

"There is no place for you here," he calmly told her. "You will be taken back down to your holding cell to wait for execution."

"No!" The word was out of Thaniel's mouth before he even realised he had thought it. "Please, she's a healer."

Doyen flicked his hand, dismissing Thaniel's comment. "We already have healers."

"But surely you can never have enough? She can do other things; she must be able to. You can teach her, like you taught me. She'll learn, won't you?" He shot a frantic look at Amelia, who was sitting stock-still, her mouth open, her eyes liquid pools of fear. She could feel both their hearts racing now as dread locked its hold on them. She couldn't have spoken even if she'd tried.

"You can't just kill her."

"I can." The words were cold, hard, and final. Doyen pulled his phone from his pocket and tapped out a short message. Within minutes, the two chaperones had arrived.

"Take her back to her cell," Doyen ordered Janson. "The holding cell. And tell Brown that we will be needing a new grave dug." Janson nodded, her face impassive. She held her hand out for Amelia, grabbing hold of her arm as she led her out of the door.

Thaniel watched them go with the same feeling of helpless dread he was so used to from their dreams.

Doyen pointed to the ink. "Clear that up before you leave."

The second chaperone, Barker, looked around the room at the mess. She nodded, stepping out of the way as Doyen strode from the room. "Come on," she told Thaniel, "If you are quick, you'll be in time for lunch."

It was surreal, Thaniel thought as he willed the ink to detach from both wood and wool, flowing it neatly back into the broken inkwell. Barker gasped, and he realised too late that it was seeping straight back out through the cracked glass. He transferred the ink into a cup, not caring if it stained the fine bone china. How could anyone just carry on as if nothing had happened when Amelia had been sentenced to death? How could he keep going when his heart was being ripped in two?

Barker looked pointedly at the cup. "Are your problems solved now?"

Thaniel wanted to rage, scream, and smash the room up as Doyen had done. Barker's face blurred before him as hot tears tiptoed from his eyes. He didn't want them to fall, to admit that this was all actually happening; yet holding them back was proving impossible. He gave one rasping breath, then dragged the back of his hand across his face. Barker was only trying to do him a favour. Defiance would not save Amelia.

"Come on." Barker bent to pick up the stapler that had been knocked from the desk along with everything else.

"You fuse that back together and replace the ink, and I'll help with this lot."

When the room was back to normal, Thaniel turned without a word and made for the door. He didn't feel hungry but made no argument as Barker led him to the refectory. A few of the magicians were still away at Marlborough House, Stephen included. Thaniel sat with Toby, who picked at his food, barely speaking.

What's the matter?

Thaniel glanced around, catching sight of Evans at the back of the room. He was sitting with a tall, dark-skinned girl who Thaniel hadn't seen before. *I wouldn't know how to explain.* He pushed away his plate, the food barely touched.

"You not hungry either?" Toby asked him, shoving his own away with a sigh.

Thaniel shook his head. The noise in the refectory was the usual din, just as it would be this time tomorrow when Amelia was gone. He banged his forehead on the table a few times, making both Toby and the cutlery jump. The chair beside him scraped back.

"Careful," Evans said as he came to sit down beside Thaniel. "You're drawing attention to yourself." He plastered a big grin on his face as he looked over to where one of the guards was eyeing their table.

Thaniel couldn't muster enough care to do the same. He felt so detached from everyone around him, even his two good friends. Doyen was going to kill Amelia, and there was nothing he could do about it. His eyes blurred again, and he hastily blinked them clear. He pushed his seat back, as if to get up, then realised that he didn't want to be alone.

"Are you going to tell us what's wrong?" Evan held a hand out, as if he would stop Thaniel from leaving. "Is it about why you came back from Fenton Woods before everyone else?"

Considering Thaniel had no idea how he and Amelia had connected before ever seeing each other, he managed, somehow, to explain about her and what had just happened in Doyen's office. He kept the more private parts to himself and revealed nothing about Amelia's secret. Even so, it was clear to Evan and Toby that this girl was something special.

"It must be a mind magician thing," Evan said after a few moments. "I've never heard of anyone doing anything like that before."

"Me neither." Toby was finding it hard enough having Stephen miles away. He couldn't begin to imagine what it would feel like if Doyen had ordered his death. He rubbed the back of his neck, wishing, not for the first time, that he had Tisha's ability to hear her friends. "I didn't know Stephen even existed until I met him here, but I know what you mean about someone else making you feel whole." He bit his lip, though the words were already out.

Even through his desperation, Thaniel found a smile. "I hadn't realised you two were an item."

Toby flushed a little, looking sheepish.

"You do right to keep that sort of thing quiet." Evan lifted his head and checked no one was nearby. When he lowered it again, both boys were glaring at him.

"You've got to be kidding!" Thaniel got in before Toby could even open his mouth. He shook his head in disgust. "Sorry, but you can sod off back to your own table if that's what you think."

"Shit, what?" Evan looked from Thaniel to Toby and back again. Toby's neck and face had turned a deep, blotchy red. The light dawned. "Bloody hell, no. I'm no homophobe." He dropped his voice even lower. "I just meant that if Doyen or the tutors find out you are close to someone in here, they might use it against you. You don't want them knowing anything you can keep quiet."

The charged atmosphere cooled as instantly as it had heated. "Sorry." Thaniel shrugged. "I guess you can stay then." He punched Evan lightly on the arm.

"We've never told anyone," Toby admitted, ducking his head. "It's always been our secret."

"Well, don't ever think that I don't approve." Evan glanced over at the clock on the wall and pulled a face. "Look, I've got to go. I've got a private lesson in a few minutes.

As he stood up, he squeezed Thaniel on the shoulder. The last person he'd called a good friend in here had been taken away a year or so ago. He remembered that desperate, helpless feeling all too well. There was nothing he could say to make it any better, so he didn't try. "Just keep talking to us," he said instead. "You can trust us."

"Thanks for that," Toby said when Evan was out of earshot. "I can't believe you would have chased him off for me. He's your mate."

Thaniel attempted a smile. "No worries, though I'm glad it didn't come to that."

There was silence between them for a few minutes, but it was not the isolating silence of earlier. After another check to make sure no one was close enough to overhear them, Toby leaned forward again. "So, it's not obvious, about me and Stephen, I mean?"

"Not at all; I just thought you were good mates, but I'm really pleased for you both." Thaniel meant it. Everyone needed someone close in here, though it didn't help ease how he was feeling about Amelia. He rubbed at his eyes and sniffed. The last thing he needed was to get emotional in front of everyone.

Toby pushed his glass of water over to Thaniel. "I'm so bloody thoughtless. I'm sorry. I was trying to distract you and doing a really bad job. Look, I'm here for you; what do you need?"

Thaniel took the glass. The water was cold, and he focused on the feel of it in his throat. A little more composed, he said, "I just don't know what to do. I feel so fucking helpless."

"What about admitting to your telepathy? That must be enough to get Doyen to change his mind. No matter how pissed he is at her."

Thaniel shook his head. "I think that all comes from me, but there is something..." He sat a little straighter. He hadn't had time to process the fact that Amelia had managed to morph into someone else. Despite Doyen being desperate to know how she had evaded everyone during the nexus fire, there had been such a strong sense of secrecy and self-preservation about the memory that Thaniel hadn't thought twice about keeping it quiet. His shoulders sagged again as he remembered that conviction. "... No, I can't. I would be giving away her only chance at escape." He slumped even more. "But if I don't tell, I'm as good as killing her myself."

"You can't escape from Blackwell. It just isn't possible. All they have to do is trigger our implants. It doesn't matter what it is she can do; with one of those in her, she'll still be as trapped as the rest of us." Toby paused while Niall wandered past. The younger boy was a renowned gossip and probably a snitch too. Toby dropped his voice even lower. "But, if what she can do is so good, then just think what they would make her do with it in here."

The last of the colour leached from Thaniel's face. They wouldn't need elaborate setups to make their targets look like magicians anymore. Amelia could just transform into them, appear in public, perform some magic, and voila, target caught red-handed. The oligarchs would have their own secret spy, able to change into whoever was required to retrieve information from someone of concern, or even, Thaniel shuddered, to get close enough to kill them. He could not be the cause of that happening.

He was still thinking about Amelia hours later when the lights went out in his room. She was still alive; he was certain of that. He hated thinking of her frightened and alone in a holding cell. So close, but still impossibly far away. She must feel so abandoned.

****

"What do you mean, she isn't lying? Have you tried everything?" There was an edge to Nirim's voice that Alistair could not, at first, place.

"I have had someone go into her mind and read what is there. The girl is no threat; she doesn't even want to be a magician."

"Pah! She is playing with you. I thought you were better than this, Alistair. I will send Armitage. He will make her talk."

This time, there was no doubt, and Alistair bristled. The oligarch was laughing! At him! He bit his lip, the coppery taste of blood filling his mouth. To be overruled was one thing; to have your expert opinion dismissed out of hand and a subordinate brought in to do your job for you was quite another. Humiliation seeped from every pore. He fought to keep it out of his voice. It would not do to let Nirim know he could get under his skin this easily. As soon as the call ended, Alistair sent a message to Brown. The grave would still be needed, but Amelia wouldn't be going in it tonight.

****

Nirim sat in Blain's office chair and sucked in a deep breath. That had been very unprofessional of him, but he found that, for once, he didn't care. He was going to enjoy telling Elon about this latest development. He would have liked to have done it face to face but couldn't be sure he would be able to keep his own face straight. Watching the news discomposing the Master Oligarch would be even more amusing than hearing Alistair trying to maintain his composure.

It had taken years for this first crack in Elon Kelby's armour to appear. All the while, Nirim had stood by patiently, a firm advocate that 'all things come to those who wait.' When Jane died, Nirim had thought the chance to step into his ancestor's shoes had finally arrived, but he'd been over-eager. Elon had clung onto the reins, turning his personal turmoil into the most ingenious political plan ever, one that would ensure the oligarchy's lasting control. Nirim had to hand it to him; the man certainly knew his business. Never before had anyone tried to wrestle the power of magicians into their own hands. It was an idea Nirim would always regret not having himself.

The Purge had been successful in every way but one, and the last few years had been focused on putting that right. The Tome of Time and Reason was the key to Elon's master plan. Without it, they remained vulnerable. The magicians could always have used the Totar against the oligarchy; that was part of Elon's argument against them, but they'd had no real reason to do so. Now, with their freedom gone and their children taken, there would be nothing stopping them. Elon's key was turning out to be their biggest weakness. Nirim let his breath back out. He might like to see Elon squirm, but his loyalty to the oligarchy was absolute.

He would obtain the leadership, of that he had no doubt, but he would not risk the organisation for the pursuit of personal glory. Now was not the time for power struggles. The oligarchs needed to unite in the face of uncertainty. The magicians were making fools of them all, and it could not be allowed to continue. Starting with that girl. There was something about her Nirim did not trust. She had escaped from right under their noses, challenging both his and Blain's authority. She might have convinced everyone else that she was innocent, but he was convinced she was dangerous. Alistair was right to kill her; he was just being a little premature. They had not tried everything yet. Armitage would be there tomorrow, and if he got anything more out of the girl, no matter how slight, Nirim had ordered him to interrogate whoever it was that had read her mind.

He trusted Alistair, though he never told the man as much. He did not, however, trust any of the magicians in his charge. He would not put it past them to collude in hiding important information.

****

Armitage had been eager to end his recovery time at home; there was only so much small talk that he could stomach. Izzy was a good-looking woman, but she was too shallow, only bothering about her horses and luncheons with her friends. Besides, he had no interest in country living. He liked to be mobile, moving from place to place as work demanded. Staying still bored him.

He threw some clothes into his holdall and was ready to go within the hour. He would find a motel to catch a few hours' sleep and be on the road again at dawn.

33

THERE WAS A WOODLOUSE SCURRYING ALONG THE floor beside the skirting board. The lights coming on had startled it from the shadows. It hurried to find refuge in a crack by the bathroom doorway. Amelia watched it with envy, wishing she could escape so easily. The lights had startled her too, jolting her awake with her heart hammering in her chest.

They were going to kill her today.

In the time since Doyen had told her she was to die, she'd tormented herself about how they would do it: imagining she could feel the constriction of a noose around her neck or the barrel of a gun pressing against her temple. Would Doyen do it himself, or would he get someone else to pull the trigger? Her mind had played over every scenario possible and many that were not.

Two or three times, she had thought she'd felt a surge of hope, but unlike the time she had been captured, these were too fleeting to be anything other than her imagination. Somehow, she had fallen asleep, though it felt like barely any time at all had passed since she had drifted off. Behind the modesty curtain, she looked into the rectangle of reflective metal pinned to the wall. She wondered what was the point in sorting her dishevelled appearance. They could hardly expect her to make much of an effort to look good for her own execution. For the

401

lack of anything better to do, she splashed cold water on her face and brushed her hair, hoping that the normalcy of the action would go some way to distracting her. It didn't. Still yawning, she flicked a hairband from her wrist and went to tie her hair into a low ponytail. She stopped before the elastic was twisted tight and dragged it from her hair. If her head was going to be on a block, she would not reveal her neck for them.

An hour later, she was still waiting. She wasn't hungry. In fact, she knew that she would never eat again, but with no breakfast tray arriving, the lack of routine was adding even more to her frayed nerves. An hour after that, she decided they must be trying to starve her to death. That was one method she hadn't thought of before. She'd heard somewhere that it took three weeks to die from no food, three days with no water, and three minutes with no air. The timings had always seemed a little too poetically convenient, and she wondered how accurate they were.

She was so tired. She sat back on the bed, and Thaniel's face swam into her mind. Had all those dreams been some sort of twisted premonition? If so, then they were going to drown her today, and he was going to be there to watch. She gave a sob; it was just too cruel.

****

"A little longer and we should be good to go," Armitage told Alistair and Brown as they watched the only one of the four screens in front of them that was turned on.

There was a tap at the door. Brown opened it to reveal his colleague, Wilson, holding a tray. The smell of hot coffee and bacon sandwiches filled the small room.

"Perfect timing," Brown said, eyeing the food eagerly. "She's almost ready."

Wilson flicked her eyes to the screen where Amelia sat, head in hands, on the edge of her bed. It had been a clever idea to wake her early. Sleep deprivation was disorientating enough when you knew the time. Add to that the fear the girl must be feeling, fear which Armitage was allowing to build as much as possible before they got started, and most of the fight would already be drummed out of her.

Wilson had not liked the idea that Armitage was to have a go at Amelia. Commonly referred to by the staff at Blackwell as The Ratcatcher, he was responsible for acquiring all captured magicians, young and old. Those who were underage were brought straight to Sheldon Wing and rarely ever caused him a problem. The older magicians, well, they were another matter entirely. Wilson had heard plenty of rumours about *that* side of his work.

She had expected him to be far too rough, but he'd dispelled that fear when he'd called late last night and explained the plan. Of course, the girl was to be terminated; Wilson did not shrink from that fact. However, she did not believe in being overly excessive. There was a line between necessity and brutality. These magicians, whatever their age, were dangerous. They might be young, but they could still do immense harm if they were not kept sufficiently under control. She ate her sandwich, watching as Amelia sobbed. It was good that the girl was winding herself up; she would crack all the quicker for it. Her end was inevitable; to prolong it would just make it distasteful.

Finally, Armitage put down his empty mug and stood up. "Let's go." He nodded to Alistair and followed him out of the room.

****

Thaniel woke slowly, rain spattering his window in an echo of the misery he was feeling inside. He still swung between wanting to tell Doyen about Amelia's transforming ability and knowing that he would be sealing her fate if he did. He had been inside her mind, had felt the goodness of her soul; it would not be right to subject her to a lifetime of puppetry at the whims of Doyen and the oligarchy. He had seen the utter devastation on the face of Krystal when she'd learnt that she was about to lose all knowledge of her healing abilities. For a caring person to have their gifts twisted and abused by those in power was not something Thaniel ever wanted to be a part of again. But how could he just let Amelia die?

The bell sounded, announcing breakfast. Thaniel pulled on jeans, a clean t-shirt, and his favourite hoodie and headed for the refectory. Toby was already sitting at one of the tables. Thaniel grabbed himself some toast and orange juice and joined him. Evan arrived shortly after, the girl he had been speaking to yesterday just behind him.

"This is Sally. She's new."

Thaniel wasn't really in the mood to get to know anyone else, especially someone they couldn't trust yet, but he smiled anyway. "Hi."

Toby welcomed the distraction. He was worried about Thaniel; hopefully talking about something other than Amelia would take his mind off her for a while. "What house did you come from? I haven't heard of anyone mentioning a Sally before."

"I came from my aunt's." She brushed a stray hair away from her face. Her nails were bitten so badly she'd made two of her fingers bleed. "Her and my uncle had been hiding me. I think they are in jail now."

The sadness in her voice was like a plectrum plucking at Thaniel's strung nerves.

"How did you get caught?" Toby had heard so many stories over the years. They never got any better.

"A neighbour shopped us. I've known them years. I even used to babysit their kids, but they just turned on us. Claimed I'd threatened to flood his house, which is so stupid. I mean, I can't even use Water."

"People turn on you so quickly," Thaniel said, pushing his plate away. He had only managed one bite of his toast, and it sat like a lump in his gullet. "My stepdad turned me in. The bastard even hit my mum when she tried to stop him. I don't know what's happened to her now."

Sally looked at him with sympathy.

"Your aunt and uncle not magicians then?" Toby asked before stuffing the last of his egg roll into his mouth. He was starting to regret bringing the subject up. It was hardly the kind of thing Thaniel needed right now.

Sally shook her head. "Nah, they took me in when my parents were taken by the oligarchy. I was twelve."

"That sucks."

"Yeah, Doyen threatened me with awful things to make me do what he wanted. He's so frightening. I hate to think what they did to my parents before they were killed." Sally looked to Thaniel, a slight frown on her face.

Thaniel was too busy trying to dislodge the food in his throat with a long drink to notice.

"Wilson's been giving her private tutoring up till now," Evan told them. "Doyen's been too busy with Fenton Woods and Thaniel to do much more than threaten her yet, but apparently he has an interest in her."

Without warning, Thaniel was gripped with an overwhelming sensation of terror. His insides turned to liquid, and he had to grip the table to keep himself upright. The cup fell from his hand, spilling the remains of his juice across the table. He didn't hear his friends calling to him.

"What's happening to him?" Sally asked in panic.

"I don't know." Evan could see one of the guards across the room start to walk in their direction. He hadn't noticed anything amiss yet, but they didn't have long. "Did you sense anything?"

"Maybe, I wasn't sure."

Evan reached out to Thaniel with his telepathy. *What's wrong?*

Thaniel's breath was coming in shallow gasps; his vision was darkening at the edges, and the room around him was spinning. He didn't feel Toby lean over and shake his arm.

THANIEL! Evan forced his way past the confusion in Thaniel's mind. It was like wading through dense fog. He had never felt anything like it. The guard was getting closer; soon he would pick up on the fact something was wrong. *THANIEL.*

This time, he felt a glimmer of response. The fog thinned, and Evan heard one word.

Amelia.

He realised what was happening just as Thaniel managed to pull out of his stupor long enough to grasp that they were all watching him.

"Guard," Sally hissed under her breath.

Toby grabbed the spilt cup and pushed his chair back. "Sorry about that; I'll get you another." He grinned at the guard. "I was sure if you spun it fast enough the liquid would stay in." He mimicked spinning the glass full circle, clockwise. "Maybe I should have turned it the other way?"

The guard gave him a withering look. "Maybe you should just leave it alone and let your mate drink it?" He nodded to the spilt juice. "One of you, clean that up."

Evan, the only one of them other than Thaniel who had any ability with Water, pulled the juice into a neat little pool before syphoning it into his empty coffee mug. The guard glared at them for a moment longer and then resumed his rounds with a look that said his pay wasn't worth half the aggro these delinquents gave him.

Toby arrived back with another cup and pushed it at Thaniel. "Take a drink; you look like you need it."

Thaniel downed the orange in two gulps. The terror was still coursing through his mind, though thanks to

Evan's intervention, he was able to find a little separation from it. "They've got her."

The boys knew what he meant, but Sally looked confused. "Got who? Are you a psychic or something? Did you just have a vision?"

"Shh." Evan gave her a warning look.

"Sorry," she lowered her voice.

"They're killing someone Thaniel knows today. He can sense how scared she is."

Sally's eyes widened. "They threatened me with that," she whispered. "I knew they meant it. I was so scared. It's the only reason I started to do as I was told." A shadow passed over her face, and she grabbed for Evan. "He's going to..."

Thaniel's knuckles whitened as he gripped the edge of the table. Another wave of fear had crashed through him, building to such a level he felt he would pass out with the intensity of it. He could hear screaming, drowning out everything else around him. Evan tried again to reach him. The fog cloaking Thaniel's mind was even thicker this time. Evan closed his eyes and pushed feelers of thought through whatever gaps he could find.

You have to disconnect yourself from it, he urged before Thaniel's mind went black.

"Shit!"

Evan heard Toby's exclamation as he pulled out of Thaniel's mind. Opening his eyes, he saw his friend face-down on the table.

"... pass out," Sally belatedly finished her sentence. "What do we do?"

Toby laid a hand on Thaniel's. He frowned as he felt more resistance than usual to his healing. "It's like something is pulling him under that I can't reach."

"I think he is connected to her; I could sense something clouding his mind." Evan checked the refectory. It was quite late now, so not many people were left. Most of those were busy clearing their tables. "Try again. We need to get him out of here before anyone realises something's wrong."

"He'll come round this time," Sally said confidently as Toby focused.

Thaniel finally lifted his head. His face was ashen. Amelia was calm now, nothing at all emanating from her mind. "She's passed out," he told them. "I don't know what was happening to her, but she was so scared she literally went out cold."

"So did you," Toby said. "Good job Jarrett is still at Fenton Woods; he'd have reported you for sure."

Evan was keeping an eye on the guard at the door. "You have to keep yourself at a distance from her. You can't risk them knowing about your connection. You know they'll use it against you."

Thaniel's eyes flared wide for a moment, then he shook his head. "She's gone."

He had felt the connection break. One moment he could feel her; the next she was gone. As if someone had taken a knife and cut their souls apart.

"You need to get out of here." Sally jumped to her feet. "You're going to be sick really soon."

Thaniel was already bolting from his seat. He tore out of the refectory, heading for the toilets.

Toby gave Sally a questioning look.

"I know what someone's going to do just before they do it. It just isn't long enough to be of any real use yet." She began gathering their dishes onto a tray. "Doyen's convinced that with enough training and practice, I'll be able to lengthen the premonition time and," she pulled a face, "become an even more valuable asset to Blackwell."

At Toby's worried frown, she quickly added, "I'm determined to give as little help as I can possibly get away with."

"It's true," Evan added. "She even made me check her mind to prove she wasn't lying."

The guards barely gave them a glance as they passed. Their only concern was what went on in the refectory and day rooms. Besides, no one did much to disobey here; the punishments were far too harsh. It was a far cry from working in the lower levels or in Jacob Wing.

34

THE SOUND OF THE OUTER SECURITY DOOR WAS MASKED by Amelia's sobs. Thinking of Thaniel had been a mistake. It had broken down the last of her resolve, and once the tears started again, Amelia hadn't bothered to try and check them. She had been over every dream they'd shared: every smile he had given her, every tortured grasp of his hand as he'd failed time and again to pull her free before the various waters closed over her head.

She had longed for him to be real, to be a tangible part of her life. Amelia still had no words to describe the moment she'd found out that he was. Once over that initial shock, she had found him equal and more to the person she had fallen in love with. Even the touch of his hand as it brushed hers had felt exactly as she'd dreamed it would. It had stirred an excitement deep in her stomach, swirling and churning her emotions until she'd felt she could burst from it all.

Then Doyen had torn them apart, throwing her back into this cell where she could not feel Thaniel calling to her. It was as if the dreams had been premonitions, warning her over and over what would happen when they finally met. How cruel, to have offered her love, only to show her she would never be able to keep it. It didn't make any sense. There must be something she was missing. She was drowning in fear, grasping at thoughts that came and went before she could hold onto them. Drowning; she was always drowning. Hope flickered deep in her soul only to be snuffed out a heartbeat later, but not before it had triggered a new line of thought. Could water be the warning?

The cell door burst open, and Doyen stood before her. She yelped in fright, her heart hiccupping for a moment before hammering violently in her chest. He made no comment about her red, swollen eyes. In his usual impassive manner, he simply said, "Follow me." Then he turned and walked from the room.

Once out of the holding cell corridor, Amelia could feel Thaniel with her. She almost sighed with relief. Even though he could not help her, his presence meant more than she could say. Their connection was just as strong as it had been up in Doyen's office, though this time it vibrated with anxiety. Amelia couldn't tell where hers ended and Thaniel's began.

Water! It was a warning after all. How had she missed it? Water was linked with emotions, just as Earth was linked with stability, Fire to passion, Air to thought, and Ether to spirit. They reached the stairs, but instead of going up as usual, Doyen led the way down into the shadowy reaches of Blackwell's underbelly. On the fifth step, Amelia stumbled. She pitched forward, catching herself just in time before she barrelled into Doyen's back. She recoiled, not wanting to touch the corvid man, who was everything she had ever believed evil to be. He was the one who controlled her fate, and it had nothing at all to do with emotions. Her heart sank. Not emotions at all; with him, it was pure, calculated thought.

She gasped; just as water pushed air out of a drowning person's lungs, so strong emotions took away the ability to think straight. Well, Amelia was certainly guilty of letting her emotions control her; hadn't she shown that time and time again? Only the dream in the maze had been different. Then, her fear had been overwhelmed by the signs of strain Thaniel had been exhibiting. Though water had been present in the tears that had dripped from his face onto hers, no doubt dripping down to pool impossibly beneath them, it hadn't been drowning that had woken her that time. It had been the realisation that he was not acting of his own volition. Were the dreams telling her that she needed to use her head and not her heart?

They had reached the bottom of the steps now. In front of her, Doyen was heading towards a heavily barred door. Amelia couldn't see much further down the unlit corridor. For once she was glad of the darkness. She did not want to see what the ominous gloom was concealing. Her connection with Thaniel had faded as she'd neared the bottom of the stairs. It pushed its way back to her now like a voice carried much too far on a wavering breeze. Once again, it gave her strength. Sucking in a deep breath, she held on to it as Doyen pushed the creaking door open.

Only the sloping floor with its central gully could be seen in the dimly lit room beyond. She pushed away thoughts of spilt blood as dread settled in a hard knot around her racing heart. As she took a step closer, the single, uncovered lightbulb hanging down from the ceiling flickered. From the dark recesses behind the reach of its pale glow, Armitage stepped forwards. He held a heavy wooden baton and a fake smile.

"Come in, Amelia."

She thought her heart would stop right there. Shivers electrified her spine at the flat, almost disinterested tone of his voice. How could her life mean so little to them? Armitage weighed the baton in his hand before hitting it into his palm with a satisfying slap. Beside her, Doyen hovered, one arm outstretched to stop her from backing away. He nodded towards the room.

"You have been given a final chance. Your grave is already dug, and if it were up to me alone, you would already be in it. Luckily for you, Nirim would like you questioned once more." He pulled a large brown envelope from his pocket and loomed towards her, the corners of his mouth twitching into an almost smile. "This is your grave soil; I had some gathered especially." He tipped the contents over her head, "Though you won't be able to feel it when the full weight is shovelled on top of your lifeless body."

It was only soil; still, she screamed as it tumbled down, finding its way into her mouth and beneath her clothes. It felt like death was scrabbling its dirty fingers all over her body. Inside the room, Armitage pulled at something Amelia couldn't see. "Telling us what we want to know is the only way to save yourself from that eventuality." A pair of leather cuffs, each inset with a single crystal, swung into view, suspended from a long chain connected to a bar set into the ceiling. Armitage flicked a switch, and more lights came on. He leaned back against a table laden with lethal-looking instruments and nodded to Alistair. "Get her restrained and let's get on with it."

Amelia felt a hand on her back, the slight pressure intending to move her forward. She couldn't do it. Not even Thaniel's tenuous presence could give her enough courage to step into that room. Cold sweat layered her skin, her lungs bound tightly by fear's embrace. She opened her mouth; the gritty residue of her own grave had dried it to sandpaper. Her head began to swim. She could feel Thaniel's terror mixing with her own. Then the blackness of the corridor engulfed her, dragging her from the horror into blessed darkness.

Alistair shoved Amelia's unconscious body over the threshold with his foot. He wasn't gentle. There had been those before who had not wanted their powers. Foolish children who could not see how wonderful the gift they had been given was. Alistair bit back a flare of jealousy, stepped over her, and quietly closed the door with a firm click. He turned the key and slipped it into his pocket.

At the table, Armitage set down the baton he had been holding and took a seat, stifling a yawn. Unable to make it all the way to one of the better motels last night, he'd pulled over at a roadside inn. The food had been rewarmed and basic. He'd eaten it in grateful silence, so tired that he'd forgone a drink in the bar afterwards and headed straight up to his room. The bed had been far too soft, a dodgy caster causing it to rock every time he'd turned over. The blackout curtains might have blocked the glow from the streetlights, but they'd done nothing to dull the raucous sounds of the smokers congregating down in the beer garden beneath his window. Tuneless, blaring disco music thumped out every time the outer door opened, which it had done with annoying frequency until almost three in the morning. He'd been up and away again by six, feeling as if he had barely slept.

Alistair took the seat next to him, and they stared at Amelia's crumpled body for a few moments before Armitage sighed. "I have a feeling this is going to be a long session." She wasn't his first unconscious prisoner, but most of the time he'd actually got around to using at least one of his implements on them before they'd collapsed. "Do you think she will be out long?" He yawned again. "Might be an idea to call for a jug of water."

Alistair was twisting a cruel-looking set of pincers around in his hand with a malicious look in his eye. "Let's give her a few more minutes." Dousing her was all very well, but he hated getting the hems of his trousers damp on wet floors.

The first thing Amelia noticed when she came round was that Thaniel was no longer with her. Just as before, she felt incomplete, a desolate hollow where his warmth had been. The second thing was that her left temple hurt. She touched the spot gingerly, her fingers coming away red and sticky with blood. She noticed smears of it on the concrete floor and realised, with a clenching of her stomach, that she had been moved. She could see where particles of dirt had tracked in with her; yet more had ridged up against the door, as if it too would rather be on the other side.

"Ah, you're awake."

Armitage sounded bored. He wanted to get this tiresome business over with, find a decent hotel, and catch up on his rest. How Alistair had been unable to get the information from this innocuous-looking girl was beyond him.

"Before we begin, I feel it only fair to warn you that this is a highly protected area. Magic cannot work in here." The soles of his leather brogues tapped on the concrete floor as he walked towards her. He bent forward, lowering his voice in tiresome mimicry. "Nor can anyone hear you scream."

He gestured to her to stand and hold her arms out. The hanging chains rattled as he took the leather cuffs and fastened them snugly around her wrists. Amelia could see where other holes on the strap had pulled out of shape. People far larger than her had struggled in these cuffs. She felt breathless for a moment, her head strangely heavy. Then the feeling was gone. The chains winched tight, dragging her arms high above her head so that they took most of her weight.

She should have been petrified, yet the terror she had been feeling ever since Doyen had told her she was to die had gone. It had taken her long enough to understand the lessons of her dreams: emotions would get her killed; thoughts and her mind would save her.

Armitage stifled a yawn. "Do you have anything to tell me before we begin?"

Amelia said nothing; she had to concentrate on clawing for answers.

Thaniel had been a pawn.

She flinched as Armitage lifted a hand towards her.

He hadn't wanted to hurt her.

Armitage did not appear to have the same qualms. She closed her eyes and braced herself.

Thaniel had been hurting just as much as she had.

Instead of striking her, Armitage stroked her cheek, menacing and peremptory.

In that instant, she knew.

It was as if, with his touch, she had been transported into his body. She could feel how his chest moved with each breath, how his fingers tingled, and how his head ached. The damage his body had taken during the explosion in Fenton Woods was as clear to her as blood on fresh snow. His lack of reaction told her that she had not transformed. This was something new. It was the warning she had been unable to decipher.

Her eyes flew open. "You're in danger."

Armitage laughed, producing a small silver necklace. It had no fastening, simply winding around her neck, each end weighted down with a crystal. From his pockets, he produced two matching gems, holding them up for her to see. Slowly, he brought his hands together, and all four crystals glowed. The pain was intense. Amelia had no recollection of starting to scream. Armitage rolled the crystals around one another, and the pain crescendoed throughout her body. He parted his hands, and it stopped as suddenly as it had begun, leaving her breathless and gasping.

"This chain is a wonderful piece of my arsenal," Armitage said, his face slightly more animated now that his work was underway. "It can inflict the most exquisite pain on the wearer. All controlled by what I do with these." He bounced the crystals in one palm. Each time they touched, they sent spasms ricocheting through Amelia's body. He smiled. "They're usually only used on adults. I'm happy to make an exception with you." He separated the gems again and dropped his hands. "Now tell me, what kind of danger could I possibly be in?"

Amelia looked straight into his eyes. Though her breath was still coming hard and fast, her voice was steady. "You are going to die."

Armitage had been threatened more times than he cared to remember, but there was something chilling in the way this girl said the words.

"I felt it when you touched my face. You're hurt. I think I can tell you more if you do it again." Amelia wasn't quite sure how she knew this. It was like their physical contact had opened up a doorway, one she instantly recognised even though she had never known of its existence until now.

Armitage wasn't having any of her nonsense. "Did I come down in the last shower?" He lifted his hands again.

"In your head, in your chest, in your... agghhh!" Her words tore into screams as the crystals touched. Her legs buckled, transferring the last of her weight to her shoulder joints. She didn't feel it; there was nothing but the agony of the crystal chain.

"Stop!" Alistair leapt from his chair. "Let her speak."

Armitage parted his hands with a frown. "They will say anything to save themselves."

Alistair held up a conciliatory hand. "That is as maybe, but I need to hear what she has to say. Indulge me a little."

With a snort of derision, Armitage put away the crystals.

Again, the inflection of Amelia's words spoke more of fact than threat as she repeated what she had already told them. Alistair heard it loud and clear even if Armitage did not. "Touch her again. This time, hold your hand against her face."

Armitage glowered, though he did as Alistair asked. Just as before, the instant their skin touched, Amelia could feel the exhaustion within his body. There was a strange weight inside her head. Her lungs seemed to take in less air with each breath, and the skin on her chest and face felt almost numb.

"You were in the explosion?" Amelia asked, feeling the blast damage as easily as if she herself had endured it.

Armitage rolled his eyes. "You know I was; you were at the house."

"You just want to sleep. There is some kind of damage in your head, you aren't breathing properly, and the feeling has gone in parts of your body."

Armitage snatched his hand away and stepped back, rubbing his palm as if it had been scalded.

"Well?" Alistair demanded. "Is she right?"

He knew she was. It explained perfectly why Armitage had been acting so strangely. There were glimmers of his old self; that ploy of turning on Amelia's lights a few hours early had been simply genius. Yet Alistair had seen him yawning a number of times, fumbling with his tools and forgetting what he'd been about to say. He had covered it well; men like Armitage did not admit to weakness readily, but his poker face had failed him as soon as he'd realised what Amelia was saying. His jaw was set firm now, his teeth clenched tightly together. Amelia had definitely hit a nerve.

Armitage's skill was getting people to talk: tough, defensive magicians with nothing but challenge in their eyes. He'd never had any qualms at all about using his instruments on the men, though if truth be told, he had never liked torturing females, whatever their age. Frustration got the better of him now, though. He grabbed the front of Amelia's clothing, bunching it in his fist and pulling until her face was only inches away from his.

"Your magic won't work on me, girl." The words carried the faintest trace of panic. "Not only is this room covered in dampening charms, but see this?" He shook his other arm at her, the gold band around his wrist glinting in the dim light. "This protects me from all magic. Nothing can touch me. Nothing." He let go of her with a shove and stepped back, trying not to acknowledge how much that small excess of emotion had cost him.

"Is she right?" Alistair's question was quieter this time.

Armitage threw him a look that could have twisted iron. He'd always been safe from magicians, no matter what they had tried to do to him, and they had tried a lot. This girl was not even twenty, yet somehow she possessed the ability to see right inside him, despite the protections. It scared him more than he would ever admit.

"You're tired all the time." Amelia shouldn't have felt concern for the man who was here to torture her, but she'd felt the neurotrauma inside him, and even though she didn't know its name, she could tell that it was deteriorating rapidly. "It's only going to get worse. You need to get to a hospital before it's too late."

This time, Armitage grabbed her by the throat, pulling her right up onto her toes. "You cannot use your powers on me." His grip was not tight, the pressure being under her chin rather than across her windpipe. "Gypsy tricks count for nothing here." He wavered, his vision blackening for a moment. He made an effort to pull himself together before staggering backwards, leaving Amelia swinging.

She managed to twist back around and looked at Doyen. Surely this was something worth keeping her alive for? She opened her mouth to speak, to beg him to test this power further, but before she had a chance to say anything, Armitage collapsed to the floor like a lead weight.

35

Doyen glared at Amelia, then back to Armitage. A second later he spurred into action, slamming his hand onto a big, red button on the wall. Instantly, an alarm began wailing. Doyen didn't even pause. He lowered the chains and released Amelia from her cuffs. She cried out as pain lanced up her stiff arms when they dropped, barely even noticing as the crystal necklace fell uselessly to the floor. She cried out again as Doyen flicked one of Armitage's crystal cords towards her. It lassoed around her body with a bolt of pain. Then he was shoving her towards the door. She just had time for one last look at Armitage lying prone on the cold floor.

Out in the corridor, a red light above the door was flashing, pulsing along with Amelia's thumping heartbeats. Doyen marched them back to the stairs. They had to press themselves against the wall halfway up to allow three men, including one in a white coat, to run down. Doyen used the time to check that his phone had a signal. He jabbed out a two-word message, then pulled Amelia on. Paroxysms of pain accompanied almost every step as the cord bounced between them. At the top of the first flight, he turned and continued going up, taking the stairs two at a time. Amelia stumbled as she tried to keep up, but he gave her struggles no heed.

The going was easier on the flat, and though Doyen's strides were twice the length of Amelia's, she managed to avoid the worst of the cord's punishment by jogging along beside him, like a cowed dog being hauled along by its unforgiving master. When they reached his office, Doyen pushed her inside.

"Sit." He barked, letting go of the cord but not removing it. It fell to a loose belt around her waist. She sat perfectly still, too anxious of its vicious bite to move.

Still with a sense of urgency, Doyen unlocked one of his desk drawers and pulled out a pair of wide metal cuffs. He clamped them onto Amelia's wrists. She could see crystals mounted into each one. From one of the cupboards, he pulled out a metal head cage adorned with yet another crystal. He slid the scold's bridle over her head, slotting the curb plate into her mouth before fastening the contraption in place. Finally, he removed the crystal cord from her waist, using it to bind her tightly against the chair.

"Stay still, and be quiet, and you might just stay alive," he told her. "I am sure I have no need to tell you what will happen if you try to move, shout, or use your powers. You have felt a little of what these crystals can inflict. Let me assure you, you have not felt the worst of what they can do." He paused for a second and then almost yelled, "Are you listening to me?"

It was hard to answer with the metal plate pressing down on her tongue, but she managed to force out a noise of agreement. The resulting pain from the bridle was excruciating. It radiated right through the bones of her jaw, into her skull, temples, and down the top of her spine.

She jolted forward, letting out a strangled scream. Immediately, the bridle gave another pulse. At the same time, the crystal cord activated. She bit down hard on the metal plate, managing to swallow the next scream along with the pain. Through her tears, she saw Doyen nod as if satisfied, then leave the room. There was an audible click as the key turned in the lock.

Amelia's breath was ragged, her pulse thumping in her neck and wrists. The iron plate in her mouth had a blood-like tang to it, and the flattened bars enclosing her face were numbingly cold. Her throat was hurting, and her bones felt brittle enough to shatter at the slightest touch. In the oppressive embrace of the bridle, she felt violated and very vulnerable.

Her cheeks were slick with tears, but lifting her hands to wipe them away would trigger the cuffs. She dared not risk it. She had no doubt what Doyen's veiled threat had meant. If she triggered all three devices and could not control her reaction, the pain would just keep on going. She would never endure it.

****

The ambulance pulled out of the car park. Doyen did not watch it go. He had sent Brown with Armitage, giving the man strict instructions to inform him the moment there was any diagnosis. He was also to find out the name of the specialist who would be overseeing Armitage's care or, if need be, the pathologist who would be performing his autopsy. Alistair knew the hospital would report straight to a member of the oligarchy. He needed to make sure that he was not kept out of the loop. If Amelia had been correct about the explosion damage, then her powers were far too important not to investigate further. There was a slight tremble in his hand as he pulled out his phone.

****

The aromatic scents of lavender and lime were doing nothing to calm Peyton Lanford as he paced the room, his mind furiously turning over what Nirim had just told him. There was so much about magic they still did not know. He wished he could speak directly to Alistair and find out exactly what had happened, but Sheldon Wing was Nirim's department, not his, and the lines of communication had been set for a reason. Blackwell was the oligarchy's hub of magical operations. Both the temptation for and the suspicion of malfeasance would be immense should any of them have free access across the site. For this reason, the various wings operated in complete isolation from one another.

Peyton ran a hand over his neat little beard and tried to control his rising excitement. The intercom on his desk buzzed. "Your car is ready, sir." His secretary's voice sounded tinny through the speaker.

Peyton pressed the talk button. "Thank you, Paula, I shall be right down. Can you call Lillian and tell her I have to cancel our plans for tonight? I will be late back. In fact, I probably won't be back at all. Tell her I'll call her when I can." He imagined his wife's disappointed face, but if this lead turned out the way he hoped, she would not be disappointed for long.

Ninety minutes later, he pulled into Blackwell, swinging his car into the small car park next to Jacob Wing. He smiled up at the great Gothic building, its gargoyles and grotesques jutting out with screaming, tortured faces. The sight of them always made him think of magicians turned to stone as they'd tried, and failed, to escape.

He pressed his thumb to the metal pad on the wall, and the door opened silently. Peyton didn't need to hear it to know that an alarm had sounded on each of the guards' radios. There was no sneaking into Jacob Wing, not even by him. The door closed just as quietly, the bolts automatically shooting home. Peyton headed straight to the guardroom, where a bank of screens displayed live feeds from the numerous security cameras covering the wing. He focused in on the one showing Inmate 1.

"Has he been any trouble?"

Unlike Nirim, Peyton was actively involved in his department, visiting often and taking a hands-on role when here. The guard on surveillance duty glanced at him briefly before returning his gaze to the screens.

"He's been writing on the walls again. Spinner has ordered pictures to be taken of everything. Feller and Tinman are ploughing through them, trying to decipher what it all means."

Peyton nodded with satisfaction before leaning forward to peer closer at the monitor. The man in question was sitting on the side of his bed. He was bent forward with his head in his hands, his dark crop of dirty hair as unruly as ever. He lifted his head and stared straight at the camera. His voice could not be heard in the guardroom, but what he said was clear enough.

"Hello, Peyton."

The oligarch's lip twitched; otherwise, he did not move. He was used to these displays of otherworldly abilities. The man could not see him, no matter how unnerving his words or how piercing his glare. One of the transient screens to Peyton's left switched location, and movement caught his attention. A short, hunched-looking man was making his way down one of the corridors. Without another glance at Inmate 1, Peyton nodded to the guard and headed the same way.

All the staff in Blackwell, no matter what their work role, initially undertook an intensive course of self-defence, unarmed combat, and weapons training. Providing they satisfied their trainers, they were then given a completely new identity. Their old lives were wiped away, and any previous criminal record, misdemeanours, debts, or obligations no longer applied. Those who didn't make the grade were terminated.

People came to work at Blackwell for a number of reasons, but it was generally accepted that they had all been running from something. Head of Jacob Wing, Spinner, was reputed to have killed his commanding officer and turned to Blackwell instead of facing a lifetime in prison. He had, in fact, killed two of the prisoners he had been guarding before turning on his superior and finishing him off as well.

It made no difference to Peyton. Spinner had proved himself to be a capable and efficient leader many times over and did not shrink from the unsavoury aspects of his job. If he had a history of violence, well, that could only be considered the perfect experience in this line of work. Besides, it was made clear to all prospective members of Blackwell staff that this was a job for life. How long that life would be was down to the individual. There would be no more second chances, no more wiping the slate clean, and certainly no time served for bad behaviour.

Spinner's office was not the conventional desk, chair, and filing cabinet type. Whilst it did contain those things, it also had a small kitchenette, a couple of easy chairs—both of which reclined at the push of a button—a fireplace, and a pile of blankets tucked away in the corner. Spinner often spent his nights at Blackwell. He considered nighttime interrogations to be an excellent way of weakening his inmates and making them more malleable.

Not bothering with a hello, Spinner got straight down to business. "It's a very rare power that works only by skin-to-skin contact. It doesn't alter or harm the person being touched in any way."

Peyton was more than happy to forgo any small talk. "That does not explain how such a power could circumvent the best magical screening protections we have."

"Apparently it's not transmitted as all other powers are." Spinner ran a hand over his bald head, frowning as he felt some stubble. "It's more that the magician assimilates their knowledge of the victim through skin contact, pulling it out of them, so to speak. Supposedly, long ago, such people gave rise to the term 'psychic'."

Peyton could see fresh bruises on Spinner's knuckles and a smattering of dried blood on his sleeve. He nodded thoughtfully, his levels of anticipation rising even further. "Is this power only connected with health?"

The two men were still standing. Spinner could feel heat on his leg where a shaft of sunlight cut across the room from the barred window. He stepped sideways to let it fall on his back, sighing inwardly as it warmed his stiff muscles. "Inmate 37 has not mentioned anything else so far." Regrettably, Spinner moved, switching on the kettle and spooning instant coffee into two mugs.

Peyton sighed and sat down on one of the recliners. There was a roil of emotions going on inside him: frustration, hatred, excitement, hope. "What more are these bastards keeping from us?"

Spinner banged the spoon down onto the sideboard and ground his teeth, almost growling. When he finally answered, his voice was tight. "Will you be wanting my... resignation?"

A little over two hours ago, when Peyton had phoned to tell him that a new power had emerged in one of the youngsters, Spinner's surety in his abilities had begun to fragment. Whilst he accepted that magicians could hold out for years against his immeasurable abilities to extract information, to have missed something as big as this, Spinner could not believe it. The failure sat hard on his already stooped shoulders.

"Why on earth would I want that?" Peyton took the offered mug.

Spinner found that he couldn't hold the oligarch's eye. "This is information I should have got out of those bastards years ago. I failed. You deserve better."

Peyton dismissed his words with a wave of his hand. "Nobody could question your methods or your determination." He nodded towards the biscuit tin, helping himself to a handful when Spinner passed it over. "I just wonder what else they have managed to keep to themselves and what could come out in the future." He bit a bourbon in half, pointedly ignoring the fact that Spinner knew full well what his Blackwell resignation would have entailed.

****

Inmate 37 was still chained to a chair in the centre of the room. He'd aged visibly since the day Peyton had first seen him, but those cunning eyes were still the same. Peyton took a step closer, fixing his own look on the magician. "Does this power show up all damage, however caused?"

The prisoner grinned back at Peyton.

"Answer." Spinner thrust a crystal rod against the man's upper arm until he grunted in pain. "Or the next one will go in your neck."

"Then how will I answer?" The prisoner's grin had turned to a look of contempt, even though he knew he would no doubt suffer for the insolence later. His already split lip and swelling eye would not be the only new injuries he would finish the day with.

Surviving here was a game; play it wrong and your life ended. He'd seen magicians who had complied with everything that had been asked of them; they had blabbed information freely, thinking it would save them. It had not. Jacob Wing was not a holding prison for magicians; its purpose was solely to extract every last ounce of magical information from its inmates. Once that was accomplished, the magicians were surplus to requirements and killed.

Others refused point-blank to co-operate. They were subject to increasingly rigorous torture until their hearts finally gave out. The game, therefore, was to balance somewhere in between, allowing bits of information to be tortured out of you, whilst always giving the impression that there was much more to be revealed. Of course, the more experienced and powerful the magician, the easier that was to do. Inmate 37 was not in the same realm as some of those confined within these thick stone walls, but he was still good at the game.

"Damage is damage," his split lip pulled tight as he spoke, "whatever its cause. If she is skilled enough, she may also be able to tell the how of it, but that hardly matters."

Peyton could feel his pulse quicken. The glimmer that had awoken at Nirim's call was gaining momentum. He knew Inmate 37 could see it inside him, and he hated the fact, but not enough to leave the questioning to Spinner and his cronies.

"So nothing will be hidden?" He pressed the point.

Inmate 37 leaned as far forward as the chains would allow, splayed his fingers, and whispered dramatically, "Nothing."

The showman in him was still there after all these years. Peyton saw again the crowd that had gathered to see the bracelet float through the air to wrap around his wife's wrist, heard the calling of the gulls, and smelled the salty tang of the sea air. He ground his heel into the floor, remembering the yellow beads he'd crushed to dust on the cobbles. "And can this power be used to heal?"

The magician's face was suddenly serious. "Knowledge is a power all of its own. It is how you use that power that proves your worth."

Spinner raised the rod threateningly.

"It may be," Inmate 37 hurried on before he used it, "that the girl also has healing powers. There have, I believe, been magicians who've wielded both the power to Read and the power to Heal, but the two do not necessarily go hand in hand." He thought sadly of this poor girl who had ended up in the clutches of these men, her life weighed in balance against their need to control her. Peyton's interest would ensure her immediate survival, but when she couldn't tell him what he wanted to hear...

"Most powers work by sending out magic; that is how you are able to block them. The power to Read is different. It works only on skin contact, by drawing knowledge into the magician's own body. It is a purely benign power. If she cannot heal the injuries she Reads, she should be able to direct a healer to. Either way, it would be a good idea to get her medically trained so she can describe the things that she finds."

He had not divulged everything there was to know about Reading powers, and unless they asked the right questions, he would be saying nothing further. He closed his eyes and hoped that in trying to save the girl, he had not said too much.

36

The relief Amelia felt as Doyen removed the scold's Bridle was immense. She swallowed a few times, trying to rid herself of the metallic taste in her mouth. Once he took off her cuffs, she rubbed at her cheeks, trying to get some warmth back into her face. Lastly, Doyen loosened the cord enough to allow her body a little movement. She eased her aching back, careful not to stretch too far.

A few raindrops pattered against the window, gentle forerunners warning of an impending deluge. It came on suddenly and without mercy, as if the heavens were throwing all they could at Blackwell.

"Is that you?" Doyen strode to the window, his words stabbing at her as he went.

"No, I..." she stopped. Could she affect the weather? It was certainly matching her mood. "I don't think so," she finished lamely.

Outside, the gargoyles clung to their mountings, their grinning faces seeming to grimace under the onslaught. Dark clouds scudded across the sky as far as Doyen could see. It was no isolated downpour. For a few seconds he rapped his fingers, now clad in black leather gloves, thoughtfully on the window ledge before seeming to satisfy himself that the weather was natural.

"It will be interesting to see what the hospital's diagnosis is." Doyen spun on his heel to face Amelia. "Of course, should it prove that you yourself somehow caused the injuries to Armitage, your life will once again be forfeit."

You are going to die. Why had she said those words? She was supposed to have been thinking, not saying the first shocking thought that came into her mind. It had hardly done her any favours.

"Because you are able, somehow, to get around our protections, you are to be fitted immediately with a security implant. All our trusted magicians have them." Doyen paused to let the seemingly oxymoronic statement sink in.

"It is an extremely useful device capable of inflicting full incapacitation in a matter of seconds and can be triggered at any distance." He brought a small controller out of his pocket. "Amazing things." He tossed it into the air and caught it. "I carry one everywhere. It is designed to operate quickly and easily using only one hand. All I have to do is slide this safety catch, say the name of the intended magician, press this button, and," he indicated a small circular dial on the front, "set the pressure."

Amelia's insides were as turbulent as the sudden storm outside. All this vacillating, was he ever going to tell her she was safe? There was a knock at the door, and the doctor they had seen hurrying down the dungeon steps came in. He was a short, squat man with watery blue eyes and grey, balding hair. He set down a medical bag on the desk and proceeded to take out a number of implements.

"This is all highly improper," he muttered. "It should be done in my surgery under the proper conditions." He pulled on a pair of rubber gloves.

Doyen ignored his complaints and nodded to the gloves, "I would double those at least."

The doctor's mouth opened in surprise. He looked at Amelia, back to Doyen, then, saying nothing, pulled on a second pair. Doyen took hold of the crystal cord. Unwinding it from Amelia's body, he coiled it loosely in his hand.

"You will remain still while Dr Goad does his work, unless you wish me to put the bridle back on you."

Dr Goad approached, needle in hand. He gulped the excess saliva from his mouth. "Lean forward, please. You will feel some slight discomfort whilst I give you the local anaesthetic, then you will feel nothing at all."

Amelia stayed as still as possible as the doctor tugged the back of her t-shirt right up and slid the needle under her skin. After all the pain she had suffered that day, it was barely noticeable. She closed her eyes and tried not to feel so vulnerable. Doyen was watching her closely. Even though he thankfully showed no interest in the fact that half her body was now exposed, her flesh still crawled.

Ten minutes later, the doctor was pulling off his gloves and packing away his things. "Your dressing will be changed in two days' time. Do not get it wet."

The thought of not being able to have a relaxing hot shower sprang immediately to mind, making her feel even more dejected. Still, at least it meant that she would be alive in two days. What was a shower compared to her life?

The door was just closing behind the doctor when a bone-deep pain throbbed through her body. A cry tore from her as she slid from the chair onto the rug. The pain stopped. She opened her eyes to see a pair of brightly polished shoes inches away from her face. Doyen loomed over her, brandishing his controller. She hadn't even heard him say her name into it.

"You may be able to get around our other protections, but you cannot get around this." He watched impassively as she struggled to pull herself to her feet. "You are mine now. I can control you easier than a puppeteer controls his puppets." He indicated to the chair. "Sit."

Amelia retook her seat. There was no need for the low-level hum vibrating through her body, but Doyen kept it there, a not-so-gentle reminder of what would happen if she disobeyed.

For the next hour, Doyen grilled her about what had happened with Armitage, coming at her from every conceivable angle until her head ached. Though she insisted that nothing like this had ever happened before, she remembered feeling a strange wrongness between her shoulder blades when Thaniel's hand had touched hers yesterday. It had been right where her own implant now sat. Any lingering doubt that he might have been a willing participant in that meeting vanished in an instant.

Doyen's mobile phone pinged. He read the message quickly before raising an eyebrow at Amelia. "It seems as if our friend has indeed suffered from internal blast injuries." The words were barely out of his mouth when the phone on his desk rang. "Nirim, yes, yes, I have her here...the implant is fitted and working fine... no trouble at all... Ah, yes, Brown has just sent me a message." He listened intently for a long time, his eyes flicking between the desk and Amelia. His unguarded face was bright with excitement and greed. The call ended, and he placed the handset carefully into its cradle.

"It seems you are someone very special indeed, Amelia."

Hope trickled over her skin.

"It is not unusual for the full range of someone's powers to take their time in coming out. Who knows, maybe there will be even more that you can yet do?"

She hoped the slight flush spreading over her cheeks would be put down purely to relief.

After one of the chaperones had taken Amelia away to her new room, Doyen rubbed his hands together. Despite the disappointment at not finding the Totar, this was proving to be a great few months: not only had they finally got their hands on a mind magician, they now also had someone with a power hitherto unknown. Alarming as that should have been, the girl was meek; he would be able to control her easily enough with the implant. The possibilities that would open up to them now he had these new magicians under his control were infinite. He was going to enjoy moulding them both.

Too busy focusing on the prestige that would come from his accomplishments, he never stopped to consider the implications of why they had turned up so close together.

Elon looked at the devastation in front of him. The search had been widened to include the area of the first cottage, but still there had been no magical tome to be found. The young magicians had been unable to pick up any trace of it, and the girl taken from Marlborough House had turned out to be a hope soon dashed. The magicians were all gone now, Pazia had returned home, and only Nirim remained. After his call to Alistair, they had come out to walk the site together. Barely a word had been spoken between them until Elon finally voiced the words no one else had dared say aloud.

"He bested us right to the end. He placed this curse just to keep us looking in the wrong damn place."

Much to Nirim's surprise, there was no sign of temper in the Master Oligarch's voice. Elon had already vented his frustrations in private, where only the shade of his wife could witness them. Now he was calm again, his emotions sealed shut by his determination to succeed. The Tome of Time and Reason was far too important a manuscript for every copy to have been destroyed. They would find one. They must. He would see Jane again in the flesh if it was the last thing he ever did.

...to be continued

Acknowledgements

The Dark Days of Magic has proved to be a monumental project. When I started it, way back in 2019, I expected to have the first book published the following year, with the next two coming hard on its heels. Ha, look how that turned out. Life with ME/CFS is a life that loves to throw curveballs, no matter how well you plan. Despite fighting against it for years, I had to give up working full-time and turn my writing back into a hobby. Still, I kept plodding on. There have been months when I couldn't even open my laptop and countless days when the words just didn't want to play, no matter how hard I tried.

If only I could have found myself a magician.

For those of you who have waited patiently through every missed deadline, I can only apologise and thank you for sticking with me.

For their help with Secrets, I would also like to thank the following:

Firstly, Sam Whyatt, who has no doubt forgotten all about the forensic pathology help she gave me so long ago. Also the lovely Lucy Horrocks, for putting me in touch with her. I am sure it is not every day someone wants to know what a head looks like after it has been immersed in water for months. Honestly, the search history of authors can be really alarming if you don't know what you are looking at.

Analyst Researcher, Neil Gunfield of Hampshire & Isle of Wight Fire and Rescue Service for all his advice and patience. It can't be easy trying to work out the best way to deal with a fire that can never actually happen in real life. Good job he is also an avid LARPer and fantasy fan.

Also from Hampshire & Isle of Wight Fire and Rescue Service, retired Station Master & wildfire expert, Dave Hodge, for pointing out a vital flaw in my original thinking.

As always, I must thank Katharine Smith for her editing skills and help with beta reading and story flow. Her patience with me over this series has been immense. I cannot thank her enough for sticking with me. After years of trying to line up our diaries, it was great to finally get to meet up with her in person a few months ago. Chatting over fries and a coffee is so much better than scribbling emails, even if it is only in a motorway services. If you are a fan of Cornwall, why not check out her bestselling Coming Back to Cornwall series?

I was working at Corfe Castle for the summer, many years ago, when I first told Katherine Willis that I'd written a book. She immediately offered to beta read it for me, just as she has for every book of mine since. I am so grateful for her assistance and suggestive input. When she isn't teaching people how to use a medieval longbow or turning people into zombies with her fabulous make-up skills, she somehow finds the time to narrate audiobooks.

Joanne Paulsen is a writer from New Zealand who has been my online friend for many years. Her advice, support, and encouragement have really helped to keep me sane. She has been a massive help with beta reading, suggestive input, chats about characters, writing flow, style, and consistency. It is thanks to her that I ended up completely rewriting sections of the book. It set the books back months, but they are so much better for it. Thank you, Joanne. This is our year!

Did you enjoy this story?
If so, please consider leaving a review on Amazon and/or Goodreads.
Reviews are vital to authors. They tell them what they are doing right, and what can be improved upon. They also help potential readers chose books they will enjoy.

Reviews do not need to be in-depth. Just say what you liked about the story and why you liked it.
Please remember to avoid spoilers.

Also by Nelly Harper:

The Albion Chronicles:

Queen of Betrayal

The Girl of Two Worlds

Seven Druids

The Battle for Brigantia

The Jet Necklace

A POWERFUL SPELL, ONCE UNLEASHED WILL NOT
STOP UNTIL ITS WORK IS DONE.
~ However long it takes ~

Centuries have passed since the jet necklace was made
and imbued with a magical calming spell capable of
stopping even the strongest hate and hostility.

Oonagh is forced to flee the invading Vikings, hiding
the necklace from them as she runs. With everyone
she knows dead, she builds a new life far away from
the troubles.
When an act of ultimate betrayal brings the past
crashing back, her daughter Bethoc, must return to her
mother's homeland and try to retrieve the necklace
before it is too late.

www.ingramcontent.com/pod-product-compliance
Lightning Source LLC
Chambersburg PA
CBHW031154310726
48969CB00001B/80